"If you are a Stephen King/Dean Koontz fan, THE HOMING is a book you will only open once. You will not put it down until its last page has been absorbed. John Saul takes the psychological suspense novel to a new height."
—*The Dayton Voice*

Suddenly Julie became aware of a humming sound.

She stepped into her room, and instantly knew something was wrong.

The light from the window.

It was an odd color—dim, and yellowish.

Her eyes went to the window, raised high to let in the cool night air, and her breath caught in her throat.

The screen was covered with bees; covered so thickly she couldn't see out at all. . . .

"EERIE . . . CHILLS APLENTY."
—The West Coast Review of Books

Trembling, Julie went to her bed and crept under the covers, pulling the quilt over her head. . . .

Outside, the bees found a tiny crevice in the siding on the house and set to work. . . .

"SAUL CAN MAKE YOUR SKIN CRAWL."
—St. Petersburg Times

THE HOMING

John Saul

FAWCETT CREST • NEW YORK

This book contains an excerpt from the hardcover edition of *Black Lightning* by John Saul. This excerpt has been set for this edition only and may not reflect the final content of the hardcover edition.

A Fawcett Crest Book
Published by Ballantine Books
Copyright © 1994 by John Saul
Excerpt from *Black Lightning* copyright © 1995 by John Saul

All rights reserved under International and Pan-American Copyright Conventions. Published in the United States by Ballantine Books, a division of Random House, Inc., New York, and simultaneously in Canada by Random House of Canada Limited, Toronto.

Library of Congress Catalog Card Number: 93-50606

ISBN 0-449-22379-5

Manufactured in the United States of America

First Hardcover Edition: August 1994
First Mass Market Edition: August 1995

10 9 8 7 6 5 4 3 2 1

FOR

BRUCE AND BETH BECKER

AND

ED AND MARIE MORRISON

*Whose support and friendship over the years
have been both invaluable and greatly appreciated.*

Also, a special acknowledgment to Larry O'Bryant,
who was more than generous with his time
and knowledge. Thanks, Larry, and
I hope I got most of it right!

DAWN

PRELUDE

"*You been wantin' me the way I been wantin' you, ain't you, kid?*"

Dawn Sanderson froze, her hand still on the half-open kitchen door. Her mother's boyfriend, Elvis Janks, was slouched at the kitchen table, an open bottle of beer in front of him, the redness of his eyes a sure sign that the bottle on the table wasn't his first.

Probably not even his third.

But it wasn't the redness in his eyes that scared her—she'd seen that so many times she didn't even pay attention to it anymore.

What scared her was the look in those two bloodshot slits, a leering gaze that seemed to slash through her clothes, ripping away her blouse and bra so he could see—

She cut the thought off, terrified that he might actually be able to read her mind, and think . . . what?

That she was interested in him?

Dawn knew Elvis was a drunk, but was he crazy, too? What could she ever have done to make him think she might like him? She couldn't even see how her mother could like him, he was such a creep! His hair was greasy, and his fingernails were always dirty, and he smelled bad, too. And not just from the beer he was always drinking.

1

It was like he never even took a bath.

She'd known this moment was coming. For the last two months, ever since she turned sixteen, she'd felt him watching her, staring at her when he didn't think she was noticing. She'd even told her mother about it, but her mother hadn't believed her, had even told her she wouldn't believe her unless she saw something herself. But Dawn knew Elvis Janks wasn't dumb enough to let her mother see anything—whenever Mavis Sanderson was around, Elvis always acted like he didn't notice Dawn at all.

This afternoon, though, with her mother safely at work, Elvis was looking at her in a whole new way. A way that sent shivers down her spine and made her feel sick with fear. Her heart pounding, she tried to edge out the kitchen door, but suddenly her knees threatened to buckle beneath her.

Sensing her fear, Elvis Janks rose from the table and lurched toward her, his lips twisting into a mocking sneer. "Come on, baby," he rasped, a rivulet of saliva dribbling from the corner of his mouth. "You know you want it as bad I wanta give it to you." An ugly cackle bubbled up from the thick phlegm in his throat. "You want to do it right here, or go into your mama's bedroom?"

Legs shaking, Dawn backed away from him, but before she was out the door, Elvis Janks was on her. His sinewy fingers closed so hard on her wrist that a squeal of pain erupted from her throat.

The sound seemed to excite him, and as his fingernails dug even deeper into the flesh of her wrist, Dawn silently cursed her lack of control. Maybe if she hadn't uttered the sound, he would have left her alone.

But she couldn't help it—it felt like he was breaking her wrist!

Oh my God, oh my God, oh my God. Dawn clamped her jaw against the scream that was pressing up from her throat. She wanted to scream with the pain and the fear. She wanted to scream her head off.

But who would come? The house across the driveway was abandoned, and the people on the other side of the Sandersons worked all day. Besides, people around here yelled and screamed all the time, and no one paid any attention anymore. And even if they did, so what? Elvis would deny everything, and her mother would believe him instead of her, and nothing would change.

Nothing at all.

Elvis was fumbling with her blouse, and Dawn felt his callused, filthy hand touching her breast.

It was his touch that finally set off her temper, releasing the pent-up resentment that had been building in her ever since her mother had let Janks move in with them. And as anger flooded through her, so also did a renewed strength. She jerked her wrist free from Elvis Janks's grasping fingers and hit him, slapping him hard across the face. It surprised him so much that he let go of her breast.

As he moved to grab her again, Dawn shot out the door, neither looking back nor slowing down until she was out of sight of the house.

Without making a conscious decision, Dawn knew exactly what she was going to do. She walked purposefully toward the mall ten blocks away—and the cash machine that would give her access to the secret bank account she'd been building up for almost a year, stashing away nearly all the money she earned from her baby-sitting jobs. She realized now that she'd been moving steadily toward this decision for months.

She wasn't acting on an angry whim, or trying to punish her mother over some petty issue.

She wasn't failing in school, or running around with the wrong crowd, or getting into drugs.

She just didn't want to get raped by her mother's boy-

*friend, and she was certain that if she stayed around, that
was exactly what would happen.*

Better just to leave quietly, and begin her own life.

*Dawn knew what she wanted to do—she'd known for a
long time. She wanted to go to Hollywood and take acting
lessons, and become an actress. Not a star—just an actress. She was pretty sure she could do it—she'd been in
the school play this year, and last year, too, and everyone
had told her she'd been really good.*

*Given a chance, and the right training, she knew she
could be even better.*

Good enough, maybe, to earn a living at it.

*As she stood in front of the cash machine, taking out
just enough money to feed herself while she hitchhiked
down Interstate 5, Dawn Sanderson had already mentally
left her past in Los Banos behind, and begun to make her
plans for a future in Los Angeles. By the time she walked
out of Los Banos, heading for the interstate ten miles to
the west, her dreams were already taking shape. She would
find a little apartment, and a job, and spend whatever free
time she had taking acting lessons and getting her high
school diploma.*

*Her stride quickening to keep pace with the rapid work-
ing of her mind, Dawn walked along the edge of the pavement, barely aware of the passage of time as she put mile
after mile behind her. It was just starting to get dark by the
time she reached the massive expanse of concrete that ran
straight down the valley as far as she could see, unwaver-
ing in its southward route, absolutely featureless.*

*Should she start hitchhiking now, in the fading light of
evening?*

No.

Better to wait until morning. It would be safer then.

*If she wasn't going to be raped by Elvis Janks, she sure
wasn't going to be raped by some faceless stranger, either.*

* * *

What seemed like endless hours later, Dawn looked up into the first faint light of morning. The sky was clear, but the stars, which had been twinkling above her all night long, were fading quickly as the blackness of the night was washed away by the rising sun, until finally there was only one star left.

The morning star.

She gazed at it for as long as it remained visible, feeling an odd connection with it that she didn't quite understand until the point of light finally disappeared into the brightening of the new day.

Only when it was gone did Dawn take it as an omen.

After all, this was the first morning of a new life, and in the brightening light, she realized she'd actually survived all the fears that had closed around her last night while she tried to sleep in the semishelter of a bridge over the interstate. All through the restless night, she'd awakened with every sound—every howling coyote and rumbling truck—to stare up into the vast sky while struggling to control her fear of the darkness surrounding her and all the unseen creatures that might be hiding in it.

Demons so close she had sometimes felt she could almost reach out and touch them.

Now, though, after making it through the dark, menacing night, and seeing the morning star, it seemed everything was going to be all right after all. And not only would she have a new life, but she'd have a new name, too!

Dawn Morningstar.

That's what she'd change her name to the minute she got to Hollywood.

Lots better than Dawn Sanderson.

Dawn stretched her aching muscles and stood up. She was hungry, but there were no fast-food places on this part of the interstate, and she didn't want to waste any of her money on breakfast anyway.

That was one of the fears that had crept up on her in the night. What if her bank account, which had seemed so large yesterday, wasn't enough for her even to rent an apartment? Then what?

She resolutely put the thought out of her mind, stood up and brushed the dirt and leaves off her clothes. What should she do first? Start hitchhiking south, or try to find a place to wash up?

The decision made itself when she realized that it was so early there was practically no traffic on the highway.

Hunger gnawing at her stomach, Dawn began trudging southward. Far in the distance she could just make out what looked like a gas station, where at least she could rinse the worst of the dirt off her hands and face, and maybe get a cup of coffee to see her through the morning.

And maybe a doughnut, too.

She was still a mile from the exit leading to the gas station when she heard a car slow down behind her. A moment later it passed her, then pulled off onto the shoulder. By the time she drew even with it, a man had gotten out.

"You okay?" he asked.

Instantly, all the training Dawn had grown up with, all the admonitions she'd heard never to speak to a stranger, rose up in her mind, and for a moment she was tempted not even to reply, but to simply walk past the car and keep going until she got to the gas station.

But then what?

If she wouldn't even speak to an ordinary-looking man who was asking her if she was all right, how was she ever going to hitchhike?

She stopped a few yards short of the car and eyed the man cautiously, reassuring herself that he looked just like anyone else, like hundreds of men she'd seen in Los Banos every day of her life.

"I'm trying to get to that gas station," she said finally. "I slept under the bridge back there last night."

The man glanced back at the overpass, which was barely visible in the distance. "Running away?"

Dawn hesitated, then shrugged. She'd never been very good at lying, and besides, what was the point? Still, she didn't think she was so much running away as simply leaving home. "Sort of, I guess. I just decided it was time to move to Los Angeles."

"Did your folks agree?" the man asked.

"I don't have any folks," Dawn replied, deciding it wasn't quite a lie, since her father had died before she was born, and her mother was far more interested in Elvis Janks than in her.

The stranger seemed to accept her words. "Well, if you want a ride, I can get you to the gas station. I got to fill up anyway." He got back into the car and glanced at Dawn.

She hesitated, and a second later the man shrugged. The car started forward, pulling quickly away as it moved back into the traffic lane.

"Wait!" Dawn called, breaking into a run as she dashed after the fast-accelerating car. For a second she was certain the man had neither seen nor heard her, but then the car slowed again. She caught up with it, and when it stopped, pulled the passenger door open and slid inside. "I guess I better take what I can get, huh?" she asked.

The man grinned at her, then started up again and turned his attention back to the road. Less than a minute later, just as he had promised, he pulled off at the exit and into the gas station. "Use the bathroom while I fill up," he told her. "And I'll get us both some coffee."

Ten minutes later, when she came out of the women's room, he was waiting behind the wheel, the engine idling. The scent of fresh coffee drifted from the open window. Sliding back into the passenger seat she found a steaming plastic cup perched on the dashboard in front of her, along with a doughnut. "Thought you might be hungry," the man said as he pulled back onto the southbound lanes of I-5.

"Thanks," Dawn said, biting hungrily into the doughnut, and washing it down with gulps of the hot coffee.

A few minutes later, just when the coffee should have been doing its work in reviving her, Dawn realized that she was feeling sleepy.

So sleepy she could hardly keep her eyes open.

"Wow," she said, trying to shake the gathering fog from her head. "What did you do, put something in my coffee?"

The man next to her said nothing. Slowly, he turned his head to look at her.

The expression on his face had changed.

His eyes glittered oddly. A vein throbbed in his forehead.

His hand reached out to her.

Dawn Sanderson raised her own hand, tried to fend him off, tried to pull away from him.

But the sleepiness was closing on her, and her whole body felt heavy.

So heavy she couldn't move.

As a blackness even darker than last night's closed around her, Dawn Sanderson knew that she had made a terrible mistake.

Elvis Janks would only have raped her.

This man, she knew, was going to do worse.

Far worse. . . .

CHAPTER 1

Julie Spellman still couldn't believe this was happening to her.

Not even sixteen yet, and her life was basically over.

She stared disconsolately through the windshield, trying once more to figure out how such a thing could have happened.

Mothers—at least not *her* mother—weren't supposed to do things like this!

She twisted restlessly in the front seat of the old Chevy, trying to get comfortable, then wished she hadn't, for now her mother was giving her that awful, encouraging smile that Julie had come to hate almost as much as she hated the place they were going.

How could she be smiling?

As if there could be—ever would be!—anything to smile about again.

Right up until last week Julie had still refused to believe her mother would go through with it. But now here she was, sitting in the front seat of a car that barely ran, with her kid sister in the backseat and everything they owned packed into a trailer that made the car sway so badly on every turn that Julie thought she might have to throw up.

Except there hadn't been any turns for the last hour.

No turns in the road, no towns, not even any signs to read except the ones that told you what kind of gas or pukey food you could get at the next exit.

9

With a sinking heart she caught a glimpse of the latest sign to flash past, for a place called Kettleman City, then heard her mother confirm her worst fear: "Almost there. Pleasant Valley's only seven miles west of I-5."

Out of the corner of her eye Julie saw her mother getting that disgusting wistful look on her face again. That was almost as bad as the encouraging smile. "Of course, it's not like when I was your age," her mother said, "and we were so far off the main highway that you never saw a stranger from one year to another."

"I bet you still don't," Julie said. "Why would anyone want to get off the freeway around here?"

Once again she gazed out the window at the endless miles of flatland that made up this part of the San Joaquin Valley. To the east, the Sierra Nevada mountains weren't visible at all; in fact, there wasn't even a horizon—just a sort of blurry spot where the brownish-green of the fields blended in with the brownish-blue of the sky, so indistinct that you couldn't quite tell where one left off and the other began.

Not like L.A. at all, with its hills covered with houses from the floor of the San Fernando Valley right up to Mulholland Drive, where the really big mansions were, and where Julie used to dream of living. Now she wondered if she'd ever even get a glimpse of those huge houses on Mulholland Drive again.

Or see her friends, either.

Or anything else she'd been familiar with all her life.

It had been bad enough five years ago, when her dad had died. For a while she'd thought it might have been better if she'd died herself, she missed him so much. For almost a year she'd cried practically every night, and sometimes, when she was alone and something reminded her of him, she still cried. Then they'd had to move out of the house in the hills above Studio City, and she'd had to start sharing a room with Molly. That was pretty awful, but she'd gotten used to it, just as she'd gotten used to the fact that her dad wouldn't ever be coming home again. They all had to get used to things being different, but at least she hadn't had to change schools, and most of her friends hadn't cared that she lived in an apartment now, instead of a nice house with a pool.

So at least she'd still had her friends, and gone to the same school she was used to, and done the same things.

But now what was she supposed to do?

Now nothing was the way it should have been.

She stared bleakly at the little town they were coming into.

If you could even call it a town.

There wasn't even a shopping mall!

Just a bunch of frame houses sitting side by side, all looking alike, without even any fences between their yards.

They passed the school, and with a sinking feeling Julie saw that the elementary school was in the same building with the high school. Great, she groaned silently. Just terrific! She and Molly would be in the same school.

"Look," the nine-year-old piped from the backseat, as if she'd read Julie's mind. "The school's all together here. We're going to be in the same one!"

"I can hardly wait," Julie muttered, then felt her mother's eyes fix disapprovingly on her and wished she'd kept the words to herself.

"Now come on, honey, give it all a chance."

They were driving through the downtown area now, and Julie had to stifle another groan as she spotted the movie theater.

One screen? Was that really all it had?

Hadn't they ever heard of multiplexes here?

Two more blocks, and they left the town behind. Once again there was nothing to see but the broad expanse of cropland, now backed by some hills rising in the west, with a few clusters of farm buildings here and there. Paralleling the road was an endless row of huge stanchions supporting high-power electric lines.

"You know, it still isn't too late, Mom," Julie said, deciding she might as well try one last time to talk her mother out of this terrible mistake. "I mean, like we could just stay a few days, and then go back to Studio City. I bet you could get your job back, and I could get one, too, and then we could even afford a better apartment!"

Her mother didn't even glance her way, let alone answer her.

As the fields rolled endlessly by, bringing them closer and closer to their destination, Julie's spirits sank still lower.

She would die out here—she just knew it.

And why?

Just so her mother could get married again!

It wasn't fair—didn't her mother even care how miserable she was?

Well, if it got too bad, and she hated it too much, there was still one thing she could do.

She could run away.

Maybe, just maybe, she would.

Karen Spellman sensed the darkening of her daughter's mood, and finally, if surreptitiously, glanced over to see her slouching against the passenger door. Should she say something? But what good would it do? Each time she'd tried to talk sensibly with Julie, her daughter had refused to listen, standing with hands planted on hips, shaking her head and repeating over and over how stupid she thought her mother was. But despite what Julie thought, Karen was still certain that what she was about to do would be the best thing she'd ever done.

Her life, which had seemed to end that night five years

ago when Richard Spellman had died, was about to begin again.

And it had all started with a letter from someone she barely remembered. A letter she'd been about to discard when a tiny voice inside her head had whispered that going to the reunion might be fun.

Fun?

A reunion of her class at Pleasant Valley High, *fun*?

*Un*pleasant Valley was what she and her mother had always called the town in which she'd grown up, and the week after she graduated from high school, she left for Los Angeles, a check from her mother carefully folded in her purse.

"I saved it from my household allowance," Enid Gilman had told Karen almost twenty-one years ago. Her mother's thin lips had set bitterly as she once more rehearsed what her life might have been like had she not married Wilbur Gilman and settled down in that godforsaken town lost in the barrens of the San Joaquin Valley.

Karen had listened willingly to her mother's familiar lament of growing old with all her dreams unfulfilled, all her aspirations withered away under the unrelenting glare of a sun that seemed to burn the life from everything it touched.

Turning her tired face away from the sunlight, Enid had pressed the cashier's check into her daughter's hand. "It's not much, but it should get you started. You go do all the wonderful things I didn't do."

And Karen had tried.

She'd found a little apartment in Hollywood, found a job as a waitress, and set about the business of becoming the movie star her mother had always dreamed of her being.

But it hadn't happened, and Karen—finally out of Pleasant Valley—had quickly shed the illusions her mother had nurtured in her for the first eighteen years of her life.

She was pretty, but not nearly beautiful enough to make it on her looks alone. Thousands of girls had hair as dark and luxuriant as hers, eyes as blue, and figures as good. She'd realized within a week of arriving in L.A. that her mother's appraisal of her had been wrong: even if she'd been the prettiest girl in Pleasant Valley, which she doubted, she certainly wasn't going to catch any eyes at the studios. Still, her mother's voice ringing in her mind, she'd enrolled in acting classes, faithfully trudged through the rounds of agents and casting directors, patiently listened to Enid's assurances that stardom still loomed just beyond the next corner.

Two years later, when her father finally died of heart failure while dozing on the porch of the tiny house in Pleasant Valley, her mother had moved to Los Angeles.

For a while Karen and Enid had lived together. And within a month of Enid's arrival, it became clear to Karen that the dream of stardom was far more important to her mother than to herself.

When she married Richard Spellman, Karen had been more than happy to give up the struggle. To her mother's unending, undisguised disgust, she'd settled down to have children and make a home for her family.

"You're going to throw your life away, just like I did," Enid had wailed. "Do you want to end up like me, worn-out, with nothing to show for a whole life? You could be a movie star, Karen! Don't waste yourself the way I did!"

Karen had refused to argue, refused to pay attention to this sad, bitter woman who, Karen now saw, looked far older than her years.

For more than a decade Karen's life had been almost perfect. First Julie had been born, and six years later Molly came along. Then, five years ago, her whole life had come apart. Richard had been driving her mother home after a long and not-too-unpleasant dinner on the terrace next to their pool. He'd just pulled onto the Ventura

Freeway when a drunk driver smashed into his car, killing both Richard and Enid.

Karen had barely begun to deal with the shock of the two deaths when she discovered that Richard's estate couldn't begin to cover their debts. Within a year she and the girls had been forced to move into a cramped apartment that, tiny as it was, had been barely affordable on what she was able to make by going back to work as a waitress.

Los Angeles began to grind her down.

Karen worked hard, fitting classes in with as many shifts in the restaurant as she could manage, and was finally able to leave waiting tables behind her, going to work as a legal secretary in one of the big firms in Century City. But no matter how hard she worked, she couldn't quite get ahead. Rents always went up just as fast as her income, and she never quite managed to get herself and her daughters out of that first cramped apartment they'd moved into after Richard died.

And every year the streets grew more violent, the traffic more congested, while the schools the girls went to declined.

The last few years, Karen had been afraid to go anywhere, as the drive-by shootings came steadily closer and the gangs moved in. L.A. had become a war zone.

When she discovered that Julie had started experimenting with drugs, she hadn't been terribly surprised. The surprise was that she'd been able to put a stop to it.

Life had ground on, getting a bit harder every day. It left her recalling Pleasant Valley with more fondness than she'd ever thought she could summon for that quiet, sun-baked place.

Then she'd come home one day and found the invitation to her high school class's twentieth reunion.

Twenty years? Had it really been two whole decades since she'd seen the town she grew up in?

Instead of throwing the invitation away, she put it on the refrigerator door.

For a week it had stayed there, held in place by a magnet shaped like a ladybug. She found herself wondering what her hometown might look like as seen through her own eyes instead of her mother's. What the kids she'd grown up with had become. Not that she'd had many friends as a child; Enid had seen to that, discouraging her from becoming close with any of her schoolmates, and forbidding her outright from associating with any of the farm kids who came into town for school every day. Indeed, she'd grown up in a farming community without ever having set foot on a farm!

In the end, it was the realization that she actually knew very little about the town she'd grown up in that made up Karen's mind.

"You can take care of Molly, and I'll only be gone one night," she told Julie. "And there's twenty dollars in it."

For Julie, the bother of taking care of Molly was counterbalanced by the promise of freedom from her mother—not to mention the twenty dollars. She accepted the job with no argument, and Karen had sent in her reservation for the reunion.

The town was exactly as she'd remembered it.

Familiar.

And strangely comforting in its familiarity.

And with comfort came dawning realization: she had never hated Pleasant Valley at all. It had been Enid who hated it.

As she embraced old classmates and renewed old acquaintances, Karen realized that she still had more friends in Pleasant Valley than in Los Angeles, even after having been gone for more than half her life.

Friends who treated her as if she'd never moved away at all.

And one friend—Russell Owen—who had suddenly become more than just someone she'd known ever since kindergarten.

After the reunion, all through the gray California winter, he drove the 200 miles down to L.A. to see her each weekend, and at spring vacation she brought Molly up to see the town and Russell's farm.

Julie, totally involved with her friends at school, had refused to come, and in the end Karen let her stay in the apartment by herself.

And now, six months after the reunion, she'd driven back to Pleasant Valley yet again. This time to stay.

Though Julie had cried and protested, Karen stuck to her guns.

"If you'd gone up at spring break with Molly and me, you'd know it's not anything like what you think it is," she told Julie. When her daughter tried to continue the argument, Karen put an end to it by reminding her of what had happened at her school only a few months earlier—a student had opened fire on a teacher, killing the teacher and three teenagers before finally turning the weapon on himself. "At least in Pleasant Valley you'll have a pretty good chance of surviving high school," she said. She'd reached out and pulled Julie close. "Come on, honey, it isn't the end of the world. In fact, if you just give it a chance, it could be the beginning of something wonderful for all of us, not just me. That's all I'm asking, sweetheart. Just give it a chance. Okay?"

The argument had ended, but as they'd driven through Pleasant Valley a few minutes ago, and Julie saw the town where she would finish high school, Karen felt her older daughter's smoldering anger flare up, though so far she'd confined her feelings to a few muttered grumblings.

Molly, on the other hand, was bouncing in the backseat, clutching the ragged teddy bear she'd refused to leave behind and chattering in high-pitched excitement about the colt she was going to see as soon as she got to the farm.

Next week, Karen thought, despite Julie's attitude toward Pleasant Valley, she was getting married.

Married to a man she'd grown up with, who had spent his entire life farming half a section of prime land in Pleasant Valley.

Her mother, Karen was certain, must be spinning in her grave, even angrier than Julie.

And Julie, from what she could see as she ventured a glance at her daughter out of the corner of her eye, was plenty angry—angry enough for herself and her grandmother, too.

The car left the paved county road and began bumping farther west along a rutted dirt track that followed a straight line between two emerald-green fields. "Does it get any worse than this?" Julie asked. "I've been afraid the car was going to die ever since we came down the grapevine three hours ago."

"What's the grapevine?" Molly demanded from the backseat.

"It's what they call that long steep grade we came down near Gorman," Karen explained to her younger daughter. And if this doesn't work out, I'm going to need a new car just to get back to L.A., she thought to herself. "And no, it doesn't get any worse than this," she told Julie. "In fact, this is Russell's driveway."

Despite her determination not to be impressed by anything in Pleasant Valley, Julie's eyes widened. "You mean all of this is Russell's?" she asked, surveying the expanse of fields all around them. "How much land does he own?"

"Three hundred and twenty acres," Karen replied. "The buildings are right up ahead."

A quarter of a mile away, Julie could make out a large barn, a silo, and a few smaller buildings. Then, separated from the outbuildings by a large yard dotted with immense old walnut trees, she saw two houses.

The smaller one, only a single story high, resembled a rectangular box with a front porch tacked onto it.

The other one, though, was much larger and looked sort of Victorian, with a large covered porch that wrapped around both the sides of the house that she could see. There was a big picture window, and several gables breaking the line of the steeply pitched roof above the second floor. At one end there was even a corner room that appeared to be in a turret, its windows glazed with curved glass that matched the nearly circular walls.

The house was painted white, and trimmed with black, gray, and a deep burgundy that matched the roof.

"Is that . . . ?" Julie began, but left the question hanging, not daring to let her hopes rise to the point of finishing the thought.

"That's Russell's house," Karen told her, a smile playing at the corners of her mouth. "The little one is his father's, where Russell grew up."

"No fair!" Molly cried from the backseat. "You said we were going to tell her the little one was ours!"

"Russell built the big one just after he got married," Karen told Julie, ignoring Molly's protest. "They were going to have half a dozen kids, but—"

"What happened?" Julie interrupted, her eyes narrowing. "Did she decide she didn't like it, being stuck way out here in the middle of nowhere?"

"No," Karen said, her voice cool and her eyes staring straight ahead as she carefully slowed the car, still not used to the feel of the trailer. "She died, just like your father." As soon as she uttered the words and heard Julie's shocked gasp, Karen wished she could retract them, but knew it was too late. She reached out and took Julie's hand. "I'm sorry," she said. "I guess I didn't have to put it quite that way." Julie's eyes were glistening, and Karen knew she was thinking about Richard. "If you hadn't managed to change the subject every time I tried to talk to you

about Russell, or if you'd been willing to get even a little
bit better acquainted with him, you'd have known what
happened."

Julie stared down into her lap, feeling suddenly
ashamed of herself. Why had she said that about Russell's
first wife? "I—I'm sorry, Mom," she mumbled. "I
guess—I don't know, I—well, sometimes I guess I say stupid things."

"You say stupid things *all* the time," Molly announced
from the backseat, garnering a nasty glare from her sister.

Again Karen chose not to respond to Molly's words.
"Just give it a chance, Julie," she said. "Please? For me?"

Julie hesitated, then nodded. "I guess," she whispered.
"But Mom, it's all so different here. I don't know anyone,
and—well, what if no one likes me?"

Instantly, Karen's eyes went to the rearview mirror, and
she saw Molly gleefully preparing to seize this perfect opportunity to needle her sister. "Not a word, Molly," she
said, "I'm warning you." As Molly subsided back onto the
seat, Karen turned to Julie. "Everybody's going to like
you, honey," she said softly. She reached out to brush a
strand of Julie's long dark hair away from her face. Even
with no makeup, Julie's eyes were large and heavily
lashed, and her features, inherited from her father, were far
finer than Karen's own. "You're pretty, and most of the
time you're very, very, nice," she said.

Julie looked up, and for the first time since they'd left
Los Angeles, a smile broke through her gloom. "But when
I'm bad, I'm really, really, rotten, right?" she asked.

Karen pulled Julie close and gave her a quick hug. "You
said it, not me. Now come on—it's time for you to meet
your stepbrother. In fact," she added, nodding toward the
house, "there he is now."

Julie followed her mother's gaze to see Russell Owen
standing on the wide veranda that fronted his house. Next
to him was a boy about Julie's own age. His hair was dark

blond, and even from the car she was pretty sure he had blue eyes.

But he also looked to Julie like he had the kind of good looks that usually made boys so conceited that they never even spoke to her. He also looked like he might be a couple of inches taller than her, and maybe a year older.

But so what? She wasn't looking for a boyfriend, and even if she were, it sure wasn't going to be her hick stepbrother!

The car shuddered to a stop. Molly threw the back door open and raced up the porch steps to hurl herself on Kevin Owen, to whom she had attached herself like a small limpet the moment she'd met him the previous spring. At the same time, a large dog of indeterminate breed pushed the screen door open and leaped onto Molly. "Hi, Bailey," Molly cried, letting go of Kevin to throw her arms around the dog's neck. But as she petted the dog, her eyes fixed once more on Kevin. "Will you show me the colt?" she asked. "Is he okay? How big is he?"

Kevin hoisted Molly off her feet and held her high in the air, then lowered her just enough so they were eye to eye. "How 'bout I meet your sister and say hello to your mother, first?" he asked.

Molly giggled happily. "Okay." Kevin swung the little girl around in a circle while Bailey barked wildly, chasing after them. When Kevin set the little girl back on the ground, the dog happily lunged at her, toppling her over and licking at her face.

Julie, watching her sister play with Kevin and the dog, wondered if maybe she should've come up here for spring vacation after all.

It was as if somehow everyone had already formed a family.

A family to which she didn't belong.

* * *

Ten minutes later Kevin finally let Molly drag him off toward the barn where she'd witnessed the birth of the colt only ten weeks earlier. "Can I ride him yet?" she begged as she tugged at his arm, trying to get him to walk faster.

"No, you can't ride him yet," Kevin patiently told her. "But you can pet him, and feed him, and wash him and groom him."

"Really?" Molly asked, her eyes shining with excitement. "I can groom him? Will you teach me how?"

As they disappeared into the barn, Karen slipped her arm around Russell's waist. "I'm sorry, but I think the colt means more to her than anything else right now. It's all she talked about on the way up—in fact, it's all she's talked about since we were up here."

"Then I guess she'll like her wedding present," Russell said as he pulled her close and inhaled the scent of her hair.

"Her wedding present?" Karen echoed blankly.

"Mmm-hmm," Russell replied. "I think we ought to give Molly the colt."

"*Give* it to her?" Karen asked, her eyes widening. "But—"

"Every kid who lives on a farm should have a horse," Russell broke in, silencing her objections with a gentle finger on her lips. "So I thought we should give Molly the colt, and Julie its mother." He turned to Julie. "Do you know how to ride?"

Ride? Julie echoed silently. When would *she* ever have had a chance to learn to ride? And who cared about riding, anyway? Back home, only the snobby girls with rich parents rode horses.

But even so . . . a horse of her very own?

Despite her conviction that Pleasant Valley was going to be the worst experience of her life, she felt a thrill of excitement run through her.

A thrill she was determined not to reveal even to her

mother, let alone to Russell Owen. "I—I don't like horses very much," she said.

"They just take some getting used to," Russell replied, choosing to ignore Julie's sulky tone. "Why don't you go have Kevin show her to you? Then you can make up your mind whether you want her or not."

Julie hesitated, still torn between her determination to hate everything about the town and the farm, and her growing interest in the animal Russell had just offered her. In the end, her curiosity won out. "I—I guess I could go see it," she finally conceded. She set off toward the barn, walking slowly, determined that it appear she couldn't care less about the horse.

Russell and Karen watched her walk away and exchanged a glance, both positive they could detect a certain eagerness in her gait that Julie couldn't quite conceal.

"I think we just found the first chink in her armor," Russell observed, pulling Karen close.

Karen smiled up at him gratefully. "I don't know what to say," she began, then realized she'd brought nothing at all for his son. "But I—well, I'm afraid I didn't bring anything for Kevin. . . ." Her voice trailed off as she saw Russell eyeing her barely functional Chevy.

"I wouldn't be so sure of that," he said. "He's sixteen, and he got his driver's license two weeks ago."

Karen's jaw dropped as she realized what he was saying. "My car?" she gasped. "You want me to give him my car?"

"Well, why not?" Russell asked. "What else are we going to do with it? We've already got two almost-new cars and a truck on the farm, and I don't think we should just turn one of them over to Kevin."

Karen's brows arched. "But I should turn mine over to him?" Then, as she replayed his words in her mind, she began to understand what he was saying. "It's in really terrible shape," she said, her voice speculative. "It tends to overheat, and the brakes are almost shot. And it's eating oil like crazy."

"Which means he'll have to do a lot of work on it," Russell went on, nurturing her logic. "And that means he'll be a lot more careful of it than if we just give him a car that's already in good condition."

Karen pressed herself close to him, wondering how she had ever been lucky enough to find this wise and loving man.

It was going to be all right.

It was going to work.

They were going to be married, and live happily ever after.

She and Russell and Kevin and Molly, and even— maybe—Julie.

Except there was one other person on the farm.

Otto Owen—Russell's father—who had barely even been polite to her when she'd been up here at spring break.

And now he was nowhere to be seen.

She looked once more up into Russell's strong, handsome face—an older, more weathered version of his son's. "Where's Otto?" she asked, her voice apprehensive.

Russell hesitated, but finally tilted his head toward his own house, the bigger one. "Up there," he said.

There was something in Russell's voice that sounded a warning bell in Karen's mind. "He doesn't want us to get married, does he?" she asked.

"It's not his decision to make," Russell said, but there had been just enough hesitation before he spoke the words—and just enough anger in his voice as he uttered them—to tell Karen that something unpleasant had happened between the two men. But before she could say anything, Russell spoke again: "I'm afraid he's being a little old-fashioned about all this." His face reddened with obvious embarrassment. "Aside from not wanting me to marry

what he keeps calling a 'city girl,' he's also decided that
you shouldn't stay in my house before the wedding."

"You're kidding," Karen said, barely able to believe
what she was hearing. Then, as she saw the abashed expression on Russell's face, her mouth dropped open. "And
you're going along with him?" she asked.

Russell's feet shuffled nervously. "It's only for a few
days," he said. As Karen started to interrupt him, he
plunged on. "Come on, honey—he's lived out here all his
life, and he's too old to get with the modern world. Can't
we just humor him on this one? At spring break, you
stayed at the motel—"

"And at spring break we hadn't decided to get married,
either," she reminded him. "Russell, it's ridiculous!"

Russell nodded, but his hands spread in a gesture of
helplessness. "I know," he sighed. "But I figure if I gave
in on this one, at least he might behave himself at the wedding." His eyes twinkled mischievously. "Or do you really
want him to stand up in the middle of the ceremony and
call you a harlot in front of the whole town?"

"He wouldn't," Karen said. Then: "Would he?"

Russell shrugged. "He might. Anyway, it's only for
three nights, and it occurred to me that you and the girls
might like to have a few nights by yourselves before you
get swallowed up by all of this." His right arm moved in
a graceful arc that encompassed the surrounding acreage.
"So I agreed that you'd stay in his house until the wedding, and he'll use the guest room in the big house.
Okay?"

What was she supposed to say? Karen wondered. That
she didn't want to stay in a house owned by a man who
obviously disapproved of her? That she wanted to be with
Russell, and that she didn't really care what his father
thought? But then she realized that Russell was right—it
was only a few nights, and it was quite possible that the
whole idea of having three new people on the farm might

be as upsetting to Otto as the idea of moving to Pleasant Valley was to Julie. She would simply think of the next few days as a buffer zone—a time of transition for all of them. "Okay," she agreed.

"Then, let's get your suitcases inside," Russell told her.

He began pulling her baggage out of the trunk of the old Chevy. Karen was about to pitch in, too, when suddenly she felt an eerie chill run down her spine.

The kind of chill you feel when you know someone is watching you. Certain she knew the source of the chill, Karen turned to gaze up the hill at the house that, in just a few more days, would become her home.

In the front window she could see a silhouette.

Otto Owen, watching her.

Watching her, but not coming outside to greet her.

What if, after all, Julie had been right?

What if coming back to Pleasant Valley wasn't the best thing she'd ever done?

What if it turned out to be the worst?

Shuddering at the thought, she instantly rejected it. The day was perfect, and she was in love, and Pleasant Valley was beautiful, and she wouldn't let anyone ruin it for her.

Least of all Otto Owen.

When she glanced up at the window again, he was gone.

CHAPTER 2

Molly Spellman awoke with the first crowing of the cock, threw the cotton quilt back and scrambled out of the bed she was sharing with Julie for the last time. While Julie grabbed the blanket and wrapped it around her, rolling over to bury her face in the pillow against the brightening morning, Molly scurried over to the window and gazed rapturously out over the broad expanse of countryside surrounding the house. To her, every day on the farm brought a new adventure, and today's was going to be the biggest yet.

Her mom and Kevin's dad were getting married.

It seemed to Molly as if she'd been thinking about it forever, but she still hadn't quite decided how she felt. Mostly, she thought it was going to be great, since after her mother married Russell, Kevin would be almost like her real brother, and a big brother was what Molly had always wished for most—even more than a horse.

Now she would have both—the colt, whom she'd named Flicka, after the one in her favorite book, and a brother, too!

And she really liked Russell, although she still didn't know what she was supposed to call him. She couldn't call him Dad, since he wasn't really her father, and "Uncle Russell" seemed kind of stupid. Why would her mother be married to her uncle, anyway? So far, she hadn't been call-

27

ing him anything. Pretty soon she'd have to make up her mind.

The only thing that made everything less than perfect was Kevin's grandfather. Whenever he looked at Molly—or her sister and mother—he always appeared angry.

And he hardly ever even spoke to them, unless he absolutely had to.

Yesterday she'd asked Kevin why his grandpa was mad all the time, but Kevin had just told her not to worry, that after a while he'd get used to having them all around and then it would be okay.

But what if he didn't get used to them?

And what was it he had to get used to, anyway? There wasn't anything wrong with them!

A vision of Otto Owen's angry face, his eyes smoldering deep in the wrinkled folds of his leathery skin, suddenly rose in Molly's mind. In her imagination he was staring at her, his gaze boring into her, making her heart pound with fear. Then, as she struggled to banish the terrifying face from her imagination, the old man himself appeared in the yard outside.

Molly felt a chill as he glanced toward her, and she quickly backed away from the window. She began getting dressed, fishing yesterday's jeans out from the jumble of clothes on the chair in the corner, and scrabbling through her open suitcase for a clean T-shirt. Stopping in the kitchen to get a glass of orange juice from the pitcher in the refrigerator, she peered warily out the window, searching for Otto Owen. If he was in the barn, she didn't want to go down there at all.

But what about Flicka?

Her eyes moving away from the barn, she searched the pasture next to it, but neither Flicka nor any of the other horses were out yet, which meant that Kevin must still be asleep.

Should she go down to the barn by herself? Kevin had

shown her what to do the day after they'd come to the farm, and yesterday she'd gotten all the chores done without forgetting anything. Maybe by the time Kevin came down, Molly thought, she could have the chores finished.

But what if Kevin's grandfather was there?

She thought it over, then made up her mind. The horses needed to be fed, watered, and turned out into the pasture, and even if Kevin's grandfather was in the barn, he wasn't going to hurt her. He was just a cranky old man, and she wouldn't pay any attention to him.

She picked up some sugar lumps from the bowl on the kitchen table, pulled on her windbreaker against the morning chill, then resolutely marched out the back door and crossed the yard to the barn.

But when she got there, the courage she'd carefully constructed in the security of the kitchen failed her.

What if he was inside?

What if he yelled at her?

She listened at the door, but all she could hear from inside was the sound of the horses nickering quietly in their stalls. Finally, working her nerve up once again, she pulled the big barn door wide open, then stood at the center of the opening, staring into the gloom within.

"M-Mr. Owen?" she called out, her voice cracking slightly. "Are you in there?"

There was no reply, and her voice echoed hollowly back at her.

As she took a tentative step into the shadowy interior of the barn, the courage she'd felt in the bright sunlight deserted her. She'd been in the barn yesterday morning, and the morning before that, and it hadn't been scary at all, she told herself. But Kevin had been with her yesterday, and the morning before, Julie had been there, too.

Now she was alone. And the barn seemed much bigger than it ever had before.

"H-Hi, Greta," Molly called to Flicka's mother, who was gazing placidly over the door of her stall. Though she'd spoken more to hear the sound of her own voice than to greet the horse, the big bay mare whinnied in response. Encouraged by the sound, Molly screwed up her courage to move farther into the barn, stepping carefully through the gloom to the stall shared by Flicka and Greta.

She reached into her pocket and pulled out some of the sugar lumps, feeding one to the colt, then one to the big mare. As the animals munched the sugar cubes, Molly moved across the stall and opened the outside door. The horses followed her into the pasture, nuzzling at her pockets in search of more sugar. Molly, giggling, pushed them away, then went to the trough and turned on the water tap, letting it run until it flooded over, just as Kevin had showed her. While the water ran, she filled the feeding trough with fresh alfalfa, then returned to the barn to get a coffee can full of oats to add to the fodder.

It was while she was scooping the oats from the barrel near the tack room that she first heard the sound.

A faint humming noise, coming from somewhere in the barn.

Molly peered upward into the darkness of the loft, but could see nothing.

She frowned, wondering if she ought to find Kevin, or maybe even his father, but when she looked around again and still saw nothing, she decided to ignore the strange noise.

She took the oats out and added them to the fodder, then turned the other two horses out of their stalls into the pasture.

Returning to the barn, she began mucking out the stall that Flicka and Greta shared. She raked up all the soiled straw, shoveled it into the wheelbarrow, and took it outside to add to the big compost heap over by the kitchen garden, where Kevin had promised that she'd have her very own rows of squash and tomatoes. "They grow real fast," he'd told her the day before yesterday. "With a lot of stuff, you can hardly see anything. But with squash, you can practically watch them grow." Maybe this morning, before they had to get ready for the wedding, he'd help her plant the seeds.

The wheelbarrow empty, she started back to the barn, pausing to shrug off her jacket now that the sun was fully up. The day was starting to get hot. Leaving the jacket on the ground by the door, Molly went back into the barn, intent on finishing the cleaning of Flicka's stall.

The humming sound in the barn seemed louder at first, but as Molly swept the last of the dirty straw out of the stall, it began to fade away into her subconscious. She worked steadily, concentrating hard to be sure she didn't forget any of the things Kevin had taught her. Only when she was finally satisfied that the stall was as clean as Kevin himself could have gotten it did she move to the bin beneath the hayloft to gather fresh straw.

Now the humming was much louder. When Molly looked up, she saw its source at last.

High up, just beneath the eaves that soared above the hayloft, bees were circling, barely visible except when they flashed across the beams of sunlight that filtered through the cracks and knotholes in the barn's siding.

Fascinated, her eyes fixed on the darting insects, Molly started up the ladder to the loft. She had barely gotten to the top when she heard a voice from below.

Otto Owen's voice.

"You stop right there," he said. Though his voice wasn't really loud, there was an urgency in it that stopped Molly cold. She froze on the ladder, and then, looking slowly upward, she saw it.

Her heart began to pound.

Not more than five feet away from her, clustered around

one of the posts that supported the barn's roof, was an enormous, crawling, humming mass.

A swarm of bees.

Terrified by the sight, Molly nearly lost her grip on the ladder.

The swarm was almost two feet across, black with the bodies of thousands of insects crawling all over each other while hundreds more hovered in the air around the undulating mass.

"It's all right, Molly," she heard Otto tell her, his voice low but very clear. "Just start coming back down, real slow. Don't move too fast, and don't startle them, and they won't hurt you."

For a long moment, her gaze fixed hypnotically on the writhing mass of insects, Molly didn't move at all. Only when Otto spoke to her again, his voice much sharper, did she come out of the spell and begin to creep back down the ladder.

Otto Owen was waiting for her at the bottom. Callused hands seizing her by the shoulders, he carried her out of the barn, not setting her down until they were halfway across the yard. "Why did you go up there?" he demanded, his deep-set, frightening eyes fixing on her. "Didn't you hear the bees? Didn't you see them?"

Molly, terrified, began to cry. "I j-just wanted to see what they were doing," she wailed. "They didn't sting me or anything."

Otto glared down at her, and for a second Molly was afraid he was going to hit her. Then the angry set to his expression faded away and he stiffly knelt down so his eyes were level with hers. "Now you listen to me, young lady," he said, his voice still severe, but no longer threatening. "If you ever see that many bees again, you stay away from them, all right?"

Molly's chin trembled as she struggled to stop crying. "B-But they weren't coming after me."

"No, they weren't," Otto Owen agreed. "But if you'da bothered them, they mighta come after you." Molly's eyes widened. "They coulda killed you, Molly," the old man went on. "Don't you never, ever go near that many bees. Not unless you know exactly what you're doing."

As the words sank in, Molly turned to look back at the barn. A few bees hovered in the air, and more were clinging to the barn's siding. From the yard, though, they looked completely harmless. Then the slamming of the screen on Otto's back door distracted her, and she turned to see her mother hurrying toward her.

"Molly?" Karen called. "What's going on? Are you okay?"

Molly pointed to the barn. "Bees!" she called out, her fear of a moment before suddenly forgotten in the presence of her mother. Running toward Karen, she started to tell her what had happened, pointing toward the barn. "They're up there, Mom. A whole swarm of them!"

Karen's eyes shifted to the barn's second story.

What was Molly talking about? There were a few bees up there, going in and out, but—

Then it happened.

Suddenly the barn itself seemed to erupt into life as thousands of bees churned through the cracks and knotholes. In seconds the air was black with them, their humming a deafening drone that seemed to shake the very earth. Then they were swirling toward her. Karen grabbed Molly's hand and began racing back toward the house, half dragging her daughter behind her.

"What are they doing, Mom?" Julie asked, a hard knot of fear forming in the pit of her stomach as she gazed at the mass of bees that roiled just beyond the window. "Are they trying to get in?"

With an arm around each of her daughters, Karen stared out the window at the swarming insects. As soon as she'd gotten Molly safely back inside Otto's house, she'd phoned up to Russell's. Kevin had answered, telling her not to worry, that he and his grandfather could take care of bees. "I don't think so," Karen finally replied, more out of need to reassure her daughters than because she herself felt that the insects would remain safely outside. "We'll just stay right here, and let Kevin and Otto deal with them."

An enormous old walnut tree spread its limbs toward the house, and it was in a crotch where the main trunk split into two huge branches that the bees were now swarming. The mass of insects was steadily growing, and both Julie and Karen were staring at it in awe. "My God," Julie breathed, barely conscious that she was speaking the words aloud. "How big can it get?"

Molly, emboldened by the protection of the glass between her and the cloud of insects beyond the window, gazed at the swarm in fascination. "It was a lot bigger in the barn," she announced. "See? They're still coming out!"

As Karen followed her younger daughter's gaze, her arm tightened around the little girl. Thank God Otto got her out of harm's way! she thought, repressing a shudder. And Kevin had said it was "No big deal." No big deal! she repeated silently to herself. With millions of bees out there, how could it be no big deal?

"What are they going to do?" Julie demanded, instantly sensing her mother's doubts.

"I don't *know*," Karen replied, her taut nerves starting to fray. "Maybe they'll spray them with insecticide or something."

Molly grabbed her mother's arm with one hand and pointed toward the barn with the other. "Wow! Look at that, Mom!"

Following Molly's gaze, Karen stared at the two figures emerging from the barn.

Otto and Kevin Owen, their heads covered with netting,

but wearing nothing else to protect themselves from the bees, were moving quickly across the yard, Kevin carrying a folded aluminum ladder, while Otto bore a large cardboard box. As Kevin began setting up the ladder, Otto put the box down, opened it, and took out what looked to Karen like a thin brush, perhaps a foot long, with a handle at one end, and an odd-looking contraption that seemed to be a metal can with an inverted funnel on top and a leather bellows fastened to one side. The ladder in place, Kevin knelt down and grasped the can. Pulling a match from his jeans pocket, he struck it against the bottom step of the ladder and dropped it into the metal can. He blew into the can for a moment, then, apparently satisfied that it was burning properly, put the top back on.

As Karen and her daughters watched, Kevin climbed up nearly to the top of the ladder, where his head and shoulders were almost level with the swarm, which clung to a branch two feet away from the boy. Otto handed him the brush, then picked up the box. Climbing up to the third step of the ladder, Otto held the box out so it was just below the swarm.

As Kevin worked the bellows attached to the canister, smoke began pouring from the funnel top, enveloping the bees, which promptly began flying away from the noxious fumes, until the body of the swarm was two-thirds dispersed. Then Kevin gently brushed what remained of the swarm into the box.

For a moment bees appeared to rise out of the box almost as soon as Kevin brushed them into it, but then everything changed. The flow of bees reversed, and the hovering horde began settling into the box.

Moving carefully, Otto climbed back down the ladder and eased the box onto the ground.

A moment later Kevin, too, had climbed down. As bees eddied in the air around him, he folded up the ladder and carried it back to the barn, Otto following him with the smoker and the brush.

By the time they were done putting the equipment away, all but a few of the bees had settled into the cardboard box, and when Kevin and Otto emerged from the barn, Otto was carrying a cover for it. Otto put the lid on, picked up the box and carried it to the pickup truck parked next to the barn. Kevin, meanwhile, came into the house.

"Are you all right?" Karen asked, barely able to believe what Kevin had just done. "Didn't you get stung?"

"Why would they sting me?" Kevin asked. "I wasn't hurting them."

Karen sank onto one of the straight-backed kitchen chairs, feeling drained by what she had just seen. "Where did they come from?" she asked, her voice hollow. "Were they in the barn all along?" She remembered Julie and Molly running in and out of the barn all day yesterday, and the day before. Had the swarm been there all along, concealed in the loft, an unseen danger to her two girls?

Kevin shook his head to her question. "They probably just came in this morning," he said. "It was too cold for them last night. Once it gets down around fifty, bees can't fly much at all."

"But where'd they come from?" Karen pressed.

Kevin shrugged. "Probably one of the hives."

"The hives?" Karen echoed. "I don't remember seeing any hives here."

"They're here," Kevin said. "All the farms have hives—we have to have bees to pollinate the crops. But when a hive gets too full, they produce a new queen, and the old one takes off with about a third of the bees. That's how they start new colonies. We'll take 'em back to the hives and set up a new one for them."

"Where are they?" Molly demanded, curiosity washing away the last of her fear. "How come you haven't shown them to me?"

"Because they're way over on the other side of the far pasture, as far away from the house as you can get," Kevin told her. "And they're out there because little kids like you should stay away from them."

"I'm not a little kid," Molly shot back. "I'm almost ten."

"In ten more months," Julie interjected.

"I still want to see the bees," Molly insisted, glaring at her sister.

"That's enough, Molly," Karen told her. "Kevin and Mr. Owen can take care of the bees, and you can stay here with me."

Outside, Otto had finished loading the cardboard box into the back of the pickup truck and was beckoning to Kevin.

"Want to go along?" Kevin asked Julie, his face reddening slightly and his eyes avoiding hers with such bashfulness that Karen, watching from the table, had to hide a smile.

Julie stared at Kevin. "Tell me you're kidding," she said. "You want me to get in that truck, with millions of bees in the back?"

Kevin's blush deepened. "It's not dangerous," he said. "The top can't come off."

"Isn't it dangerous when you put them in the hive?" Karen asked. "You have to open the box then, don't you?"

Kevin nodded. "But Julie won't be anywhere near it. She can even stay in the truck, and keep the windows closed if she wants to," he explained, his eyes fastening on Karen's in a mute appeal.

"Why don't you go, Julie?" Karen said, giving in to Kevin's puppy-dog look. "I'm sure Kevin and Otto know exactly what they're doing."

"Mo-ther," Julie groaned. "Come *on*. Why would I want to—"

But this time, Karen didn't let her finish. "I think you

ought to go," she said. "If I didn't have so much to do, I'd go myself. It sounds interesting." Before Julie had a chance to say anything more, Karen turned to Kevin. "Go tell your grandfather to wait a minute, will you? Julie will be right there."

Kevin, sensing that something was about to happen between Julie and her mother, hesitated. "If she doesn't really want to—" he began, but Karen quickly interrupted him.

"She'll be down in a minute," she insisted. "Just tell Otto to wait." As Kevin left through the back door, Karen turned to her daughter, who was glaring at her angrily.

"Mother, I don't want to go!" Julie began. "I mean, like, beehives? Who cares about beehives? I don't see why—"

Karen held up her hands against Julie's torrent of words. "Will you please listen to me? All I want you to do is go with them. Can't you see how important it is to Kevin that you go? Please, Julie. You can stay in the truck and look the other way if you want to. But we're going to be living on this farm, and we all have to get along together. Even with Otto Owen. And I might remind you that he got Molly out of the barn, and helped Kevin get the swarm out of the tree while we were hiding in the house. No wonder he doesn't think much of us—we acted like a bunch of cowards! So just go with them, and thank Otto for taking care of the swarm. All right?"

Julie took a deep breath, about to argue some more, but then saw the expression her mother always got when she'd decided there wasn't going to be any more discussion. "Oh, all right," she sighed. "I'll go. But I won't get out of the car—I *hate* bees!"

"Really?" Karen asked, her brows arching and her eyes sparkling with mischief. "But they've always spoken so well of you!"

Julie stared at her mother in exasperation, then turned and started across the kitchen. Maybe seeing the hives wouldn't be so bad after all, she decided. In fact, though she wasn't about to admit it, she was already feeling a little curious about exactly how they were going to maneuver the bees out of the box into the hive.

"But what about me?" she heard Molly complaining as she pushed the screen door open. "Why can't I go too?" Hurrying, Julie quickly moved away from the house before her mother could decide she might as well take her sister along.

"Because someone has to stay here and help me get ready," Karen replied, reaching down and lifting Molly off her feet to distract her from trying to chase after Julie. "After all, you don't want your old mother to look like a hag when she gets married, do you?"

"But I want to see the bees!" Molly demanded.

Karen held her so the tip of Molly's nose just touched her own. "Tell you what. You stay here and help me get dressed, and tomorrow you and I will sneak off without anyone knowing where we're going, and look at the beehives together. But you have to promise not to bother the bees. Okay?"

Molly, her ruffled feelings somewhat soothed, nodded reluctantly, and Karen set her back on the floor. Outside, Julie was sliding into the cab of the truck next to Otto, and though the old man barely nodded an acknowledgment that she was there, Karen smiled to herself. She had been certain she'd seen at least a flicker of interest in Julie's eyes, and she suspected that by the time Julie got back, she'd have pumped Otto dry on the subject of beehives.

And Otto, perhaps, would have warmed to at least one of her daughters.

An hour later, when the truck came back and Julie came into the house, Karen realized she'd been wrong.

"Julie?" she said. "What happened?"

Julie, already on her way to the room she shared with Molly, turned to glare at her mother.

"Mr. Owen," she said. "I hate him! I really hate him! He wouldn't even speak to me, even when I asked him a simple question. All he did was tell me to stay out of the way! All I wanted to do was watch! As if I care about the stupid bees! As if I care about any of this!" Bursting into tears, she dashed into the little bedroom and hurled herself onto the bed, burying her face in the pillow.

Karen groaned inwardly. Why did this have to happen on her wedding day? And worse, what did it mean for the future? Wasn't Otto *ever* going to accept them being there?

Maybe she should go up and talk to Russell about his father.

Or maybe even postpone the wedding . . .

No! That was exactly what Otto wanted. And not for her simply to postpone the ceremony, either, but for her to cancel it entirely, and take her daughters back to Los Angeles.

Well, to hell with him! Deciding she simply wouldn't worry about the cantankerous old man for the rest of the day, Karen set about the task of calming her daughter down.

But even after she'd stopped crying, Julie's eyes remained stormy.

"We should go home," she said. "We don't belong here. We should just go home."

Saying nothing of her own fleeting thought of postponing the wedding, Karen silently prayed that Julie was wrong.

CHAPTER 3

*T*he afternoon sun was hot, and Karen was beginning to wonder if she'd made the right decision about the dress she'd chosen to get married in. It was a good dress—one she bought years ago, before Richard died—and its pale green was a shade she'd always thought flattered her skin and contrasted nicely with her dark hair. If it was somewhat dated, so be it—she hadn't had any money to buy a new dress, and refused to let Russell buy her one. "Farmers' wives do not waste money on a dress they're only going to wear once," she told him when he suggested she buy a new dress in Los Angeles before the move up to Pleasant Valley. She'd meant the words when she uttered them, but now, as she gazed at the carefully altered and pressed garment hanging on the closet door, she wondered.

The temperature had soared into the high eighties, and the heavy silk dress had long sleeves. Nervously, she imagined herself walking across the wide yard and up the hill to Russell's front porch with dark stains spreading under her arms. Just the thought of it made her skin go clammy. But what else was there to wear? She was just about to make a quick inventory of the clothes she'd brought with her when a car horn startled her. She looked out the window to see a gray Jeep Cherokee pulling into the yard. As it rolled to a stop, Karen gazed at the man behind the wheel. Though he looked vaguely familiar, she couldn't quite place him.

And what was he doing here so early? The guests weren't supposed to start arriving for another half hour. Her nerves getting edgier by the second, Karen abandoned the idea of searching for another dress, and hurried toward the door to take up her duties as hostess. But even before she got Otto's front door open, she heard the voice of the old man himself.

And, as usual, he sounded mad.

Pushing the screen door open, Karen stepped out onto the front porch just as the man, heavyset, and a few years older than herself, was climbing out of the Cherokee. His eyes were hidden behind dark glasses. He wore jeans and a western shirt, and as he stepped out into the heat of the sun, he reached back into the car for a stained and battered cowboy hat with which to protect his balding head from the sun. Then, with an amused grin playing at the corners of his mouth, he leaned against the Jeep as the angry Otto Owen bore down on him.

"What the hell are you doin' here?" the old man demanded as he strode across the yard. Stopping before he was close enough for the visitor to offer his hand, the old man folded his arms belligerently across his chest.

The younger man's grin broadened into a smile in the face of Otto's hostility, but to Karen the pleasant expression looked forced. "The wedding, Otto," he said. "Russell *did* invite me, you know. I just came out early to see if I could lend a hand with anything."

"He don't need nothin' from you," Otto growled.

The man nodded in apparent resignation, as if he'd heard all this before. Finally he shrugged, almost sadly. "I don't get it, Otto," he said. "What is it you've got against making this place pay off?"

"Pay?" Otto Owen repeated, the color in his face rising along with his voice. "You don't know what the hell you're talking about, Henderson!"

And suddenly Karen realized who the man was, and

why he looked familiar. Although he was older and had put on some weight, she remembered Carl Henderson perfectly clearly, from her childhood. He was four or five years older than she was, and he used to help her and her friends catch butterflies in the fields. In fact, hadn't he gone to Cal Poly to study entomology? The two or three times she'd thought of him over the years, she'd assumed he'd wound up in a museum somewhere. But apparently he was still here, where he'd grown up.

"This farm paid pretty damned good for a lot longer'n you'd know about!" she heard Otto Owen sputtering as she turned back to the scene before her eyes. "First for my pa, then for me. And if it wasn't for you bastards, it'd do just fine for my son and my grandson, too!"

"Come off it, Otto," Henderson replied, his eyes narrowing as they fixed on the angry old man. "You know damned well these fields weren't producing like they used to. And it's not like anyone meant for that fertilizer to sterilize the hives! What the hell do you want from us? We've paid more damages than the crops were worth, and we're still paying. Besides, if you and your precious pa hadn't farmed the fields out, you wouldn't have needed that fertilizer in the first place! Left to yourself, you'd have gone broke in another five years."

"The hell I would!" Otto roared. "And I don't need no more of your kind of help! Buncha damned chemicals polluting the place! No wonder you hafta have all them fancy hybrid bees. Regular ones couldn't stand the pollution! Why don't you just stay the hell away from here?"

"Oh, for Christ's sake, Otto," Henderson said. "The fields still have to be fertilized, and the crops still have to be pollinated. All I'm trying to do is make things better for you! We're working on your fields, and we're supplying you with bees, and if you want to know the truth, I'm doing you a favor looking after the hives. If it was up to you—"

But Otto didn't let him finish. Shaking his finger in the younger man's face, his querulous voice rose once again. "We let you and the bastards you work for keep on taking care of us, and we'll *all* be poisoned in five years! UniGrow, my ass—Uni*Dead* is what they should call your outfit!"

"I don't believe it." Karen realized she'd been holding her breath, half expecting Otto to take a swing at Carl Henderson. "Otto?" she called as she hurried off the porch and started toward the two men. "What's going on? What's wrong?"

Otto's concentration on Carl Henderson broken, he turned to glare at Karen for a moment, then swiveled on his heel and strode back to his son's house, slamming the front door behind him.

"I'm afraid it's my fault," Carl Henderson said, taking a tentative step in Karen's direction. "I'm—" He stopped abruptly, then a look of recognition came into his eyes and a smile spread across his face. "My God—Karen Gilman! Even after all these years, I'd recognize you anywhere. And just as pretty as when you were a kid." His smile faltered slightly. "You probably don't even remember me, do you?" he asked. "I'd already gone to college by the time you got to high school. I'm—"

"Carl Henderson," Karen finished for him, moving toward him and extending her hand. "I *do* remember you! You used to help me and the other kids catch butterflies! But I haven't used 'Gilman' since I married my first husband."

"Sorry to cause such a stir," Henderson said as he waved a greeting to Russell, who had just emerged from the house up the hill, the tails of a half-buttoned dress shirt hanging over his pants. "I just figured I'd show up a little early, so Otto could get done with his yelling before everyone else got here." As Russell came across the yard, Henderson leaned conspiratorially toward Karen, though

when he spoke, he made sure his voice was loud enough
for Russell to hear. "I'm going to tell you a secret, Karen.
Your prospective father-in-law is crazy. Just plain out of
his mind!"

As Russell clapped Carl Henderson on the back and
suggested they have a quick drink—"just to get me
through this hog-tying"—Karen retreated back into Otto's
house, wearily wondering what fight Otto might try to
pick next, and if she was ever going to get married at all,
let alone that very afternoon.

"I guess that will have to do it," Karen pronounced half an
hour later, checking her makeup in the mirror one last
time. "You both look gorgeous, so let's go get me married
to Russell."

She held still while Julie carefully set the minuscule hat
and veil on her head. Molly looked up at her mother, her
head cocked as her brows knit into a deep frown.

"How come your veil doesn't cover your face?" she
asked.

"Because I hate the feeling of them," Karen replied. Or
was it because for her second wedding she felt foolish getting all dressed up, let alone putting on a long veil? "Now
let me see you." Molly struck a pose, then pirouetted to
show off her best dress, a soft pink that set off the little
girl's rosy complexion. Smiling, Karen turned her attention
to Julie, who was wearing the one new dress Karen had
purchased for the occasion, when neither her own ward-
robe nor Julie's had yielded anything that could be com-
fortably altered. She also suspected she might have bought
the dress as a form of bribery. Now she found herself
searching her daughter's eyes for a last-minute change of
heart about the wedding. "All set to walk down the aisle
with your old mother?" she asked.

Julie hesitated for just a split second, and Karen could
see her wrestling with the desire to make one last attempt

to talk her out of going through with it. But to Karen's relief, Julie managed instead to produce a smile that looked almost genuine.

"All set," her daughter said. "And you look beautiful."

They left the bedroom and Karen and Julie paused in the living room while Molly went outside and waved to the musicians on the porch of Russell's house, signaling them to begin playing. A moment later the first strains of the wedding march drifted across the yard, and Molly, picking up a basket she'd filled with wildflowers that morning, stepped off the porch. The yard was filled with people—so many of them that for a second Molly almost forgot what to do. But then she saw Kevin, standing next to his father at the top of the porch steps in the big house, winking at her.

I can do it, she thought to herself. And I won't mess up, either!

Taking a handful of petals from the basket, she tossed them in front of her and started down the steps. Concentrating as hard as she could, she stepped slowly across the yard spreading petals in front of her. When she heard the crowd murmur a few seconds later, she knew her sister and mother must have emerged from the house, too. She had to resist the impulse to look back, but managed to keep on going until she was finally at the bottom of the steps that led up to Russell's porch.

Julie waited until Molly had descended the steps from Otto's house and begun to cross the lawn before following her. Now that the wedding was actually happening, and she had no more opportunity to argue with her mother about it, she found that she was actually enjoying it. Despite the fact that she'd resisted to the very last moment, showing no enthusiasm at all for the plans her mother had made, she loved the pale blue dress she and her mother had chosen, and now, as she followed her sister up the slope to Russell's house, she realized that everything about the wedding was truly beautiful. The June day was perfect—clear and bright—and the hills, still green from the winter's unusually heavy rains, made a perfect back-drop to the farm, and to Russell's house.

Even the guests assembled on the lawn—though they were mostly complete strangers to her—looked open and friendly. Not at all like the people in L.A., who either didn't look at you at all or stared at you like they were go-ing to slit your throat at any moment. But here, not only was everyone looking at her, but they were all actually smiling!

Almost against her will, Julie found herself smiling back at them, glorying in the friendliness of the attention riveted on her, feeling that today, in the pretty, new dress and with her dark hair cascading loose down her back, she looked nicer than she'd ever looked before.

But then, as she was halfway up the slope to the house, she suddenly felt something else.

The sharp, unpleasant sensation of someone staring.

A stare that penetrated her sunny mood like cold steel, and made her suppress a shiver, despite the warmth of the afternoon.

For a moment her eyes met those of the man watching her, then she quickly looked away. There was something about him that frightened her, and as Julie continued up the hill, she found herself wanting to circle around, away from him.

But that's stupid, she told herself. Just because he's looking at you, it doesn't mean he wants anything. He's just an ordinary man. Yet as she walked past him, con-sciously keeping her eyes fixed straight ahead, she felt again the chill blade of his gaze boring into her.

It was as if he was looking right inside her.

Once again she shivered, then found herself glancing at

the man, despite her determination not to. Their gazes held for a fraction of a second, and he flashed a smile at her.

Julie felt herself flush and quickly jerked her gaze away. Now, as she kept walking, she had to struggle to keep her pace slow and measured. Just before she got to the steps to Russell's porch, she dared to glance back once again.

Carl Henderson's eyes were still fixed on her.

Suddenly Molly forgot.

She was at the foot of the porch steps, but what was she supposed to do next? Was she supposed to go on up, or was she supposed to stand somewhere else?

She felt a surge of panic, but then saw Kevin signaling to her. Quickly, certain her sister and mother must be right behind her by now, she tossed the rest of the petals onto the steps and darted up onto the porch to stand next to Kevin, who took her hand as a ripple of laughter moved over the crowd. Then she felt Kevin squeeze her hand, and saw her mother smiling at her, and decided that maybe she hadn't messed up after all.

Julie, a slight frown betraying her feelings, joined Molly on the porch, then her mother came up the steps and moved next to Russell, who'd come out of the house to stand beside the minister.

The ceremony began.

Molly tried to listen to what the minister was saying, but just as he started the ceremony, the buzzing of a bee distracted her. She glanced quickly around, afraid at first that maybe the whole swarm was coming back.

Then she saw it.

A single bee, hovering over the flowers she'd dropped on the steps.

She tried to ignore it, but it came closer.

What if it stung her mother, right in the middle of the wedding?

The bee was on the porch now, still exploring the flowers. If Molly stuck her foot out, she could just reach it. And if she squashed it, then it *couldn't* sting her mother! She edged her foot out, moving her white patent leather shoe closer to the bee.

It darted away, then instantly circled back, closer to Molly's foot than before.

She edged her foot closer.

She glanced up, but nobody seemed to be watching her at all. And the bee was only a couple of inches away from her toe!

She lifted her foot, but just as she was about to reach for the bee, it flew away, and for a moment Molly didn't know where it had gone.

And then, as she felt it on her leg, she knew.

Under her dress!

The bee had gotten under her dress, and now it was crawling up her leg!

She stifled the urge to jerk her skirt up over her head so the bee could fly away. If she could just hold perfectly still until the minister finished and the wedding was over . . .

Molly stood rooted to the spot, trying not to feel the insect's movement tickling her skin as it crept up her calf to the spot on the back of her knee where she'd always been ticklish. Finally she could stand it no longer and moved her leg.

Not much—just enough to make the bee move a little.

That was when she felt the searing heat of the stinger sinking into her flesh.

She gasped, but managed to hold back the scream that rose in her throat.

How long? How much longer before the minister would be done?

She tried to listen, but the burning was spreading rapidly through her leg now, and she was starting to feel funny. Then, through the pain, she heard the words:

"I now pronounce you husband and wife. Russell, you may kiss your bride!"

She looked up and saw Russell kissing her mother. She reached out toward her mother, but before her fingers even touched her mother's arm, she felt it starting to get harder to breathe. She moaned, then lurched against Kevin, who looked down at her.

"Molly?" she heard him ask. "Hey, short stuff, you okay?"

Molly's eyes widened and she struggled to speak, but her throat seemed to be closing, and all she could utter was a tiny gasp: "A . . . bee . . . st-stung me . . ." Her eyes glistening with tears, she reached down to press her hand against the spot on her leg from which searing heat was spreading rapidly in every direction. Yet even though the pain was almost more than she could bear, when she touched the place where the bee had stung her, she could hardly even feel her fingers against her flesh.

Pulling up her skirt, she stared in horror at her leg, inflamed to a red that looked even worse than the sunburn she'd gotten last summer. There was a bloodless white spot where the stinger had pierced her skin. She could still see the stinger itself, torn from the bee's body when it tried to withdraw the weapon from her leg. She tried to pluck the stinger from her swollen flesh, but now she was losing control of her nerves, and all she could do was prod helplessly at the tiny black needle that had inflicted such agony on her. A scream of pain and terror rose in her throat, but emerged only as a helpless gurgle.

Her attention caught by the strange sound, Julie glanced at her sister, gasped, then clutched at her mother's arm. Startled, Karen pulled away from Russell and looked down. "Honey—?" she began. Then Kevin broke in and told her what had happened.

"She's having an allergic reaction to a bee sting," he said. "I'll get the kit."

As Karen knelt beside her young daughter, whose breathing was quickly dissolving into labored gasps, Kevin darted into the house, returning almost instantly with a first-aid kit. Taking the kit from his son, Russell opened it, found an Epi-Pen, and quickly injected a dose of epinephrine into the muscle of Molly's thigh.

A moment later, as Molly's breathing took on a terrifying feathery quality, Russell picked her up. "Come on," he told Karen. "She's going into shock and the shot isn't working. We've got to get her to the clinic. Fast!"

With Molly whimpering helplessly in his arms, he pushed his way through the crowd, Karen following close behind him. Julie, stunned by how quickly it had all happened, tried to follow her mother and sister through the crowd, but before she could catch up her stepfather had gotten them into a car and was already heading down the driveway.

Feeling totally useless, Julie could only watch them go.

CHAPTER 4

"*I*t's all right, Molly," Karen crooned. "It's going to be fine." But as she held her daughter in her arms, she wondered if her words were true. Molly's leg kept swelling, and her knee—which she could no longer bend at all—had practically disappeared into her puffy flesh. The little girl's breathing seemed to be getting worse by the second, and her skin was bright red all over.

"Can't you go any faster?" she asked Russell, her voice taking on an urgency she hoped Molly wouldn't understand.

"We'll be there in less than a minute," Russell told her. "Someone will have called ahead to let Dr. Filmore know we're coming. Molly's going to be all right."

"But what's happening to her?" Karen asked. "She's been stung by bees before. She's—"

"I don't know any more than you do, honey," Russell told her. The town was still a quarter of a mile away when he hit the brakes and swerved off the road into the parking lot of the small clinic that had been finished just a year ago, built with funds raised by the townspeople over a period of almost a decade. As Russell had promised, the front door opened as they approached it, and a woman of about thirty-five held it wide as Karen, still clutching Molly in her arms, hurried inside.

"Take her straight through that door," the woman instructed, indicating one of the two doors at the back of the waiting area.

Karen lurched through the door, surprised to find the room empty. A wave of panic threatening to strangle her, she twisted her head back toward the woman who'd met them at the door. "Where's Dr. Filmore?" she asked. "Russell said—"

"I'm Ellen Filmore," the woman announced. "Let's get some of those clothes off her." While Karen supported Molly's weight, Ellen Filmore, whose prematurely graying hair framed a pretty, oval face highlighted by warm brown eyes, expertly unfastened the row of buttons that ran down the back of Molly's dress, then pulled the little girl's arms free of the sleeves. "All right, let's lay her down."

Gently, Karen lowered Molly onto the examining table. Molly's breathing was becoming more and more labored, and the color in her face was changing from the bright red it had been a few moments before to a pale bluish tinge. "Oh, God," Karen cried. "She can't breathe! You have to—"

But Ellen Filmore, a strange-looking plastic object in her hands, was already pushing her firmly aside, and now a young man clad in white pants and a pale green smock had appeared at the other side of the table. "Do you want to give her a sedative?" the man asked.

"I don't think she needs it," the doctor said. Speaking quickly, she explained to Karen what she was doing as she began working the object, which consisted of two tubes, divided in the center by a large plastic plate, into Molly's mouth. "Her throat's swelling, blocking her trachea. If we can get this airway in . . ." The doctor's voice died away as she focused all her concentration on her task. The nurse held Molly's mouth open and used a depressor to move the little girl's tongue aside. Karen winced as the plastic tube began to slide into Molly's throat, causing her daughter to gag, but a moment later Molly's chest suddenly expanded

as she drew a deep breath of air into her lungs. Soon, the
bluish tinge to Molly's face gave way, but the unnatural
redness remained. "Don't worry too much about her
color," Ellen Filmore said. "It means she's getting air
again. With any luck, the worst of it's already over." Her
attention shifted to the nurse. "Let's give her a shot of epinephrine, Roberto."

Russell, who was hovering just inside the door, spoke
just as the nurse started out of the room. "I already used
epinephrine. It didn't seem to have any effect at all."

Frowning, Ellen Filmore looked up from Molly, onto
whose arm she was wrapping a sphygmomanometer cuff.
"You're sure you gave her the shot from the bee kit, not
the snake kit?" she asked as she pumped the cuff. Molly's
blood pressure was perilously low.

"I gave her the right shot," Russell declared. "And it's
fresh, too. I just replaced it a month ago."

"Then we have a problem." Ellen's frown deepened as
she began jotting notes on a blank chart. "We're going to
have to get her over to San Luis Obispo."

Karen felt her growing fear begin to give way to panic.
She reached out to lay a protective hand on her daughter,
who, mercifully, no longer seemed able to hear what was
being said. "San Luis Obispo?" she echoed. "Why can't
you treat her here?"

Ellen Filmore ignored Karen's question, turning instead
to Russell. "Was Carl Henderson at the wedding?"

Russell nodded.

"Good. Call your house and ask him if we can use his
plane. If he's already left, find him." As Russell strode out
of the examining room, Dr. Filmore turned her attention to
Karen, talking as she began setting up an IV in Molly's
right forearm. "I'm going to try another shot of epinephrine, just in case, but if she still doesn't respond, then we
have a problem," she repeated.

"A problem?" Karen echoed, immediately thinking the

worst. "Oh, God, Molly's not going to—" She cut off her words, unwilling to let Molly hear her even utter the word "die."

Ellen Filmore, though, understood exactly what Karen was trying to ask, and shook her head firmly. "We're a long way from even thinking about that," she assured Karen. "Has your daughter ever been allergic to bee stings before?"

Karen shook her head, repeating what she'd told Russell in the car. "Lord knows, she's stepped on her share of bees, but all she's ever done is cry while I've pulled out the stinger, then gone right on with whatever she was doing. She's never even swelled up before." She looked down into Molly's pain-contorted face, and her eyes flooded with the tears she'd been struggling to control.

As the nurse came back into the room with a hypodermic needle, Ellen Filmore took it, administered the shot, then watched for any sign of a reaction from Molly.

There was none.

"Stay with her, Roberto," the doctor instructed. "She seems stable for the moment, but if there's any change, call me immediately." She led Karen out of the room, closing the door behind her. "It appears that your daughter has developed an allergy," she explained. "It happens sometimes—people go along for years with no reaction to bee venom at all, and then, wham! With some people it seems to be a cumulative effect. But what bothers me," she went on, her eyes clouding with worry, "is that she isn't responding to the epinephrine. Unless what stung her is a different strain of bee from what we're used to, it should have pulled her out of the reaction."

For a moment Karen didn't grasp what the doctor was saying, but then she remembered all the stories she'd seen in the Los Angeles papers over the last couple of years, and the meaning of the doctor's words finally sank in.

"You mean, killer bees?" she whispered, her face paling slightly.

"I didn't say that," Ellen replied. "In fact, I'd be very surprised if that's what it is. The African strain hasn't reached this far north as far as anyone knows, and even if it has, this isn't what it does. It's more aggressive than our bees, but individually, it's no more dangerous. It almost seems as though something else must have stung Molly."

Before Karen could say anything more, Russell came in from the reception area. "I talked to Carl—he's on his way to the airport now. We'll meet him there."

"All right," Ellen Filmore said. She led them back into the examining room, and Russell stared at the IV in Molly's arm. Even to his unpracticed eyes, he could see that the swelling had grown worse, and though she was still able to breathe through the airway, she was struggling for each lungful of air. Could she even survive the flight?

"How—" he began, but his voice choked as he gazed at the helpless child, and all he could do was gesture toward the array of equipment that was keeping Molly alive.

"It'll be okay," Ellen told him. "We'll take the van to the airport, and I'll fly over to San Luis Obispo with you. Carl has a cellular phone in the plane, so I can talk to the hospital on the way. He can radio ahead for an ambulance to meet us. Let's go."

Issuing instructions as she began transferring Molly, who was now barely conscious, to a gurney, the doctor showed Russell how to regulate the oxygen that was feeding into Molly's breathing tube, and explained to Karen how to regulate the IV. "Neither of you should actually have to do anything at all," she said as she began wheeling the gurney toward the main door. "But if her condition should change while we're in the air, I might not have time to tell you what to do. The important thing is to keep the bottle higher than Molly, so the fluid keeps dripping into her arm. And if I tell you to turn it off, do it with the valve. What we don't want to do is detach the tube from the bottle or the needle, and absolutely we don't want to let the needle come out of her arm. Ready?"

Working as a team, with Ellen Filmore and Roberto Muñoz guiding the gurney while Russell carried the oxygen canister and Karen the IV bottle, they moved out of the clinic to the parking lot. Within minutes they had Molly loaded into the van, Russell cradling the little girl in his arms. Ten minutes later they arrived at the airport, where Carl Henderson already had the tie-downs off his plane and the engine warming.

They maneuvered Molly into the plane, stretched out on the middle of the three cramped rows of seats. As Russell climbed into the co-pilot's seat, he looked back at Karen, who was crouched in the backseat with Ellen Filmore.

"Will you look at us?" he asked, forcing a smile he didn't feel at all. "We're going to be the best-dressed parents the hospital in Obispo's ever seen."

Karen tried to return the smile, but when Molly shuddered in her stupor, she had to bite her lips to keep from crying out.

Don't let her die, she prayed silently. Please, God, don't let her die.

Julie hung up the phone in the kitchen. Beyond the closed door to the dining room she could hear the murmur of the few guests who were still at the farm, waiting to hear if Molly would live. Steeling herself to answer their questions, she opened the door and began moving as quickly as she could through the small group of her stepfather's best friends. "It doesn't sound like they're coming home today," she told Maddy Brewer, whose name was one of the few she could remember. "Molly's really sick, and Mom sounds scared." Catching sight of Kevin on the front porch, Julie moved quickly to the front door and stepped outside, gratefully sucking the fresh air into her lungs. "Mom just called," she reported. "They've taken Molly to the hospital in San Luis Obispo, and she isn't sure when they're going to be able to get home. Maybe tomorrow, but maybe not until the next day."

Kevin sighed heavily, uncertain what to say. The memory of the pain he'd seen in Molly's eyes an hour ago tore at his guts, and as he tried to ask Julie how she was, a knot formed in his throat that choked the words off. So instead of exposing the deep fear he was feeling for Molly, he tried to act a lot braver than he was feeling, and forced his mouth into a wry smile. "Some wedding, huh? I guess we better tell everyone who's left that they might as well go home." He glanced back into the house, where tables were laden with food. "Kind of a waste, isn't it?"

Julie stared at him. "Is that all you care about? A bunch of food? What about my sister?" What did Kevin think? That Molly had deliberately gotten stung? "She didn't do it on purpose!"

"Who said she did?" Kevin replied, stunned by Julie's flare of anger. What the hell was going on? Why was she all of a sudden so pissed off? "All I said was—"

"I *heard* what you said," Julie shot back, cutting him off. "And it sounded like you think Molly deliberately tried to—"

"I didn't say anything about Molly at all!" Kevin protested, his own voice rising now.

The screen door banged open and Otto Owen stepped out, scowling at both of them. "What's going on out here?"

Before Kevin could say a word, Julie blurted out her accusation.

"Well, he's right," Otto grumbled. "If you kids and your mother had stayed where you belonged, your sister wouldn'ta gotten stung, now would she?"

Julie's mouth dropped open with mute astonishment and she burst into tears. Covering her face with her hands, she stumbled down the steps and ran across the yard toward the barn.

Kevin glared at his grandfather. "Jeez, Grandpa!"

"Well, it's true, isn't it?" the old man snapped. "They don't belong here!"

Kevin's temper erupted. "Dad and Karen are married, Grandpa! He loves her! And I like her, too." His words came faster and faster, tumbling from his mouth. "She's not my mom, but so what? Mom's dead, and nothing's going to change that! And I like Julie and Molly, too! If Molly dies, I don't know what I'll do! She's just like my little sister. So just cut it out, Grandpa! Okay?" Before Otto had a chance to reply, Kevin turned, took the steps to the ground in one leap, and set off after Julie.

Otto's jaw tightened and a vein in his forehead started to throb. He took a tentative step after Kevin, but then stopped, wheeled around and went back into the house, pushing his way through the cluster of guests until he came to the punch bowl on the dining room table. He started to pour himself a cup, then changed his mind and stalked to the sideboard where several bottles of liquor stood. Pouring himself a generous shot of Jack Daniel's, he drained it, then poured another.

Kids! What the hell were they coming to? If he'd ever spoken to his grandfather the way Kevin had just spoken to him, his father would have given him a licking he'd never forget.

Knocking back the second shot of whiskey as quickly as the first, he refilled the glass once more.

Maybe he'd just get drunk.

And maybe he'd just give Kevin the whipping he deserved, too!

"Julie?" Kevin stepped into the shadows of the barn, pausing to let his eyes adjust from the bright sun outside. "Julie?" he called again. "Where are you?" He listened carefully, but at first heard nothing other than the normal sounds of the barn. In their stalls, the horses were snorting softly, and a few chickens were scratching at the planks as they searched the floor for stray grains of food. Then, from the loft, Kevin heard another sound.

A sob.

Going to the foot of the ladder, he started to mount it, but stopped short when he heard Julie's voice from above.

"Don't come up!" she called, her words strangled by the sob he could hear in her throat. "Just leave me alone!"

Kevin hesitated on the ladder, then climbed up until he could see into the loft. Julie was sitting on a bale of hay fifteen feet from the top of the ladder, and as Kevin's head and shoulders came through the hatchway, she turned her back to him, her shoulders hunching defensively. "Didn't I just tell you not to come up?" she demanded.

"I came anyway," Kevin told her. He climbed into the loft and moved tentatively toward her. "I just wanted to—I don't know . . ." He shoved his hands deep in his pockets and stared at his feet. "I guess I just want to apologize," he mumbled. "I mean, I never meant I thought Molly wanted to wreck the wedding, and I guess it was a really dumb thing to say. Jeez! I like Molly. She's really neat. And Grandpa shouldn't have said what he did, either. I don't know why he says things like that."

"Well, maybe he's right," Julie said, still not turning around, but shifting slightly as her shoulders relaxed. "Maybe we shouldn't have come. It sure wasn't *my* idea."

Though the pain in her voice caused Kevin's stomach to tighten, he resisted his sudden urge to move closer to her. Instead he sat down cross-legged on the floor of the loft and picked up a piece of straw, which he twirled nervously between his fingers as he spoke. "You mean you didn't want to come here?"

"Why would I?" Julie demanded, still not looking at him. "Why would I want to leave all my friends and change schools to come here? I mean, do you know how boring this town is?"

Kevin's jaw tightened, and if Julie had been looking at him, she would have seen—just for an instant—an eerie resemblance to Otto. But then Kevin carefully checked his anger. "I—I guess I never thought about it," he admitted, choosing his words carefully, not wanting to make Julie any more miserable than she already was. "I guess just because I love it here, I thought everyone else did, too. That was kind of stupid, huh?"

Julie nodded, but said nothing.

"Well, anyway, I'm sorry," Kevin said. "I'm sorry Molly got stung, and I'm really sorry she has to stay in the hospital. And I'm sorry Dad and Karen's party got wrecked, too." He hesitated. "And I really didn't mean to hurt your feelings." He waited a moment, hoping Julie might say something. When she didn't, he got to his feet, embarrassed at having exposed his feelings, and started back down the ladder. "I guess I was just really stupid, and I don't blame you for not wanting to talk to me." His head was about to disappear through the hatchway when Julie turned around.

"Kevin?"

He paused on the ladder, waiting.

Running the fingers of her right hand through her long dark hair, Julie tried to smile. "I—I guess—I don't know—it's just that everything's different here, and I don't have any friends, and—"

Quickly, Kevin climbed back into the loft and went to her, crouching down on the floor next to the hay bale on which she sat. "You've only been here a few days," he told her. "And I know lots of kids. I was going to introduce you to them at the party, but you were hiding in the kitchen."

Julie felt herself blushing. "I—I was worried about Molly," she stammered. "What if she dies?"

Kevin took her hands in his own. "She's not going to die, Julie. People don't die of bee stings. They'll just give her a shot and she'll be fine. You'll see. Now come on. Let's go meet some people."

Still Julie hesitated.

Her worry about Molly hadn't been the only thing that had kept her in the kitchen.

First there had been Carl Henderson. She had caught him staring at her at least three times before he'd left to fly Molly to the hospital, and each time she'd felt even more disturbed by the intensity of his gaze. Should she ask Kevin about him? But she already knew he was a good friend of her new stepfather's. If she asked if he was some kind of pervert or something, Kevin would just think she was trying to make trouble.

But avoiding Carl Henderson was only one reason she had retreated from the party. The truth, which she knew she would rather die than admit to Kevin, was that the three girls who'd clustered around Kevin almost the minute their parents had taken off with Molly had totally terrified her. How could she tell him she'd been afraid he might not introduce her to his friends, or even notice her if she tried to join the group?

"There's something else, isn't there?" Kevin asked.

Julie hesitated, but in the end she shook her head, unwilling to tell him what was wrong. Better to just keep it to herself, she decided.

When she said nothing, Kevin stood up and pulled Julie to her feet. "Then come on," he told her. "Molly's going to be just fine. Let's go back to the house." He glanced out the open door to the loft to the yard below. "There're still some people here, and there's lots of food, and if our folks aren't here, shouldn't we be taking care of things? I mean, it's kind of like we're the host and hostess now, and our folks did get married today."

Julie's eyes drifted toward the house. "I can hardly even remember anyone's name—" she began.

"I'll be right beside you, and I'll introduce you to everyone who's still here," Kevin told her. "Now stop worrying, and brush the hay off your dress."

Julie gazed down at the skirt of the beautiful blue dress that had been brand new only a few hours ago. Now it was a mass of wrinkles, and covered with flecks of straw. "Oh, God, I look awful!" she moaned.

For the first time since he'd come into the barn, a grin played around Kevin's lips. "No you don't," he said. "You look great. You're a lot prettier than any of the other girls."

"But my dress—" Julie began.

"People will just think we've been making out up here," Kevin said, starting to laugh as Julie flushed a deep red. "It'll be great for me! Every guy down there will be totally pissed off! They've all been begging me to introduce you."

"But we haven't been making out!" Julie protested.

Kevin's grin broadened. "I won't tell if you won't tell," he offered.

"But everyone will think—" And then she realized what he was really saying, and for a moment felt herself floundering. Her hands instinctively tightened in his. "I'm sorry I got mad at you," she said softly. "I just—" Again she had that strange feeling of confusion, and when she felt his fingers pressing her hands, her heart fluttered. "I don't know what happened."

"Well, it's okay now," Kevin told her. He chuckled. "Or anyway, you're not mad at me, and I'm not mad at you. But Grandpa's totally pissed at both of us."

"Both of us?" Julie repeated. "Why should he be mad at you?"

" 'Cause I told him to cut out what he's been doing," Kevin replied. He shivered as he remembered the fury in his grandfather's eyes as he'd left the old man standing on the porch. "He looked like he was ready to give me a licking." Still holding Julie's hand, he started once more for the ladder that led down to the barn floor. "We'll just stay out of his way, and he'll cool off. He gets mad real fast, but he gets over it almost as fast. Come on—let's go find you some friends. But if any of the guys tries to hit on you, they'd better watch it!"

As he stood aside to let her start down the ladder first, Julie wondered exactly what he'd meant by his last words.

Did he mean they'd better watch it because he was sort of like her older brother now?

Or did he mean it another way?

To her own surprise, she realized with clear certainty that she hoped he meant it another way entirely.

The last thing she wanted right now was for Kevin Owen to start acting like her brother!

Karen Owen stood frozen with terror in the emergency room at the hospital in San Luis Obispo, her eyes fixed on her daughter. Talking to Julie on the phone, she'd forced herself to sound calmer than she really was, but now, as she gazed at Molly's unnaturally red face and her grotesquely distended leg, she felt panic rise in her again. The little girl's breathing was still coming in heavily labored gasps, her face so swollen that her big blue eyes were reduced to slits.

Why wasn't anyone doing anything?

Why was the doctor talking to Ellen Filmore instead of doing something to help Molly?

"Does she have a history of allergic reactions?" she heard someone ask, then realized that the resident had turned his attention to her.

Though his name badge identified him as Dr. Paul Martin, he looked barely old enough to have graduated from high school, let alone from medical school. "Never," she replied, shaking her head.

Martin frowned, then began what seemed to Karen to be an absolutely endless process of duplicating the same examination that Ellen Filmore had already given Molly back in Pleasant Valley. A nurse stood at his elbow, taking notes, but just as Karen thought she would scream in frustration, the resident finally murmured something that sounded to Karen like it might be an order for some kind of medicine. The nurse left the room, returning a few seconds later with a vial and a hypodermic needle.

"What is it?" Karen asked, her voice sounding unnaturally loud. "What are you giving her?"

"It's a new kind of antivenin," the doctor replied. He jabbed the needle into Molly's arm, then pressed the plunger, injecting clear liquid into Molly. A moment later he pulled the needle out of Molly's flesh, dropped it in a wastebasket, and carefully dabbed at the tiny wound with a cotton swab.

"I'll do that, Doctor," the nurse immediately said. Martin made no objection to the nurse taking over the swab, but neither did he move back from the bed. Instead he leaned over and gently peeled one of Molly's eyes open.

"I-Is something wrong?" Karen whispered. Before the doctor could reply, Molly's hand twitched, and a second later her color began to change, the bright red starting to ease. "What's happening?" Karen gasped, uncertain whether Molly was responding to the medicine. "Isn't it working?"

"Give me a hand with the airway," Martin told the nurse, still not replying to Karen's question.

While the nurse held Molly's head firmly in place, preventing her from instinctively moving away from the doctor's hand, Martin gently drew the plastic tube out of her throat. Karen, unconsciously gripping the back of a chair so hard her fingernails were cutting into its vinyl upholstery, found herself holding her own breath as she waited for Molly to begin breathing without the aid of the tube. Only when the little girl's chest heaved did Martin finally glance at Karen, smiling.

"The swelling in her throat's already down enough for her to breathe, and her color's almost back to normal. She's going to make it."

As if in response to the doctor's words, Molly's eyes fluttered, then opened, and an almost inaudible word escaped her lips. "Mommy?"

"I'm here, darling," Karen replied, moving quickly to the head of the examining table and taking one of Molly's hands in both of her own. "I'm right here, and you're going to be fine. Just fine!"

Molly glanced around, then frowned deeply. "Where am I?"

"In the hospital in San Luis Obispo," Karen explained.

As her mind began to clear, fragments of what had happened came back to Molly. Her frown deepened. "I wrecked the wedding, didn't I?" she asked. "Is everybody mad at me?"

Tears of relief ran down Karen's cheeks, and she kissed Molly's fingers. "Of course no one's mad at you. You just got stung by a bee and had a bad reaction to it, that's all. It wasn't your fault. Everything's going to be fine."

Molly, still not satisfied, tried to sit up. "Where's everybody else?" she asked. "Is Julie here, too?"

Karen shook her head. "Just me and Russell and Dr. Filmore. There wasn't room for anyone else in the plane."

"The plane?" Molly echoed, looking puzzled.

"Mr. Henderson flew us over," Karen explained. "He works for a company called UniGrow that helps Russell raise better crops."

"And I'll fly you home, too," a voice said from behind her.

Karen turned to see Carl Henderson, along with Russell, standing just inside the door.

"They told us we could come in," Russell said, moving across to lean down and kiss Molly on the cheek. He made as if to tickle her ribs, a game he and the little girl had discovered early on. "How's my favorite girl?"

Molly giggled and wriggled away from his fingers. "I thought Mommy was your favorite girl!"

"Next to you, she is," Russell replied. "Feeling better?"

Molly nodded. "Except my leg still hurts."

"That should go away pretty soon," Dr. Martin said. He turned to Carl Henderson. "That's some stuff you guys are making. She responded to it in less than a minute." As Henderson's brows rose questioningly, the doctor looked confused. "Didn't you say he works for UniGrow?" he asked Karen.

Before Karen could reply, Henderson nodded. "I do, but what's that got to do with Molly?"

Martin's look of confusion deepened. "You don't know what your pharmaceutical division's doing?"

Henderson's questioning look cleared. "I don't have anything to do with them. I'm an entomologist, specializing in agricultural insects. It's a big company, and most divisions don't know what the others are doing. And I'm lucky. I work out in Pleasant Valley, pretty much by myself."

Martin handed him the vial that still sat on the counter running the length of one of the emergency room's walls. "Amazing stuff. It seems to work much faster than anything else we've got."

Ellen Filmore stepped forward. "What is it?"

Martin smiled wryly. "It doesn't even have a trade name yet. Right now, they're still identifying it by the chemical compound, and I'm not about to try to pronounce it." He winked at the nurse. "We're calling it 'that new stuff UniGrow made for bee stings.' Real scientific, huh?"

"Works for me." Ellen chuckled. "Maybe that's what they should market it as. Then us docs could speak the same language as the patients." She inclined her head toward the vial that was still in Carl Henderson's hand. "Can you get me some of that?"

"I don't see why not," Henderson replied. "If it's in the catalog, there won't be any problem at all. If it's not, it might take a little doing."

Ellen Filmore shrugged. "Even if it's not on the general market yet, I want to know all about it. If push comes to shove, I can try to get us in on the final testing phase. If we're going to have any more stings like Molly's, epinephrine just won't cut it."

Henderson nodded. "I'll see what I can do." His eyes shifted back to Dr. Martin. "Can Molly go home?" he asked.

Paul Martin shook his head. "Not a chance," he replied. "I've just given her a pretty strong dose of a brand-new drug, and I'm not about to let her out of here until I'm sure there aren't any side effects." He turned to grin at the little girl. "Sorry, but I'm going to have to stick you in a private room tonight, without anything except a television, a VCR, and a whole stack of movies."

Molly's eyes brightened instantly. "Do you have *Bambi*?" she asked. "I love *Bambi*."

"I think we just might," Martin replied. "And if we don't, I bet you could talk your dad into going out and renting it for you."

Molly's grin wavered as her eyes flicked toward Russell. "He's not my dad, he's—"

"I'm her stepfather," Russell said. "And I think we can probably produce a copy of *Bambi*." He slipped an arm around Karen's waist. "What do you think about a honeymoon in San Luis Obispo?" he asked. "I know it's not Paris . . ."

"It'll be perfect." Karen smiled. "And I know just where we'll stay—the Madonna Inn!"

"Perfect," Russell agreed. "I've always wanted to have an excuse to stay there, and this is it." He leaned over and kissed Molly. "Thanks, Princess. I don't know how you managed it, and I'm sorry you're stuck in the hospital for the night, but you've pulled it off. The wedding is now perfect. Your mom and I don't have to deal with that huge party at the farm, and we get to have a honeymoon at a place we've always wanted to go. I owe you, and so does your mom. Before we go home tomorrow, we get you a present. So start thinking about what you want, okay?"

Molly, finally certain that neither her mother nor her stepfather was angry at her, nodded happily as an orderly began wheeling her toward the room in which she would spend the night.

By the time she was settled into her bed, the swelling in her leg was beginning to ease and the pain of the sting was almost gone.

She had no idea how close to dying she had come.

DAWN

INTERMEZZO

*I*t was a nightmare.

It had to be a nightmare, and in a few more minutes she would wake up.

She would be in her bedroom in Los Banos, and through the thin wall she would hear the sound of Elvis Janks and her mother having their usual quarrel while they tried to treat their hangovers with coffee.

The darkness would lift, and she would get the covers untangled from her arms and legs, and she would look up and see the light of morning flooding through her bedroom window.

But as her mind slowly floated up through the dark waters of sleep, no trace of light appeared to brighten the blackness around her, and as the realization that what she was experiencing was far worse than any nightmare could be, Dawn Sanderson began to feel hope fading away.

She had no idea how long she'd been in the blackness.

No idea whether it was hours or days.

Perhaps weeks?

She had no way of knowing.

Time no longer had any meaning for her.

Should she try to scream?

She remembered that she'd tried that before.

How long before?

70

She didn't know.

A sob wrenched her body, but it was a nearly silent sob.

As she came fully awake, she waited for the familiar searing pain in her arms. They were tied above her head, the rope from which she hung cinched so tight that if she bent her knees at all, her feet lifted off the floor of her prison and her arms felt as if they were being torn from her shoulders.

This time, though, the pain seemed to have disappeared. For a brief moment of unutterable joy Dawn thought she must have been released from her bonds. But as she tried to move her naked body, she felt her bare feet lift off the floor. With a terrible sinking feeling Dawn realized what had happened.

She wasn't free of the rope at all. Rather, she had simply lost all feeling in her arms and hands.

As that realization seeped through her consciousness, she also became vaguely aware of a new pain.

A terrible cold, deep within her, that seemed to be emanating from her numbed shoulders.

Why?

Why had this happened to her?

Every time she'd awakened from those periods of sleep that seemed to bring neither rest nor escape, she'd tried to put what was happening together in some way that made sense.

All she'd been trying to do was escape!

And the man had seemed so nice. It wasn't like he'd tried to drag her into the car.

All he'd done was offer her a ride. And she'd only taken it because he didn't really seem to care if she went with him or not.

He'd bought her a cup of coffee, and she started feeling funny.

And the next memory she had was of coming slowly awake in the blackness, her arms on fire not only from be-

ing held high above her head, but from the chafing ropes she'd been able to feel around her wrists.

She'd screamed—screamed as loudly as she could—until finally her vocal cords had given out and all that would emerge from her throat was a rasping gasp.

The door had opened while she was screaming, and for a few seconds she'd been able to look into his face.

The friendly grin he'd worn when she first met him was gone. His lips were twisted into an ugly sneer, and his eyes were glazed over with that same strange look he'd had just before she passed out.

"It won't do any good," he told her. "It never does."

Then the door closed, and despite what he'd said, Dawn kept screaming until her voice gave out.

She'd seen him twice more.

He'd opened the door, stood staring at her for a few moments, saying nothing at all, then closed the door again, plunging her back into the terrifying darkness.

She clung to the few images she'd caught when the door was open.

A basement.

She was in a basement, with concrete walls, and heavy beams supporting the floor above.

But that was all she knew.

She'd heard him, though.

Sometimes, when she woke up, she heard him outside her dark prison, muttering softly, as if talking to someone.

She never heard another voice, though, and finally decided he was talking to himself.

Now, as she hung in the darkness with the terrible cold in her shoulders seeping inexorably into the rest of her body, hunger began to gnaw at her belly, and the terrible thirst she'd been feeling rose up in her parched throat once again. She tried to lick her lips, tried to summon up at least enough moisture to slake the terrible dryness, but *her tongue felt like a thick pad of cotton in her mouth, dry and swollen, threatening to choke her.*

Slowly, very slowly, the truth began to sink in.

Dawn Sanderson was dying.

That's what the cold meant.

She could no longer feel her arms and hands because they had died, and now the cold of death was creeping down into the rest of her body as well.

How long would it take?

Would it end in a few minutes, or would the terror and agony of the darkness stretch on to eternity?

Would she even know when she'd died?

Tearlessly, soundlessly, Dawn Sanderson began to cry.

Then, out of the silence beyond the confines of the darkness, she heard something.

It was him—he was in the basement again.

Dawn listened, praying that the door would open, and that this time, instead of simply staring at her, he would hold a cup of water to her lips, let her dampen them at least, even if he wouldn't let her drink.

The sound drew closer.

Whistling.

He was whistling softly, and then she heard something else.

A scraping, as if a drawer had opened or something had been dragged across the concrete floor.

Unconsciously, Dawn found herself holding her breath in the darkness, waiting for whatever was going to happen next.

Would the man come back again, to stare at her?

To taunt her?

To do to her whatever he had intended when he brought her here?

But when the attack finally came, it was so unexpected, and so terrifying, that a new scream was wrenched from Dawn Sanderson's exhausted vocal cords.

Her feet!

Something was on her feet!

At first it was only an odd tickling, but within a few seconds the tickling turned into a red-hot burning, a searing sensation that felt as if her feet and legs were on fire.

She jerked her legs up, pulling her knees up to her chest. Now her whole weight was suspended from the rope tied around her wrists, and she heard a popping sound as her right shoulder dislocated. A scream built within her, and she could feel the agony in her throat as her larynx protested against this latest abuse.

The burning in her feet scorched its way up her legs, and then she felt something else.

Something warm, something slimy, oozing down her legs and feet, then dripping off her toes.

Blood!

Panic seized Dawn. She thrashed against her bonds, struggling to escape her unseen attackers, but a few seconds later the terror and agony overcame her once more and she dropped back into blessed unconsciousness.

And while she slept, her attackers continued their work, slowly devouring her, a few cells at a time.

CHAPTER 5

*S*unlight flooding in through the window woke Karen. The sheer white curtains were drifting softly on the light breeze that caressed her face.

A week.

A week since she had married Russell, and six days since they had brought Molly, fully recovered from the bee sting, back from San Luis Obispo.

But only this morning—this perfect June morning—had she actually awakened and known instantly where she was, and felt as if she truly belonged.

She stretched, then relaxed back into the coziness of the bed for a few moments, luxuriating in the sounds and smells drifting in from the open window, gazing contentedly at the patch of turquoise-blue sky, untarnished by even a hint of the smog she had finally become inured to in Los Angeles.

She rolled over to look at the clock.

Already six.

Russell would have been up for at least an hour, meeting with Kevin and Otto in the tack room to plan the day, then setting about the earliest chores.

Molly and Julie would be up, too, their horses already turned out to pasture, the stalls cleaned, and the rest of the animals fed and watered.

It was all starting to work just the way she'd hoped it would, even after those first few days before the wedding, when everything had seemed to go wrong, and she began to think their two families might never be able to meld into one. Since she and Russell brought Molly back from the hospital, though, everything had gone much more smoothly. Part of it, of course, was simple logistics: The family was all under one roof now, except for Otto, who was back in his own house, where—as far as Karen was concerned—he could make himself as unpleasant as he wanted, and pay for it with loneliness. At least he no longer had every day and night to poison the atmosphere in what he still insisted on calling "Paula's house."

It was Paula Owen's house no longer. Every day, Karen felt it become more and more her own. When they'd arrived, of course, she felt as if she'd stumbled into a nightmare reenactment of *Rebecca*, with Otto only slightly miscast as Mrs. Danvers. But Russell had encouraged her to make the house her own, and, tentatively, she began to make small changes, adding her possessions, rearranging furniture.

At first, she was fearful of hurting Kevin's feelings by changing the house from the way his mother had set it up, but all he'd said so far had been complimentary, and the day before yesterday he even asked her if she'd help him pick out some new things for his room, waiting until his father was out of earshot to confide that "Mom had some funny ideas about what kind of stuff I should like." When her eyes moistened as she thanked him for making her feel so much at home, he'd flushed scarlet and hurried out.

But it was enough. It was her house, and her family, and Otto wasn't going to be able to poison the atmosphere, no matter how hard he tried.

Even Julie had almost stopped complaining about the change in her life. Part of it, of course, had to do with her horse. She was spending more and more time with Greta, and with Kevin, too, who was teaching her how to ride the big mare.

On the other hand, Julie still was barely speaking to Otto, and apparently wasn't about to try to bury the hatchet with the old man.

Karen finally rolled out of bed and began running through a mental inventory of the contents of the refrigerator as she took a quick shower, toweled her hair dry, then dressed in what was becoming her standard daytime costume: jeans, and one of the shirts Russell had been about to consign to the thrift shop when he'd begun cleaning out the closet in their bedroom to make room for her clothes. By the time she made it downstairs, she had already decided on omelettes, stuffed with the last of the ham left over from the wedding reception, and some of the green onions she'd spotted in the garden earlier in the week, which she hoped would be ready for picking this morning.

Or did one pull onions? Well, pick or pull, who cared?

Humming quietly to herself, she went into the kitchen, then stopped abruptly, her lighthearted tune dying on her lips.

Sitting at the kitchen table, a cup of coffee held halfway to his lips as he regarded her darkly through his deep-sunk eyes, was Otto Owen.

It was the first time since the wedding that he'd set foot in this house, and though Russell had tried to convince her that his absence was motivated by a desire to give them their privacy, Karen was certain she knew better. Now the first words Otto spoke proved she'd been right.

"When Paula was alive, she always had breakfast ready by the time Russell came downstairs."

A knot of anger formed in Karen's belly, and the cheerful mood that had flooded over her when she'd awakened this morning shattered. But she kept her voice even, determined not to rise to his bait. "I guess she was a better woman than I am," she observed. "But I think I'll wait until fall to start getting up before the sun." The back door opened and Julie came in, hesitating when she saw Otto, and giving her mother a questioning glance. Hoping Otto would miss her silent exchange with her daughter, Karen rolled her eyes just enough to let Julie know that Otto was on the warpath.

Otto didn't miss the gesture. "I'm not any blinder than I am deaf," he growled, his eyes fixing on Karen as she went to the refrigerator, pulled out the egg container, and began cracking eggs into a bowl. "And you don't need to keep those in the fridge," he went on. "Fresh eggs keep just fine on the counter. 'Course, you'd be used to the store-boughten ones, and those are a week old by the time you see 'em. And they call 'em *fresh*!" He drained his coffee, then held his cup out for a refill.

Karen's eyes flicked to the pot of coffee that stood at the far end of the counter.

Closer to Otto than to herself.

Did he really expect her to stop what she was doing, take his cup, refill it for him, and then hand it back to him?

He wasn't an invalid, for heaven's sake!

She opened her mouth, about to ask him if he'd turned into a cripple during the night, when she changed her mind. He's just old, she reminded herself. He's set in his ways, and the only women he's known his whole life were farm women. Saying nothing, she took Otto's cup, refilled it, and returned it to him.

Julie, her eyes darkening with anger at what she'd just seen, seemed about to say something to Otto, but Karen signaled her to let it go. "Can I pour you a cup, too, Julie?" she offered, as Otto accepted his cup without a word of thanks.

"It's okay, Mom," Julie said, her eyes on Otto, who seemed oblivious to her furious gaze. "Some of us can do things for ourselves." Taking the pot from Karen, she carried it to the table and mimed pouring the steaming liquid over Otto's head as she passed behind him.

Karen was just starting to cook the first of the omelettes when the rest of the family trooped in through the back door.

"Uh-oh, we're early," Russell said, pausing at the stove to kiss Karen on the cheek before moving on to the sink to scrub his hands.

"Or I'm late," Karen replied. "Kevin, could you give Julie a hand setting the table? There's orange juice in the refrigerator, and I think there's still some jam left. If there isn't, get a new jar from the pantry."

"What can I do?" Russell asked.

"Make some toast, while I finish the omelettes." She hesitated, then glanced at her father-in-law. "Will you be having breakfast with us, Otto?"

Otto's brows arched. "Not if you're plannin' to put me to work, too. It's one thing doing women's work when you don't have a woman in the house—"

Russell started to interrupt his father, but before he could say anything, Julie broke in, her voice taking on a syrupy tone that instantly caught not only Otto's attention, but everyone else's as well. "Why, Mr. Owen, we simply wouldn't think of asking a *man* to do anything around the kitchen," she drawled. "You just sit there, and let us womenfolk take care of you." Quickly shoving a place setting in front of him, she moved to the stove and took the plate containing the first omelette from her mother. "Molly, you're a girl, too, so you can pour Mr. Owen's orange juice for him. And don't worry about filling it too full, because if he spills any of it, we'll just clean it right up for him, won't we?"

Molly, not quite understanding the game but anxious to play it, scurried toward the refrigerator.

Knowing the showdown between his grandfather and the three newest members of the family had finally come, Kevin backed away from the table to see what would happen next.

Karen, about to put a stop to Julie's performance before it went too far, glanced at Russell, who read her intentions perfectly.

And silently signaled her to let the scene play itself out.

Julie set the omelette in front of Otto. "Can you feed yourself, Mr. Owen, sir?" she asked with exaggerated servility. "Because I'd just be more than happy to sit right down and help you." As she dropped onto the chair next to Otto and began cutting his omelette up for him, Karen decided the game had gone far enough.

But before she could say anything, both Kevin and Russell began to laugh.

Otto's face went scarlet and the vein in his forehead throbbed. He stood up and stomped out of the kitchen, slamming the screen door behind him.

Julie, starting to giggle herself, suddenly saw the look in her mother's eye. "But he acts like you're nothing but a maid around here—" she began.

"And I can deal with it myself," Karen told her.

"Oh, come on," Russell said, but this time it was Karen who motioned to him not to interfere.

"He's an old man, and nothing you or I can say is going to change him," Karen told her daughter. "All we can do is be tolerant of him, and hope people are tolerant of us when we get to be that age."

Julie hesitated, about to reply, then reconsidered. Argument would be useless. "I—I guess I'd better go apologize to him . . ." she said, deliberately leaving the words hanging in the hope her mother might yet give her a reprieve.

"I guess you had," Karen said.

"I'll go with you," Kevin offered as Julie started toward the back door.

"Oh, no you won't," Karen told him. "Julie got herself into this alone, and she can get out of it alone, too. The rest of us will have breakfast."

As Julie started off in search of Otto Owen, Karen began serving the rest of her family.

Carl Henderson had been about to turn up the Owens' driveway when he'd seen first Julie, then Russell, Kevin, and Molly, head from the barn up to the kitchen door.

Otto, he assumed, was either already there or in his own house, if he was still acting the way he had been last week.

Which meant that no one would be anywhere near the beehives, and he could take as much time as he wanted without having to answer anyone's questions.

He parked his Jeep on the county road, carefully positioning the Cherokee so the barn stood between it and Russell's house, then opened his field pack and took out one of the small brown vials he'd filled in his lab only the night before.

Henderson didn't think the job would take more than half an hour, since he'd already identified the queen cells in half of the three dozen beehives on the Owen farm. Much bigger than the other cells, they were easy to spot, and there were never more than a few of them in any given hive.

A single drop of fluid in each cell would be enough, and then all he'd have to do was wait.

Wait, and watch, and mark the new queens as they hatched.

If he was right, and the contents of the vials did the job, Carl Henderson would be a hero.

If it failed, nothing would happen at all, and he would simply keep working steadily in his private lab, laboring over a new solution until he finally got it right and the problem was solved at last.

The Problem.

That was how everyone thought of it now. As if it were capitalized, like the title of a movie or something.

It had started three years ago, when UniGrow released a new fertilizer that the company promised would double the alfalfa crop. It had been tested against everything anyone could think of, and no one had seen *any* problems, let alone what had become known as The Problem.

The fertilizer seemed perfect, containing nothing poisonous to any living being, no pollutants to taint the water or contaminate the soil.

Totally biodegradable, totally environmentally neutral.

And it hadn't killed the bees—that had been one of the first things UniGrow had tested for, since no one could raise alfalfa—or much of anything else—without bees.

Carl himself had led the apian tests, and been as enthusiastic as everyone else.

He had also been the first, a few months later, to discover the one big flaw of the fertilizer: though it didn't kill the bees exposed to it, it made them sterile. Slowly, all the hives in the area had died.

And that, a year later, had become The Problem.

For two years UniGrow had been working on a solution, but so far had come up with nothing.

Carl Henderson, in the meantime, had been conducting his own research in the privacy of his own lab, applying all the knowledge of his years of study and experimentation to the problem. And today, contained within the brown vial, he held in his hand what might finally be the solution everyone was looking for.

A biological solution to a biological problem.

If it worked the way Henderson thought it would, the queen cells into which it was injected would produce bees whose descendants were immune to the effects of the fertilizer, and would continue reproducing new generations.

Not only would UniGrow be relieved of the burden of having to bring in new hives each time a crop season began, but relieved as well of having to pay the enormous damages the courts were already beginning to award the local farmers whose fields had been affected by the fertilizer.

Instead the company would begin to enjoy the profits the new fertilizer, marketed in conjunction with Henderson's altered strain of bees, would generate. And Carl Henderson, whose genius had discovered the answer, would reap at least a percentage of those profits.

The Problem would be solved; everyone would be happy.

If it worked. Henderson was not yet quite certain it would. In fact, the last refinement he'd experimented with had resulted primarily in the increased virulence of the bees' venom.

It was that venom, Carl knew, that Molly Spellman had reacted to the previous week, though he'd been careful not to contradict the various doctors who had simply assumed the girl had had a violent allergic reaction to an ordinary bee. The child, after all, had recovered, so no real harm had been done, and Henderson was almost certain that his newest creation would have no bad side effects.

Carefully removing a hypodermic needle from its case, Carl filled it, returned it to the case, then put the case into one of his shirt pockets, snapping the flap closed just to be on the safe side.

Leaving the Cherokee unlocked, he crossed the road and started along the dirt track that led to the beehives which he himself had placed on the far side of the farm, well out of sight of the house.

There were thirty-six of them, placed in three well-spaced rows of twelve hives each. Each of the hives was four boxes high, and Henderson had marked several of the boxes with the numbers of the frames that contained the queen cells he planned to treat. Glancing around to be sure he was alone, he set to work, carefully lifting off the first two half-depth supers that formed the highest levels of the hive. Setting them aside, he turned his attention to the now exposed full-sized super, which was nothing more than a white-painted box designed to hold a rack of brood frames. The design was simple, and hadn't changed substantially since L. L. Langstroth had invented it in 1851. The key to it was the precise spacing of the frames inside, which allowed a bee space of exactly three-eighths of an inch. Had there been less space between the frames, the bees simply wouldn't have used them; more, and they would have begun filling it in. Very gently, Henderson lifted the fourth frame out of its slot. Heavy with comb, the wooden rectangle was covered with bees, but as Carl lifted the tray into the sunlight, most of them quickly took off, or dropped back into the squirming mass below.

Easily finding the queen cell he'd identified earlier in the week, Henderson carefully pierced its wax cap with the hypodermic needle and injected a drop of the fluid from the brown vial into it. Withdrawing the needle from the cell, he plugged the tiny hole by scraping a fragment of wax over it, pressing the wax into place with his little finger. As soon as he slid the frame back into its slot, the bees would go to work, trimming the plug or adding wax to it until it would blend so perfectly as to be undiscoverable.

And inside the cell, the contents of the solution would go to work on the developing bee. If it worked, the descendants of that queen would be impervious to the ravages of the fertilizer.

If it didn't, the queen would simply die, and Henderson would return to his lab to begin again.

Finishing with the first hive, he replaced the top supers, then moved on to the second. He was just about to lift its lid when he heard a sound behind him.

A slight gasp.

The kind of gasp someone makes when he comes upon something unexpected.

Or frightening.

Stiffening, Carl Henderson straightened up, then slowly turned to face whoever was behind him, already prepared to explain his presence as nothing more than a routine check on the hives.

Henderson's own breath caught as he recognized Julie Spellman. It was the first time he'd seen her since the wedding, and now, as his eyes locked on hers, he felt his hands clench into tight fists.

Once again, her long black hair was cascading down her back, and once again her dark eyes were fixed on him, just as they had fixed on him at the wedding.

His emotions churned and his fingers began to work.

Don't! he told himself. Don't go near her. Don't touch her. Don't even look at her!

Yet he couldn't keep himself from looking at her.

His eyes fastened on her, and in the deep recesses of his mind, darkness began to close around him.

A terrifying darkness—a darkness filled with nameless horrors that were reaching out to him.

He could already feel talons of fear sinking deeply into his soul, and hear a mocking laughter in his ears.

It was a laughter out of the past, as the fear that threatened to overwhelm him was also a terror out of the past. The laughter triggered a blind rage within Carl Henderson, and though he had no conscious memory of the source of either the laughter or the rage, he knew where they would take him.

Voices were whispering to him now, urging him to vent the fury within. He wanted to give in to the voices, wanted to let them lead him, let them show him how to quench the hatred that burned inside him.

But it was impossible!

This girl knew him.

Even worse, her mother and stepfather knew him, too. If he gave in to the demons that dwelt within him—to

the cold fury and the deep hatred that he had kept closeted
for so many years—his secrets would be exposed.

Everyone would know what they made him do.

Yet even as he tried to struggle against the blackness inside him, the battle was already lost, for his eyes remained
fixed on Julie, remained fixed on that face that taunted
him, mocked him, tortured him.

The darkness closed around him, and his ears were
filled with the familiar humming that had haunted his
nightmares for as long as he could remember.

His eyes glazing with the same dark look that had
chilled Julie to the core only a few days ago, he started toward her.

Julie instinctively backed away as she saw Carl Henderson
move forward. "I—I was looking for Mr. Owen," she
stammered.

"He's not here," Henderson said, his voice rasping in a
way that sent a shiver through Julie. "Just me. Me, and
you."

For an instant Julie didn't understand. He was staring at
her the way he had stared at her at the wedding. As though
he hated her. But he didn't even know her.

She took another step backward, but suddenly Carl
Henderson's hand was on her arm, holding her.

"Stop it!" he said. "Stop laughing at me!"

Julie's eyes widened as fear formed a cold fist in her
belly. What was he talking about? She wasn't laughing at
him. She hadn't even known who he was when she'd first
seen him! "I wasn't laughing—" she began, trying to pull
her arm loose from his grip.

"You were!" he snarled. His free arm rose into the air,
then arced downward, his hand lashing across her face.
"You're always laughing at me! Always!"

A scream erupted from Julie as Carl Henderson's palm
smashed across her cheek, then she cowered back, whim-

pering in terror. "N-No," she stammered. "I was just look-ing for Mr. Owen! I wanted to—"

But Carl Henderson heard nothing of her words. His consciousness was filled only with Julie's image and his own rage, which was urging him on, whispering to him, telling him to do to her what she had done to him.

The darkness, the voices in his head whispered. *Put her in the dark with the other one. Do to her what she did to you. Now, Carl. Do it now. No one is here . . . no one can see you. . . . Do it, Carl . . . do it. . . .*

His grip on Julie tightening, Carl twisted her around, and she stumbled, falling to the ground.

She felt him drop down on top of her, and now, as his weight held her immobile, she felt his hands closing on her throat. "No!" she screamed once more. "Noooo!"

Otto Owen emerged from his house. His anger had finally abated. In fact, if he wanted to be dead honest, he felt kind of stupid.

When Julie had come knocking at his door a few min-utes ago, he'd known why she was there: all she'd wanted to do was apologize.

But he'd refused to listen—hell, he'd even refused to admit he could hear her, even though he was pretty sure she'd known he was right inside the door.

And it's not like she was a bad kid—not really. After all, weren't all kids mouthier now than when he'd been her age? But whose fault was that? If he was going to be mad at anyone, he should be mad at Karen, not Julie. It was just the way the girl had been raised, that's all. And if he was going to be completely honest, he didn't really think Karen had been such a bad mother, though he wasn't about to admit that to anyone but himself.

Besides, even now that he was close to eighty, Otto could remember a few times when he was Julie's age, and had wanted to tell off his own grandfather.

Still, he wasn't going to pretend he was happy about what was going on at the farm. It just seemed like nothing was the way it used to be—the way it should be.

All his life the farm had run just the way it was supposed to. He and his father—then he and Russell—had worked the fields and the livestock, and his mother, then his own dear wife, Emily, then Russell's Paula, had taken care of the house.

After Emily died, Paula had taken care of his house, too. Never complained about it, either.

She'd seen her duty and she'd done it!

Of course, after she died, he and Russell and Kevin had to pitch in and do the housework themselves. And it wasn't that he hadn't wanted Russell to get married again—he had! Hell, they had to have someone to take care of them, didn't they?

He'd waited all week, hoping that sooner or later Karen would come down and offer to clean up the growing mess in his house, but she hadn't showed up at all, so this morning he'd gone up to talk to her about it, and she'd hardly even been civil to him.

He'd seen the way she looked at him when all he asked for was a simple cup of coffee!

Of course, he *had* only been a couple feet from the pot, and Karen *had* been pretty busy.

Maybe he could have poured the coffee himself.

In fact, if he really wanted to be fair, he supposed he *should* have poured the coffee himself.

Abruptly, he started chuckling as he remembered the act Julie had put on. And now that he thought about it, hadn't Enid Gilman once told him years ago that Karen was off in L.A. trying to be an actress?

Well, from what he'd seen that morning, it was Julie who had the talent.

Otto stood on his back porch, looking around the empty yard. No sign of Julie—but why would there be? He'd been a cantankerous old man, just as rude to her as she'd been to him, but at least she'd had a point to make, and he resolved to find her and let her finish apologizing. It would do her good.

But where had she gone?

He glanced up the hill toward his son's house. Would she have gone back up there?

What if she hadn't known he was in his kitchen, listening to her? She'd still be looking for him.

He set out toward the barn, but stopped when he caught sight of the vehicle parked at the bottom of the drive.

Carl Henderson's Jeep.

His anger surged back as he glared at the UniGrow man's dusty gray Cherokee.

What the hell was Henderson doing parked down here? Where was the man? If he was on the farm, how come he hadn't gone up to talk to Russell?

Then he knew.

The beehives!

That was it: Henderson was doing something with the hives.

Wasn't it enough that Henderson and his company had already destroyed his own hives? The old man's fury increased as he remembered what had happened after Russell had let UniGrow treat their fields with that new-fangled fertilizer, despite his own objections.

After the hives went bad, Russell should have just run Henderson and the rest of them off the property. There were lots of people they could have rented bees from, but oh, no! Russell had to go along with UniGrow again!

Sometimes Otto wondered if he'd raised an idiot.

Scowling deeply, he crossed the county road and started along the dirt track that edged the pasture. As he skirted a pile of boulders that had been cleared out of the field by his own father before he'd even been born, he spotted Carl Henderson.

But he wasn't messing with the hives at all.

Instead he was on the ground, sprawled out on top of Julie Spellman, who was struggling to escape him.

Breaking into a stiff-legged trot, Otto ran toward Henderson as quickly as he could. "Henderson!" he roared. "God damn you!"

Otto Owen's enraged bellow cut through the darkness in Carl Henderson's mind. Instantly he released Julie, scrambling to his feet.

"Mr. Owen!" Julie screamed, scrabbling away from Henderson and struggling to stand up herself. "Help me!"

Otto glowered at Carl Henderson as he hurriedly approached, certain he knew exactly what was going on.

"This isn't what you think," Carl said quickly. "She tripped, and I was just—"

Otto's anger boiled over. He hurled himself at Henderson, grabbing his shirt in both hands. "You think I'm blind, Henderson? Well, I'm not, and you're goin' to jail, you son of a bitch! You know how old that girl is?"

Carl Henderson's arms thrust up between Otto's, breaking the older man's grip on his shirt. A second later his right hand clenched into a fist and he swung at Otto.

Julie, her terror of a moment before giving way to fury, hurled herself at Henderson, her right arm going around his neck as she tried to drag him off Kevin's grandfather.

Twisting himself free from her grip, Henderson shoved her away, and Julie, staggering, lost her balance and fell against one of the hives. Instantly, bees swarmed out of the white box and began buzzing angrily around her.

"Watch out," Otto yelled. "Get up, Julie! Run!"

Julie scrambled to her feet. Waving her arms wildly in a vain attempt to fend off the bees' furious attack, she tried to spin away from the swirling insects. She lurched toward Otto and Carl Henderson, then turned away and raced off in the other direction. After she'd run some thirty yards, the bees abandoned their pursuit and began returning to the overturned hive, around which a cloud of insects still hovered in churning confusion.

The three stings the bees had inflicted on her already beginning to burn, Julie started back toward Otto and Carl, but she'd taken no more than three or four steps when a wave of dizziness struck her and she felt her knees begin to buckle.

"Julie?" she heard Otto Owen ask. "You okay?"

It sounded to Julie as if the old man's voice were coming from a long distance away. She opened her mouth to answer; she tried to shout.

No sound came out.

A second later Julie collapsed to the ground.

Otto stared in shock at the fallen girl. "Jesus Christ," he gasped. "What the hell did you do to her?"

Carl Henderson's mind had been racing.

If Otto told what he'd seen, and Julie backed him up— Henderson's blood ran cold as he realized what would happen.

They'd search his house, and they'd find—

No! He couldn't let that happen! If they found what was in his house, they'd send him to jail for the rest of his life.

But then his eyes went to Julie, and suddenly he realized he might be all right after all.

Because Julie—like Molly a week ago—was having a reaction to the bee sting.

An even worse reaction than her sister had had.

If she died, no one would believe Otto, no matter what he said. Everyone in town knew how much the old man disliked him.

But if it looked as though he'd been trying to save Julie's life—

"She's going into shock," he told Otto, his mind working furiously as he bent down and picked up Julie's unconscious body. "I've got to get her to the clinic, fast." Cradling Julie in his arms, already seeing a way out of his predicament, Carl Henderson started back along the track toward the county road and his Jeep.

Otto followed, struggling to keep up with Henderson's fast pace. "You're not takin' her anywhere!" he protested. "Not after what you were tryin' to do!"

Henderson glanced at the old man with a carefully constructed expression of bafflement. "What the hell are you talking about, Otto?" he began. "All I was—"

"You were trying to rape her, you damned pervert!" Otto bellowed. "I saw you!"

They were at the Jeep now, and after loading Julie into the backseat, Carl Henderson stared coldly at Otto. "You don't know what you saw, Otto," he said. "But I'm gonna tell you, so listen good. Something's wrong with the bees again, Otto! That's why Karen's kids are having reactions to them! That's what I was trying to do! I was taking a sample of the bees, so we can figure out what's wrong with them!" As Otto's mouth worked in fury, Henderson smiled. "Don't try to tell anyone anything different," he said. "Nobody will believe you. They'll all think you're just a crazy old coot!"

Otto's expression hardened. "Julie knows what you did," he grated. "When she wakes up—"

"*If* she wakes up," Henderson interrupted. He started the Jeep, put it in gear, and was just pulling away from Otto when the old man shouted after him.

"I'm calling the cops, Henderson," the old man yelled. "I'll have you in jail, you bastard!"

With Otto's words ringing in his ears, Carl Henderson sped away, his mind still working, knowing he wasn't safe yet. If Julie woke up—

He glanced into the backseat.

The girl was unconscious, and her breathing seemed to be getting more labored by the second.

If he slowed down, and she died before he got her to the clinic—

But he couldn't slow down. Not if it was going to look as if he'd done his best to save her life.

For that, he'd have to get her to the clinic, where Ellen Filmore—whom someone at the farm would probably be calling even now—would set to work.

And then she would ask him for the antivenin he'd promised her.

The antivenin that he'd promised to deliver today. The antivenin that was in his briefcase.

And that she *knew* was in his briefcase, because he'd told her so yesterday when she'd called to ask him when it would be available.

Ellen Filmore would administer the antivenin to Julie, and in a few minutes her breathing would return to normal—as would the color in her face—and the swelling would begin to go down.

She would wake up.

And she would talk.

Carl Henderson's mind continued to work, even as he turned into the parking lot of the clinic.

And then, as the car slowed to a stop, the answer suddenly came to him.

An answer that was simple, and elegant.

And would ensure that Julie Spellman never woke up.

CHAPTER 6

"*I*'ll kill him, Russell," Karen said. "If what Otto says is true, I swear, I'll kill him with my own hands!"

They were in Russell's Chrysler, she in the front seat with her husband, Kevin and Molly in back. Ahead she could see the clinic, and a terrible sense of déjà vu rolled over her. Only a week ago she had made this exact same ride, and for the exact same reason.

A bee sting.

First with Molly, who had almost died.

Now with Julie, who was already unconscious.

And who, according to Otto, had been raped as well.

They'd met Otto halfway down the driveway, all four of them drawn from the kitchen by the sound of his shouting voice, suddenly muffled by the roar of a gunning car engine. By the time they'd arrived outside, Carl Henderson's Jeep was already speeding away.

Karen had listened in shock as Otto told them what had happened. Barely able to control her fury at Carl Henderson, she hadn't even wanted to wait while Russell called Ellen Filmore at home to let her know that Julie was on the way to the clinic. And as they'd gotten into the car, Russell had told her to try to keep calm.

"Let's just take this a step at a time," he cautioned. "I just can't believe that Carl would—"

"No one ever wants to believe it," Karen interrupted, her voice cold as she stared straight ahead out the windshield. "That's why so many of these perverts get away with it! But Otto *saw* it!" She turned to glare angrily at Russell. "He—" She saw Molly sitting next to Kevin in the backseat, listening to every word, and cut herself short, falling into a furious silence.

Otto's words rang in her ears. "I better not go," he'd told them. "If I even see that son of a bitch Henderson, you'd be hard-pressed to keep me from tryin' to kill him! You go ahead, and take care of Julie. I'm gonna call Mark Shannon—I told Henderson I was going to see him in jail, and by God, I meant it. And I got to get the hives straightened out, too."

The hives, Karen thought. The hives that had almost killed Molly last week and Julie this morning. "We'll have to get rid of the hives," she said now, reluctantly abandoning the problem of Carl Henderson for the moment.

Russell shook his head at Karen's statement. "We can't just get rid of them," he said. "We need them."

"Need them?" Karen broke in. "With what's happened? How can you even—"

"Now calm down," Russell said, pulling into the clinic's parking lot and sliding the car into a space near Carl Henderson's Jeep. "Let's just see what the situation is, okay?"

Karen said nothing, but as she got out of the car and hurried across the nearly empty lot, she knew she'd already made up her mind, no matter what arguments Russell might come up with.

By the end of the day, Carl Henderson would be in jail, and the hives would be off the farm.

The front door of the clinic stood open, but the waiting room—and the reception desk, too—were empty.

But of course they were—it wasn't even seven in the morning yet!

"Where are they?" Kevin asked. "How come no one's here?"

"They'll be in the examining room," Russell said, striding across the waiting area toward a closed door from behind which he could hear murmuring voices. Without knocking, he pushed the door open and went through, Karen right behind him.

Julie was stretched out on the examining table, Ellen Filmore hovering over her, checking her vital signs, just as a week ago she'd checked Molly's.

Carl Henderson stood at the counter that ran the length of the far wall, his back to the door, his briefcase open in front of him.

I'll know, Russell thought. The second I see his face, I'll know if what Dad said is true. "Carl," he said, his voice low.

Carl Henderson turned around. He'd known this moment was coming—had already been preparing for it in his mind even as he'd carried Julie into the clinic. Now he faced Russell and Karen, and knew by the looks on their faces that Otto had told them exactly what he'd seen. Instantly, he put on an expression of good-humored exasperation: just the slightest trace of a wry grin; a helpless shrug of his shoulders. "Obviously Otto told you about me raping Julie," he said. As he'd hoped, both Karen and Russell looked totally nonplussed by the unexpected words. Henderson instantly pressed his advantage. "I think he may have actually gone around the bend this time."

Karen opened her mouth to speak, but suddenly caught sight of Julie, lying on the examining table. Her words dying in her throat, she gazed at her daughter's face.

It was flushed the same bright red as Molly's had been a week ago, and three large welts were swelling on her neck. Her eyes were closed and her breath came in tortured gasps, just as Molly's had.

"Have you given her anything yet?" she asked Ellen Filmore.

The doctor nodded. "The same things we tried on Molly

last week." Her eyes fixed on Julie. "She's not responding to it any more than Molly did."

Karen tried to stifle an anguished whimper as she relived in vivid detail Molly's terrible ordeal on the day of the wedding. Next, they would take Julie to the airport and fly her to San Luis Obispo.

But even as the thought came into her mind, she heard Ellen Filmore speaking. "I need that antivenin *now*, Carl," she snapped.

"Right here," Carl said. He turned to his briefcase and handed Ellen Filmore a small, brown glass vial with a rubber top. Glancing briefly at the polysyllabic words identifying the vial's contents, she looked up at Carl. "You're sure this is it?" she demanded.

"I'm as sure as I can be," Henderson replied. "It's what the pharmaceutical guys gave me, and I was damned lucky to get it. It's not supposed to be available except to the test hospitals for another three months, but when I told them about Molly, they let me have some in case she got stung again."

Still, Ellen Filmore hesitated. If the stuff wasn't even on the market yet, it meant the FDA hadn't given final approval. And if something happened . . .

If Julie didn't respond . . .

On the examining table, Julie's whole body suddenly jerked spasmodically, and her breathing, which only moments ago had been labored but fairly strong, turned into the same kind of gasping rales that Molly had exhibited just before they put the airway in her throat.

Making up her mind, Ellen Filmore tore the paper from a disposable hypodermic, slid its point through the vial's rubber cap, and drew a dose of the clear fluid into the instrument's body. A moment later she slid the needle into the muscle of Julie Spellman's upper arm and pressed the plunger.

All of them waited.

For a moment nothing happened.

Then Julie jerked again, and her chest heaved with her struggle to push air through her fast-closing throat.

Ellen Filmore picked up an airway that was already waiting on the counter.

"Is she dying?" Henderson asked quietly, barely able to mask the eagerness he was feeling. *Die, Julie, die. Die, and I'll be safe.*

Not only safe, but with the monsters within him satisfied, at least for now.

"Not if I can help it," the doctor replied. "But we might need your plane again." Her eyes fixed on Julie for a second, and she shook her head. "If she even makes it that long," she added, so quietly that only Carl could hear her. "Hold her head, Russell," she said as she stepped back to Julie's side. Russell moved into position at the end of the examining table, his hands on either side of Julie's head, ready to hold it steady.

Karen, her face ghostly white, had taken one of Julie's hands in both of her own. "Hang on, baby," she whispered. "You can do it, Julie. Just keep listening to me!"

Then, just as Ellen Filmore was about to insert the airway through Julie's mouth and down her throat, something changed.

The cherry-red color of her skin began to return to normal, and the swelling in her neck began to ease.

As the swelling went down, she began to breathe with a slow, even rhythm.

No more than ten seconds later, Julie's eyes opened and she struggled to sit up.

"J-Julie?" Karen stammered, barely able to believe that the miracle was happening again.

Julie turned to look at her mother.

Something was wrong.

She felt hot, as if she were running a fever.

A high fever, the kind where your skin gets covered with sweat, and then suddenly you're freezing cold.

But when she touched her own forehead, her skin felt dry.

Dry, and cool.

The chill hit her then, and she felt her whole body shiver.

A split second later the icy fingers released her from their grip.

And nausea clutched at her stomach.

What was happening to her?

Was she dying?

A terrible panic rose in Julie, and she opened her mouth to cry out for help, to beg the doctor to do something before she died.

But before the words could even be formed, Julie's throat closed, and for a moment she thought she was going to strangle.

No! she screamed silently to herself. Don't die! Relax . . . take a deep breath . . . Summoning her will to overcome the fear that was still building within her, Julie opened her mouth again, determined this time to get the words out, despite the horrifying strangling sensation that was once again gripping her throat.

"I—" she began. "I—" She reached out, and instantly her mother took her hand.

"What?" Karen asked. "Julie, what is it?"

Once again Julie tried to speak, and finally words came to her, words that she actually managed to utter.

Unbelievable words.

"I'm fine," Julie heard herself say. Sliding off the examining table, she stood up. Immediately, her mother was at her side. A wave of dizziness hit her, but, like the horrible chill, it passed as quickly as it had come. "I—I just have to go to the bathroom."

Once more feeling the heat of the fever, her stomach

threatening to rebel at any second, Julie flung herself out of Karen's embrace and hurried down the hall toward the bathroom. Karen rushed after her.

Molly and Kevin were waiting just outside the examining room door, and as Julie passed her, her younger sister looked up at her. "Are you going to have to spend the night in the hospital, like I did?" the little girl asked.

Her gorge rising, feeling as if she might faint at any second, Julie paused, but once more found herself saying words that had nothing to do with the reality of what was happening to her. "I'm fine," she heard herself repeat. As her stomach heaved once more, she turned away. "I just have to go to the bathroom, that's all."

Moving past Molly and Kevin, with her mother right behind her, Julie rushed down the hall. "I'll be okay, Mother," she said when they were finally at the door to the bathroom. Worriedly, Karen searched her daughter's face.

Was it really possible that she was all right? But only a couple of minutes ago ... She left the thought hanging, unwilling to finish it, even in her mind. Then, as Julie was about to go into the bathroom, she once again remembered what Otto had told them just before they'd left the farm. "Julie," she said, reaching out and laying a hand on her daughter's arm. "Did Carl Henderson do anything to you?"

Julie gazed uncertainly at her mother. "Do something?" she repeated. "Do what?"

Now Karen hesitated, taking a deep, steadying breath. Julie was fifteen—nearly sixteen—and not naive. "Otto said when he found you, it looked as if Carl Henderson was trying to—well, trying to rape you."

Julie's eyes widened.

Rape her?

What was her mother talking about?

Why would Carl Henderson have tried to rape her?

"I really need to go into the bathroom, Mom," she said.

"I'll be right out." Before her mother could say anything else, Julie slipped into the tiny cubicle that contained only a toilet, a sink, and a mirror, automatically locking the door behind her.

She knelt down on the cold tile floor, her head over the toilet, and felt bile rising in her throat.

In a second her mouth would fill with the foul-tasting fluid, and then the contents of her stomach would spew out from her mouth.

She waited, her mouth open, her body braced.

But the nausea passed as suddenly as it had come.

Julie waited a few moments, then stood up and stared at her image in the mirror.

Though she still felt hot with fever, though all her joints were aching, though she felt as if she were suffering from the worst flu she could ever remember—she looked absolutely normal.

Her eyes were bright, and her cheeks glowed with apparent good health.

She looked perfect.

But she felt terrible.

Then she remembered the strange words she'd spoken, telling everyone she was fine, even though she felt as though she was about to die.

What was happening to her?

Was she going crazy?

Her blood ran cold as a new thought formed in her mind.

Maybe she *was* crazy! Maybe she'd lost her mind.

A dream!

That was it! None of this was really happening at all! It was just some kind of nightmare, and if she pinched herself, she'd wake up!

She sank the fingernails of her right hand into the flesh of her left wrist, digging so deeply that the pain almost made her cry out.

A second later, though, as the pain began to fade, she still found herself caught in the nightmare.

She stared at herself once more.

Her eyes were still bright and clear, her skin still its normal color.

But inside, she felt as if some monster had taken over her body and invaded her mind, twisting at her guts and making her feel sicker than she ever had before, and attacking her brain, forcing her to lie, forcing her to pretend she was all right.

Then, still staring at her image in the mirror, she remembered what her mother had told her just before she'd come into the bathroom.

About Carl Henderson trying to rape her.

Suddenly she recalled the way he'd been staring at her at her mother's wedding, and how creepy it had made her feel. But even then she hadn't gotten the feeling that he was attracted to her.

In fact, it had been just the opposite—she'd felt, for some reason she couldn't understand at all, that he *hated* her. She closed her eyes and tried to imagine Carl Henderson raping her.

She couldn't.

And yet, when she'd gone up to the hives looking for Otto, Carl Henderson had been there.

He'd been there, and . . . what?

He'd spoken to her, and she'd said something to him, and . . .

. . . and after that, all she could remember were the bees swarming out of the hives she'd knocked over, surrounding her.

Even now she could still hear the hum of their vibrating wings and feel them crawling on her skin.

She shuddered, instinctively trying to brush them away.

But they weren't there! There was nothing there!

But she could feel them! She knew she could! Even as

the panicky thoughts tumbled in her mind, the itchiness on her skin seemed to penetrate inside her, reaching all the way into her bones.

Terrified, she unlocked the door, pulled it open and stepped out into the hall, determined to tell her mother what was happening to her, how she felt, that she couldn't remember if Carl Henderson had done anything to her.

As she started back toward the examination room, though, she felt her resolve already slipping away, as if something inside her were sapping her will as well as her strength. When she spoke, it was as if she'd lost control of her own words. "I'm done," she said, her voice sounding unnaturally steady to her own ears, reflecting none of the turmoil that was churning within her. "Can we go home now?"

Karen hesitated. A wave of relief washed over her that her daughter looked none the worse for what had happened to her, but with part of her mind, she had a terrible feeling that something was wrong, that Julie couldn't possibly have recovered so quickly. Then she thought she understood:

Shock.

Julie was in shock.

"In a little while," she said gently. "But first, let's have Dr. Filmore look you over, just to make certain you're really all right, okay?"

A surge of hope rose in Julie. Despite her words, her mother hadn't believed her. Now the doctor would find out how sick she really was and would help her! Eagerly, she smiled and nodded her agreement to the examination.

They went back to the treatment room. The men were no longer there, and Ellen Filmore was working on Julie's medical record. Glancing up from her work, the doctor smiled briefly and was about to complete her notes when she suddenly found her eyes locking onto Julie, gazing at her in utter disbelief.

Only five minutes ago the girl had been on the examining table, unconscious, her neck grotesquely swollen, barely able to breathe.

Now she was standing in the doorway, smiling, and looking perfectly normal. This, as far as Ellen Filmore knew, was impossible. "Julie?" she asked. "How do you feel?"

Once again Julie struggled to tell the doctor the truth, carefully formulating the words in her mind.

Fever.

Chills.

Nausea.

But when she spoke, the nightmare world closed in on her once more: "I'm fine," was all she could make herself say.

Ellen Filmore frowned. *Fine?* But that was impossible, given her condition a few minutes ago, and given what Russell had told her while Julie had been in the bathroom. If Julie had been raped—or even come close to it—she might very well have gone into shock and closed down. "I think maybe I'll be the judge of how 'fine' you are," she told Julie gently, handing her an examination gown. "Why don't you put this on and lie down again, and let me have a look?" As Julie started undressing, Ellen led Karen out into the hall and pulled the door closed. "Why don't you stay with me while I look her over?" she asked. "And what, exactly, was Carl talking about when he said he guessed Otto had told you about him raping Julie?"

Trying to keep her emotions in check, Karen repeated what Otto had told them. "I asked Julie about it," she said. "But she didn't really answer me."

"She could be in shock," Ellen Filmore told her, confirming Karen's own thoughts. "If what Otto said is true, she'll remember it sooner or later, and I suspect I'll also find some physical evidence of it. If not of actual penetration, at least there might be some soreness and bruises from a struggle." She smiled encouragingly, but privately reflected that another possibility existed as well. There was still the chance that, as Carl Henderson had insisted, Otto Owen had completely misread the situation and there was no truth to his accusations at all. Together, the two women went back into the examining room, and Ellen Filmore began her examination of Julie, sticking a thermometer under her tongue and wrapping the cuff of a sphygmomanometer around her upper left arm.

She examined Julie's tongue and peered down her throat.

She checked her eyes, and tapped her knees with a small rubber reflex hammer.

She examined her pelvic area for both penetration and bruises.

In the end Ellen Filmore shook her head.

"Well," she sighed when she was finished, smiling wanly at Julie. "I'm not going to pretend I know how that antivenin worked, but you're right. You *are* fine. And you're darned lucky, too. If Carl Henderson hadn't had that antitoxin, I'm not sure you would have made it at all, even if we'd been able to get you to San Luis Obispo."

Julie felt a chill of pure terror pass through her.

The doctor must have found something! She must have! It wasn't possible to feel this bad and look perfectly normal.

And yet, as she slowly sat up, she realized that finally she really was beginning to feel a little better. The aching in her joints was still there, but not quite as bad as it had been before, and it seemed the fever was easing a little, too.

Her stomach still felt like she might throw up any second, but she had a feeling she wasn't actually going to do it.

Was it possible that maybe there really wasn't anything wrong with her, and that she was just feeling some side effects from the shot they'd given her? "You mean I can go home?" she asked, starting to get dressed, but still hoping the doctor would stop her, would refuse to let her leave the clinic.

Ellen Filmore hesitated. "Julie, do you remember if Carl Henderson did anything to you before the bees attacked? Anything at all?"

Once again Julie struggled to remember something—anything—that might account for what was happening to her. But all she could remember was talking to him—she couldn't even remember what had been said—and then being surrounded by the swarm of insects. She shook her head. "He didn't do anything at all," she said. "All he did was try to help me."

At last, hearing Julie's words, the tension that had been building in Karen through the examination was finally released. Apparently Julie really was all right, after all, and Otto, true to form, was just trying to make more trouble. "Come on," she said, giving Julie an affectionate hug. "Let's get home and thank our lucky stars Carl Henderson was there and had that medicine. Okay?" she asked, turning to Ellen Filmore.

"I don't see why not," the doctor agreed, though reluctantly, her eyes still on Julie. "But if anything happens—if she starts feeling anything unusual—you call me." She picked up the brown vial, which was still two-thirds full, and held it up for Julie to see. "If there are any side effects from this stuff, I want to know about them."

There are! Julie wanted to scream. Can't you see? Can't you see any of what's happening to me? But once again she found herself powerless to utter the words, felt herself nodding and smiling though every fiber of her body was screaming, *Help me, help me.*

One last time she tried to tell the doctor about the fever, the aching joints, the nausea and chills.

But all she could do was smile. Weakly, she repeated the lie once more.

"I'm fine."

Defeated by the strange and terrible power she felt inside her, Julie left the examining room and went out to the lobby, where Carl Henderson, his face pale, waited at one end of the room, and her stepfather at the other.

She hesitated at the door, wanting to run to her stepfather, wanting to feel his arms around her, protecting her from whatever had invaded her body and her mind, wanting to beg him to help her.

Instead, against her own will, she found herself walking over to Carl Henderson. "Thank you," she heard herself say, the words coming from some part of her mind she hadn't known existed. "If you hadn't been there, I guess— well, just thank you."

Carl Henderson managed to betray nothing of the terror he'd been feeling as he waited for the results of Julie's examination. He'd hoped she would die. She *should* have died! But she hadn't. Yet, now, listening to her words, he realized he was safe. Though the shot hadn't killed her, it had obviously done *something* to her.

She remembered nothing.

Taking her hand in both of his own, Carl Henderson squeezed it. "Any time," he said. "Any time at all." But even as he spoke the words, his eyes fixed on Julie's face once more, and once more that unfathomable fury rose up inside him.

Even now, right here in the hospital, he wanted to reach out and crush her.

Why? *Why?*

He had no idea.

Julie, seeing his eyes begin to darken, seeing once more that spark of hatred, felt the edges of a fleeting memory stir in the depths of her mind. She jerked her hand away, but as quickly as the fragment of memory had come, it slipped beyond her reach.

She hesitated, once more trying to grasp the fragile wisp of recollection, but then turned away.

The memory was gone.

A few minutes later, sitting in the backseat of the Chrysler between her mother and her sister, with Kevin and Russell sitting up front, Julie saw her stepfather peering at her in the rearview mirror.

"You're really sure you're okay?" he asked. "Maybe you'd better take it easy the rest of the day."

Once again Julie opened her mouth to try to tell her stepfather exactly how she felt.

Once again the words refused to come.

"I'm fine," she said yet again. "I really am."

But both her mind and her body told her she wasn't fine at all.

Something, she knew, had happened.

Something inside her had gone dreadfully wrong, and she no longer had any control over what she said.

How long, she wondered, would it be before she lost control over what she thought, too?

But what if it had already happened?

What if she was already crazy?

That, she realized, was the scariest thing of all. Because if she really had gone crazy, what would she do next?

Her eyes went to Molly, sitting beside her, her little hand clutching her own much bigger one.

She trusts me, Julie thought. She trusts me, but she doesn't have any idea what's happening to me.

What if I hurt her?

What if I kill her?

What if I kill everyone?

The thought seemed to expand in her mind, filling it up, slowly blotting out everything else.

Was this how the people she'd read about felt? The ones who suddenly started killing their friends, or their families, or even complete strangers?

Had they felt like they were dying, and not even been able to ask anyone for help?

Terror built in her once again.

What if I've gone crazy? What if I start killing everyone?

Silently, tearlessly, giving no clue of what was happening to her, Julie Spellman began to cry.

CHAPTER 7

Mark Shannon had been a deputy in Pleasant Valley for almost fifteen years. He and his partner, Manny Gomez, knew most of what was going on in the small community at any given time, and—or at least so Mark liked to think—everything that was going on, given enough time.

Mark had come to Pleasant Valley from San Francisco, where after only five years he'd decided he'd had enough of being a big-city cop. He wanted to work somewhere where he was part of the community—where people would like him or dislike him simply because he was Mark Shannon, not because he wore a blue uniform.

Overall, it had worked out pretty much as he'd hoped. He'd been absorbed into the life of the town years ago, and his only problem at present was that a couple of the kids he'd watched grow up—even coached in Little League—were turning into troublemakers, and he suspected that sooner or later he was going to have to arrest someone who only thought of him as a friend. On balance, though, it made his job easier that at least he and Manny were on a first-name basis with most of the local creeps and perverts.

Until that morning, Carl Henderson had not been on the C-and-P list, but after listening to what Otto Owen—definitely a character, but neither a creep nor a pervert, so far as Mark knew—had to say, he wasn't averse to adding

Henderson to the short list of people upon whom he and Manny would keep an eye.

The problem was that even though Otto's story had sounded plausible, nothing else seemed to add up. Ellen Filmore, with whom Mark had talked for almost half an hour, had assured him that if any attack had been made on Julie Spellman, it couldn't have been nearly as violent as the scene Otto Owen had described. Julie Spellman was not only most assuredly still a virgin, but Dr. Filmore's examination had shown no signs of any kind of struggle, nor any bruises in her genital area.

Now, for the last half hour, he'd been talking to Julie herself, and the whole thing was becoming murkier.

He glanced at his scribbled notes. According to Otto, there was no question of what had been happening by the beehives. But according to Julie, nothing had happened, and her story had been backed up by Dr. Filmore.

His next stop would be Carl Henderson, for all the good it would do him. No matter what had actually happened, he couldn't imagine that Henderson was going to admit to an attempted rape.

And that was the weird part, as far as Mark Shannon was concerned, for despite what both Julie Spellman and Ellen Filmore had told him, he had this feeling that something had, indeed, happened up by the beehives. For one thing, there was a place on the ground where it sure looked as if there'd been a struggle: deep gouges in the hard-packed earth where the gravel with which the area was littered had been ground down under some kind of force.

Of course, it was just possible that Otto had doctored the scene himself; Mark was as aware as everyone else in town of how much Otto hated Henderson. On the other hand, Otto himself had told the deputy how angry he'd been at Julie earlier that morning. "But just 'cause she was rude to me doesn't mean she should get raped," he'd grated as he made his report.

For the moment, despite his gut feeling, Shannon was pretty much stymied. Unfolding his six-foot-four-inch frame from the creaking rattan chair on Russell Owen's shady front porch, he gazed out over the valley. The morning wasn't too hot yet, and the air was clear enough today that you could see all the way across to the peaks of the Sierras, just visible in the distance.

In the pasture adjacent to the barn, the horses were grazing; in the field to the north of the pasture, he could make out Russell's small dairy herd.

On mornings like this Pleasant Valley looked so ridiculously peaceful that it almost made Mark Shannon wonder why they needed his services at all.

But of course he knew why they needed him: every now and then, he got a call like the one Otto had made this morning. This problem, though, looked like it was going to go away by itself, once Otto settled down a bit. "Well, I'll talk to Carl Henderson," he told Russell and Karen, who were flanking Julie on the wide glider that creaked even more than the wicker whenever it moved. "But if Julie says nothing happened, I guess that's pretty much gonna wrap it up." As he placed his hat carefully back onto his thick thatch of blond hair, he decided there was no point in telling them he also planned to keep a weather eye on Carl Henderson, just in case. After all, even though Julie seemed like a nice kid, there was just the off chance that she might have been leading Carl on, in which case there wouldn't have been any bruises for Ellen Filmore to find.

Time, Mark Shannon knew, would eventually tell the tale. As he said good-bye to the Owens, he made a mental note to keep his ear to the ground for any rumors about Julie Spellman, as well as Carl Henderson. Jail-bait was jail-bait, but if Pleasant Valley was going to have a Lolita on its hands, he wanted at least to be able to warn a few folks to give her as wide a berth as possible.

That, he decided as he left the farm, was the major part of his job—keeping the wrong folks from getting together, so as few sparks would fly as possible.

When Mark Shannon was gone, Karen turned worriedly to her daughter. "Maybe you ought to go upstairs and lie down for a while," she mused.

Julie shook her head. "I'm fine," she said. This time the words she uttered were almost true, for in the time that had passed since Dr. Filmore had given her the shot, she'd finally begun to feel better. The feverishness was almost gone, and the strange itchiness deep inside her had all but disappeared.

Perhaps, after all, she wasn't losing her mind.

"All right," Karen sighed. "If you say so." As Julie got up and went into the house, Karen focused on Russell. "The hives," she said, her tone telling Russell there was going to be no putting this discussion off any longer. "I told you I want those hives off the farm, and I meant it, Russell. First Molly almost died, then Julie."

"But they're both fine," Russell protested. "They both responded to the antitoxin."

"What if Carl Henderson hadn't had it with him today?" Karen asked. "Julie was worse than Molly! She wouldn't even have made it to San Luis Obispo!"

"But he did have it," Russell reminded her.

"What if Dr. Filmore runs out of it?" she pressed. "My God, Russell, it's not even on the market yet, and any of us could get stung any time!" She shook her head. "I just don't want those hives anywhere around. Those bees are dangerous."

"They're not that dangerous," Russell replied doggedly. "And besides, we can't just get rid of them. Without the bees, the alfalfa won't pollinate. We can't run the farm without them."

Karen stared at him. "You're telling me that we're totally dependent on them?"

"It's part of how a farm like ours works," he said. "Alfalfa is a terrific crop, but it can't pollinate itself. It has to have bees."

"There's got to be another way," Karen began, but Russell didn't let her finish.

Instead he explained to her what had happened when they'd used UniGrow's fertilizer on the fields and the hives had been inadvertently sterilized. "We lost more than eighty percent of the crops," he finished. "Without the bees to pollinate the fields, the alfalfa just disappeared." His eyes fixed on hers. "We can't let that happen again, Karen. One more year like that, and we'll be wiped out. I mean *wiped out*, Karen," he repeated, reading the doubt in her expression. "We'd lose the farm."

Karen took a deep breath, held it a moment, then let it out slowly in a long sigh. "All right," she said, getting to her feet. "Then let's think of something else. Come on."

They left the porch and started down the driveway toward the road. Crossing it, they walked hand in hand along the dirt track that led toward an immense berm of rocks. Behind the boulders lay the hives. "What if we moved them farther from the house?" Karen asked.

Russell shook his head. "It's not that easy to move hives. You have to move them at least five miles, or you lose the workers. Any distance much less than five miles, and the day after you move them, they'll head out to gather pollen and nectar, but instead of returning to the new hive, they'll go back to where the hive was before. And that's the end of that. Since the homing pattern doesn't change unless the territory is completely unfamiliar, they'll just go back to the previous site and hover there until they die. The only way around it is to move them into a completely new environment, where nothing at all is familiar to them."

Karen turned to look at him. "Then we'll have UniGrow bring in new hives and put them as far from the house as we can," she said, as if the solution to the problem should have been as obvious to him as it was to her. "Or is there some reason why we can't do that, either?"

"I don't know," Russell admitted. "But I can talk to Carl Henderson about it. I suppose it depends on whether they have any hives available right now." He put his arm around her shoulder and pulled her close. "We'll figure it out, hon. And once we know what's going on with the bees, and how come both the girls reacted to them, we'll know what to do. But we have to give Carl a chance to check out the bees." He bent over and kissed her. "I didn't really know how worried you were, either."

"I wasn't, until today," Karen told him. "I thought Molly's reaction was just a freak allergy, but when Julie—" She shuddered as she remembered her older daughter in the clinic, her flesh distended with swelling, her breathing labored and ragged, looking as if she might die at any moment.

"We'll get it solved," Russell promised her. "Carl's working on it, and he'll get the UniGrow labs fired up, too. The worst scenario is that we live out the summer with these hives. Because of the contamination in the fields, the bees we have will be starting to go sterile, so we'll have to get new ones next year anyway. But one way or another, we're always going to have to have bees here. Without them, there's just no farm at all."

Feeling less than mollified, Karen nevertheless slipped her arm around Russell's waist. Something, at least, was being done, and if they were all careful, maybe nothing else would happen.

The sun was low in the western sky. In another fifteen or twenty minutes it would drop behind the foothills of the coast mountains, sending a shadow racing swiftly across the Owen farm, then across the breadth of the San Joaquin Valley toward the Sierras. For an hour after the shadow had fallen, dusk would linger. After only a little more than a week in Pleasant Valley, Karen had already discovered that the long evenings of slowly fading light were her favorite time of day. This evening, with the heat of the afternoon already broken and a cool night breeze already creeping from the ocean into the valley, promised to be nearly perfect. "I want to go for a walk," Karen told Russell as they sat on the front porch, rocking the glider gently and gazing out over the farm. "I want to go down by the creek and listen to the running water, and I want to smell the fresh air. And I want you to hold my hand. I want us to pretend that we're in one of those dumb romantic novels where no one ever has to deal with the real world."

Supper was over, and in the kitchen Julie and Kevin were doing the dishes. Molly was playing on the lawn with Bailey, though Karen wasn't sure whether the dog had quite figured out that Molly was a nine-year-old girl, rather than a recalcitrant calf. The two of them had invented a chasing game, the rules of which, as far as Karen could tell, only the dog and the little girl could possibly understand.

Inside the house the phone began to ring. Karen was about to get up when Russell stopped her. "Let one of the kids get it. If it's for us, they'll tell us." Karen sank back onto the creaking contraption upon which they were sitting. A moment later Kevin appeared at the screen door.

"Can we go to the movies?"

"By 'we,' do you mean you and Julie, or you and Julie and Molly?" Russell countered.

Kevin's eyes clouded. "Come on, Dad—nobody else is taking little kids."

"Who all's going?" Russell asked.

Kevin reeled off four names that sounded vaguely familiar to Karen, though she could attach a face to none of them.

"What do you think?" she heard Russell ask.

She shrugged. "If Julie really feels well enough, I guess it's okay."

Ten minutes later Kevin and Julie came out. "We're going to walk over to Jeff's house," he said. "He's going to drive."

Karen looked questioningly at Russell, who pointed toward the next farm toward town, which spread out from a haphazard group of buildings a half a mile away from their own house. "Marge Larkin's oldest son," he explained. "She rents an old tenant house from Vic Costas, next door."

Karen, still worried about what had happened that morning, gazed up at Julie. "You're sure you're all right?"

Julie's eyes rolled with adolescent scorn. "How many times do I have to tell you?" she said. "I'm fine, Mom!"

"All right," Karen sighed. "Just checking. What time will you be home?"

"One?" Julie asked, obviously using the hour as an opening bid.

"Ten," Karen countered.

"Mom!" Julie wailed. "The movie won't even be over by then! And it's summer—we shouldn't have to be in until midnight."

"And this is a farm, where everyone has to get up early," Russell interjected. "You'll be home by eleven, and that's it."

Julie, unused to having to bargain with anyone but her mother, looked as if she were about to argue with Russell. And Karen, in that instant, knew the moment had come to establish the rules of the new family unit. "Eleven it is, then," she said. Her eyes held her daughter's, and for a moment she thought Julie might still try to argue. But before she could say anything, Kevin spoke.

"Nothing's open later than ten-thirty, anyway. Let's go."

"What about you?" Russell asked as Kevin and Julie left the porch and started off across the fields toward the farm next door. "Ready for your walk?"

"What about Molly?" Karen countered. "We can't just leave her here."

"Why not?" Russell asked. "This isn't L.A., honey. Dad's right next door, and she's playing with a dog who would cheerfully tear the throat out of anyone or anything who tried to hurt her. She's fine by herself."

Karen shook her head. Not tonight—not after what had happened just that very morning. This evening, at least, she wasn't about to leave her daughter alone with no one but the big dog to look after her.

Russell, reading her worries perfectly, whistled to Bailey, then called out to Molly. "Come on! We're going down by the creek!" As Molly and Bailey dashed off across the field, Russell stepped into the house and picked up the flashlight that always sat on the table in the foyer.

When he'd come back out of the house, Karen slipped her hand into his and they started toward the stand of scrub oaks that bordered the field. Through them a brook wound its way down from the foothills to the valley floor. A few minutes later, sitting on a rock at the edge of the stream, Karen peeled off her sneakers and socks, and dipped her feet into the water, sighing in contentment as she felt the coolness of it penetrate her skin, and watched Molly and the dog explore the shore a few yards downstream. "Perfect," she sighed. "This is just perfect." She leaned back, resting against Russell's chest, and felt his arms tighten around her. "It's all going to work out, isn't it?" she asked.

"Of course it is," Russell assured her. "From now on, everything's going to be wonderful."

DAWN

FINALE

*D*awn *had no idea how long she had been praying for death. A while ago—maybe minutes, maybe hours, maybe only seconds—she had thought her torture had finally ended. The blackness around her had begun to recede, and she heard music playing. Heavenly music, like she had always imagined the harps of angels would produce.*

She felt a gentle caress, as if loving fingers were stroking her skin.

But then everything began to change—the swirling colors turned into a glaring light, and what had been music before was now the furious buzzing of thousands of insects.

The stroking fingers became instruments of torture as mandibles and stingers sank into her naked skin.

Her mind felt as if it were about to shatter as it was wrenched once more out of the safety and comfort of sleep by the torture her body was undergoing, and again she tried to force a scream from her ruined vocal cords.

All that emerged was a bubbling gasp as her final plea for rescue dissolved into a barely audible gurgle of defeat.

It was the laugh—the shattering, maniacal braying—that cut through the last defenses of her crumbling mind and made her open her eyes.

He was standing in the open doorway, silhouetted

against the glare of the naked lightbulb behind him, a black shadow against a blinding white background.

She knew who it was, though, even knew why he had come.

She was dying, and he wanted to see it happen.

A surge of rage energized Dawn, and from somewhere deep within herself she found the strength to lash out once more, to kick out at him, even though she had no hope of reaching him. As he laughed once more, she fell limp and her head flopped forward.

For the first time, her eyes beheld what was happening to her.

Paralyzed and totally muted by the awful sight, she gazed in horror at the thousands of insects crawling over her skin. But they weren't just crawling on her.

They were killing her.

Killing her and eating her at the same time.

Ants.

Thousands of them. Hundreds of thousands of them.

They were everywhere, not just on her body, but on the floor around her as well. For a second Dawn tried to pull her feet up, but her strength was gone now. Her bloodied feet, the skin gone from the raw flesh, dropped back to touch the sticky mass of insects—mixed with her own dripping blood—that squirmed beneath her.

Some of the insects were attacking each other, responding to ancient instincts of enmity, but most of them were answering a much more powerful call.

The summons to feed.

To feed, and to kill their prey.

They swarmed over her, and in the glare of light streaming in from the open door, Dawn could see tiny fragments of her own flesh clutched in the mandibles of the ants as they scuttled down her legs, over the mass of their blood-ensnared cohorts and across the floor, to vanish into the shadows.

Eaten alive!

She was actually being eaten alive!

As her gorge rose in a violent and involuntary protest against what was happening to her, and her throat filled with the taste of vomit, she heard the man yell at her.

"Look at me!" he screamed. "Look at me and let me see your eyes!"

But it was no longer possible for Dawn to obey his order, for the last of her strength was ebbing from her body now, and the realization of how she was dying had, finally, crushed her sanity.

Though her body still breathed, Dawn herself was dead. . . .

He stood in the doorway, watching Dawn die, as he'd watched others die before her.

But he'd experimented with Dawn.

With the others, he'd simply brought them home, put them in the room, and turned the insects loose.

He'd gagged the other girls, to keep their screams from being heard, but with Dawn, he'd left the gag off, so he could sit outside the door and listen to her screams as she cried out in the darkness before he even loosed the insects.

With the earlier girls, he'd enjoyed listening at the door as they thrashed around in the darkness, trying to escape the swarms of insects.

With Dawn, though, he'd decided to try something new, and suspend her from the floor joists, leaving her in helpless immobility when at last the insects attacked.

His greatest joy, though, was now, as he watched her die.

It was the fire ants—his beloved Solenopsis saevissima—*he knew, that were actually killing her. They'd been swarming over her for hours, each jab of the tiny stinger at the end of their abdomens releasing a minute drop of poison into her system, making her feel as if her body was on fire.*

Now, though, she was dead, and suddenly he had an idea.

Turning away from the room at the back of his basement, he went in search of something to use. When he returned, he carried with him a rusty piece of reinforcing bar and a large mallet. Holding one end of the re-bar—the end he'd carefully ground to a point—against Dawn's chest, he began hammering it with the mallet, driving it through her chest and into the old wood of the post behind her.

Mounting her, adding her to his collection.

He wondered how long he could keep her there before her body would begin to rot away.

The girl, he decided as he surveyed his work, wasn't nearly as good as an insect.

Insects, at least, didn't deteriorate after he mounted them, but stayed eternally in their state of perfection, hovering on pins, always waiting for him to admire them.

Yes, in so many ways insects were superior to humans. Perhaps that was why he loved them so much.

CHAPTER 8

Julie stared at the car that sat in front of Jeff Larkin's house. She'd seen some pretty crummy cars in L.A., but nothing quite as bad as this one. "This is it?" she asked Kevin as Jeff came out the front door of his house. "This is what we're going to the movies in? Does it even run?"

"Most of the time," Kevin told her.

"All it needs is a little body work, and some paint," Jeff told her, his voice defensive as he moved almost protectively to the ancient, rusting station wagon. He'd discovered the car in a shed right after he, his mother, and his kid brother had moved onto the farm two years ago. He'd finally managed to get it actually running a few months ago, and Vic Costas had told him he could use it as long as he insured it and kept it going. So far, though it had cost him almost every nickel he managed to scrape up, Jeff thought it was worth it. "It's better than walking, isn't it?"

Julie shrugged, got into the car, and tried to pretend she didn't notice the moldy smell that permeated the upholstery. But as they started driving toward town, she suddenly started feeling funny again.

It began as a hum in her ears, right after they turned out of Jeff's driveway.

For a few minutes it didn't bother her too much—nothing at all like the terrible things that had happened to her at the doctor's that morning—but the closer they got to town, the worse it got, and finally, certain it must be coming from somewhere outside the car, she cranked her window closed, even though the smell emanating from the seats was making her feel nauseated again.

But the humming didn't let up at all, and now something else was happening to her.

She was starting to feel as if the car itself were closing in around her, and her whole body was starting to itch again.

Within a few minutes she wanted to jump right out of her skin.

A couple of times she felt Kevin's eyes on her.

Could he see that something was wrong with her? But if he did, why didn't he ask her what was wrong?

Even as the question took shape in her mind, a knot of fear constricted her chest, for she could almost hear herself repeating that she was just fine, even though she felt awful and was afraid she was going crazy.

Oh God, what was she going to do?

What was happening to her?

Her nerves kept getting edgier and edgier. Finally, as the heat in the car built up, she rolled down the window, and breathed deeply of the night air. And then, as they came into the village itself, the humming died away, and a few seconds after that, the terrible itching inside her body began to ease as well.

Was she going to be all right after all?

But for how long?

Jeff found a place to park the car, and they walked the half block to the theater, where the rest of the kids were waiting for them.

Inside the theater, for a few minutes, things were fine.

Then, as soon as the lights went down and the previews began, the humming started in her ears again.

But now it wasn't just the humming sound that threatened to drive her crazy.

It was the flickering image on the screen, too.

At first she tried to ignore it, but even before the feature began, her head was starting to throb with pain, and the nausea was rising in her stomach.

Leave, she told herself. Just get up and go sit in the lobby until you feel better.

But when she tried to leave her seat, to stand up, her body refused to obey.

It was as if some force inside her were holding her down, commanding her to stay where she was, taking control of her body from her own mind.

The fear she had felt in the car seized her, ballooning into terror.

Now she tried to ignore the humming and the headache and concentrate on the movie itself. She'd already seen the first six—or was it seven?—movies in the series, and had been waiting for this one to come out.

But tonight she just couldn't follow the plot at all. Even glancing at the screen made her head throb.

Now the itching she had felt as a vague, restless sensation deep inside her body had crawled outward, onto her skin. It felt as if thousands of tiny insects were creeping all over her—under her clothes, in her hair, her nose, her eyes—everywhere.

But no matter how she tried to scratch herself or wriggle in her clothes, she couldn't get rid of the itch.

The worst of it seemed to be in her fingers, and she kept scratching and kneading them until she became afraid she might dig right through her skin and make them start bleeding.

And as the humming in her ears and the pounding in her head and the itching in her body continued to worsen, so also did the terror inside her.

It was happening—she was sure of it now.

She was going crazy.

* * *

Kevin gazed up at the screen in the darkened theater and tried one last time to get involved with the plot of the movie.

But it was impossible.

And not just because the movie, which was the seventh—or maybe the eighth?—in a series involving some kind of rampaging slasher, made no sense, though he suspected it didn't since he remembered enough of the plot to know that so far none of the killings he'd witnessed seemed to have a motive.

It wasn't just the movie.

It was Julie, too.

Ever since they'd gotten into the car at Jeff Larkin's house, she'd been acting weird.

Now they were sitting next to each other, with Jeff and Shelley Munson to Julie's left, and Andy Bennett and Sara McLaughlin to Kevin's right. Right after the lights had gone down, he'd nudged Julie. "Look at the ceiling," he whispered, and she looked up, giggling at the phony projected clouds that swirled overhead.

He'd slipped his hand into hers and squeezed it, and she'd squeezed his back.

But as the previews had played, and then the movie's opening credits had begun to run, she pulled her hand away from his. Ever since, she'd been fidgeting in her seat, her hands twisted together, rubbing and scratching her fingers so constantly that even he was starting to get nervous about it.

A couple of times he'd glanced over at her. Although she didn't look back at him, he didn't think she was watching the movie, either. In fact, her head was down, as if she were deliberately not looking at the screen.

Once, he leaned over and whispered to her, asking her if she was okay. She hesitated, then nodded and said she was fine.

And for a few minutes it seemed as though she was.

Then she'd started fidgeting again, and scratching her hands and fingers.

When she looked away from the screen again, he leaned over to whisper in her ear. "Why don't we just get out of here? If neither of us likes the movie, why don't we leave, and go get a Coke or something?"

Saying nothing at all, nearly certain that her body would refuse to obey, just as it had earlier when she'd wanted to get up and flee from the theater, Julie tried to stand.

And to her own shock and relief, she found herself rising from her seat.

Barely trusting her ability to move, she quickly began working her way past Jeff Larkin and Shelley Munson.

"Where're you going?" Shelley whispered as Kevin struggled by a second later.

"We're leaving," Kevin whispered back. "The movie's so dumb I can't even follow it, so we're going for Cokes or something."

"We'll come too," Shelley said. When Jeff Larkin groaned, she shrugged elaborately. "Stay if you want," she told him in a voice that clearly belied her words. "I can walk home alone."

"Come on, Shelley," Jeff protested. "We all wanted to see this movie!"

"You mean you and Andy wanted to see it," Shelley replied. "And I just told you—I can walk home!"

As people in the area began to shush them, Shelley Munson, followed an instant later by Jeff Larkin, hurried up the aisle. A few seconds after that, Andy Bennett and Sara McLaughlin emerged into the lobby as well.

"What's going on?" Andy demanded. "The movie was just getting good! Did you see that last one? Jeez, I never saw so much blood in my life!"

"Gross!" Sara told him. "I hate that movie! It's so dumb!"

"It's not dumb," Jeff protested. "It's neat!"

"So you and Andy go back and watch the rest of it," Shelley Munson suggested. "The rest of us are going for Cokes."

"How about beer instead?" Andy asked. "Jeff and me got—"

"Will you just shut up?" Jeff demanded, turning to check out the lobby of the theater. "What if someone hears you, man? What if we get caught?"

"Nobody's gonna catch us," Andy told Jeff. "The only person here is Josh Carter, and he'd go with us if he didn't have to work." From behind the candy counter one of their classmates looked up, his eyes hopeful.

"I get off as soon as the next show starts," he began.

"Too late," Jeff told him. "We'll have it all drunk by then."

The six kids left the theater, with Julie breathing deeply of the night air. Away from the flickering movie screen, she felt all right again.

They all piled into Jeff's car.

"Where we going?" Kevin asked.

"The power lines," Jeff replied.

Five minutes later the car pulled into an old county park that, having been built under the high-voltage power lines that supplied the town with electricity, had years ago been all but abandoned by the town as people began worrying about what the magnetic fields under the lines might do to their children. For the last ten years or so the park had been left pretty much to the teenagers.

Tonight, as dusk was rapidly turning to darkness, it was totally deserted.

Jeff pulled the station wagon to a stop as Andy Bennett fished around under the seat, then triumphantly held up a six-pack. "Here it is," Andy crowed. "Right where I left it!" Pulling the cans from the plastic web that held them together, he began passing them forward.

As one of the cans was put into her hand, Julie's fingers

closed on it. She'd started feeling better as soon as she'd escaped from the theater, and by the time they pulled into the park, the weird itching was completely gone. But now it was starting up again, and she could once more hear the strange humming sound in her ears.

Trying not to think about it, she looked at the can of beer she still held clutched in her hand.

She'd tasted beer a few times, back in L.A., but hadn't really drunk it before.

Maybe it would make her feel better.

Popping open the top of the can, she raised it to her lips. The fluid, warm and bitter, filled her mouth, and for a moment she thought she was going to choke on it. Then, out of the corner of her eye, she saw Sara McLaughlin drinking thirstily from another can.

If that's what the kids in Pleasant Valley did . . .

She choked down the mouthful of beer, and took another one.

The humming in her ears was getting worse now, and so was the itching that seemed to come from somewhere deep inside her.

And now something else was happening to her—she felt an urge to get out of the car.

Pushing the door open, she scrambled out, and a moment later Kevin got out, too. "You okay?" she heard him ask.

Nodding her head, Julie took another swallow of beer, and moved away from the car into the shadows of the evening. Kevin hesitated, then started after her.

"Hey," Sara McLaughlin asked. "Where are you guys going now?"

"Want to go with them?" Shelley Munson teased, seizing the opportunity to needle Sara about her ongoing crush on Kevin Owen. "Can't you stand to have Kevin out of your sight for a few minutes?"

Sara burned with embarrassment, and told herself never again to trust Shelley with any of her secrets. Besides, she was pretty sure that since Julie had arrived in town, Kevin hadn't been interested in anyone else, let alone herself.

Kevin, though, appeared not to have heard what Shelley said. "We're just going for a walk," he called back. He glanced toward Julie, who was still moving quickly away from the car, and wondered what was wrong with her. "We'll be back in a few minutes."

Jeff leered at him knowingly. "Taking a walk, my ass," he said. "Get real, man—we all know what you guys are going to do." He started giggling. "Want to borrow a blanket?"

But Kevin was hurrying after Julie. "Hey," he asked as he got closer, "you okay?"

Julie, who was once again starting to feel better, smiled at him. "Of course I am," she said. She cast around for an excuse not to go back to the car. "I—I just thought it might be fun to walk home," she said. "I mean, it's so warm. . . ."

Kevin stared at her, but in the last of the rapidly failing light, her face was completely unreadable.

Was it the other kids? Didn't she like them?

Then another thought came to him.

Maybe she just wanted to be alone with him.

"I—I guess we could walk," he stammered. "It's a couple of miles, but we can just follow the power lines." He pointed up to the thick wires above the car. "The right of way goes straight out to our place." He started toward the twin rows of enormous stanchions that supported the high-voltage lines, but Julie reached out and took his hand, stopping him.

"No," she said.

Kevin, puzzled, strained once more to see her face in the darkness.

"No?" he asked. "What do you mean, no?"

Julie's mind raced, for the moment he pointed to the high-voltage wire, she realized where the humming she'd thought was inside her head must have been coming from.

The power lines!

First it had happened on the way to the movie, when they'd been driving along right next to them.

Then again, when Jeff had parked under them a few minutes ago.

"I—I just don't want to," she said. "I mean, everyone says power lines are really bad for you."

"Come on," Kevin teased. "It's not like we're gonna be living under them or anything!" Once more he started toward the double row of stanchions and the utility road that ran between them.

"No!" Julie said again, her voice rising sharply. She dropped his hand and started off by herself. "You can go that way if you want to, but I'm not!"

Kevin stared after her. What was she, nuts? For a second he had half a mind to let her go off by herself, and to take the easy path home himself.

But what if she got lost?

So what if she did? a voice inside him asked. Who cared?

But he already knew the answer to that question.

He cared.

Abandoning the power lines, he went after Julie, wondering how they could get home without having to walk along the country road, where the lines would be practically over their heads.

It seemed really stupid, but if that's what she wanted . . .

Kevin suddenly had a sinking feeling, as he realized how he was acting.

He was acting like he was in love with her.

His heart suddenly throbbing with excitement, he ran to catch up with her, and once more slipped his hand into hers.

Julie smiled at him and squeezed his hand happily.

Now that they were away from the power lines, she felt fine again.

CHAPTER 9

*L*iar!

Otto Owen sat on the sagging sofa in his living room, his eyes fixed on the television screen but his mind so consumed with anger that he was barely aware that the set was even on.

Liar!

That's what they'd called him, even though no one had actually come right out and said the word.

Liar!

That's what Mark Shannon thought he was.

Either a liar or a confused old geezer who didn't know what he'd seen that morning.

And Karen thought he was a liar, too, even though she hadn't had the guts to say the word any more than the deputy had.

But what really hurt was the way his son and grandson had looked at him as he told Mark Shannon what he'd seen Carl Henderson doing to Julie. Not that they'd said anything, but after a while Kevin had looked away, and he'd seen Russell shaking his head.

Like he was pitying me! Otto thought bitterly. They all thought he was old, or blind, or didn't know what he saw.

Or that he was lying.

How the hell could they have believed that scumbag Carl Henderson?

'Course, it hadn't helped that Julie couldn't even remember, but after what had happened to her, how could anyone expect her to? She'd almost died from the bee stings, hadn't she? So how could anyone expect her to remember what Henderson had been doing to her?

Otto had been turning it over in his mind all day, trying to figure out if maybe he could have been wrong, if maybe his eyes had deceived him some way. After all, he wasn't as young as he used to be; he couldn't even read without glasses anymore. Finally, that afternoon, he'd gone back up to the hives and taken another look.

He'd paced off the distance from the spot where he'd come around the berm of rocks to the place where Henderson had been sprawled out on the ground, Julie pinned under him.

No more than fifty feet.

Then he'd gone back to the spot by the rocks and started looking around.

He'd not only been able to see the hives perfectly clearly—and they were ten feet or so past the spot where Henderson and Julie had been—but had even been able to read the word "UniGrow" stenciled all over them, as if someone was just waiting to steal the damned things.

He'd come back home and spent the rest of the afternoon and evening stewing about it.

And the more he stewed, the madder he got.

By tomorrow everyone in town would be talking about him, spreading the word that Otto Owen was starting to lose it and couldn't be trusted anymore.

Which was a damned lie! He'd seen what he'd seen perfectly clearly, and he didn't care what anyone said, or didn't say, or couldn't prove.

Even if Henderson hadn't actually been raping Julie, he had sure as hell been on top of her, and she had sure as hell been struggling. And whatever the son of a bitch was trying to do, he was going to get away with it, Otto thought, unless he himself did something! And there was something he could do, too! He could go over to Henderson's and make him tell the truth.

He might be pushing eighty, but he was pretty damned sure he could still take a creep like Carl Henderson!

His mind made up, Otto picked up the remote control, switched off the television, and left the house.

Ten minutes later he turned his three-year-old Ford pickup onto Walnut Road. At the end stood the house where Carl Henderson still lived. The man must be nuts, Otto reflected. What with his mother having died years ago and his sister gone to live somewhere back East, the house was far bigger than any normal person would ever need. Not that he could consider Carl Henderson any kind of normal, Otto reminded himself, not after what he'd seen!

He slowed the truck as he approached the house. Standing a half mile from its nearest neighbor, it was almost concealed in a grove of trees, and didn't appear to have been painted in twenty years. Though still occupied, it had begun to take on a derelict air that told Otto even more about what kind of man Carl Henderson was. A man who didn't take care of his own house couldn't be trusted, not as far as Otto was concerned.

Darkness was falling rapidly and he saw no sign of Henderson's car. Swearing under his breath at the loss of the confrontation he'd spent the whole afternoon working himself up to, Otto was about to start back home when suddenly he slammed on his brakes.

Almost completely hidden in the trees in front of the house, he spotted Henderson's gray Cherokee. His lips tightening into a thin line, Otto backed the truck up a few yards and turned into Henderson's driveway. A few seconds later he was parked in front of the house. Getting out of the truck, he mounted the steps to the front porch, pressed the button next to the door, and, when he heard no sound from within, knocked loudly.

Otto waited, but still heard nothing from within the house.

Scowling, he moved to the front window and peered inside. He was looking into the living room, where a bright bulb burned in a brass lamp. The room contained a Victorian sofa, two overstuffed chairs, a coffee table, and two side tables, both of which were covered with the kind of knickknacks Otto's wife had loved but which he himself had cleared out of his house within a year of her death. Framed photographs, china figurines, a collection of cheap glass objects of the sort Otto could remember winning at the midway of the county fair years earlier. Dust collectors was all they were, as far as Otto was concerned.

Then Otto's eyes were drawn to the walls.

Everywhere he could see, the walls of Carl Henderson's living room were covered with display cases.

Display cases filled with insects mounted on pins.

Even in the failing light, Otto could make out dozens of glass-covered boxes, some of them filled with butterflies and moths, others with beetles, wasps, grasshoppers, and locusts.

Though many of the insects were as familiar to Otto as houseflies, some of the boxes on the walls contained exotic specimens he'd never seen before.

Beetles with immense horns and midsections that looked strong enough to break your finger.

Flies twice the size of any Otto had seen before.

Otto's eyes swept the cases and he felt a faint shudder as he tried to imagine living with these morbid displays, confronted by dead insects everywhere you looked.

Finally moving off the porch, he slowly circled around the house, but it wasn't until he was in the backyard that he noticed, through a dirt-encrusted window in a small ventilation well, a dim glow of light coming from the basement.

Climbing the steps to the back door, Otto rapped sharply

twice more, waited, then called out Carl Henderson's name.

Nothing.

His scowl deepening, he pulled the screen door open and tried the doorknob.

Locked.

Locked, but so loose in its frame that the latch seemed barely to be catching in the striker.

In fact, if he were to just sort of push on it . . .

A second later he was standing in the utility room of Carl Henderson's house.

Barely glancing at it, he moved on into the kitchen, treading so lightly that he made practically no sound as he crossed the worn linoleum floor.

And yet, despite the care with which he stepped, there was sound in the near darkness of the kitchen.

The sounds, Otto realized, of a summer night. Except that here the sounds were coming from within the house, instead of from the fields beyond the walls.

Groping in the gloom, Otto found a light switch and flipped it on. Bright fluorescent lights flickered for a moment, then came on, flooding the room with a harsh white light almost as bright as day.

In the kitchen sink were the dirty dishes from a make-shift supper, most of which looked as if it had come out of the microwave oven that sat on the counter next to the refrigerator.

Otto, though, barely noticed the dishes, the microwave, or even the leftover mess from Carl Henderson's supper.

For everywhere in the kitchen—arranged on metal shelving that covered one of the walls, spread across the area of the counter that the microwave wasn't occupying, even covering all but a tiny corner of the kitchen table— were glass tanks. Terraria.

Instead of containing the usual lizards, turtles, or even

small snakes, each and every terrarium in Carl Henderson's kitchen was alive with insects.

Insects, and spiders.

Unlike the house itself, the glass enclosures were carefully tended, each of them filled with a carefully constructed environment developed to suit its primary tenants.

One of them, sitting on the corner of the table closest to Otto, seemed to be empty save for some leaves scattered across its bottom, but when he leaned closer, he was able to make out dozens of green caterpillars feasting on the leaves.

Others had already spun cocoons and were starting the metamorphosis from pupa into butterfly.

In one of the smaller tanks a large, hairy tarantula crouched, seeming to stare out at Otto as if ready to pounce.

Otto shivered as he gazed at the ugly spider, and quickly turned away.

Leaving the kitchen, he moved through the dining room into a hall that led toward the front door and the stairs to the second floor. Like those in the living room, the walls of the hall were covered with more display cases containing Carl Henderson's vast collection of insects, each creature carefully mounted and labeled, all arranged in precise rows in their boxes.

Beneath the staircase was a door, and when Otto opened it, he found exactly what he was looking for.

The stairs to the basement.

He paused, listening, but heard nothing from below save the same soft humming that was coming from the tanks of insects in the kitchen.

"Henderson?" Otto called.

There was no answer from below, nor could he see any light.

Then there must be more than one room in the cellar below the house.

Again Otto groped for a light switch, and again he found one almost exactly where he expected.

A naked bulb came to life in a socket above the door. His shadow preceding him, Otto started down the stairs into the basement. At the bottom of the steep flight he found three more light switches, and flipped one of them on.

As in the kitchen, a bank of fluorescent lights flickered on, filling the basement with bright light. Blinking as his eyes adjusted to the glare, Otto looked curiously around.

The basement had been converted into a laboratory, and the stale air contained within its walls was heavy with the smell of strong disinfectants. Along one wall ran a long counter made of white marble, broken only by a gleaming stainless steel sink. Several different kinds of microscopes sat on the stone counter, and above it were bookshelves filled with reference volumes.

Along the back of the counter was an array of chemicals and tools.

A display case sat open, partially filled, and on a thick piece of cardboard next to it were a dozen insects, each of them mounted on a pin, awaiting labels before being added to the case.

Against the opposite wall were more shelves filled with terraria. Even from ten feet away Otto could see that several of them contained large ant farms, though not of the sort you could buy in any toy store, meant to amuse children for a few days and then be thrown away. Carl Henderson's ant farms were large, and only a few tunnels were visible, but the surface of the ground within the farms was teeming with the tiny insects, assuring Otto that thousands of ants were thriving in each of the large tanks.

Otto was still staring at the tanks when he heard a sharp voice behind him.

"What are you doing in my house?"

Startled by the sound, Otto jumped, then turned to see Carl Henderson standing in a doorway on the far side of the basement. It was so lost in shadows that Otto hadn't noticed it when he'd come downstairs, and now Carl's figure, framed against the light in the room behind him, was no more than a black silhouette. But as he snapped off the lights in the room behind him and stepped into the larger portion of the basement, Otto caught a glimpse of something.

A girl.

A girl with long, flowing dark hair.

Hair like Julie's.

But that wasn't possible—he'd seen Julie leave with Kevin a little while before he himself had left. They'd been heading over toward Vic Costas's, where Kevin's friend Jeff Larkin lived.

And yet, even in that fragmentary glimpse he'd caught before Carl Henderson pulled the door closed, Otto was almost certain it was Julie who was in the back room.

"What's going on down here, Henderson?" he growled now, taking a step toward the much younger man. "What's Julie doing here?"

"Julie?" Henderson echoed, his eyes fixing on the old man. When he spoke, his voice was low, but steady. "She's not here, Otto. You interrupted me this morning, remember?"

Otto paused. Was it going to be this easy? Was Henderson going to admit what he'd done? But why wouldn't he? There was no one here but the two of them. Why would Henderson care what he said?

Carl Henderson's lips twisted into a dark parody of a smile. "It wasn't what you think, Otto," he said. "I wasn't trying to rape her. I wouldn't do that."

Otto's jaw began to work as anger rose in him once

again. "I saw it, Henderson," he rasped. "I know what you were doing."

"No you don't," Henderson told him. "You don't know at all. But I'll show you." He paused for a moment, his smile broadening into a twisted grin. "Would you like to see my collection, Otto?"

Collection?

What was Henderson talking about? Wasn't that what he'd been seeing all over the house? "I already saw it, Henderson," he growled, "and if you ask me—"

"I *didn't* ask you," Henderson cut in, his voice low, but suddenly as cold and hard as a marble counter. "I didn't ask you to come here at all, Otto. I didn't ask you to break into my house." His eyes narrowed as he saw Otto flinch at his last words. "You *did* break in, didn't you, Otto? You must have, because I always lock the house before I come down here." He paused for a fraction of a second, then repeated one of the words he'd just spoken: "Always."

There was something in the way Henderson spoke the word that made Otto Owen's blood run cold, and instinctively he took a step back. It was as if the action triggered something in Carl Henderson. Suddenly the younger man was beside him, the fingers of his right hand closing on Otto's shoulder.

Fingers that were far stronger than Otto had imagined they would be.

"You can't leave, Otto," Carl told him. "After all, I can't have you spreading stories about me, now can I?"

"Get your hands off me—" Otto began, but again Henderson cut his words short.

"But you've only seen part of my collection, Otto. The rest of it is back here." He began moving Otto toward the closed door at the back of the cellar, his fingers digging painfully into the flesh of the older man's arm. "Come along, Otto. Don't you want to see my best specimens?"

As a terrible premonition began to expand in Otto

Owen's mind, Carl Henderson propelled him toward the door. When they were finally in front of it, Carl reached out with his free hand and grasped the knob. Then he paused, and his eyes fastened on Otto as he spoke. "You understand that after you see my collection, you won't be able to leave."

Before Otto could answer, Henderson twisted the knob and pushed the door open.

The harsh smell of disinfectants instantly grew stronger.

The lights inside the room were off, and as the door swung slowly and silently on its hinges, the scene within was revealed in a strange kind of slow motion.

It wasn't Julie that Otto had seen in that brief glimpse when Henderson had first come out of the room only a few moments ago.

It was someone else.

Someone Otto didn't recognize.

A girl with long dark hair.

Hair that spilled down her shoulders, hanging almost to her waist.

She was suspended against the far wall, hanging from one of the floor joists by a thick rope tied around her wrists. Her hands, blackened and distended, must have turned gangrenous before the rest of her body had died, for even though her arms had paled as blood had drained from them after death, her hands had not, and their mottled dark purplish hue stood in stark contrast to the alabaster tone of her forearms.

From her chest the head of a large spike protruded; a spike that had been driven completely through her body and into one of the original support posts of the house's foundation.

Her head hung down, as if she was staring at the floor, but Otto could still make out her features.

She appeared to have been about Julie's age.

Otto had no idea how long the girl had been dead, nor

exactly how she had died. But even as his gorge rose in protest against the horrific sight, a fleeting prayer ran through his mind.

A prayer that the girl had died before Carl Henderson had administered the final indignity of pinning her to the wall in a grotesque parody of the way he'd pinned so many thousands of insects into the boxes that were displayed all over his house.

The girl, though, unlike the insects, was no longer intact.

Rather, her body was in the process of being devoured.

Ants swarmed over her legs, picking at her skin and flesh.

Her feet, suspended only a few inches above the floor, had already been stripped almost clean of their meat, the bones of her toes held together now only by threads of cartilage.

The girl's belly was grotesquely distended, and as Carl's eyes fixed on her rotting flesh, a maggot appeared, erupting from her skin like a pustule, then dropping—squirming—to the floor, only to be instantly overrun by the ants that were working their way up her legs, devouring everything they touched.

Otto stared at the grotesque figure, stunned into mute immobility by the sheer horror of it.

"She'll be gone soon," he heard Carl Henderson say. "But it's all right." Henderson's lips curled once more into the dark smile he had shown Otto a few minutes ago. "There are lots of girls out there, Otto. Even if I can't bring Julie down here, I'll find someone."

Otto's lips worked helplessly for a moment, but finally a single word emerged from his throat: "Why?"

Carl Henderson's cruel smile froze. His eyes darkened, glazing with a manic fury that set his entire body trembling. "It's the way they look," he rasped, his teeth clenched as his crazed eyes fixed on the girl. "It's not my fault. Something happens when I see them. I can't—" Abruptly, he cut himself off and forced his gaze away from the body on the wall, to stare contemptuously at Otto. "Maybe I just want them to feel what you're going to feel right now, Otto."

In one quick motion Henderson stepped out of the room, snapping the light off and closing the door behind him.

In the scant second before the door clicked shut, Otto turned around and took one lurching step toward it. But it was too late. As he was plunged into darkness, Otto heard the rasp of the lock being turned.

Carl Henderson savored the look he'd seen in Otto Owen's eyes in that last half second before he closed the door, locking the old man into the room where he kept his most valuable specimens.

It was a look of pure terror, a look that told him Otto knew what was coming next—knew he was about to die.

The only thing Carl wished now was that he could watch Otto's face for the next few minutes—or hours, depending on how long it actually took for death to come to the old man. But that, of course, was impossible.

In order to do that, there would have to be light in the room, and light was the one thing Carl's victims were never allowed.

Their fear, he'd long ago learned, was far more intense when they were unable to see what was happening to them; when their imaginations made their agonized deaths more terrifying than even the most grotesque torture he himself could devise.

The only problem with Otto Owen was that Carl couldn't take nearly as much time as he would like.

The last girl—the one who was even now pinned to the wall of the pitch-black room—had taken days to die, though her mind had shattered into fragments even before the first night was through.

Like all the others, he'd found the girl hitchhiking south on the freeway, as he was on the way back from an overnight trip to Sacramento. And like all the others, she was just about fifteen years old, with long dark hair.

He'd known the minute he'd seen her that he was going to bring her home. He'd begun to feel the familiar rage when he spotted her walking along the shoulder of the highway.

He'd concealed it, though, smiling at her, acting as though he didn't care whether she got into his car or not.

She'd seemed like a nice girl, too. Her name was Dawn.

Dawn Morningstar, according to her.

He hadn't believed her, of course—no one's name was Dawn Morningstar. But it didn't make any difference, either. Not in the end.

Carl let his mind drift back to the day he'd met Julie Spellman. From the moment he'd caught his first glimpse of her, he'd known that he had to make room for her in his basement.

Which had meant it was time for Dawn Morningstar to die.

And die she had, while he'd savored every moment of her final agony. Now, though, it was time to put the delicious images of Dawn's last moments back into the recesses of his mind, and turn his attention to Otto Owen.

Should he, perhaps, kill and mount Otto as he'd mounted Dawn? But no—he simply wouldn't have the luxury of time. Not that it mattered, for to Carl, Otto himself didn't matter.

He wasn't like the girls. In fact, if Otto hadn't come here tonight, he wouldn't have bothered with him at all. But now that Otto knew his little secret, Otto would have to die.

A simple matter of logistics, really. Otto must die

quickly, and in a way that wouldn't send anyone else to his house.

Even as Carl Henderson posed the problem to himself, the answer came to him.

Moving to one of the terraria on the rack against the wall, he paused for a few seconds to admire its contents.

Centruroides limpidus. Scorpions.

Dozens of them.

Small, pale in color, nearly indistinguishable from the local variety.

But more dangerous. Far more dangerous.

Carefully, using a long pair of tweezers, he began transferring the arachnids from the terrarium into a box he had constructed especially for the purpose of moving his prized specimens from their glass homes to the darkroom.

When the box was full of the aggressive creatures, Carl closed its top, then took it to the chute that led through the wall into the darkroom. The box fit perfectly, and when he was certain it was properly secured, Carl pressed a button that opened one end and released the scorpions into the lightless concrete chamber.

Then he sat down to listen.

Otto Owen struggled to control the fear that had gripped him the moment the velvety darkness had closed around him. Suddenly he felt dizzy, as if he'd lost not only his ability to see the walls of the room, but even to distinguish up from down.

He stood swaying on his feet for a moment, trying to regain his bearings.

He was facing the door, which couldn't be more than three feet in front of him.

The body pinned to the wall was behind him, maybe six feet away.

He shuddered as he thought about it, then determinedly put it out of his mind.

The main thing right now was not to give in to the panic that seemed to be an almost palpable force in the darkness.

And certainly not to think about the corpse on the wall, nor the ants that were devouring it, nor the maggots that infested it.

Instead he must concentrate on escaping from the trap he'd been stupid enough to walk into.

Because if he didn't, Carl Henderson was surely going to kill him.

Otto moved finally, stepping gingerly forward in the darkness, his hands held out in front of him. As his fingertips touched the solid wood of the door, the fear that had only a moment ago threatened to overwhelm him abated slightly. Now, at least, he no longer had the terrible sensation of being adrift in the darkness.

His legs suddenly weakened beneath him, and he instinctively let himself sink to the floor, his back resting against the wall behind him.

His heart was thudding in his chest, and for an awful moment Otto wondered if perhaps Henderson wouldn't have to kill him at all, if perhaps he was simply going to die of a heart attack right now.

The moment passed, though, and slowly his heartbeat began to return to normal.

He was about to get back to his feet and continue exploring the blackness of his prison when he heard something.

On the opposite side of the wall, something was happening.

He listened, trying to figure out what it might be.

A moment later he heard a click, followed instantly by a sound almost like that of a mousetrap snapping shut.

He paused again, listening, but heard nothing else.

Then, just as he was about to stand up once more, he felt something.

Something crawling up his leg, under his pants.

Instinctively, Otto tried to brush it away.

And instantly felt the first burning sting as the scorpion's barbed tail lashed into his flesh.

Otto tried to scramble to his feet, but as he put his hand on the floor to push himself up, another of the creatures attacked him. As he felt the second stinger plunge into the flesh between his thumb and forefinger, he jerked his hand away from the floor and reflexively put his palm to his mouth to suck the poison from the wound.

The scorpion, still clinging to his fingers, leaped to his face and whipped its tail again.

Otto screamed then, and tried to roll away from the attack, but now the floor seemed to be covered with the deadly creatures, and he felt first one, then another penetrate his shirt.

He was thrashing helplessly now, the poison surging through his system. Everywhere he moved, another scorpion waited.

"No!" he screamed as he felt one of them scuttle onto his face. "Help me!" His voice rose into a keening plea: "For the love of God—"

But even as he uttered the words, more of the stingers sank into him, lashing into his face and chest, and finally, whimpering, he sank back against the wall.

A new and even darker kind of blackness began to close around Otto.

A blackness from which he knew he would never emerge.

He whimpered, tried to lift his hand against his unseen tormentors once again, but then the darkness overwhelmed him and his hand fell back to the floor.

Mercifully, Otto Owen felt no more of the scorpions' stings.

CHAPTER 10

*J*ulie had never experienced anything like it.

Growing up in the San Fernando Valley, the nights had never been like this.

Always, there had been lights.

In the neighborhood where the Spellmans had lived since her father died, brilliant halogen bulbs had glared down from high overhead, casting an almost shadowless light over the streets and sidewalks, washing away the night in an attempt to tear the protective shield of darkness from the drug dealers and gang members whose rule had spread over wider areas every week.

Even before that, when they'd lived up in the hills above Studio City, where the warm glow of the glass-enclosed bulbs sitting atop their concrete posts had only created small pools of illumination in the nighttime streets, nothing had ever been truly dark.

Not like it was out here.

Everything, always, had been dimly lit by the indirect glow of the hundreds of square miles of lights that carpeted the entire Los Angeles area.

But tonight, avoiding the power lines and the road, she and Kevin had headed across country, making their way through the perfectly cultivated fields that spread over the valley floor.

Soon even the glow of the little town was behind them, and though Julie could still see an occasional light twinkling in the distance, the blackness around her was almost complete.

Overhead, filling the sky, were more stars than she had ever seen before—millions and millions of them, glimmering in the blackness, the great swath of the Milky Way slashing across the cosmos like a cascade of diamonds on black velvet.

But even more than the stars, it was the sounds of the night that touched something deep inside Julie, resonating within her in a way she'd never felt before.

Back in Los Angeles there had been a steady drone of traffic noise, always there, always in the background. Most of the time she'd simply tuned it out, becoming conscious of it only when its rhythms changed: the sudden squeal of brakes; a scream of tires spinning on the pavement.

In the summer, sometimes, she was vaguely aware of crickets chirping in the night.

But nothing like the symphony of sound that enveloped her tonight as she walked through the fields.

The thrumming of crickets formed a steady rhythmic background, but over that she could hear other sounds—sounds she couldn't even begin to identify.

"Listen," she whispered to Kevin. Her pace had been steadily slowing as they moved through the darkness; now she came to a complete stop and her hand tightened on Kevin's.

"What?" Kevin asked, turning to look at her in the darkness, but seeing only a dark shadow against the backdrop of the night.

"Don't you hear it?" Julie went on, her voice so low Kevin could barely hear her. "It sounds like music, doesn't it?"

Kevin frowned in the darkness. Music? All he could hear were the sounds of millions of insects all around them, chirping and buzzing as they worked their legs or wing covers together to attract mates out of the darkness.

"What are you talking about?" he finally asked, lifting the can in his free hand to his lips and draining off the last few drops of beer. "It's just a bunch of crickets and stuff."

Julie shook her head. "But it's not," she told him. "It's like music! I've never heard anything like it before."

Kevin rolled his eyes. "Except last night, and the night before, and the night before that! This time of year it's so loud you can hardly sleep."

"I like it," Julie said. "Let's just listen for a while, okay?"

Kevin glanced around, feeling vaguely uneasy. Why did Julie want to listen to a bunch of insects chirping? "Let's just go on home, okay?" he said.

Julie turned to look at him, but her face was still lost in dark shadows. "You're not scared, are you?" she asked.

Her voice suddenly sounded different to Kevin; there was a quality to it that sent a chill through him.

Not a chill of fear.

Another kind of chill, an exciting one.

He swallowed nervously. "I—I just think we should at least get back to the farm," he said. "I mean, I'm not even sure whose property we're on. What if they catch us?"

"What if they do?" Julie countered. "Who cares?" Her voice dropped again. "I mean, it's not like we're doing anything we shouldn't be, are we?"

A nervous flutter churned in Kevin's belly. Was it just his imagination, or was she thinking the same thing he suddenly was? "W-We could go down by the creek," Kevin stammered, not quite answering her questions. "It's really neat down there at night."

Almost to his own relief, Julie didn't answer him, but when he started across the field, she moved along with him, her hand in his.

Half an hour later, coming to the edge of a field that Kevin knew belonged to Vic Costas, they found a dirt road that wound along the edge of the valley, following the contours of the foothills. Perhaps a quarter of a mile away, he could see the lights of their house, beckoning in the darkness.

Fifty yards down the road an old wooden bridge spanned the creek, marking the boundary between the Owen farm and the one next door. When they came to the bridge, Kevin led Julie off the road and down the low bank to the edge of the water. "There's a neat place just downstream," he told her. "Come on." Edging along the rocky bank, he worked his way toward a small copse of oaks that flanked the creek. There was a sandy area there, a miniature beach, where he and Jeff Larkin had often gone swimming.

And just as often fantasized about bringing girls, who, in their imaginations, would be more than willing to join them in skinny-dipping, and afterward . . .

Kevin shuddered with excitement as the fantasy played out in his mind.

Then he groaned silently—here he was with Julie, almost to the beach that was the site of his very best fantasies, and he hadn't even brought a blanket!

But maybe it wouldn't matter—maybe, if Julie wanted to go swimming, they could just sort of stretch out in the sand afterward . . .

Kevin's imagination shifted into high gear, and he felt once more that thrill of excitement in his groin. Maybe, just maybe, tonight was the night he was finally going to—

And then the fantasy exploded in his mind, blasted to smithereens by the sound of a voice.

His father's voice.

"Better get back to the house," he heard his father say as a flashlight came on. "I think Molly's just about to fall asleep."

Kevin froze. Molly? His dad and Karen? What were they doing down here? Why weren't they in the house, where they belonged? He took a step backward, about to turn around and lead Julie back the way they'd come, when he suddenly felt his foot slip. Losing his balance, he reached out and grabbed Julie to steady himself, and heard a clatter as the loose rocks shifted beneath his feet.

"Shit!" The word exploded unbidden from his throat. A second later, out of the blackness, a dark form hurled itself at him. His balance completely destroyed by Bailey's joyful assault, he collapsed to the ground as the big dog licked at his face. "Will you get *off*!" Kevin cried, struggling under the dog as a beam of light pierced the darkness, momentarily blinding him.

"Kevin?" he heard his father say. "Julie? What are you two . . ." The words died on Russell's lips as he realized that he knew exactly what they were doing. Or at least what Kevin had been planning to do. "Perhaps," he said, doing his best not to laugh out loud at the expression of acute embarrassment on his son's face, "we all ought to go back to the house."

"You want to see my bug?" Molly asked her sister as the family came in through the kitchen door. "Where's a jar, Mommy?"

Karen retrieved an empty mason jar from one of the shelves in the pantry and handed it to Molly, who dropped a large june bug into it and screwed its lid tight. The beetle, which Molly had been clutching in her fist for almost half an hour, despite Russell's insistence that they could catch another one just by turning on the porch light, lay on its back for a moment, struggled, then managed to right itself, apparently none the worse for wear.

"Isn't it neat?" Molly demanded, handing the jar to Julie for her inspection.

Julie looked at the insect, which was now circling the container, searching for a way out. "Why don't you let it go?" she asked Molly. "It'll just die in the jar."

"No!" Molly insisted. "It's mine, and it won't die if I feed it!"

"You won't do anything till you put your pajamas on," Karen interrupted, shooing her youngest daughter out of the kitchen. Then, as Molly headed through the dining room toward the stairs, Karen finally got a good look at Julie under the bright light of the kitchen's fluorescent tubes.

Her daughter looked pale, and there was an unhealthy sheen of sweat on her forehead, as if she were running a fever. Frowning, Karen laid her wrist on Julie's forehead.

To her surprise, Julie's temperature seemed normal.

"You're sure you feel all right?" she asked. "You don't look very good. Maybe you're finally having a reaction to the shot Dr. Filmore gave you." Her eyes shifted to Russell. "Do you think we ought to call her?"

"It's the middle of the night, Mom," Julie protested. "And I'm not sick."

"Maybe she just picked up some kind of bug," Russell suggested. "Let's not bother Ellen if we don't have to. If she's not all over it by morning, we'll take her to the clinic then."

Julie's eyes rolled. "There's not anything to *get* over," she groaned. "I'm going to bed! Good night."

She started out of the kitchen, but Russell's voice stopped her. "Not quite yet!"

Julie turned back to look nervously at her stepfather.

Russell's glance flicked from Julie to Kevin, who was standing near the back door, studiously avoiding his father's gaze. "Have you two made up a story you think we'll swallow, or do you just want to tell us the truth and get it over with?"

Julie's demeanor turned stormy. "You're not my father—" she began, but now her mother stopped her.

"This is one family now, Julie. Russell's your stepfather, and you'll treat him with proper respect." Julie started to protest again, but this time her mother's words stopped her completely. "Before you say anything else," Karen said with deceptive gentleness, "I think you should know the beer is still on your breath."

Julie's eyes widened. "We only had one apiece," she said.

"Which is one too many," Karen told her. "You two said you were going to a movie," she said, her glance going to the clock. "Obviously, you didn't, since you haven't even been gone two hours."

Julie and Kevin glanced at each other, and then Kevin spoke: "The movie wasn't any good, so we left. And I guess when Andy said he had some beer, we should have just walked home right then." He shrugged helplessly. "But we didn't. We went up to the power lines, and when Andy started passing out the beer, we each took one. Then we split."

Russell eyed one teenager, then the other. "Why did you leave?"

This time it was Julie who answered. "I just didn't like it up there," she said, shrugging. "So we decided to walk home."

"And that's it?" Russell asked.

Kevin and Julie's eyes met for a second, and they both nodded.

"All right," Russell said. "Karen and I will discuss it, and let you know in the morning what we've decided. But I suspect you can both count on being grounded for at least a week."

"A *week*—" Julie began, but Russell held up a cautioning hand.

"I suppose if you want to argue about it, we could make it two weeks," he offered.

Julie was still glaring at him, shocked into silence by his words, when Molly's june bug began to hum.

As she listened to the humming from the bottle, something inside Julie responded to it. Her anger toward Russell was completely forgotten. "I'm sorry," she said. "Is it all right if I go to bed now?"

Karen, too surprised by Julie's sudden acquiescence to say anything, nodded mutely.

"I'll take this up to Molly," she said, picking up the jar with the june bug in it. Saying good night to Kevin and Russell, she headed upstairs, pausing at Molly's door as she started down the hall toward her room. "How about if I take care of this for you tonight?" she asked.

Molly's eyes narrowed suspiciously. "How come?" she asked. "Are you going to let him go?"

Julie shook her head, her eyes fixed on the buzzing creature. "I just want to look at him for a while, okay? And tomorrow I'll help you figure out what to feed him. How's that?"

Molly hesitated, then nodded in agreement, and Julie continued down the hall to her room, still listening to the humming of the insect trapped in the bottle.

Julie's eyes were open and unblinking in the gloom of her room. Moonlight streamed in through the window, refracting on the iridescent shell of the insect captured in the jar at her bedside.

Though her neck was twisted into what should have been a painfully unnatural position, she was unaware of any discomfort, for her entire concentration was fixed on the constantly moving creature trapped within the confines of the glass.

As she fixed on the june bug, mesmerized, she gradually became aware again of the noises of other creatures as they moved invisibly through the summer night.

Crickets, chirping softly.

Cicadas, emitting their whirring drone.

The high-pitched whine of mosquitoes as they zeroed in on their prey.

In her mind, Julie didn't distinguish one sound from another, at least not in any typical way.

No images flashed into her head, attaching a specific creature to a certain sound.

Instead the music of the insects blended into a strange, hypnotic symphony, and as its rhythms penetrated deeper and deeper into the consciousness inside her, she finally rose from her bed and left her room.

Moving with the steady pace of a somnambulist, and clad only in her thin nightgown, Julie silently descended the stairs, padded on bare feet through the dining room and the kitchen and out onto the back porch.

The sounds of the night were clearer here, the song of the insects more insistent than ever.

Leaving the porch, Julie started across the yard. The cool breeze drifting down from the hills to the west caressed her nearly naked skin as she walked slowly across the yard and out into the pasture behind the barn.

She kept walking, letting the sound of the insects guide her.

She moved to the center of the pasture and lay down beneath the pale glow of the star-filled sky, spreading her limbs sensuously, like a pagan priestess presenting herself to the gods.

The nocturne swirled around her, and she stretched her body languorously, nestling deep into the grass of the pasture.

And deep within the earth beneath her, sensing her presence, a colony of ants stirred, then began making their way to the surface.

In the grass, the crickets paused momentarily in their song, then began to chirp again.

A cloud of gnats, disturbed when Julie lay down in the grass, swirled in the air above her, then began settling once more. Now, though, instead of settling back into the vegetation from which they had risen, they drifted down to alight on Julie's exposed skin.

From the ground the ants appeared, creeping up her arms and legs, their legs clinging to her flesh, their antennae exploring her skin.

Insects seemed to come from everywhere, flying through the darkness, creeping through the grass, scurrying up from their subterranean nests.

Julie felt a horrible crawling wave of terror come over her as she felt the insects begin to cover her skin.

She wanted to leap to her feet and run screaming through the night.

Wanted to dig her fingernails deep into her own flesh as millions of tiny legs made every square inch of her skin tingle with a burning itch unlike any she'd felt before.

But she could do nothing, for once more that terrifying force within her held her in its thrall, strangling her cries in her throat, turning her muscles against her, holding her paralyzed beneath the teeming horde that swarmed around her.

She finally gave up, exhausted by her efforts to make her body respond to her own will, and soon she was covered with an undulating mass of life, protected from the chill of the night by a constantly moving blanket of living creatures.

Their thrumming drone filled her ears, steady, insistent, swelling until the unending whir overtook all thought and at last she lay still beneath the shroud of insects.

She stared up into the night sky, barely even aware of the rising moon that shone down upon her or the stars that twinkled above her like a billion tiny fireflies.

Numbed finally, her mind overwhelmed by the sheer mass of the swarms of insects that crawled over every millimeter of her skin, Julie at last drifted into sleep.

Dark, deep, dreamless sleep.

* * *

Three hours later the eastern sky began to brighten, and in the field, Julie stirred. As consciousness began to return to her, and the fog of sleep lifted slowly from her mind, she became aware of a strange sensation on her skin.

The kind of sensation she might have felt if millions of ants had been crawling over her.

She came fully awake then, and as her mind cleared, she realized that she was no longer in her bed, nor even in the house.

Her eyes snapped open in the graying light of dawn.

She was staring up into a cloudless sky.

All around her, tall grass was growing.

And something—something vile—was on her.

She could feel it distinctly now.

Her skin was crawling. For a moment she didn't dare to look at herself. But finally, slowly, she raised one of her arms.

Ants!

Red ants!

She remembered stumbling across a nest of them last year, in the park five blocks from the apartment in North Hollywood.

They'd swarmed up out of the ground, overrunning her sandal to creep up her leg, and within seconds it seemed her whole calf was on fire.

Now they were covering her whole body!

A horrible confusion overwhelmed her.

What was she doing outside, wearing just her night-gown?

She had no memory of coming outside at all!

The last thing she recalled was going into her room, to bed, and taking Molly's june bug, trapped in its mason jar, with her.

Yes, she'd gone to bed, and then stared at the large bee-tle, listening to its muffled whir as it tried to escape.

But how had she gotten here?

Had she walked in her sleep?

She began brushing the ants from her body as a terrified whimper emerged from her throat. Her heart pounded as she anticipated the terrible burn of the ants' bites.

A dark thought rose in her mind: What if they *all* bit her?

There were millions of them! If they all sank their mandibles into her at once, each of them sending poison into her system . . .

She shuddered and tried to banish the thought, but it kept growing in her mind.

A tidal wave of panic built up within her, towering over her, threatening to crush her will.

The creek!

If she could get to the creek—get into the water—she could wash them away.

Wash them off her skin, out of her hair, off her face.

She could feel them in her ears now, and in her nose.

A scream rose in her throat, but she stifled it, terrified of opening her mouth for fear that the teeming creatures would invade that space, too.

She began running then, racing across the field, her nightgown swirling about her legs, her hair streaming behind her.

In less than a minute she came to the creek. Stripping off her nightgown, she waded into the water, moving quickly out to the center, where pools almost three feet deep lay between the boulders that lined the banks.

Ignoring the chill of the water—barely even conscious of it—Julie dropped to the bottom of the creek, totally submerging herself, her fingers working furiously as she tried to dislodge the insects from her skin and claw them from her hair.

Finally, when she could hold her breath no longer, she broke the surface, opening her mouth wide to fill her lungs with the fresh morning air.

She stayed in the water until the chill of it began to penetrate to her very bones. When she finally waded ashore, naked and dripping, she was almost afraid to look at her skin.

In her mind's eye she could still see the angry red welts that had covered her calves after the attack last summer.

As the sun began to creep above the mountains to the east, and the icy chill of the water wore off, she waited for the burning sensation to begin.

It didn't come, and at last, realizing she felt no pain at all, she looked down at her legs and torso.

She frowned, then examined the skin of her hands and arms.

Nothing!

Nowhere could she find even the tiniest bump that would betray the presence of an insect bite.

Her hands trembling, she reached down and picked up her nightgown. She shook it violently, expecting to see hundreds of the vermin fall from its folds.

Again there was nothing.

The ants were gone—gone so completely that she wondered if they'd ever been there at all.

She slipped the nightgown over her head and pulled the soft material down over her still-damp skin.

Could she have imagined the whole thing?

But it wasn't possible, was it?

How could she have imagined her skin being entirely covered with red ants?

How could she have felt them?

And not just on her skin, either.

They'd been in her hair, her ears—even her nose!

Panic welled up inside her once again, and she shuddered at the memory.

Struggling to control the panic, she started back toward the house, breaking into a stumbling run.

What if someone saw her? What if Otto were already

up, fixing his morning coffee? If Kevin spotted her, running around in just her nightgown ...

How would she be able to explain it? What reason could she give for having gone out into the field in the middle of the night, almost naked?

There wasn't any reason, and now Julie ran faster, ducking around the corner of the house so that even if Otto was up, he wouldn't be able to see her.

At the back door she paused, listening, but heard nothing from inside the house. If everyone was still asleep, she could get back upstairs and—

Suddenly she became aware of a humming sound.

She turned, her eyes widening as she beheld a cloud of bees—thousands of them—moving toward the house.

Instantly, her mind went back to the previous morning, when she'd bumped into one of the hives and the bees had attacked her. Now here they were again, coming toward her.

And she was wearing nothing but a thin nylon nightgown!

As the first of the bees streaked across the yard, Julie jerked the back door open, slipped inside, and quickly shut it again. She paused just inside, listening again, but the house was still silent, and she padded through the empty rooms and up the stairs as quietly as she'd come down a few hours earlier.

She stepped into her room, and instantly knew something was wrong.

The light from the window.

It was an odd color—dim, and yellowish.

Her eyes went to the window, raised high to let in the cool night air, and her breath caught in her throat.

The screen was covered with bees; covered so thickly she couldn't see out at all. They were layers deep, climbing over one another, the humming of their wings filling the room. For a moment Julie stood frozen, just staring at them. Then she darted to the window, slammed it closed, and pulled the drapes as well, plunging the room into a darkness almost as deep as night.

Still she could hear them, their humming muffled through the cloth and glass, but clearly audible.

What was wrong? What was happening to her?

Trembling, Julie went to her bed and crept under the covers, pulling the quilt over her head despite the already building heat of the summer morning. She buried one ear in her pillow and clamped a hand over the other one, attempting to shut out the terrifying sound.

Outside, the bees found a tiny crevice in the siding on the house and set to work.

Soon they had expanded the crevice.

Then they began creeping in, filling the empty space in the wall that separated Julie's room from the one next door.

Karen was carrying a picnic basket.

It was filled with champagne, caviar, and little sandwiches, and she was walking in one of the pastures, feeling the sun on her back, listening to the birds singing and watching the butterflies flit among the blossoms. The afternoon was perfect, and soon Russell would come and join her.

They would walk down to the stream, open the champagne, and lie in one another's arms, sipping the bubbling wine and feeding each other morsels of food. Then, as the afternoon turned into evening, Russell would begin opening the buttons on her blouse. . . .

Her reverie was interrupted by a new sound, a low tone that made the birds fall silent around her. As the sound filled her ears, Karen turned, half expecting to see Russell coming across the field toward her.

But it wasn't Russell.

Instead it was the giant threshing machine, moving toward her, its huge blades spinning, a green arc of fresh-cut hay pouring out of it, a mist of pale green seeming to hang over it.

She stared at the machine, abstractly wondering where it had come from.

It hadn't been in the field when she'd arrived; of that, she was almost certain.

Time seemed to stand still as she watched the mower come slowly closer, and it wasn't until it was only a few yards away from her that she saw the empty driver's seat.

But that was impossible—with no one at the controls, how could the mower operate?

Then, quite suddenly, she knew it was coming for her.

The mower was going to run her down!

She turned, fleeing through the field, but the faster she tried to run, the harder it became for her to move her feet.

The drone of the mower grew louder, and she looked back over her shoulder.

It was gaining on her!

In another few seconds it would be on her and she would be sucked into its blades!

She redoubled her efforts, struggling to make her legs work harder, to force them to respond to her commands, but then she tripped. She sprawled out in the field, and her mouth opened as she tried to scream.

Where was Russell? Why didn't he come and save her?

Her scream finally emerged, but it was a pitiable sound that she knew no one could hear.

The mower was almost upon her now, and already she could feel the first agonizing slash of the huge blades as they tore into her flesh.

Once again she screamed.

And this time, as she screamed, she woke up, sitting bolt upright in bed, still in the grip of the nightmare.

"Honey?" It was Russell's sleepy voice. "Honey, what is it? What's wrong?"

Karen sat still for a moment, her heart pounding, her skin covered with the cold sweat of terror. Very slowly the dream began to release her from its grip. She eased herself back against the pillows. "The mower," she began. And instantly fell silent.

The drone!

She could still hear the drone of the mower, even though she was awake!

The panic of the dream flooded over her once again, and she clutched at Russell. "What is it?" she begged. "Russell, what do I hear?"

Finally coming fully awake, Russell listened for a moment, then got out of bed and went to the window.

Outside, the sun was rising and bees were buzzing in the warmth of the morning.

Closing the window, he went back to bed. "It's just a few bees, honey," he told her, nuzzling her ear. "They're always all over the place this time of year. Go back to sleep." Snuggling up against her body, Russell sighed contentedly, drifting back into a peaceful sleep.

Karen, though, remained awake, Russell's unconcerned voice echoing in her mind: . . . *just a few bees . . . all over the place this time of year.*

But what about Molly and Julie?

What if they got stung again?

Stop it! she told herself. You're starting to sound like the kind of hysterical overprotective mother you've always hated! They didn't die—they aren't even sick! It was just a freak reaction, and it's over!

This morning, though, she would talk to Carl Henderson or Ellen Filmore about getting a supply of the antivenin for the farm. If she had the antitoxin, she decided, she could live with the bees.

At least for the rest of the summer.

At last, secure in Russell's arms, she, too, fell back into sleep, and when she woke again an hour later, the humming didn't seem nearly so frightening.

Indeed, even the memory of the dream the humming had induced had all but disappeared from Karen's mind.

But in the wall, the swarm of bees had grown.

CHAPTER 11

"*J*ulie, get up! We have to take care of the horses!"

Julie groaned, rolled over, and pulled the covers over her head, but when Molly refused to give up—jerking at the quilt until finally it came loose from Julie's grip—she opened her eyes just enough to glare at her sister. "Just leave me alone, will you?" she said. "I'll get up in a few minutes."

"But we have to—" Molly began, but Julie cut her off.

"I *said* I'll get up in a few minutes." She grabbed the quilt back from Molly and snuggled under it. "Just get out of here, okay?"

Molly eyed her sister, carefully calculating how far she could push before Julie took a swing at her. If Julie actually hit her, then she could tell her mother, and Julie would get in trouble. But then Julie might stay mad at her for two or three days, and if *that* happened . . .

Overwhelmed by the complexity of possible results if she jerked the quilt away again, Molly left her sister's room and headed downstairs to the kitchen. The rest of the family was already there, sitting at the table drinking coffee, and Molly began reporting her sister's laziness even before she sat down. To the nine-year-old's great disappointment, her mother was more worried about Julie than angry at her.

"Is she all right?" Karen asked. "Is she sick?"

"She's just lazy," Molly told her. "And she's supposed to help me with the horses, too! She's supposed to—"

"I know what she's supposed to do," Karen told her, unwilling to let herself get involved in either a condemnation or a defense of her older daughter.

"But she—" Molly began again, only to be cut off once more by her mother.

"Enough!" Karen said, holding up a hand to silence her. "If she's not down in a few minutes, I'll go check on her."

"Why don't you come with us?" Kevin asked Molly as he and his father stood up and started toward the back door. "Dad and Grandpa and I always have a meeting in the tack room to decide what needs to be done."

"Can I?" Molly asked, her sister's laziness instantly forgotten at the prospect of going with Kevin. "Can I, really?"

Kevin winked at his stepmother. "I don't see why not. Of course, you might wind up having to help plow the east forty."

"Really?" Molly piped, skipping after Kevin as her mother mouthed him a silent thank you for having redirected the little girl's energy. "Could I drive the tractor?" Molly's questions continued pouring from her lips as they started toward the barn, but before Kevin could even begin to answer them, she ran ahead, eager to make sure her colt was still in its stall and had made it safely through the night.

By the time Russell and Kevin got to the barn, Molly was already in the stall, opening the outside door to turn Flicka and Greta out into the paddock. Kevin stopped to give the little girl a hand with the two horses, while Russell went on to the tack room where his father would be putting a pot of coffee on the hot plate and already planning the day.

Except that this morning the tack room was empty. The coils of the hot plate were cold, and the dregs of yesterday's coffee, an unappetizing brown sludge, coated the bottom of the unwashed pot.

Frowning, Russell went to the small window that faced out into the yard and glanced up toward his father's house.

Otto's truck was parked in its usual spot.

But where was his father?

If he'd still been in his kitchen, he'd have called out to them as he and Kevin passed his house on their way to the barn.

Could he still be in bed?

His father never slept in—Russell couldn't remember the last time Otto hadn't been up with the sun.

Unless he was sick . . .

But his father was never sick, either.

A knot of apprehension began to form in Russell's stomach. His father was almost eighty, after all.

Russell put the thought out of his mind. His father was perfectly healthy—Ellen Filmore had given him a physical less than a year ago, and found him as strong as a man of forty.

Damn it, where was he?

Unable to rid himself of apprehension, Russell left the tack room and started back toward the barn's main doors. Less than a minute later he let himself into his father's house through the kitchen door, which was never locked. "Dad?" he called. "Hey, Dad, do you know what time it is?"

There was no answer. As he listened to the silence, Russell's sense of apprehension grew stronger.

Steeling himself against what he might find, he strode through the kitchen and small living room, then into his father's bedroom.

The bed was empty, fully made up.

The fear of finding his father dead in his bed instantly dissipating, Russell started back to the barn. Not in his house. Not in the barn. Where in hell was he?

Then, as he scanned the horizon, he had an idea.

The hives!

Of course—after what had happened yesterday morning, and with his deep suspicion of Carl Henderson, Otto had probably headed over to the beehives, just to make sure everything was all right. His sense of relief increasing, Russell stopped at the paddock to tell Kevin and Molly where he was going, then headed out toward the hives. At least Carl Henderson's car was nowhere to be seen, so today wouldn't start off the same way that yesterday had.

As his father started down the long drive, Kevin went back into the stall to begin mucking it out, while Molly set about filling the water trough in the paddock. She had just turned the valve to start the water running when she heard a bark from somewhere behind her. Turning, she saw Bailey over by one of the toolsheds. He was crouched down, his tail laid out on the ground, and as Molly watched, he barked again, scooted forward a foot or so, then quickly backed up until he was back where he'd started.

"Bailey!" Molly called out. "Come on, boy! Here, Bailey!"

The dog looked over at her, but instead of jumping up and bounding toward her the way he usually did, he only barked again, then darted toward the area behind the toolshed.

Curious, Molly forgot about the water trough and climbed between the two lowest rails of the paddock. Her eyes on the dog, she started toward him. "What is it, Bailey? Did you find something, boy?"

The big dog wagged his tail eagerly as Molly came closer, and began whimpering as if trying to tell her something. By the time she was close enough to squat down and pet him, his whole body was quivering with excitement. With one more bark, he leaped away from Molly, disappearing around the corner of the toolshed.

Molly rose to her feet and started after the dog just as Kevin called out to her from the paddock.

"Hey, Molly! You left the water running!"

Molly paused, torn. Should she go back to the paddock and turn off the water, or see what it was that Bailey had found behind the toolshed?

It only took a fraction of a second for her curiosity to win out, and she called out to Kevin as she moved around the corner of the shed. "Just a sec—" she began.

Her words abruptly died on her lips as she stared at what had gotten Bailey so excited.

For what seemed a very long time to her, Molly simply stood staring at the body stretched out on the ground, facedown.

She knew who it was.

She could tell by the almost white hair, and the clothes.

She wanted to turn around and run away, but couldn't. In fact, she wasn't sure she could move at all. "K-Kevin . . ." she began, his name barely audible even to herself. Then, as Bailey sniffed at Otto Owen's body, pawing gently at it as if trying to wake the old man up, Molly finally found her voice. The second time she called her stepbrother's name, it was audible all the way up to the house.

When Kevin got there, Molly still hadn't moved. He dropped down next to his grandfather's body. "G-Grandpa?" he said. Gingerly, he reached out and touched his grandfather's neck.

Reflexively, his fingers jerked back from the cold flesh.

"Oh, Jesus," he whispered. Standing up, he swiped at the tears flooding his eyes, and reached for Molly's hand. "Come on," he said. "We'd better get help."

Half dragging, half carrying the little girl, Kevin ran up the slope toward the house.

Mark Shannon was slouched behind the wheel of his green Taurus squad car when the call came in. As usual for seven A.M., he was parked at the A&W, and also as usual, he was making his ritual attempt to convince Charlene Hopkins to marry him.

Charlene, of course, was refusing, which was just as well, considering that Mark hadn't the slightest idea what he'd do if Charlene ever accepted his proposal—an unlikely prospect at best, since she was already married to the A&W's owner, who usually came out and offered to stand them to a honeymoon if Charlene would just accept Mark's offer.

When the radio suddenly came alive and the sheriff's dispatcher interrupted their conversation, Charlene's habitual happy smile faded. "Did she say Russell Owen's farm?" she asked, hoping she might have heard wrong through the static.

"That's what she said." Mark sighed, reaching down to start the squad car. "And it sounds like it's a lot more serious than yesterday."

Charlene shook her bleached blond head sympathetically. "I hope it's not one of those girls. Seems like nothing's gone right for Karen since the day she came back here."

Having long ago learned to make no comment on anything that came over the radio, Mark put the Taurus in gear. "Talk to you later."

He pulled out of the A&W, switched on the lights and siren, and headed out of town. No more than a couple of minutes later he switched off the sound and light show as he turned into the Owens' driveway and spotted the small cluster of people behind the shed just south of the barn. Russell and Kevin were both crouched down next to someone who lay on the ground, while Karen stood close by. Molly was clinging to her mother's waist, and Karen had one arm around Julie, holding her close.

Pulling the car to a stop a few yards from the toolshed,

Mark jumped out and hurried over to Russell and Kevin, dropping down beside them.

One look at Otto's face was all he needed to know the old man was dead: Otto's clouded eyes were wide open, staring unseeingly upward, and his mouth was agape. Still, Shannon pressed his fingers to the old man's wattled neck, searching for a pulse. "What happened?" he asked, glancing up at Russell.

Russell, his eyes still fixed on his father's distorted face, shook his head slowly. "I don't have any idea," he said, his voice dull. "He wasn't around this morning, and I went looking for him. I finally figured he must have gone up to the beehives, but . . ." His voice trailed off and he shook his head again. "Molly found him," he finished. "Or I guess Bailey did, really."

"Bailey?" Mark Shannon repeated.

"My dog," Kevin told him. His own voice as numb as his father's, Kevin finished the story of how Molly had found the body. "What happened to him?" he asked. "Why did he die?"

Shannon shrugged. "Hard to say. Could have been a heart attack, or a—"

He was about to say "stroke," but as his eyes fell to Otto Owen's right hand, he cut the word off.

The palm of Otto's hand between the thumb and forefinger was clearly marked by what looked to Shannon like a tiny puncture wound. Frowning, the deputy began examining the body more closely.

There were two of the minute puncture wounds on Otto's face, and still more on his left hand and arm. He rose to his feet, strode to his car and spoke brusquely over the radio, then returned to where Russell Owen was waiting by his father's body.

"I've got Manny Gomez coming out to lend me a hand with this, Russell," he said. "And we're going to have to get Ellen Filmore involved. With cases like this, an autopsy is pretty standard procedure."

Russell Owen nodded. "But you must have some idea of what killed Dad," he said.

Mark Shannon's eyes flicked uneasily toward Karen and her daughters, and he decided to say nothing of what he suspected until he was absolutely sure.

He would not be sure until Ellen Filmore examined the body.

Ten minutes later Manny Gomez arrived in his pickup truck, and together the two deputies began putting Otto Owen's corpse into a body bag.

Karen, able to watch the oddly impersonal process for only a moment, quickly turned away and guided her daughters back up to the house.

Russell and Kevin both stayed with the deputies until the patriarch of their family had been put into the back of Gomez's truck, then walked back to the squad car with Mark Shannon. "You've got some idea of what happened, don't you?" Russell asked again.

Shannon hesitated, but now that Karen and her daughters were no longer within earshot, he decided there was no point in holding his suspicions back from Russell. "I'm not positive, but it looks like something stung Otto," he said.

Russell's jaw tightened. "You mean bees?"

"I don't mean anything," Shannon replied, more gruffly than he'd intended. "I can't tell you what I don't know." He reached out and grasped Russell's shoulder. "I'm real sorry about this, Russell. Soon as I find out anything, I'll call you. In the meantime, you just sit tight, and don't get yourself worked up until we know exactly what happened. Could be I'm completely wrong and those marks aren't even stings. Maybe he was already dead, and some kind of bug just bit on him. Might not mean a thing."

"But if it *was* bees," Russell pressed, "then I'm getting

Carl Henderson out here right away. Dad thought something was wrong with the hives . . . that there was something wrong with the bees—"

"Goddamn it, Russell," Mark Shannon cut in. "If I'd thought you were going to grab onto something like that, I would have kept my mouth shut. Just take it easy until we know what happened, okay? And if it was bees that killed Otto, you can bet I'll order every hive UniGrow has in this valley taken out before the day's over. But let's not go off half-cocked. Say the wrong thing to the wrong people, and we could have a panic around here. Just after what happened to your wife's girls, we already got people talking about African killer bees. So let's just wait and see, okay?"

Russell hesitated, as if about to say more, then changed his mind and nodded agreement. "Call me as soon as you know anything." As Shannon climbed into the squad car, he spoke again. "Mark?" The deputy looked up. "After the autopsy, do I have to, well—" He faltered and fell silent, but Shannon understood exactly what he was asking.

"Just tell me what you want done," Shannon said. "No reason why I can't take care of it."

"He wanted to be buried on the property," Russell said, and for the first time his voice began to tremble, as if the full impact of what had happened had only now finally struck him. "There won't be any funeral or anything—you know how Dad felt about that kind of thing. I guess I'll need some kind of casket, though."

"He wanted a pine box," Kevin said as his father once more faltered. His eyes glistening with tears, he repeated to the deputy what he'd heard his grandfather say so many times. "The cheapest one we can find is what he always said. No funeral, and no service. We're just supposed to bury him next to Grandma, and plant a tree. He—He said the rest was just for show, and he didn't want anything to do with it."

As Kevin tried to control the sob that threatened to choke him, Mark Shannon nodded. "I'll take care of it. And it shouldn't take too long. If you want, we can probably bury him tomorrow morning."

"We'll do it," Russell said. "Just let us know when we can come and pick him up, and Kevin and I will bury him."

As the squad car drove away, Russell and Kevin started slowly walking back up the hill toward the house, but as they came to the house in which Otto had lived all his life, and in which Russell himself had grown up, they paused, and Russell reached out to lay his arm across his son's shoulders. "It's okay," he said softly. "No matter what happened to him, it's better to go fast than to just start getting older and weaker and sicker. That's what he never wanted, and at least it didn't happen to him." He pulled Kevin closer—self-consciously, almost roughly. "You and I should be so lucky, huh, Kev?"

Kevin hesitated, then managed to nod.

But still, he wondered: What could be so lucky about being dead? And from the look on his grandfather's face, Kevin was pretty sure dying must have hurt a lot.

In fact, it had looked to Kevin as if his grandfather had been screaming when he died.

Why had no one heard him?

"Well, what do you think?" Ellen Filmore asked an hour later, after she'd given Otto Owen's corpse a thorough examination. She'd found several more of the puncture marks in Otto's skin: three of them on his left leg, one on his right, and three more on his chest.

Yet it hadn't been the stings that killed him, for despite the clear punctures in the skin, the wounds showed little of the characteristic swelling that would normally have accompanied the sort of marks she'd found on Otto's corpse.

What had killed him, she was fairly certain, was not the

stings themselves. Rather, the stings had induced a massive heart attack; an attack that killed Otto almost instantly.

Finding no more injuries, and already fairly certain she knew what had happened to the old man, she finally called in the local expert for confirmation of what she thought.

Now, looking up from Otto's body, the expert nodded his agreement.

"Scorpions," Carl Henderson said. "No question about it. And not surprising, considering where they found him. There're probably dozens of them under that shed. The question is, what was he doing out there?"

Ellen Filmore sighed deeply. "I don't see how we'll ever find that out," she said. "But what a horrible way to die." Her gaze shifted to Henderson's and she shook her head sympathetically. "At least the heart attack ended it quickly for him."

Carl Henderson nodded in silent agreement, seeing no need to say anything else.

His secret, for now, was safe.

CHAPTER 12

*K*aren paused in her unloading of the breakfast dishes from the washer and glanced at the clock over the kitchen sink.

Quarter past eleven, and there had been no sign of Julie since breakfast.

But why should that surprise her? After all, for the last two days, nothing on the farm had felt quite right, nothing had been normal.

Karen still shuddered every time she thought about Otto Owen's death.

Scorpions.

The very word sent shivers through her body now. Ever since she'd heard the results of the autopsy, she'd imagined them everywhere on the farm, lurking in the corners of the house, hiding under every rock on the property.

"But that's crazy," Russell had insisted when they talked about it yesterday. "They're here, of course—they're pretty much everywhere where the climate is fairly dry. But they're more afraid of you than you are of them, and they do their best to stay hidden."

"Well, they didn't stay hidden from Otto!" Karen had insisted. "My God, just to think of it gives me the willies! And if it could happen to Otto, it could happen to any of us! You know it could!"

"I suppose it could, if we go rooting around in places where they're likely to be, when they're likely to be

177

there," Russell told her. "But why would any of us be poking around under the sheds in the middle of the night?"

"Why was Otto?" Karen immediately challenged.

But of course there had been no answer, and since there were no witnesses to what had happened to Otto, there would never be an answer.

But when she thought of how close to dying both Molly and Julie had come before Otto finally did die, Karen's impulse had been to take her daughters, leave the farm, and never come back.

Indeed, it had been far more than an impulse—it was an almost irresistible urge. But as she thought about it, she realized that even if she could bring herself to abandon her new husband and her new life—both of which she loved—there was really no place to go.

Russell was right—there were scorpions everywhere she'd ever lived, but Otto was not only the first person she'd ever known to be killed by them, he was the first person she'd ever even *heard* of being killed by them.

Bees, of course, were even more ubiquitous than scorpions, and if the African strain had come as far north as Pleasant Valley, it either already was or soon would be everywhere else in California as well.

Besides, the hives had already been replaced—the first truck from UniGrow arrived the night after Otto died, taking away every hive on the property in the cool and darkness of night, when all the bees were inside. The new hives were delivered last night.

Yesterday Russell had sprayed insecticide under all the sheds on the property.

Yesterday, too, they buried Otto, obeying his wishes that there be no funeral and no service. The five of them had gone up to the small plot of land where Russell's grandparents, mother, and first wife were already buried, and together Russell and Kevin lowered Otto's pine coffin into the grave they'd dug the day before.

Though nothing was said aloud, Karen had silently prayed for Otto's soul.

Nothing else: no formal gathering of Otto's friends, no wake, not even a reception.

Exactly as Otto had wanted it.

And today they were all trying to pretend that things were back to normal, even though Karen was sure it would be weeks before Russell and Kevin were truly used to not having Otto around. For herself, Karen felt a certain relief that the old man was gone, which she was both ashamed of and determined to keep a secret. Yet it was true, for even the day after Otto had died, Karen found herself feeling more relaxed in the house, treating it as if it were finally her own. And she knew why: it was simply because Otto was no longer there, reminding her of the way Paula had done things, either out loud or merely with silent looks of disapproval.

But there was still a question Karen couldn't get out of her mind: Why had Otto been out at that shed in the middle of the night in the first place?

And why hadn't he yelled when the first of the scorpions struck him?

Was it possible that he had, but none of them heard him?

The questions seemed to chase each other endlessly through her mind, but this morning she was trying not to think about them, just as she was trying not to think about the possibility that Otto had lain in the darkness for hours, his body seared with pain from the scorpions' potent stings, crying out for help while the rest of them remained soundly sleeping in their beds.

The kids, too, seemed unusually subdued, and though the grounding that Russell had issued the night Otto died had not been lifted, neither had it had to be enforced. Kevin, Karen knew, was mourning the death of his grandfather in his own way, too uncertain of himself to talk aloud about his feelings, but suffering nonetheless.

Then there was Julie.

Julie seemed to be taking Otto's death harder than any of the rest of them, and though Karen had tried to talk to her about it several times, her elder daughter had obstinately insisted that nothing was wrong, that she was "just fine."

Karen, though, was pretty sure she knew better, for the last words Julie had spoken to Otto had been uttered during the parody of obsequiousness she'd put on at breakfast the morning of the day the old man died. Julie hadn't had a chance to speak more than a word or two to Otto after that, and hadn't been able to give him the apology she'd been intent on making when she'd gotten stung.

Guilt, Karen knew, could make people behave in strange ways, and Julie was certainly behaving strangely.

The first day after Otto's death hadn't been too bad. Julie had been late coming downstairs, and certainly hadn't spoken much, but Karen had expected that.

Yesterday, though, Julie had pretty much stopped speaking at all, and though she'd helped Molly with the horses, she flatly refused to vacuum the downstairs area of the house. "I hate that vacuum cleaner, and you can't make me use it!" she told Karen.

Facing her daughter's anger squarely, and preparing herself for a long argument, Karen had folded her arms over her chest. "Fine," she said. "Then use a broom. I really don't care."

To her surprise, Julie had done exactly that.

It took her three times as long to do the job with the broom instead of the vacuum cleaner, but Julie hadn't complained.

In fact, she hadn't spoken at all.

Nor had she spoken this morning, when she came down

for breakfast. She simply sat in silence at the kitchen table, consuming her breakfast.

And consuming, Karen reflected, was exactly the right word, too. Her eyes fixed unwaveringly on her food, Julie had eaten not only her normal piece of toast, bowl of cereal, and glass of orange juice, but a stack of pancakes and three pieces of bacon, as well.

Then, after helping Molly with the horses, Julie simply disappeared.

"Go see where your sister is, will you, honey?" Karen asked Molly, who was sitting at the table with a catalog of equestrian supplies, compiling a list of things she absolutely had to have "or I'll die," which would not only have filled the tack room to overflowing, but broken the bank account as well. But at least Molly was starting to behave normally, finally emerging from the shock the discovery of Otto's lifeless body had engendered.

Now, the little girl ran out of the kitchen, and a moment later Karen heard her pounding up the uncarpeted stairs, her footsteps thundering through the farthest reaches of the house. "Quietly!" Karen called after her, shaking her head. A minute later Molly crashed back down the stairs, both feet making a resounding thud as she took the last five steps in a single leap.

"She's on her bed!" Molly reported as she came back into the kitchen. "She's just lying on her bed, staring out the window."

Leaving the ham she was slicing for lunch, Karen told Molly to start setting the table, then went upstairs herself.

Julie's door was standing ajar, and sure enough, Julie was stretched out on the bed, her eyes fixed on the window.

Karen rapped gently at the door. "Julie?" she said. "Are you all right?"

For a moment there was no response at all, and then

Julie turned to look at her. "I'm fine," she said, but there was a flat tonelessness to her voice that belied her words.

"Then I think you should come downstairs and help your sister and me get lunch ready."

Julie shrugged, but made no move to get off the bed.

"Sweetheart, are you sure you feel all right?" Karen asked once more.

"I'm fine," Julie insisted for the second time. "I'll be down in a couple of minutes, okay?"

As her mother left the room, leaving the door standing open, Julie flopped back onto her pillow.

Once again she'd lied about how she felt.

She'd wanted to tell her mother about the unbearable sickness she was feeling, to tell her about what had happened early in the morning of the day they'd found Otto's body.

Ever since she heard what happened to him, she'd been thinking about how she herself had awakened in the field and thought she was covered with red ants.

At the time, she'd been sure it was just a horrible dream, that it hadn't really happened at all.

But what if the ants had really crawled all over her, just like the scorpions had crawled all over Otto?

Why hadn't the ants so much as bitten her, the way the scorpions had stung Otto to death?

For almost two days now she'd been thinking about it, but no matter how hard she tried to find an answer, there was none.

And even worse than not being able to find an answer was what had happened when she'd finally decided to tell her mother about it. It had been late yesterday afternoon, and she was in her room, lying on her bed, just as she was now. The door was open, and she could hear her mother down in the kitchen, starting supper.

They were alone in the house, and all Julie had to do

was get up and go downstairs. They could talk, just like they used to when she was a little girl.

She started to sit up and swing her legs off the bed.

Nothing happened. Nothing at all!

She tried to cry out, to scream to her mother that she was paralyzed.

Tried, and failed.

For a long time—she didn't know how long—she'd lain on her bed, and slowly, from somewhere deep within her, she began to understand.

No words were spoken, nor even formed in her head.

But as the minutes had ticked by and she was still unable to move, a concept had come into her mind.

Something—some force she couldn't begin to understand—was inside her now.

A force that had a will far stronger than her own.

The concept sank into her consciousness:

Ever since she'd almost died from the bee stings, there were things she could not talk about, and things she could not do.

She had become a slave to some new force within her that she didn't understand and was powerless to fight.

And once she accepted that, once she finally gave herself up to that force inside her, she'd been able to move again.

Move, and talk.

And pretend that everything was fine.

Pretend that she wasn't going crazy.

This morning, when she awoke, the memory of that awful night when she'd found herself in the pasture—the night Otto had died—was once again fresh in her mind.

For a moment—a horrible moment in which she'd felt cold fingers of terror squeezing her heart—she experienced again that awful crawling sensation of millions of tiny red ants creeping over her skin.

The moment passed, and with it the terrible panic that

boiled up inside her. She'd gotten up, pulled on her robe, and gone to the bathroom.

She took a shower, brushed her teeth, and combed her hair.

All perfectly normal.

But when she went back to her room to dress, she suddenly felt tired, and sat down on the bed for a minute.

And then, when the smells of the breakfast her mother was cooking had come wafting up the stairs and through her open door, she suddenly realized she was hungry.

Not just hungry—famished.

She'd gotten dressed and gone down to the kitchen, where the rest of the family were already at the table.

Not even bothering to greet Kevin or Molly, she dropped into her chair and started eating.

Eating as she'd never eaten before.

A bowl of oatmeal, with butter, sugar, and cream.

After that, bacon and pancakes.

Pancakes! She *hated* pancakes! All they did was make you fat, and you never even felt good after you ate them!

"You okay, Julie?" Kevin had asked as she piled the disgusting things onto a plate.

She'd nodded, finished the pancakes, and been about to reach for more when she felt everyone staring at her, watching her pig out!

She'd stopped eating then, even though she still didn't feel full.

But how could she still be hungry, after all she'd eaten?

After breakfast the peculiar exhaustion she'd felt before the meal came back to her, and it wasn't long before she was hungry again.

But this time, instead of giving in to the hunger, she retreated to her room, where she lay down on the bed.

What was happening to her? Was she going to turn into one of those girls she'd seen on television, who pigged out all the time, then puked it all up, until finally they starved to death?

Then, when her mother came in and asked if she was all right, she wanted to tell her about it.

But when she'd spoken, only those same awful words— the words she knew weren't true—came out.

I'm all right . . . I'm fine. . . .

But she wasn't all right! She wasn't fine!

She was terrified.

She was terrified, and she felt like she was losing control of herself, and most of the time the stinging itch within was so bad that she wanted to jump out of her own skin!

She wanted to roll over and bury her face in the pillow, wanted to sob with the fear and frustration of it.

But instead, driven by some strange force deep within her, she got up from the bed, went to her dresser, and picked up her hairbrush.

Staring at her image in the mirror, she brushed her hair until it shone.

And by the time she went downstairs to help her mother with lunch, she looked exactly as she had told her mother she felt. Indeed, as she went into the kitchen, her mother smiled her approval. "Well, you certainly look much better than you did a few minutes ago," she said. "Ready for lunch?"

Julie nodded.

She was afraid to actually speak, for she no longer knew what words might come out of her mouth.

"Karen?" the voice at the other end of the telephone line said. "It's Marge Larkin—Jeff's mother?"

Karen cradled the phone against her shoulder as she put the final touches on the potato salad she was serving with the sliced ham that was already on the table. "Hello! I keep meaning to call and have you and the kids come up for supper some night, but—well, ever since the wedding it's been hectic, and now with Otto's passing on . . ." Her voice trailed off.

Marge Larkin clucked sympathetically, though she'd never really liked Otto Owen. In fact, she'd thought he was a cantankerous son of a bitch, but it certainly wouldn't do to mention that right now. "Well, you can put off inviting us for another day as far as I'm concerned," she said. "I've got a tooth that's gone bad on me, and I've got to go over to San Luis Obispo to the dentist. Jeff promised to help Vic Costas out all afternoon, and I was wondering if maybe Julie might want to pick up some money baby-sitting Ben."

Karen was about to suggest that Marge Larkin bring her little boy—whom Karen had seen playing by himself several times in the dusty yard in front of Vic Costas's tenant house—over to the Owen farm where he could spend the afternoon playing with Molly, when she suddenly changed her mind. Much better for Julie to get out of the house for a little while, earn some money, and feel as though she were doing something on her own. "Hold on—I'll let you talk to Julie."

While Marge explained the situation to Julie, Karen put the salad on the table, then went to ring the old-fashioned triangle that hung just outside the back door. Kevin and Russell, though, were already crossing the yard, and as Kevin headed back to the laundry room behind the kitchen to wash up, Karen suggested to Russell that perhaps they ought to reconsider the grounding, given the circumstances.

Before Russell had a chance to reply, Julie appeared at the back door. "Mom?" she called. "Can I do it?"

Karen hesitated, then spoke: "As far as I'm concerned, you can, but you'll have to ask Russell, too."

For a moment Karen thought Julie might just turn away, giving up the job rather than ask her stepfather for permission. Indeed, as Julie's eyes shifted to Russell, Karen thought she saw a flash of resentment in them.

"It's a baby-sitting job," Julie finally said. "Can I take it, or am I still grounded?"

Karen held her breath, wondering if Russell had heard the note of challenge in Julie's voice, as if she were daring him to refuse. If he heard it, he gave no sign.

"No more beer?" he asked.

Julie's jaw tightened and her eyes narrowed slightly, but she shook her head.

"Then I guess it's okay," Russell decided. As Julie stepped back into the kitchen, he smiled thinly at Karen. "I guess I'd better be glad she asked me, and not demand she be thrilled about it, huh?"

Karen nodded. "We take what we can get." She sighed. "And I don't know about you, but I'm hoping maybe if she gets out of here for a while she'll start coming out of the mood she's been in ever since Otto died. It's . . . well, it's almost as if she blames herself."

Russell frowned. "But she didn't have anything to do with it!"

"I know that, and you know that, but I'm not sure Julie does. I think she's still kicking herself over what happened at breakfast that morning."

"Maybe I'd better have a talk with her."

Karen stretched up and kissed her husband on the cheek. "Thanks, but I don't think it'll work. If she won't talk to me about it, she *sure* won't talk to you. The best thing we can do is just try to get back to some kind of normal life."

"What's wrong with you?" Ben Larkin demanded, turning away from the television screen to stare scornfully at Julie. "I thought you said you could do this?"

"I *can*," Julie told him. "Anyway, I always could back at home!"

She dropped the video joystick into Ben's hands and got up from the sofa, moving restlessly to the window of the Larkins' little house.

What was wrong? Once again she was feeling that terrible itching deep inside her, making her want to leap out of her skin; a sensation of something building up inside her, on the very edge of exploding.

She shook herself, violently, as if the movement could rid her of the horrible nervousness that made her feel she was going crazy.

"It's your turn," Ben said. "I just bombed out."

"Will you just shut up?" Julie heard herself say. As Ben burst into tears, Julie's mouth dropped open in shock.

What had made her say that? None of this was Ben's fault! In fact, for a kid of Molly's age, he was pretty good. He just wanted to do the things most boys his age liked to do, and Julie had done her best to keep him entertained.

At first it had actually been fun.

They walked down to the creek, peeling off their shoes and socks to go wading in the cool water, and Ben had caught a jar full of tadpoles. Though the little creatures felt slimy in her hands, she'd enjoyed catching them, and for the next hour they'd both been engrossed in fixing up a place for the tadpoles to live while they grew up to be frogs.

Or got eaten by the birds that had already discovered the old wash pan they'd turned into a makeshift pond and put in a shady spot next to the back door. With a layer of sand and muck on the bottom of the pan, and six inches of water on top of that, Ben had been sure the tadpoles would be perfectly happy. Julie suggested they add some rocks and some of the reedy grass that grew in the creek, to give the tadpoles someplace to hide. So they'd trekked back to the creek, brought back the necessary pebbles and vegetation, and so far the tadpoles didn't seem to miss their normal habitat at all.

But an hour ago Ben had gotten bored with the tadpoles and decided they should play video games.

Ben, it turned out, was a whiz at Nintendo. Julie had always been a proficient player, but today she just couldn't seem to get the feel of it.

Maybe it was the heat.

It seemed to her the temperature had been rising all afternoon. Now, though she'd opened all the windows, the cramped living room felt like an oven. The plastic upholstery on the sagging sofa had clung to her skin, which was covered with a sticky film of sweat, and just looking at the television screen made her want to scream.

"I'm sorry," Julie told Ben, going back to the sofa, determined to try the game one more time. "It's just—I don't know. It's just so hot in here, and I feel so sticky. I guess I'm just crabby."

Mollified, Ben's wailing sob abated to a sniffle. He looked up at her curiously. "It's not hot," he said.

"It is too," Julie replied. "It feels like it must be a hundred degrees."

"It's not either," Ben protested. He pointed to the thermometer on the wall. "Look! It's only seventy-five degrees!"

"Well, it feels like a lot more," Julie said. "How about if we make some lemonade?" That, at least, might not only cool her off a little bit, but ease the gnawing hunger she'd been feeling all day.

"Okay," Ben replied, his hurt feelings completely forgotten.

Together they went out to the kitchen, and while Ben dug around under the counter for the juicer, Julie began slicing lemons in half. By the time she'd gotten half a dozen cut, Ben had found the juicer, and she began squeezing the juice out of them.

The citrus scent of the fresh fruit filled Julie's nostrils, and she felt a pang of hunger.

A pang so strong she couldn't ignore it.

Without thinking, she picked up half a lemon and bit into it.

Ben stared at her, his eyes wide. "What are you doing?" he asked. "You can't do that! Lemons are too sour to eat!"

Julie shook her head, already reaching for a second lemon. Though she knew the little boy was right, the lemon didn't taste the least bit sour to her.

Indeed, it tasted almost sweet.

Greedily, she sucked the pulp out of the second lemon half, then reached for a third.

And as the juice trickled down her throat, her hunger only increased.

She went to the refrigerator, opened it and surveyed the shelves.

There was a large bowl. Through its Saran Wrap covering, Julie could see what looked like a piece of leftover pot roast, the grayish meat sitting in a pool of congealed fat and gravy.

She pulled the bowl out of the refrigerator, set it on the counter and pulled off the plastic. Sinking her finger into the bowl, she scooped up a large brown glob of the ice-cold meat drippings and stuck it in her mouth.

Ben stared at her, his own stomach rebelling at the thought of putting that icky mess into his mouth. "Gross!" he groaned.

But Julie was already scooping up more of the slimy ooze, and tearing off pieces of the gristly meat, stuffing them into her mouth as fast as she could, barely chewing them before gulping them down.

"What are you doing?" Ben yelled as the roast began to disappear. "Mom said we weren't supposed to eat that! She said—"

Julie, though, was deaf to the little boy's words. Her entire being was focused on satisfying the hunger within her.

She tore off more bits of meat, and dipped her fingers deep into the jellied fat and gravy.

Ben, frightened now by her bizarre behavior, edged toward the back door. "I'm gonna find Jeff," he said, more to himself than to Julie. And as she continued devouring the roast, he slipped out the back door and ran toward the far field, where he could see Vic Costas's tractor.

"Look," Ben said to Jeff twenty minutes later. "Look what she's doing!" He was pointing through the window into the kitchen, his brother beside him.

Inside, Julie was still standing at the counter. What seemed to be the entire contents of the refrigerator were spread around her, and as Jeff watched, she broke a large chunk off a block of cheddar cheese, shoved it into her mouth, then pushed a wad of bread in after it.

As she chewed the mass in her mouth, her hands tore at the wrapper of some sliced bologna, finally tearing at the plastic with her teeth in her urgency to get past the packaging to the meat inside.

The bowl that had contained pot roast was empty, save for the last few gobs of gravy, which Julie scooped into her mouth as Jeff watched in awed fascination and disgust.

At that moment, she looked up and caught sight of him through the window. For a second Jeff had the eerie sense of having caught a wild animal devouring its prey.

And then she smiled at him.

Smiled at him in a way that excited him.

He remembered, then, how she'd gone off with Kevin the other night, and not come back.

Even though Kevin hadn't told him what happened, Jeff was pretty sure he knew.

After all, Julie was from L.A., and everyone knew what the girls down there were like.

And now she was smiling at him.

"Go over to Mr. Costas's house," he told Ben.

"Why?" the little boy demanded. "What are you going to do? I want to watch."

"Well, you're not going to," Jeff told him. "Just go over to Mr. Costas's and wait for me there."

Ben started to object, then saw the look in his brother's eye. The look that told him he'd better do as Jeff said. "It's not fair," he complained. "I was the one who—"

"Get!" Jeff ordered him, and finally Ben started up the road that led to Vic Costas's farmhouse, a few hundred yards away. Only when he was sure his brother was going to obey him did Jeff finally go into the kitchen.

"Julie?" he said. "What are you doing?"

Julie, her hunger still strong within her, looked at him but said nothing.

He moved closer and reached out. His fingers touched her skin.

She jerked away, but her eyes remained fixed on him, and now she was licking her lips.

Jeff knew what that meant.

He moved close to her again. "Come on, Julie," he said, slipping his arms around her. "I know what you want. And there's no one here but us." He began nuzzling her neck, his lips nibbling at her skin. She wriggled in his arms, but her movement only excited him more. "You want to go into the bedroom?"

Julie was struggling, trying to get away from him, but Jeff twisted her around, tripping her—whether accidentally or deliberately, she wasn't quite sure—and she fell to the floor. A second later he was on top of her, pinning her down, and she was looking up at him.

He lowered his head to kiss her, and Julie opened her mouth.

Opened her mouth and exhaled in a great, rasping breath.

And from Julie's mouth emerged a swirling black cloud, a dark and writhing mist that split instantly into dozens of serpentine tongues as it lashed from Julie's throat and curled around Jeff Larkin's head like tentacles, instantly paralyzing him with a horror greater than any he'd experienced before.

It wasn't just a mist—Jeff knew that even before it engulfed him.

Though the specks were so tiny he couldn't even make them out as individuals, Jeff knew they were alive, that they were flying together in a swarm the same way termites and ants sometimes rose from the ground by the tens of thousands, borne on wings they would lose within a day.

Almost instantly the mist enveloped Jeff's head like a dark shroud, and he instinctively drew in his breath to scream out in terror.

He could feel them in his mouth now—millions of them. He was choking as they filled his throat and spread through his lungs.

His scream emerging as no more than a bubbling gurgle, he rolled away from Julie, twitching as he scrabbled across the floor in a futile attempt to escape the swarming mass that now surrounded him.

He caught a glimpse of Julie for a split second, and his gorge rose as he saw a second mass emerge from her open mouth and join the cloud that now totally engulfed him.

They were settling on his skin; suddenly, every square inch of his body felt as if it were on fire.

Now they were in his eyes and his nose.

His ears were filled with them, and in his head he heard a terrible humming buzz, which he was certain was the sound of their millions of wings.

The torture went on, the nearly invisible creatures swarming around him, burrowing their way through his skin, into the membranes of his mouth and nose, his eyes and ears.

There was no way to escape them, no way to defend himself from them.

He lay squirming on the floor, and as the unbearable horror burgeoned within him, a new terror seized Jeff Larkin's mind.

He was going to die.

In some way—in some unearthly manner that he didn't understand at all—Julie Spellman was killing him.

And there was nothing he could do about it.

CHAPTER 13

Marge Larkin's jaw was throbbing with pain when she woke up the next morning, and even before she got out of bed, she swallowed one of the pills she'd left on her bedside table, washing it down with water that tasted a bit stale after having been in the glass all night. She flopped back on the pillows for a few minutes, waiting for the codeine the dentist had prescribed to take effect.

She could barely even remember coming home last night. The drive had been pure torture, since she'd refused to take any pain medication, and hadn't even dared to drive until the effects of both the Novocain and the nitrous oxide had worn off. By the time she'd gotten in, much later than planned, she felt almost delirious with pain, and instantly dosed herself with codeine. Still, she had made it home, and everything seemed to be all right. Though Julie Spellman was no longer there, she had a vague recollection of Jeff telling her that he'd sent Julie home and put Ben to bed. Nodding mutely, she'd stopped only long enough to kiss Ben good night before going to bed herself.

Now, though, she recalled Ben trying to tell her something—something she'd been far too miserable to listen to.

Not that she felt much better this morning.

Still, no matter how much her jaw hurt, she was going to have to get up.

Get up, take care of her kids, and go to work today.

The thought of trying to work made her groan softly to herself. Though her official title at the weekly community newspaper was that of secretary, in fact she and Jim Chapman—owner, publisher, editor-in-chief, and jack-of-all-trades, as he liked to say—were pretty much the whole staff. There were a few people in town who wrote stories now and then, but Jim Chapman and Marge Larkin actually got the paper out. It wasn't much of a paper, Marge had to admit. In fact, it hadn't turned a profit in any of the ten years she'd worked for the *Pleasant Valley Chronicle*.

Not that her boss cared. Jim had plenty of money from his first career, which had involved inventing a complicated computer gadget Marge didn't even pretend to understand, and brought him checks every month that allowed him easily to make up the losses the *Pleasant Valley Chronicle* generated. "I'm having a good time, and I can afford it," he always told her whenever she suggested maybe he ought to stop throwing good money after bad. So who was she to complain? She liked Jim Chapman, and she liked her job, and she hated to miss a day's work, because all too often it meant they were a day late getting the paper out.

Not, Marge suspected, that anyone in town except she and Jim cared if the *Chronicle* was late, but it was the principle of the thing.

So, jaw hurting or not, she was going to have to work today.

She climbed out of bed, dressed, and went into the kitchen to start a pot of coffee. Tentatively exploring the gap in her lower jaw where a molar had been until yesterday afternoon, she opened the refrigerator to get out the milk. As she reached for the carton, she automatically scanned the contents of the refrigerator, putting together a mental list of things to pick up at the store on the way home from work.

Marge frowned. Not only was the leftover pot roast that

she'd planned to heat up for dinner tonight no longer there, but other things seemed to be missing as well.

The block of cheddar cheese was almost completely gone.

And the package of bologna that was supposed to serve as sandwich material for the whole week.

It hadn't even been opened yesterday morning, and now only a couple of slices remained.

And the bread, too.

Hadn't there been a whole loaf yesterday?

How much could three kids have eaten last night?

Then she remembered that they weren't supposed to have eaten anything—at the last minute she'd decided to give them money to go to the A&W for hamburgers. Hadn't they even gone? She couldn't believe they'd give up a chance to go to the drive-in in favor of staying home and eating leftovers.

Now, as Ben came into the kitchen, still in his pajamas and rubbing sleep from his eyes, she nodded toward the refrigerator. "You guys sure ate us out of house and home yesterday, didn't you?"

Ben shook his head. "Not *me*," he said with such exaggerated innocence that Marge instantly knew there was more to the story, and that she would have to dig it out of him so no one could accuse him of being a tattletale.

"Oh, really?" Marge said. "Well, if it wasn't you, who was it?"

"Jeff and Julie," Ben said, climbing onto one of the chairs and reaching for the box of Cheerios.

"Jeff and Julie?" Marge echoed.

"Well, mostly Julie," Ben said. Under his mother's prodding, he told her what had happened, up until the time his brother had sent him over to Vic Costas's house. "Then they *finally* came and got me," he finished, emphasizing the word "finally" so hard that Marge almost laughed out loud. "And we went to the A&W and had hamburgers. Can we go there again tonight?"

"No, we can't," Marge said automatically as she tried to make sense out of what Ben had just told her.

Memories of things she read about or had seen on television flipped through her mind.

Was Julie one of those girls with that disease—what did they call it, bulimia?—that caused them to gorge themselves with food, then throw it up?

But what about Jeff? If he'd been there, too—

And where *was* Jeff? Usually he was up before Ben.

In the room the two boys shared, she found Jeff sprawled out on his bed, facedown, covered only with a sheet.

Sunlight was shining through the window, and as she shook Jeff awake, he rolled over and shielded his eyes from the glare with his arm.

"Ma? Jeez, Ma, what are you doing? Is something wrong?"

"That's what I'd like to know," Marge told him. "What on earth was going on around here yesterday? Ben says—" She stopped abruptly when Jeff lowered his arm and she saw his face.

Jeff looked . . . what?

Not sick, exactly, but not really well, either.

His face seemed to her to be too pale, and despite the coolness of the morning, his forehead was covered with a sheen of perspiration. "Do you feel all right?" she asked.

Jeff groaned and sat up. "I feel fine," he told her. "Why, do I look sick or something?"

Frowning, Marge pressed her wrist against his forehead, then the palm of her hand.

Despite his pallor, he didn't feel feverish.

And yet . . .

Another idea flitted into her mind, one that disturbed

her far more than the possibility that Julie Spellman might have some exotic eating disorder.

Didn't kids on drugs like to eat a lot? The "munchies"—wasn't that what they called it?

Was that why Jeff sent Ben out of the house? Did Julie have drugs, which she'd shared with Jeff?

"I think you'd better tell me exactly what went on around here yesterday afternoon," Marge told him. Then, before Jeff could reply, she caught sight of the clock.

In ten minutes she would be late for work, and this was the morning they had to get the final layout files for the paper ready to send to the printer, no later than ten.

If she pursued this with Jeff now—provided, of course, that she could get him even to talk about anything that might have happened yesterday afternoon—it could take most of the morning.

She looked at him once more.

The eyes—hadn't she heard that kids who were on drugs had dilated pupils?

But when? Just when they were high? All the time?

She peered at him, trying to analyze the state of his eyes. They looked normal, yet something, clearly, was wrong.

What was she supposed to do? Just ask him if he was doing drugs? She suddenly realized how totally naive she was about such things.

Maybe the pallor didn't mean anything at all—maybe it was just because he'd been sound asleep a few minutes ago. "You're sure you're all right?" she asked.

"I already told you, Ma, I'm fine," Jeff replied.

Five minutes later, as she left for work, Marge Larkin knew she'd taken the path of least resistance. Something, obviously, had gone on in her house yesterday afternoon, but right now she was just too busy, and felt too lousy, to deal with it.

Tonight, she told herself as she headed into town. I'll

talk to him tonight, and if I have to, I'll talk to Karen and Russell, too. But whatever it is, it'll just have to wait.

Jeff stared into the cracked mirror in the bathroom.

Why had he told his mother he felt fine, when he didn't at all?

In fact, he had never felt worse in his life.

Last night he'd had chills and fever; all night long he'd gone back and forth between freezing to death and burning up.

He'd felt sick, but hadn't been able to throw up.

There was a terrible itching feeling, a raw, stinging, maddening sensation so deep it seemed to be rising out of his very bones.

This morning, when his mother had shaken him awake, he felt a little bit better, but not much.

Yet when he tried to tell her how sick he was, he hadn't been able to. It was as if he were paralyzed, thinking the words but unable to will them from his brain to his mouth. Instead he'd told her he was fine.

Fine!

But he felt terrible! Why hadn't he told his mother?

Was he going nuts or something?

Then, as he stared at his image in the mirror, he saw another image, one that rose out of the depths of his memory to superimpose itself on the face in the glass.

An image of Julie Spellman, smiling at him.

Beckoning to him.

Luring him.

Enslaving him.

His pulse quickened as he stared past his own reflection to the vision floating beyond the mirror, and he knew that he had to see her.

Had to be near her.

Suddenly, being close to Julie Spellman had become the most important thing in his life.

* * *

"Why can't *I* ride her?" Molly demanded. She was perched on the top rail of the corral, watching as Kevin, riding Greta bareback, cantered easily around the perimeter of the enclosure, Flicka racing along after her mother, struggling to keep up. "But what if I just walk her?" the little girl pleaded. "How am I supposed to train Flicka when she grows up, if I don't even know how to ride myself?"

Kevin grinned at Molly as he passed her. "Come on—look at how little you are. Greta's way too big for you."

"I bet I could do it," Molly insisted. Then, as Kevin ignored her, she decided to try a different tactic. "How old were you when you learned to ride?"

"Five or six, I guess," Kevin replied before he realized his mistake.

"Well, I'm almost ten!" Molly declared.

Kevin reined the mare to a stop, swung his left leg over her neck and dropped to the ground. As he dismounted, Molly jumped off the fence and ran over to take the reins. "Tell you what," Kevin said as Molly began leading the horse around the corral, walking her just the way he'd taught her to. "We'll ask your mom, and if she says it's all right, I'll put a saddle on Greta after breakfast, and you can try it. But I'll hold the reins, and you have to promise to do exactly what I tell you. Okay?"

"Really?" Molly asked. She'd been pleading with Kevin to teach her to ride Greta all week, but she hadn't actually expected him to give in. "I promise! I promise!" Almost trembling with excitement, she finished walking the horse, forcing herself not to rush and give Kevin an excuse to change his mind. Finally, after she'd walked Greta around the corral three times and Kevin agreed that the mare had been properly cooled down, Molly turned the horse loose. Instantly Flicka began nursing at the mare's nipple, finally reaching the goal she'd been trying to achieve as she'd followed her mother around the enclosure.

Feeding both the horses lumps of sugar, Molly crawled between the two lower rails of the fence and ran up the hill to the house to begin lobbying her mother for permission to ride Greta.

In the kitchen, Karen was feeling better than she had in several days, and she knew exactly why.

Julie.

This morning—indeed, ever since she'd come home from baby-sitting Ben Larkin yesterday—Julie seemed finally to have recovered from her anger over the grounding, and from the strange lethargy that had overcome her since Otto had died.

Her color appeared better to Karen, and at the table last night she'd once again joined in the conversation, as close to her old self as she'd been since they arrived in Pleasant Valley. And this morning Julie had gotten up early to help Molly turn out the horses, then cheerfully volunteered to pitch in with breakfast.

Perhaps, finally, things were going to settle back down to normal.

She was just getting ready to go out and ring the triangle to summon the rest of the family when Molly burst into the kitchen, bubbling over with the news that Kevin had finally agreed to teach her how to ride Greta. "But he says I have to ask you first," she finished. "But I know I can do it, Mom. Kevin was only five when he learned! And if I'm going to—"

Karen held up her hands in mock protest against the torrent of words. "Will you just slow down, wash your hands, and get to the table? We'll all talk about it when Russell and Kevin come in. All right?"

Though another torrent of excited words was already building in Molly's throat, she managed to choke them back until everyone had gathered around the table, but as Karen passed the platter of pancakes to Russell, Molly could stand it no longer. "You said we'd talk about it at the table," she blurted out. "And we're all at the table, so you have to talk about it!"

The discussion, as it turned out, lasted only a couple of minutes, and it was Russell who finally summed it up.

"She lives on a farm. She owns a horse. She needs to know how to ride. What's the big deal?"

"But she's so young," Karen protested, though she already knew the issue was decided.

"She's older than Kevin or I were when we first got on a horse," Russell told her. Then he faced the little girl directly, his eyes alive with humor for the first time since his father had died. When he spoke again, his voice actually took on the same timbre Otto's had had. " 'Course, I 'spose there ain't no way girls can do some of the things boys can do . . ." he added in perfect imitation of his father.

Realizing the discussion was essentially over, Karen nonetheless tried one last gambit. "It seems to me Molly's going to have to convince Julie, too. I mean, Greta's *her* horse, isn't she?" But to her surprise, her older daughter only shrugged.

"It's okay with me," Julie said. "Molly's the one who's crazy about horses. She *should* know how to ride."

"When?" Molly demanded, sensing victory. "This morning? Please? I'll do the dishes, and clean my room, and everything!"

Karen gave up the fight. "All right, if you all think it's okay, I'll go along with it. But if you fall off, don't come crying to me," she added, doing her best to glare at Molly but failing completely. "And don't bother with the dishes or your room. I'll take care of it myself."

As the rest of the family began planning the day— around the kitchen table, instead of in the tack room—

Karen leaned back in her chair and almost guiltily savored the moment.

For the first time since the wedding, all of them were together, and all of them—even Julie—seemed to be happy.

Except that Otto is dead, Karen reminded herself. And yet, despite the guilt her feelings caused her, she couldn't rid herself of the thought that perhaps, just perhaps, Otto's death might have been for the best in the long run.

He hadn't been happy about what was happening to his farm, or his family, or even himself.

And he'd died quickly. Ellen Filmore had even suggested that after the first quick sting, he might not have been conscious for more than a few seconds.

And now, finally, the rest of them seemed truly to be turning into a family.

A real family.

"Why are we going over to the Owens'?" Ben asked, still angry at his brother over his banishment the previous afternoon. Now, his fists settled stubbornly on his hips, and his legs spread wide as he glared up at Jeff's towering height. "I don't want to go, and you can't make me!" he declared.

Jeff reached down, picked the much smaller boy up, and held him at arm's length as Ben struggled to get loose. "We're going over there because that's what I say we're going to do, and I'm a lot bigger than you."

"I'm telling Mom when she gets home," Ben shouted. "She said—"

"She said I was supposed to take care of you, and I'm going to," Jeff told him. "And we're going over to the Owens', and you can play with Molly."

"She's a girl!" Ben objected. "I hate girls!"

"What about horses?" Jeff asked. "You like them, don't you?"

Suddenly Ben looked uncertain. "Horses?" he asked, sensing a trap.

"Sure. Molly has a colt, and I bet she'll let you pet it."

"Really?" Ben asked, plunging instantly into the snare his brother had laid for him. "Where'd she get a colt?" By the time they started across the field, Ben's threat to tell his mother about Jeff's imagined transgression had vanished from his mind, and as they approached the Owens' corral a few minutes later, he ran ahead to scramble up to the top rail of the fence.

Inside the corral, holding a big horse by its reins, was Molly, whom Ben had seen a couple of times but never spoken to.

"Is that your horse?" he asked.

Molly shook her head. "Mine's a colt. This one's my sister's, and Kevin's going to teach me to ride her."

"Will he teach me, too?" Ben asked.

Molly hesitated, then shrugged. "I don't know. Who are you?"

"Ben Larkin. I live over there." He pointed off toward Vic Costas's farm. "Can I watch while Kevin teaches you?"

Molly shrugged. "I guess."

A few seconds later, as Kevin came out of the barn, Jeff joined his brother on the fence. "Hey, Kev," he called. "Where's Julie?"

Kevin glanced at Jeff. Why was he asking about Julie? What did—Then he remembered that Julie had been baby-sitting Ben yesterday afternoon.

Had Jeff been there, too?

A twinge of jealousy shot through Kevin. "I don't know," he replied. "I guess she's in the house."

"She's coming down to watch me ride," Molly informed Jeff. "You can watch, too, if you want."

Kevin flushed when Molly contradicted him, and quickly turned away from Jeff. "Come on," he told Molly. "Let's get you up on Greta."

Molly watched as Kevin demonstrated how to mount the horse. Then he dismounted, and, still holding the reins in his left hand, lifted Molly with an arm around her waist till she was high enough to place her foot into the stirrup, grab the pommel, and scramble up, throwing her right leg over Greta's saddle. "I did it!" she cried as she sat up straight. "I got—"

Greta took a sudden step, and Molly, surprised by the movement, almost lost her balance.

"Hang on!" Kevin told her. Quieting the horse, he moved back to where Molly sat and shortened first one of the stirrups, then the other. "There, that's better," he said.

He showed Molly how to hold the reins properly, and gave her instruction on how to sit on the horse. Grasping the bridle, he began leading Greta slowly around the corral, letting Molly get used to the feel of the horse.

On the third circuit of the enclosure, Kevin noticed that Julie had come down to the corral, and was now seated on the top rail, watching.

Next to her, sitting very close to her, was Jeff Larkin.

As they approached Julie and Jeff, Kevin felt the mare tense. Then she snorted loudly and jerked her head, as if trying to pull away.

"What's wrong?" Molly asked. "Is she scared of something?"

Kevin, certain the horse had merely reacted to the twinge of jealousy he'd felt when he saw Julie and Jeff together, tightened his grip on the bridle.

"It's all right," he said, trying to soothe the horse. "Nothing's wrong at all." He kept walking, making the circuit of the corral yet again, and Greta seemed to relax as they moved away from Julie and Jeff. "Good girl," Kevin whispered into the mare's ear. "I don't like it, either, but we'll just act like we don't notice."

They came around the last turn in the fence, and as they approached Jeff and Julie once more, the horse shied. Her nostrils flared and her ears flattened against her head. "Easy," Kevin crooned. "Just take it easy."

But the horse, as if sensing some unseen danger emanating from Julie and Jeff, tried to pull away again, this time rearing up and jerking loose from Kevin's grip.

On top of the horse, Molly shrieked in alarm and dropped the reins. A second later Greta reared again, one of her hooves lashing out toward Kevin, who ducked away just in time to keep from being kicked in the head. As he rolled away from the spooked horse, Greta lunged off in the other direction. Molly clung to the pommel, screaming in terror now, but the next time Greta reared up, the little girl slipped from the saddle and fell to the ground. Thrashing around, trying to roll away from the bucking horse, Molly's screams grew ever louder.

From her place on the fence, Julie watched in horror as the horse lunged back and forth in the corral, its hooves striking the ground only inches from her sister. Molly scrambled first one way, then another, but no matter which way she turned, Greta seemed to be there, blocking her escape.

Any second, Julie knew, the horse's hooves would drop down on Molly and—

She felt a surge of adrenaline in her body, and from somewhere in her mind there came what seemed like a burst of pure energy.

Her eyes fixed on the horse, and in her mind she envisioned it under attack.

And then, as the horse continued to lunge in the corral, something happened.

Its bucking abruptly stopped and a shrieking whinny burst from its throat. A second later it plunged away from Molly, as if trying to escape something.

Julie kept staring at the horse, her entire attention focusing on the thrashing animal.

Jeff, beside her, felt her tense, and when he turned to

look at her, Julie's expression was a frozen mask of concentration.

Then, from behind him, Jeff heard a humming sound. When he turned to look, he saw them.

Bees.

Thousands of them, pouring into the corral from the direction of the house, swirling around the terrified horse in a dense cloud.

Greta, surrounded by the mass of stinging insects, thrashed from side to side as she tried to dodge away from the undulating swarm.

She tried to run then, but dozens of the tiny creatures had settled on her head, found the spots around her nose and eyes where the hair was thinnest, and plunged their stingers in.

Hundreds more clung to her belly and crept up the insides of her flanks, where the hair was worn away and her bare skin was exposed.

Thousands more began burrowing through her short hair until they found the skin below.

Kevin, still in the corral, scooped Molly up from the ground, then watched in awe as the bees relentlessly attacked the mare.

And Jeff, from his place next to Julie on the fence, found himself almost hypnotized by her oddly emotionless eyes as she watched the tormented creature stumble, then fall to the ground and begin rolling over and over in a vain attempt to escape the swarm of insects.

As Molly and Kevin, mesmerized by the sight, retreated silently back to the fence, the horse whinnied one last time.

Then its body trembled and it lay still.

Except for the humming of the bees, an eerie silence fell over the corral.

CHAPTER 14

Karen shut off the vacuum cleaner, sighing as she reflected that it had taken her twice as long just to do the upstairs of the farmhouse as it had taken to clean the whole apartment back in L.A. And there were still the kids' rooms to do before she could even start on the bathrooms.

The noise of the machine died away, and Karen pulled the plug out of the outlet midway down the wall of the upstairs corridor, letting the cord snake back onto the spring-loaded reel of the Electrolux. For just a second she considered the possibility that the plug might snap off the end of the cord as it hit the canister, thus ending the chore. The plug held, though—as she'd known it would—and before she dragged the machine into the master bedroom, she eyed the corridor once more, searching for any dust she might have missed.

It was while she was inspecting the hall that she realized she was still hearing a faint buzzing in her ears, though the vacuum was off.

She hesitated, then shrugged it off, telling herself it was nothing more than a residual effect from listening to the Electrolux roaring at her for the last half hour. Even Bailey, who had been asleep on Kevin's bed when she began, had abandoned the house as soon as she'd turned the machine on. A little while ago she'd seen him snoozing in a patch of sunlight out by the barn.

Pulling the Electrolux along behind her, she entered the

master bedroom and was about to plug the vacuum in
again when she noticed that the humming in her ears
hadn't disappeared, but had grown louder.

Louder, and more familiar.

The first stirrings of fear fluttering in her belly, she
moved tentatively around the room.

The sound was loudest when she stood next to the wall
separating this room from Julie's. Leaving her own bedroom, she went into the one next door.

The level of the humming was the same, and loudest
when she stood next to the master bedroom wall.

The sound was coming from inside the wall, and still
growing louder.

And now, with terrible certainty, she knew what it was.

Bees!

But how could they be in the wall?

Going to the window, she opened it and was about to
unhook the screen when she saw them.

Hundreds of them, hovering in the air just outside the
window.

Her skin prickling with goose bumps, Karen watched
them land on the wall, then creep through a crack in the siding. But even as they disappeared into the wall, more and
more kept arriving, until the air seemed choked with them.

For what seemed an eternity, Karen stood frozen at the
window, gazing at the cloud of insects just beyond the
screen.

What if they suddenly attacked the screen?

Could they get through?

The thought of them filling the room in which she stood
brought her back to life. She reached out and slammed the
window shut.

The sound of the frame thudding against the windowsill
triggered a memory in Karen's mind—of the day they'd
found Otto's body, when she'd awakened to this very same
sound.

A sound that Russell had insisted was nothing just before he'd closed the window to shut it out.

Her heart beating faster, Karen went back to her own room.

The humming was louder now, and she flushed with anger as she moved to the window and peered out.

Bees were still arriving, hovering in the air, crawling over the screen that covered her window.

At least a dozen had found a tiny hole in the mesh and worked their way into the space between the screen and the glass. Karen shuddered as she remembered the reactions Molly and Julie had had to the bee stings. What if she'd left the window open this morning, as Julie had, instead of shutting it against the heat of the day? Her eyes fixed on the growing mass of bees outside, and she felt an icy chill of horror.

Molly!

The last time she'd looked out the kitchen window, Molly had been starting across the yard on her way down to the corral! And if the bees were swarming in the yard—

She heard a shriek, then, from somewhere outside.

A shriek that she knew instantly was that of her younger daughter.

"Molly!" The name erupted from her throat, and she rushed from the bedroom, bolted down the stairs, and burst out the back door.

But Karen was barely off the back porch when she stopped short, her eyes caught by something moving only a few feet above her head. She looked up, shading her eyes against the bright glare of the sun. For a moment she saw nothing.

Then her eyes focused and she shuddered.

A steady stream of bees was flying up from the direction of the corral, one corner of which was now visible behind the barn.

Her blood ran cold as she realized that Molly wasn't alone down there.

Kevin was with her, and she was almost certain that Julie had gone down, too, to watch her sister's first riding lesson.

"Oh, God," she wailed, breaking into a run. She raced down the slope toward the corral, her mind reeling. What if they've been stung again? What if this time all the kids have been stung?

"Stick out your tongue and say 'Ahh,' " Ellen Filmore told Gareth Parker. The four-year-old gazed up at her solemnly, but made no move to comply with her order.

"Don't hurt me," he said.

"I'm not going to hurt you," Ellen promised. She held up the tongue depressor for his inspection. "See? It looks just like an ice cream stick, doesn't it?"

Gareth shook his head emphatically.

"Well, maybe it doesn't," Ellen agreed. "But I'm not going to put it down your throat or anything. I'm just going to press your tongue down a little bit, so I can see how your tonsils look. See?" Opening her mouth, she used the depressor to flatten her own tongue, then leaned over so the little boy could peer into her throat. Just as he leaned closer for a better look, she said, *"Ahh!"* loudly enough to make him jump, then reached out to tickle him. As the little boy began giggling, Ellen threw the used tongue depressor away and began peeling the paper from a new one. "Now what do you say?" she asked. "Your turn?"

Gareth nodded. "Okay," he said, opening his mouth and leaning forward slightly. Ellen pressed his tongue down, moved closer, and was just about to get a good look at the offending tonsils when she felt the little boy's fingers plunge into her ribs and heard a burst of laughter explode from his throat.

Reflexively jerking back as the depressor dropped from

her fingers, Ellen did her best to fix the little boy with a stern look, but didn't quite succeed. "You planned that," she accused.

Gareth nodded happily.

"Okay," Ellen sighed. "Let's start over again, all right?"

But as she was reaching for yet a third depressor, the door to the examining room opened and Roberto Muñoz stuck his head in. "Better get out here, Doc," he said. "We got a problem."

From the waiting room, Ellen could hear a low moaning sound, followed by a worried female voice: "It's going to be all right, Andy. Just hang on!"

It was the urgency in the woman's voice that commanded Ellen Filmore's attention more than the sound of the moan.

A moan could mean anything from a stomachache to a hangover, but whoever was with the patient in the waiting room obviously thought it was a lot more serious than either of those. Leaving Gareth Parker under Roberto's supervision, she hurried out to the waiting room.

One look told her what had happened.

It was Andy Bennett, his face flushed the same abnormal red she'd seen only a few days before on Julie Spellman, and a week before that on Julie's little sister, Molly.

Andy's right hand and forearm had already swollen grotesquely, and he appeared to be on the verge of falling into unconsciousness.

"Bee sting?" Ellen asked, though she was nearly certain it could be nothing else.

Marian Bennett glanced up and nodded, her lips clamped tightly in a harsh line as she attempted to control the fear that had bloomed inside her as she'd watched Andy's arm blow up and his face turn red.

His breathing had become increasingly strangled on the short ride to the clinic. Now he was gasping for breath.

"It's all right," Ellen assured her, already turning back

toward the emergency room. "I've got something that will take care of it."

Marian Bennett found her voice. "I don't know what's happening to him. He's never been allergic. He—"

But Ellen had already disappeared, moving quickly as she found a syringe, unwrapped it, and filled it with half the remaining contents of the vial Carl Henderson had given her the day he'd brought Julie Spellman in. She strode back to the waiting room, an alcohol-soaked cotton swab in one hand, the hypodermic in the other. "Get his shirt open and off his upper right arm," she instructed Marian Bennett.

Jerking at the front of Andy's shirt, Marian exposed her son's chest, then pulled the shirt off his shoulders. The instant his arm was exposed, Ellen Filmore swabbed it with alcohol, then plunged the needle in.

As the contents of the hypodermic needle flowed into his blood, the color of Andy's face began to change, fading quickly back to normal.

As Marian watched in amazement, the swelling in her son's arm began to ease, and his breathing—nothing more than a labored gasp a few moments ago—took on an easy rhythm.

But with Andy Bennett, as with Julie Spellman a few days before, the instant and dramatic easing of his most obvious symptoms was only part of what was happening inside his body.

What neither his mother nor Ellen Filmore could know was that Andy Bennett—though he looked better every minute—was feeling worse.

While the symptoms of the sting were easing, those of the treatment were just beginning.

He opened his mouth to tell the doctor what was happening to him, to tell her about the nausea boiling in his stomach and the feverish chill that held him in its icy grip, but when he heard the words he uttered, he felt a new kind of fear—a fear that gripped his mind as painfully as did the sudden illness that had invaded his body.

For the words he spoke were not the words he'd intended to say.

Indeed, they bore no relationship at all to the violent illness that seemed suddenly to have taken possession of his body. "Good," he sighed. "That feels so good. . . ."

"You're sure?" his mother asked, looking at him with anxious eyes. "You're really all right?"

Andy wanted to scream, wanted to fall to the floor, writhing in agony, wanted to vomit up the vile nausea he felt in his belly.

Instead he stood up and smiled.

"I'm fine," he heard himself say. "Let's go home."

Carl Henderson pulled his Cherokee to a stop in a shady spot next to the Owens' barn just as Karen burst out of the house and began running down the slope toward the corral. It wasn't until he'd gotten out of the Jeep that he caught sight of the bees streaming from the corral behind the barn up toward the house, where they seemed to be swarming above the porch roof.

But that didn't make any sense—the new hives had been on the farm less than twenty-four hours, and in Carl's experience, bees rarely swarmed unless a hive was too crowded. No hive could possibly become overcrowded in less than a day, so one of the old hives must have split before it had been taken away.

Which meant that the bees now streaming toward the house would undoubtedly be of the virulently poisonous strain that had almost killed both Molly and Julie Spellman.

Carl felt a thrill of anticipation as the thought that Julie might have been stung again—perhaps even killed—flitted into his mind. Quickly, he rounded the corner of the barn, but stopped short as he saw Julie Spellman sitting on the top rail of the corral.

The moment of hope that she might be dead faded away, to be replaced by the same deep, cold anger she'd triggered in him the day she'd gotten stung.

That day, she hadn't remembered what had happened up at the hives; but that didn't mean she would never remember. Carl had done his best to avoid her since then, not only because he was afraid of what she might suddenly remember, but also because of the fury that rose within him just at the sight of her.

The fury that made him want to reach out to her, to capture her, to add Julie to his collection.

But he couldn't do that, not now.

Maybe not ever.

He was almost certain that Mark Shannon was watching him. The deputy had come to his house the day after Otto died, and even though Shannon had pretended he only wanted to talk about scorpions, Carl Henderson knew better.

Shannon was spying on him.

He'd known it instantly, felt it in the way the deputy's eyes had fixed on him, then flicked through his house, prying into the corners, searching the crannies for . . .

What?

Whatever he was looking for, Carl knew Shannon wouldn't find it. There was nothing left to find; not upstairs, nor down in the basement, either.

Dawn Sanderson was gone—even before he'd driven Otto home in his own truck and deposited him behind the toolshed, Carl had taken Dawn off the wall and put her into his special box.

A wonderful, perfectly constructed box, eight feet long, four feet wide, and four feet deep—like a huge coffin— half filled with a special mixture of earth that he himself had compiled.

The box of earth stood in the back corner of the darkroom.

In the earth lived a colony of ants.

A special colony that had been multiplying for years and now comprised millions of insects.

Insects that needed to be fed.

When he'd taken the girl off the wall and put her into the box, the ants had swarmed up out of their underground colonies and set to work.

By the time he'd walked home from the Owen farm, Dawn's face was already gone, her jaws and cheekbones picked clean of flesh. Carl, entranced by the spectacle, had watched the insects devour Dawn for almost three hours.

By morning there was little left on the surface of the earth in the box but Dawn's skeleton—barely held together by remnants of cartilage—and her hair.

The thick, dark hair, the very sight of which had triggered Carl's fury the morning he had first seen her.

In the dead of night, Carl had driven the skeleton far up into the hills west of town, where he'd hidden it in thick brush in the midst of a huge tract of empty wilderness.

Nevertheless, Mark Shannon was watching. And no doubt waiting for him to betray himself, Carl Henderson thought.

That meant he would have to keep his dark anger under control.

He would have to stay away from Julie Spellman, who aroused more fury inside him than any other girl he'd ever seen.

But it would be all right. If he had to control his rage, then he *would* control his rage.

At least for now.

Taking a deep breath, telling himself to ignore Julie Spellman as if she weren't there at all, Carl strode toward the corral to see what had happened.

Karen Owen was kneeling down by the fence, her arms wrapped around her youngest daughter. "Are you all right, honey?" she asked. "The bees didn't sting you again, did they?"

Molly shook her head. "But they killed Greta, Mommy," she wailed. "They killed her!"

"Greta?" Karen asked. "Honey, what are you talking about?"

The little girl pointed through the rails of the fence, and both Karen and Carl Henderson followed her gesture with their eyes.

The mare lay on the other side of the corral, surrounded by Kevin and Russell Owen, Jeff and Ben Larkin.

As Karen held her sobbing daughter in her arms, trying to comfort her, Carl Henderson climbed through the fence and started across the corral. "Russell?" he called, injecting just the right mixture of curiosity and concern into his voice. "What the hell's going on out here? What happened to the horse?"

But it wasn't Russell who answered him. Instead it was Kevin, standing next to his father. The boy's eyes stayed on the fallen horse as he spoke. "The bees, Mr. Henderson," he said. "You never saw anything like it—anyway, I didn't." As Henderson moved in to join the group around the horse, Kevin tried to explain what had happened. "She shied. I'm not sure what spooked her, but all of a sudden she just jerked away from me and reared up. Molly fell off, and then . . ." His voice trailed off for a second as he remembered watching helplessly as the horse nearly trampled Molly. "I couldn't do anything," he finally went on. "I couldn't even get to Molly." He shrugged helplessly. "Then all of a sudden the bees came." He shook his head, remembering the sight of the swarm of insects streaming across the fence from the direction of the house. "It was really awesome—I mean, you wouldn't believe it unless you'd seen it!"

"They flew right over me," Ben Larkin cried, his voice piping loudly as he picked up the story. "The horse was going to kill Molly, but then the bees came and killed the horse!"

"That doesn't make any sense," Russell Owen interjected, moving closer to the fallen mare. Frowning, he turned to Carl Henderson. "You ever hear of bees that could do this?"

Carl Henderson composed a perfect demeanor of puzzlement. "Well, technically, any kind of bees could kill an animal if enough of them stung it," he offered. "But the domestic species we keep is far too docile to mount a major attack on a horse. Hell, they rarely attack much of anything—that's what makes them so perfect for domestication."

"What about Africans?" Russell pressed. "Could your hives have gotten Africanized?"

Henderson's mind worked quickly. "I don't see how," he said. "Africans just haven't gotten this far north yet. But of course," he added, carefully planting the seed that would direct any suspicion away from himself, "there's always the first incident in any area they penetrate. Down south, it was a dog that first got attacked."

Russell squatted down to begin examining the dead mare, then glanced up at Jeff Larkin. "Is that what you saw, too, Jeff? The bees just came out of nowhere and attacked her?"

Jeff opened his mouth to speak, ready to tell them how he'd watched Julie as the bees attacked, and had the strange sensation that somehow she had actually *summoned* the insects, had directed them to attack the horse.

But he couldn't speak.

It was as if something inside him had taken control of his will and was refusing to let him utter the words that formed in his mind.

He stood still, his mouth half open, terror building inside him as he struggled to make sense out of what was happening to him.

Then, without warning, the strange force that was keeping him from speaking compelled him to turn his head and look at Julie.

No longer sitting on the fence, she was standing near her sister and mother now.

But she was looking at him.

Their eyes met and, for just a moment, locked.

And Jeff gave in to the force inside him. Shrugging, he turned back to Russell Owen. "It was just like Kevin told you," he said. "Really weird."

Ben Larkin piped up once more, his hand tugging at his brother's sleeve. "But what about Julie? Aren't you going to tell them about that?"

"Julie?" Russell Owen asked, frowning. "What's he talking about? What did Julie have to do with it?"

Once again the strange force inside him wrestled Jeff's words into silence, but even as he shrugged off any knowledge of what his brother might be talking about, he heard Ben excitedly start to tell the tale:

"It was really weird, Mr. Owen. It was almost like Julie sicced 'em on the horse." Ben's voice rose excitedly as the words tumbled from his mouth. "You should've seen it, Mr. Owen! The horse was bucking all over the place, and Molly was trying to get away from it, and all of a sudden I looked up and Julie was just sitting there, watching it, with a real funny look on her face! And a second later there were bees everywhere! It was just like she made them go after the horse!"

Russell's eyes narrowed and he turned to look at Julie, who had entered the corral and was standing a few feet away from them. "Julie?" he said. "Did you hear that? What's Ben talking about?"

As she looked at her stepfather, Julie clearly remembered the strange burst of energy that seemed to explode from somewhere deep inside her brain. But when she opened her mouth to tell Russell what had happened, she, like Jeff a few moments before, found herself struggling, as if totally confused by Ben's story. "I don't know," she heard herself say as the awful, formless entity within her swelled, robbing her of the will to speak her own thoughts. Julie tried to fight it, tried to tell her stepfather the truth, but even as she struggled against the strange force, the unbidden words began to roll from her lips: "All I remember is Greta bucking, and being scared that Molly was going to get killed. And then all of a sudden the bees were all over Greta."

"But it was like you did it!" Ben cried. "I saw it, and it was just like you did it! And you looked funny, too, just like you did yesterday!"

Above Ben's head Carl Henderson caught Russell's eyes, and the two men exchanged a resigned shrug as the little boy went on talking, his words pouring out in a rush as he tried to convince them that somehow Julie had made the bees attack the mare. Only when he finally ran out of steam did Russell give him a gentle pat on the back and turn him back toward the fence.

"Okay, Ben. Now, why don't you go over there with Molly, and let us figure out what happened here?"

"But I just told you," Ben wailed, his voice reflecting his indignation. "If you don't believe me—"

"It's not that we don't believe you," Russell broke in, knowing he had no chance of convincing the boy that despite how it might have looked, Julie couldn't possibly have had anything to do with the bees' attack. "It's just that right now we've got a lot to do."

Ben, his face stormy, finally stamped away, and at last Russell turned his attention back to the horse. "Well?" he asked Carl Henderson. "What do you think?"

Henderson shrugged. "Hard to say, without an autopsy. Tell you what—I'll have one of our trucks pick up the carcass, and our lab boys can do a postmortem. And we'll check some of those bees, too." His eyes darted toward Ben, then back to Russell. When he spoke again, his voice had dropped so low, only Russell could hear him. "I think maybe we'd better keep this quiet, if we can," he said. "At least until we know exactly what's going on." When Russell made no reply, Henderson pressed a little harder. "The last thing we need around here is a panic, Russell. And if these bees *are* turning lethal, a panic is exactly what we're going to have. All I'm saying is there's no use letting it start until we know for sure."

Russell glanced at his wife, who was still crouched down by Molly, her arms wrapped around the little girl.

The panic, he suspected, had already started.

Sighing heavily, he agreed to say nothing to anyone until they got the results of the autopsy.

A few minutes later, as Carl Henderson walked back toward his Cherokee to call UniGrow's offices in San Luis Obispo on his cellular phone, a chill of apprehension crept into him.

The kind of chill that means someone is watching you.

Don't turn around, he told himself, instantly certain he knew whose eyes were boring into his back. Just keep walking, and don't turn around. But even as he silently repeated the words to himself, his step faltered and he couldn't resist glancing back over his shoulder.

Julie Spellman's eyes were fixed on him, and even though she was almost fifty feet away, he could read their expression perfectly.

She knows, he thought. She remembered, and she knows what I've done.

His heart suddenly pounding and his skin breaking out in a cold sweat of fear, he tore his eyes away from hers and almost ran back to the Jeep.

CHAPTER 15

*T*he sun was starting to drop, but the temperature was still climbing as desert heat poured into the valley on a wind that had shifted to come from the southeast. In the distance the lush green carpet of the valley floor shimmered, while out toward the horizon a mirage lake that had appeared that afternoon spreading its phantom waters over a vast area of the flatland was now rapidly vanishing as the angle of the sun dropped too low to support it. Karen Owen hadn't noticed the phenomenon, however, for though she was in the midst of fixing supper, and the view of the valley was spread out before her as she stood at the kitchen sink, she was concentrating neither on her work nor on the panorama beyond the window.

Rather, her mind was still focused on what had happened that morning.

Now she did glance out the window, but it had nothing to do with enjoying the splendor of the valley. The potato peeler she was wielding paused in its rhythmic movement for a moment as she warily eyed the bees hovering over the lawn.

Russell, following his wife's gaze, shook his head helplessly. "I don't know how else I can explain it to you," he told her, knowing that despite everything he'd told her, Karen was convinced that the bees were waiting to strike at anyone who showed their face outside.

Molly hadn't been allowed out of the house for more

223

than a few minutes at a time, no matter how much Russell insisted that what happened to the horse was a freak circumstance and none of them was in any danger.

"But they're still out there," Karen told him, nodding toward the yard where, indeed, a few dozen bees were humming around the clover blooming in the lawn.

"Of course they are," Russell replied, and Karen heard a note of irritation in his voice. But then, as he saw how truly frightened she was, he softened. "Look, I know how scared you are, and I don't blame you. But you have to understand that this is a farm, and there will always be bees around. We've gotten rid of the ones that stung Molly and Julie, so let's at least wait until Carl has a report from the lab before we jump to any conclusions."

"But the kids all said—"

Russell silenced her by wrapping his arms around her, stroking her hair soothingly. "Who knows what the kids really saw? If Greta stomped on a bunch of bees while she was spooked, it stands to reason that more bees are going to come. Injured bees exude an odor that attracts their hive mates. It's a defense mechanism of the hive, pure and simple."

Karen looked up into her husband's face. "And after they killed that poor horse, they came back here, Russell. Not to one of the hives half a mile away. Here! Doesn't it bother you at all that they're inside the house?"

Russell frowned. "You mean they're not just in the wall? Have you actually seen them in the house? In our room or Julie's?"

Karen hesitated, then reluctantly shook her head. "But I can hear them," she said. "That awful buzzing."

"It'll stop," Russell assured her. "When it cools down—"

"I know," Karen broke in, slipping out of his embrace and moving to the refrigerator. " 'Bees don't move if it gets below fifty-four degrees,' " she went on, parroting what he'd told her earlier. "But it's almost a hundred out there right now, and it's not going to drop fifty degrees tonight. What if . . ." She floundered for a moment, searching for an argument she hadn't already used. She understood that they couldn't just move the swarm, the way Otto and Kevin had taken the one out of the tree the day they'd been married. Short of ripping the wall apart, there was no way of getting at the queen, and Karen knew you couldn't move the swarm without moving the queen. Tearing a gaping hole in the wall was the one thing absolutely certain to fill the house with bees.

"All right," she sighed, pulling a head of lettuce out of the vegetable bin at the bottom of the fridge, then straightening up and facing Russell again. "I'll make you a deal. I won't leave you if you promise me we'll call someone in the morning and have them come out and fumigate the swarm."

"I promise," Russell replied.

"But I won't sleep in our room, either," she went on. "Not with that awful humming. I'd be afraid they were going to come through the wall any second."

"They're not carpenter ants," Russell observed dryly. "Those guys don't make holes, they fill them up." He grinned as Karen shuddered. "Hey, think of the money we could save on insulation if we just let them fill the walls with honeycomb!"

Karen's eyes blazed. "Don't make jokes," she told him. "You may think this is all very funny, but in case you've forgotten, both my daughters have almost died from bee stings. How would you feel if it had been Kevin we'd flown to the hospital instead of Molly?"

His laughter dying, Russell said, "You know how bad I feel about what happened. I guess I was just trying to lighten things up a little."

"Well, you can't do it by making jokes," she said. "And I mean it about having an exterminator out tomorrow. And

I mean it about sleeping downstairs. And the kids can sleep downstairs, too, if they want to."

"Sounds like it's going to be a slumber party around here," Russell observed. Then, as he started out of the kitchen, his eyes fell on the large clock that hung on the wall above the door to the dining room.

It was almost six-thirty, and he clearly remembered Karen telling Julie to be home no later than six when she'd gone into town with Jeff Larkin.

Instantly, he thought about what had happened a few nights before, when she and Kevin had come home along the back road, reeking of beer.

Now she'd taken off with Jeff in his car, and was already half an hour late getting home.

Maybe, he reflected, giving her an early release from her grounding hadn't been such a good idea after all. One day, and already she was breaking a promise.

Well, when she got home, the two of them would have a talk.

And the later Julie was, the longer—and more unpleasant—the talk would be.

Jeff Larkin banged the fender of Vic Costas's ancient station wagon, his frustration at the car's refusal to start growing with every passing second.

He'd been working on it for nearly an hour already, but was no further along than when he'd begun.

And Julie, who was sitting in the front seat, turning the key whenever he told her to, was worried about how late it was.

"I was supposed to be home at six," she'd told him a few minutes ago. "I'm already half an hour late!"

He'd checked the battery, finding the cells full. The snapping spark he'd gotten when he grounded a screwdriver across the positive pole told him there was nothing wrong with its charge. Besides, the radio worked fine, and the headlights glowed brightly even in full daylight.

After that he'd started checking fuses, but quickly realized he was out of his depth—there was no manual for the car, and he didn't know where half the fuses were, let alone what they might be for. Still, all the ones he'd found had been in good shape, so he almost eliminated a fuse problem from his list of possible causes for the car's absolute refusal to start.

What the hell could it be, anyway?

He wracked his brain, trying to think, but all day long he'd been feeling strange, and the last couple of hours, since he and Julie had taken off in the car after he parked Ben with Vic Costas, he'd been feeling steadily worse.

But not so bad that he wasn't hungry. They'd stopped at the A&W and gotten some hamburgers, and he'd been about to head up into the park when Julie stopped him.

"Do we have to go up there? The power lines drive me crazy."

Jeff had glanced over at her. "Is that why you didn't want me to take the county road when we came into town? Because of the power lines?"

Julie nodded. "I hate them." But she hadn't told him why.

So instead of going to the park, they'd driven up into the foothills, parked the car, eaten their hamburgers and talked.

He asked her about the bees that morning, but she just shrugged her shoulders. "How could I have done that?" she asked. But she didn't quite say she hadn't done it.

After that, they just talked for a little while, and then, at quarter of six, they decided to head home.

And the car hadn't started.

With every minute that passed, Jeff was more pissed off.

Dropping the hood down, he went around to the driver's door.

"I'm going to try pushing it," he said. "Put it in neutral and let the parking brake off." As Julie followed his instructions, he leaned hard against the wagon's back door and pushed the car ahead a dozen feet, until it hit the downhill grade. "Okay, set the brake again," he called to Julie. The car jerked to a stop, and as Julie slid over into the passenger seat, Jeff got in behind the wheel. Putting the car in second gear, he held the clutch in with his left foot and released the parking brake again. The car started rolling forward, gaining speed. When it was doing ten miles an hour, he let out the clutch.

The car jerked as the transmission grabbed, then the engine coughed twice and started up. Jeff shook his head in disgust as he braked the car and the engine idled.

"Almost an hour," he groused. "I messed with it for almost an hour, and all it needed was a push! Do you believe it?" Then he felt a chill wash over him, and he shivered.

Jeff felt Julie watching him and heard her voice: "You okay?"

He turned to look at her and tried to speak, but just as at the corral that morning, when he'd tried to tell her stepfather about the horse, the words died on his lips.

Fear twisted his guts as he felt that strange force—a force he could neither fight against nor identify—once more refuse to let him speak.

Julie chuckled. "You're fine, right?" she asked, her voice tense. She was leaning against the passenger door, her face pale, her voice trembling as she spoke. "Go on," she whispered, her words almost pleading. "Tell me how you feel. Just try."

Jeff hesitated, then opened his mouth, determined to tell her exactly what was happening to him.

But again something unidentifiable rose up in his mind, seizing control. "I'm fine," he heard himself say.

And then, as he saw the knowing look in her eyes, he understood.

Whatever was doing this to him was doing it to her, too.

"What is it?" he whispered, barely trusting himself to be able to utter the words. "What's happening to us?"

Julie's whole body trembled as if she were gripped in a fever. "I don't know." She hesitated, then said, "Sometimes it seems to get better. Sometimes you almost forget it's there. But then it gets worse again. And then . . ." She fell silent, as if searching for the right words. "It fills you up," she whispered at last, her voice barely audible. "It fills you up, like it did with me yesterday. Then you have to do something." Her eyes locked on Jeff's. "You have to do something like I had to do yesterday."

Jeff stared silently at her, waiting for Julie to go on, but she said nothing else. As he put the car in gear and drove them home, though, her words echoed in his mind and he remembered once again the horrifying black swarm that had erupted from her throat the day before.

Erupted out of her, and attacked him, penetrating his body through his mouth, his nose, his ears, even his very skin.

Was that the source of the terrible force inside him that twice today had seized control of his mind?

But what was it?

What did it want from him?

Was it filling him up now, too?

And when it filled him, what would he do?

And then he had another thought.

What would *it* do?

After it filled him up and took control of him, what would it do?

But even as he formulated the question in his mind, Jeff Larkin was already certain that he knew the answer.

When it was done with him, when he could serve it no
longer, the thing—the strange force inside him—would
kill him.

CHAPTER 16

*M*arge Larkin was getting angrier by the minute.

Not only had Jeff not been there when she'd arrived home from work, but he'd dumped Ben with Vic Costas, and left her a note saying only that he'd gone for a ride with Julie Spellman and would be back by six.

Julie Spellman!

Marge still didn't know what had gone on between her son and Julie yesterday, and now they were together again and half an hour late getting home.

The worst, though, was that he'd left Ben with Vic Costas!

"As long as the kids don't bother me," the old farmer had told her when he'd reluctantly agreed to rent her the little house behind his barn. The building hadn't been occupied since he'd sold most of the land off to UniGrow, keeping no more than he could easily tend himself. "I don't really want no kids around the place. If I'd wanted kids, I'd have gotten married and had some of my own, and you don't notice I ever did that, did I?" Marge had promised that not only would Jeff and Ben be no trouble, but that they'd help out, too.

Up until Jeff had turned sixteen three months ago, it had worked out just fine. But then Jeff found the old Mercury station wagon buried under a mass of weeds next to the toolshed. Though the car had been completely hidden by the dense foliage, he discovered that it looked far closer to ruin than it actually was. Fortunately, the windows had been closed tight, and the interior of the car had actually turned out to be pretty clean. So he'd hacked away the weeds and set to work getting it running again.

Vic Costas went along with it, albeit reluctantly, but again had given her a stiff warning. "Any trouble," he said, wagging his finger severely, "any trouble at all, and out you go. I'd forgotten that old car was even there, so I guess it's okay if he wants to use it. But he pays! He pays the insurance, and the license, and everything else." His canny eyes had narrowed, almost disappearing into his weathered face. "And don't forget who's responsible," he told her. "Not me—you! He's your boy, not mine."

Though Marge suspected that Vic's gruff manner was more bluff than anything else, she wasn't about to risk finding out, for the tenant house on his farm was by far the best thing she'd been able to afford in the years since Ted Larkin had left her and the kids, simply disappearing one day, never to be seen or heard from again.

If Jeff got them kicked out of the tenant house, she didn't know what she was going to do.

She glanced out the window once more. Still no sign of Jeff.

She was about to pick up the phone to call the Owens and ask if Julie was home yet when she spotted a car moving along the dirt road that edged the foothills. Her hand on the receiver, Marge didn't move until she recognized the battered station wagon as it passed their driveway on its way to the Owen farm.

Five minutes later, when Jeff finally pulled the old Mercury up in front of the house, Marge was waiting by the front door, the first words of her angry lecture already rehearsed in her mind.

"Do you know what time—" she began, but the words died in her throat as she stared at her son.

His face was pale—ashen, really—and glistening with sweat.

His clothes were dirty and his hands black with grease.

"Jeff?" she asked. "What happened? What's wrong with you?"

Jeff, his six-foot-two-inch frame looming over her own five and a half feet, felt the beast within him take over. "What do you mean?" he asked, uttering the words the force inside his mind chose for him. "Nothing's wrong."

Ben, who had sensed his mother's anger and maintained a careful silence for the past hour, came back to life.

"It is, too!" he countered, pointing at his brother's face. "You look just like Julie did yesterday! You look like you're sick!"

Jeff barely glanced at his brother. "I'm not sick," he told his mother, obeying the instructions of the dark entity hidden inside him. "I just had to work on the car—it wouldn't start."

Marge inspected her son more carefully. Her eyes narrowed suspiciously and she moved closer to Jeff. "Let me see your eyes."

Jeff instantly understood her implication. "Oh, right," he groaned. "Julie and I are going to go out and get stoned, and I'm going to come driving home drugged out! What's with you, Mom? It just took a while to get the car started. What's the big deal?"

"The big deal," Marge replied, her voice growing cold in the face of Jeff's lack of concern, "is that according to your own note, you were going to be home at six!"

Jeff's mouth dropped open. "I couldn't help it! How was I supposed to know the car wouldn't start? And I couldn't even fix it, either!" Digging in his pocket, he produced the keys to the station wagon and held them out to her. "If you don't believe me, go try it yourself!"

Her eyes steely, Marge snatched the keys from Jeff's hand. Marching out of the house, she yanked the door of the station wagon open and slid behind the wheel. Inserting the key into the ignition, she twisted it.

The engine instantly roared to life.

She gunned the engine a couple of times, then shut off the ignition and returned to the house. "I thought you said it wouldn't start," she said coldly.

"Well, don't ask me what's going on! If you don't believe me, ask Julie!" Then, with exaggerated politeness that crossed the line into insolence, he said, "May I go take a shower now, your majesty?"

Marge stared at her son, shocked more by his tone than by the words themselves. Though Jeff had never been anything close to a perfect child—far from it—he'd never been deliberately nasty to her.

Once again the question of drugs rose in her mind.

Despite what he'd said, she still wondered.

Was it possible that Julie had gotten Jeff into drugs?

She almost blurted the question out, then thought better of it. What was he going to do? Having already denied it, was he now simply going to admit that he and Julie had been out somewhere getting stoned? "Go ahead," she said almost curtly. "We can talk about this later."

When he was gone, Marge turned to Ben. "I think maybe you and I ought to have a little talk," she said. Taking him by the hand, she led Ben out to the kitchen and sat him at the table.

Ben, suddenly suspicious, looked warily at his mother. "Are you mad at me?" he asked, his voice trembling.

Realizing how her words must have sounded to the little boy, Marge felt instantly contrite. "Of course not," she assured him, reaching across to pat his hand. "I just want to talk to you, that's all."

"About what?" Ben asked, still not certain what was going on.

Marge thought quickly, wondering how to question Ben without letting him know exactly what she was thinking.

"About Julie," she said. "I mean, you said Jeff looked like she did yesterday. What did you mean?"

Ben shrugged. "I don't know," he said. "Just what I said. When she started acting so weird yesterday, she looked just like Jeff does."

"You mean she was sick?"

The little boy shook his head. "She just looked funny, that's all. And she was acting funny, too. Like when the horse—" He clamped his hands over his mouth as he realized what he'd done. He'd promised he wouldn't say anything about Greta. He'd promised Jeff, and Mr. Owen, and everybody, and now he'd broken his promise.

"The horse?" Marge asked. What was he talking about?

Ben was regarding her fearfully now. "I wasn't supposed to say anything," he told her. "Not until they know what happened to it."

"Happened to what?" Marge pressed, her exasperation growing. What on earth had gone on today? "It's all right, Ben," she went on. "I can't believe they meant for you not to tell me, sweetheart. I'm your mother."

"But I promised," Ben pleaded. "You're never supposed to break a promise, are you?"

"No, you're not," Marge sighed, trapped by her own teaching. "I'll tell you what. You go on in and turn on the television, and I'll start getting supper ready, so as soon as Jeff is finished with his shower, we can eat, okay?"

Relieved, and anxious to get out of the kitchen before his mother changed her mind, Ben slid off his chair and darted out to the living room. A moment later, when she heard the television go on, Marge picked up the phone and dialed the Owens' number.

"Russell? This is Marge Larkin. Look, I know this is probably going to sound a little paranoid . . ." She hesitated. What would Russell know about Julie and what she might be up to? She'd better talk directly to Karen. "I guess I really need to talk to Karen," she went on. "Is she there?"

In the kitchen of the Owens' farmhouse, Russell wondered exactly what to say.

Karen was there all right.

She was in the den, with Julie.

And given the way she was talking to her daughter, Russell wondered if Marge Larkin was calling because she could hear Karen's voice from her own house, even though it was half a mile away.

"Just a minute," he said, betraying none of his thoughts. "I'll see if I can find her."

"It will be a lot easier if you just tell me what you two have been up to," Karen said.

It was half an hour since she'd hung up the phone after her conversation with Marge Larkin, and she and Julie were in the front seat of the Chrysler, on their way into town. Russell wanted to go with them, but Karen insisted on dealing with the problem herself.

Drugs.

Was it really possible that Julie had gotten herself involved in drugs again? She had been so sure they'd left that problem in L.A., and when Marge Larkin first mentioned the possibility that Jeff and Julie might have been doing drugs, Karen's immediate response was to dismiss it out of hand. This was Pleasant Valley, not Los Angeles! Where would Julie even have gotten her hands on any drugs? Yet Karen knew perfectly well that a drug problem wasn't something anyone just put aside and never thought of again.

Staying off drugs simply wasn't that easy, and if she were completely honest, she'd admit the possibility that Julie might have brought something with her.

Or that Jeff had given them to her. She'd been careful not to mention that idea to Marge Larkin, who seemed to think that if drugs were involved, it had to have been at Julie's instigation.

Julie had certainly been acting strangely the last few days, and she hadn't looked right since the bee had stung her and she'd had that terrible reaction.

But if Jeff was looking the same way Julie was, and was acting strange, too . . .

And Jeff hadn't been stung.

What was going on?

It had been her idea that they take both kids to the clinic right now and have them given drug tests. After all, the test was a simple urine analysis, no more difficult than a home pregnancy test. Marge Larkin, suddenly faced with the possibility of actually confirming what was now only a speculation, hesitated, but then agreed. So immediately after their conversation, Karen called Ellen Filmore, whose home number Russell had written on the wall by the phone. When she'd explained why she was calling, Ellen instantly turned professional.

"Does Julie have a history of drug abuse?"

"It depends on what you call abuse," Karen replied, hedging. "She's smoked a couple of joints, like most kids nowadays, but—"

"Not most kids around here," the doctor pointedly interjected. "Bring her in and we'll get to the bottom of this right now."

Julie, of course, had steadfastly refused even to admit that anything was wrong at all, despite the way she looked.

Now, as Karen suggested one last time that Julie own up to the truth, her daughter only sat impassively next to her and stared straight ahead. "I don't know why you don't believe me," she said yet again. "I'm fine."

"All you have to do is look in a mirror to know that isn't true," Karen told her as she struggled to control her anger. Did Julie think she was stupid? Or did she think she could just lie her way out of this?

Minutes later Karen pulled into the parking lot of the clinic.

Marge and Jeff Larkin had already arrived, and Karen slid the Chrysler into the slot next to Marge's Chevy. Her hand clamped firmly on Julie's elbow, she led her daughter through the door into the waiting room.

Marge and Jeff were sitting in the far corner, Jeff on the orange Naugahyde sofa, his mother on one of the matching chairs that faced it across a Formica-topped coffee table.

They were neither talking to nor looking at each other, and Marge appeared almost as pale as Jeff. Ben was perched at the other end of the sofa, nervously flipping the pages of a comic book.

"I'm sorry about all this," Marge said, getting up and moving toward Karen. "I probably had a huge overreaction."

"It's not your fault," Karen assured her. "If you're wrong, we'll both feel a lot better, and if you're right, at least we'll know. Have you seen Dr. Filmore yet?"

Marge nodded. "Just for a second. She waved to us, but I haven't really talked to her yet. I think—" She fell silent as the door to the examining room opened and the doctor came out.

If Dr. Filmore noticed the ashen complexions of the two teenagers, she gave no sign. "All right," she said. "Which of you wants to come in first? Or would you like to talk to me together?"

Julie's eyes met Jeff's, and Jeff stood up. Both Marge Larkin and Karen Owen watched carefully for any signs of nervousness in their children, but there were none. Together Jeff and Julie headed toward the inner office. When Karen and Marge started to follow, Ellen Filmore shook her head. "I don't think we have an emergency here," she said pointedly, "and if you don't mind, I'd like to talk to the kids alone." Leaving the two parents in the waiting room, she turned and followed Julie and Jeff into her office.

"I assume you both know you're here for a drug test," she said, deliberately making the statement without preamble, in an attempt to catch them off guard.

Julie nodded. "My mom thinks I'm doing them," she said.

"And you're not?" Ellen asked.

Julie shrugged. "I wouldn't even know where to get anything around here."

"What about you?" Ellen asked, turning to Jeff.

"I don't hang out with kids who do drugs," he said. "Sometimes I have a beer or two, but that's all."

Ellen Filmore watched them carefully as she continued her questions. Certainly both of them looked pale, but their eyes didn't have the dilation that was a prime indicator of drugs, and nothing in their manner made her think they were lying.

"Do either of you have a problem giving me a urine sample?" she asked. Then: "And before you answer, let me tell you that I'll have the results within thirty minutes, and there is no chance at all that the results will be wrong."

Julie looked up, and for the first time since she'd come in, smiled. "Where's the jar?" she asked, almost flippantly.

"In the bathroom."

Julie rose and started out of the examining room. "Roberto's waiting for you," the doctor went on. "He'll be right outside the door while you put the sample in the jar."

Julie shrugged and continued on her way.

"How about you?" Ellen asked Jeff. "Any problem taking the test?"

"It's fine with me," Jeff replied.

Ellen betrayed no sign of the relief she felt. Surely if

they were on drugs they wouldn't be nearly so relaxed about taking the urine test. "Okay," she said. "Roll up your sleeve. Let's take your blood pressure and see if we can find out what's wrong with you."

Slowly and methodically Ellen began her examination of Jeff Larkin.

Blood pressure and temperature.

Lung capacity and reflexes.

She looked in his eyes and ears, and down his throat.

She took samples of his blood to send to the lab in San Luis Obispo, and asked him every question she could think of. Finally she sent him in to produce a urine sample.

Then she repeated the examination process with Julie Spellman.

Forty-five minutes later she was finished.

Nothing abnormal.

Not a trace of drugs of any kind.

But Ellen Filmore still wasn't satisfied.

To her, both of them just plain looked sick.

Totally baffled by the conflict between how the kids appeared and the results of her examination, she went out to speak to Karen Owen and Marge Larkin, who were waiting anxiously in the outer lobby.

"Well, I'm pleased to be able to tell you that neither of them is on drugs," she said, and gave Karen and Marge a moment to savor their relief. "The problem," she went on, "is that I agree with you that something's not right." Out of the corner of her eye she saw the two adolescents glance at each other. "I can't find any symptoms at all," she went on. "Everything seems normal, except they don't look quite right. Their complexions are too pale." She shook her head. "If it were just Julie, I'd assume it's a lingering reaction either to the bee sting or to the antidote. But that certainly doesn't apply to Jeff. So what I want to do is send them to San Luis Obispo tomorrow." As both their children groaned that it was a waste of time and there was nothing wrong with them, Marge and Karen stiffened with apprehension. Ellen Filmore hastened to reassure the worried parents. "Believe me, I don't see this as an emergency, and if they look better tomorrow, maybe I'll change my mind. But for now, I'd just feel better if they'd go over there to the hospital and get checked out. There's a guy named Michael Callahan, and he's really good." She wrote the name on a prescription form and handed it to Karen. "Maybe he can find something I missed. But for tonight, take them home and try not to worry too much. All right?"

After the two mothers had taken their children home, Ellen Filmore went back into her office to look once more at the results of the examinations she'd just given the two teenagers.

Somehow, she'd missed something.

Something she hadn't seen, which she should have.

But what?

She didn't know.

And, worse, she didn't know how to find out.

Which meant that if there was some kind of new virus loose in Pleasant Valley, some new mutation that had infected Julie and Jeff, she didn't know how to fight it.

And that scared her.

CHAPTER 17

"*I*s it possible that Otto was right?" Karen asked.

It was past ten, and Russell, already half undressed, tossed his shirt onto the back of the chair in the den where, despite all his arguments, Karen had settled in for the night.

Though Kevin had insisted on sleeping in his own room upstairs, Molly and Julie were in sleeping bags on the living room floor, Molly making it an adventure, while Julie was playing the martyr, complaining that she didn't see how she was supposed to go to San Luis Obispo in the morning if she couldn't get any sleep tonight.

"I'm not arguing," Karen had finally told her. "I'm not even discussing it. Neither of you sleeps upstairs until those bees are gone, and that's that." Julie, sensing another grounding on the horizon, had let the matter drop, but Karen suspected she would get her revenge by letting Molly watch television as late as she wanted.

Ten minutes ago, when they finally came into the den to go to bed themselves, Russell had hoped that the discussion of the bees was concluded, at least for tonight. Apparently, though, it wasn't. "Right about what?" he asked as he opened the none-too-comfortable-looking sofa bed.

"That Carl Henderson did something to the bees that we don't know about."

Flopping down on the thin mattress and propping himself up on one elbow, Russell patted the bed in an invitation for Karen to sit down. "I'm not going to say it's impossible that he was right," he said. "I just don't believe it. At least, I don't believe that there's some great plot going on, like Dad did. So for tonight, let's just forget about everything and pretend we're not even at home." He glanced around the den. "This is kind of fun," he said, pulling her down so she was lying next to him. "We can pretend we're in someone else's house, and we're all alone, and—"

And then the door opened and Molly stood staring solemnly at them, clutching her teddy bear close to her chest.

"I hear them again," she said. "I'm scared."

Sighing, Russell rolled away from Karen and stood up, knowing instantly that any chance at romance was over for the night. "Bring her sleeping bag in here," he told Karen. "I'll go up and take a look, just to make you feel better." But even as he headed up the stairs, he was certain that Molly had heard nothing at all, but simply decided she'd rather sleep with her mother than with her sister. Nor could Russell blame her for that, given the way Julie had been acting the last couple of days.

Upstairs, just as he'd expected, nothing at all had changed.

Kevin was in his room, already asleep, and when Russell pressed his ear to the wall that contained the swarm of bees, he could barely hear them.

Less than five minutes after he'd left, he was back downstairs, and when he finally climbed into the sagging Hide-A-Bed in the den and gathered Karen into his arms, Molly was already sound asleep in her sleeping bag on the floor. "Everything's fine up there," he reported. "Whatever Molly heard, I don't think it was coming from upstairs. In fact, it might not have been anywhere but in her imagination."

Karen snuggled close, feeling the strength of his body.

"I'm sorry," she whispered. "It would have been fun, pretending we were all alone, wouldn't it?"

"Mmm-hmm," Russell murmured, already falling asleep. A minute later he began to snore softly, and finally Karen, too, rolled over and buried her head in the pillow.

She was too tired to worry anymore that night, and soon she drifted into a mercifully dreamless sleep.

It was nearly two in the morning when Julie awoke the first time.

She was feeling another one of those strange chills, but as she pulled the sleeping bag tighter around her body, she realized that she was hungry, too.

Ravenously hungry, just as she'd been yesterday morning.

She'd eaten a huge dinner—three helpings of the lasagna that her mother had pulled out of the oven when they'd finally gotten home from the doctor's, and a big salad, and then a piece of pie.

But still she was hungry.

She slid out of the sleeping bag, pulled on the robe she'd left on the couch, and went into the kitchen. Rummaging in the refrigerator, she found the last piece of leftover pie, washed it down with a glass of milk, then, her appetite still unsated, began looking for something else. Fixing a sandwich, she finally turned out the kitchen lights and started back to the living room. But when she got to the foot of the stairs, she paused and gazed up into the darkness.

From above, something seemed to be calling out, drawing her up toward the blackness on the second floor.

Nothing she could see, nothing she could hear.

But she could feel it.

A vibration, resonating deep within her.

Julie stood staring up into the darkness, feeling the beginnings of that terrible loss of control over her own mind beginning to play around the edges of her consciousness.

She didn't want to go upstairs, didn't want to respond at all to the tingling sensation that was now spreading through her body or the strange compulsion that was drawing her to the stairs.

She wanted to go back to the den, slip into her sleeping bag, and drift quickly into unconsciousness, where she would be free of the forces inside her.

But a moment later—despite her own wishes—Julie walked up the stairs, almost as if in a trance, then down the hall and into her room.

Stretching out on her own bed, she began eating the sandwich.

As she ate, the vibration in her body became stronger. And now she could hear the droning hum coming from the wall. At last, the sandwich finished, she got up and went to the wall, pressing her ear against it.

The humming in the wall resonated perfectly with the strange vibration in her own body, and she began to experience something she'd never felt before.

It was as if she was actually *feeling* the droning of the bees.

Was such a thing possible?

The vibration grew steadily stronger, and Julie's own consciousness began to drop away into some bottomless darkness.

A barely audible whimper of fear emerging from her lips, she used the last of her willpower to push herself away from the wall and stagger to her bed.

Then, as she lost control of her mind to the dark force within her, a sudden bout of feverish heat swept through her, and she stripped off her bathrobe and the nightgown beneath it.

For a little while she drifted into oblivion. . . .

* * *

Julie awoke again just before dawn, when the blackness of night was just beginning to fade into the gray of morning.

For a second she felt nothing, then slowly realized that the odd vibration she'd experienced earlier was still there.

But it was different now. Now it was coming neither from within her own body nor from the wall a few feet away.

Now it was on her skin.

She came further awake, and realized that the whole surface of her body felt charged with an electrical force.

She lay still, waiting for the sensation to disappear as she came fully awake.

It struck her that the droning hum of the bees was louder than ever.

A cool breeze was blowing.

Julie turned her head toward the window.

The sheer curtains, which should have been billowing in the breeze, were hanging slack at the sides of the open window.

Then Julie felt something else on her face, and her heart began to speed up as a memory surged up out of her subconscious.

A memory from the other night, when she dreamed she'd been outside, naked, lying in the pasture, her body covered with millions of tiny red ants.

But that had been a dream—she was certain of it!

Now, though, dawn was breaking, and she was wide-awake.

Awake, but with that same feeling of millions of tiny creatures crawling over her skin.

Suddenly an image came into her mind.

Beehives!

Beehives, on the hot afternoon when she'd first seen them.

An afternoon so hot that hundreds of bees had stationed themselves on the ledge at the entrance to the hive, their wings beating as they fanned fresh air into the colony's interior.

Fanned air, creating a breeze.

For several long minutes Julie held absolutely still. Of course she knew the idea that had come into her mind wasn't possible, but try as she would, she couldn't dismiss it.

Finally she reached out, moving her arm very slowly, and switched on the bedside lamp.

Bees were everywhere.

Hovering in the air a few inches from her face.

Crawling on the walls and across the ceiling.

Covering her skin.

A violent shudder came over her now that she could see them as well as feel them.

They were clinging to her, their wings beating so fast her eyes could see only a blur.

Yet at the same time that her terror of them began to grow once more, another part of her—that unnameable force that resided within her—responded to the breeze as it gently caressed her skin.

And the morning brightened and the gray light of dawn slowly filled her room, and the entity within expanded, sapping the last of Julie's will.

Suddenly it was as it had been yesterday, when the bees swarmed over Greta and she'd known that somehow they had come in response to her own command, in response to that burst of strange energy she'd felt in her mind.

She rose from the bed and went to look at herself in the mirror over her bureau.

Her face was an undulating mask of insects, her features totally invisible, only her eyes still exposed, peering through an ever-shifting layer of bees that seemed to be moving in a pattern, almost as if they were performing some kind of ritual dance.

Fascinated by the sight, Julie gazed into the mirror for

several long minutes. Soon she began to understand that the bees weren't individuals at all, but merely tiny parts of the swarm that together comprised a single being.

A being that was communicating with her.

The pattern of movement on Julie's face kept shifting and changing, and slowly she felt something happening within her mind.

She began to understand what the dance meant.

Turning away from the mirror, her mind now totally surrendered to the will of the swarm, she left her room.

The bees clung to her skin as she moved silently down the darkened hallway and descended the stairs.

More of them gathered as she left the house by the back door and started walking across the yard.

Soon they were streaming out of the house, erupting not only from the crack in the siding through which they'd first gained entry, but from the window of Julie's room as well. Like a long ribbon fluttering on the morning breeze, the swarm trailed after Julie.

As the morning sky slowly brightened and the first cocks began to crow, Julie Spellman started up into the low, rolling hills to the east of the farm, following a force of nature that neither she nor any other human could comprehend.

The bees moved steadily on her face, and now Julie could feel their pattern on her skin, her nerves tingling as the insects' legs stimulated them.

The nerves sent messages to her brain that something inside her understood.

And Julie walked on.

Soon the low hum that had emanated from within the walls of the house was silenced. Obeying the command of their queen, the swarm had departed.

CHAPTER 18

"*M*ommy? Mommy!"

Karen groaned, tried to pull the pillow over her head, then slowly opened her eyes. Molly's face loomed in front of her. "What, honey?" she asked. "What is it? What time is it?"

"I can't find Julie," Molly told her. "It's almost six-thirty, and we should have fed Flicka and the rest of the horses by now, but I can't *find* her!"

The last vestiges of sleep fell away from Karen. She sat up, wincing as a sharp pain shot through her back. Too old for sofa beds, she thought as she swung her legs off the thin mattress. "What do you mean, you can't find her? Where did you look?"

"In the living room," Molly replied. "Then I went down to the barn, but she isn't there, either."

"Did you ask Russell?" Karen asked. She'd awakened briefly when he'd gotten up an hour ago, then fallen instantly back to sleep, intending only to close her eyes for a few minutes.

"He's already gone," Molly told her. "He went on the tractor with Kevin."

"All right," Karen sighed. Pulling on her robe, she picked up the clothes she'd left on Russell's big leather easy chair and headed for the downstairs bathroom. "I'll be out in a minute," she told Molly. "Wait for me in the kitchen." Then, as she saw her daughter's furtive glance

249

toward the ceiling: "Don't you even think about going upstairs, understand?"

"Aw, Mom," Molly groaned, but Karen silenced her with a look.

Dressing quickly, Karen started toward the kitchen, pausing at the foot of the stairs to call up to Julie. And yet, if Julie were asleep in her room at the end of the corridor, would she even hear a voice calling from all the way downstairs?

Maybe she should go up and take a look.

But what about the bees? If they were still up there . . .

Recalling what had happened to Greta yesterday, Karen shuddered, and knew that for now she simply couldn't bring herself to go up to the second floor. Besides, she rationalized, Julie had probably gotten up early and was outside somewhere. Moving through the dining room and the kitchen, she went out on the back porch and rang the triangle to summon the rest of the family.

But ten minutes later, when everyone had assembled in the kitchen, Julie was still missing.

No one had seen her that morning.

It was Kevin who finally went upstairs to check Julie's room. When he came back, he looked puzzled. "She's not up there," he reported. "And neither are the bees."

Karen blinked. "The bees are gone?"

"Practically all of them," Kevin said. "You can't hear anything at all in the wall, and there are only a few flying around the window."

Molly, once more sitting at the table, a bowl of cereal in front of her, looked up at her stepfather. "Why would they go away all by themselves, if no one made them?"

Russell pondered Molly's question, but in the end shook his head helplessly. "I don't have any idea at all," he admitted. "As far as I know, they won't go anywhere unless a queen is with them, and queens don't usually just take off. They tend to stay put."

"Then where'd they go?" Molly demanded.

"Can't we just be happy they're gone?" Karen broke in. "What I need to know is where did *Julie* go?"

"You're sure she isn't upstairs?" Russell asked Kevin, who shook his head. "Then she must be outside somewhere," he declared.

But another idea was forming in Karen's head.

Jeff Larkin.

Jeff, who had a car, and who hadn't seemed any happier than Julie about the idea of going over to San Luis Obispo for more tests this morning. What if the two of them had just decided to do something else instead?

Picking up the phone, she dialed the number that someone—probably Kevin—had written on the wall next to Jeff's name. Her fingers drummed impatiently on the Formica countertop as the instrument at the other end rang half a dozen times before Marge Larkin's voice finally came on the line.

"Hello?"

"It's Karen Owen, Marge."

"Karen! Hi," Marge began, but a split second later, as the worry in Karen's voice sank in, Marge's voice turned guarded. "Has . . . something happened?"

"I'm not sure," Karen said, attempting to keep her escalating fear under control. "I—Well, I was wondering if you've seen Julie this morning."

"Julie?" Marge echoed. "I've hardly even seen *myself* yet! What time is it?"

"Six forty-five," Karen replied. "Julie doesn't seem to be around, and I wondered if she might have gone over there."

"If she's here, she's invisible," Marge replied.

Karen hesitated, then went on. "Marge, is *Jeff* there?"

There was a moment of hollow silence at the other end of the line, then Marge spoke again. "You really know how to set up a mother's day, don't you, Karen? Hang on."

There was another silence, longer this time, and then Marge Larkin was back. "He's here, all right. In bed, but no longer sound asleep." She hesitated a moment, then, as if she could read Karen's mind: "Karen? Maybe Julie's just hiding out somewhere. I mean, Jeff's not looking much different than he did last night, and if Julie wasn't, either, maybe she just got scared of going to the doctor."

"Maybe," Karen said doubtfully, but willing to grasp at any straw right now.

"Well, try not to worry too much," Marge told her. "She could have just gone for a walk. And there's plenty of time before they should be leaving to go over to Obispo."

As Karen hung up the phone, she wasn't quite sure what to think. And yet, if Julie was still sick, maybe she was around somewhere. Maybe she'd become disoriented, or . . . or what?

She didn't know.

But at least if she was sick, she might not have run away! She turned to face the rest of the family. "I think we better start looking for her," she said. "Marge says Jeff's not any better than he was last night, which means Julie could be anywhere around here, and maybe so sick she couldn't even call to us if she needs help."

Breakfast forgotten, the family set out in search of Julie, Russell heading north, then planning to circle around toward the east forty and the area around the beehives.

Karen, taking Molly with her, would check the barn one more time, then go down toward the stand of oaks by the creek and start working her way upstream, searching the thickets as she went.

"What about me?" Kevin asked as the rest of them set out.

"Stay here," Russell told him. "Someone should be here in case she comes back." He nodded toward the triangle. "If she shows up, ring it. We'll all hear you."

Then they were gone.

* * *

Jeff Larkin felt terrible.

His whole body itched, but it was like no itch he'd ever felt before. No amount of scratching seemed to relieve it, for somehow it actually seemed to come from *beneath* his skin, as if millions of tiny ants were creeping about deep inside him, irritating every cell of his body.

He hadn't actually been asleep when his mother had come in, but he'd decided to pretend that he was, so she wouldn't start right off asking him a bunch of questions he wasn't ready to answer. When he finally heard her talking in the kitchen again, he got out of bed and went into the bathroom, where he stared at himself in the mirror.

His face was just as pale as it had been yesterday, and his eyes looked kind of funny, although he couldn't quite see how they looked different than they had before.

And he was hungry this morning, which was really strange, since he never wanted anything except coffee before lunch, except maybe a doughnut if one was handy.

He got into the shower and turned the water on cold, which eased the itching, at least a little bit. He dried himself off, then went back to the room he shared with Ben—who was nowhere to be seen—and dressed, pulling on a pair of old gym shorts and a tank top. After running a brush through his still-damp mop of blond hair, he went out to the kitchen, where his mother was just setting a stack of pancakes in front of Ben.

"Can I have some of those?"

Marge's brows rose in surprise. "You? Since when do you eat breakfast?"

"Since this morning, I guess," Jeff said, pouring himself a cup of coffee from the chipped enamel pot on the stove. He dropped down onto the chair opposite Ben, self-consciously avoiding his mother's critical gaze.

"You don't look any better than last night," Marge pronounced. "So I guess I'll have to pay for Ben to go to day care today."

"I'm fine," Jeff insisted. "I'll take care of him."

"You're going over to San Luis Obispo," Marge reminded him. Then: "If they find Julie, anyway."

Jeff looked up. "Julie?" he said. "What do you mean, if they find her?"

Marge shrugged, then began spooning batter onto the hot griddle. As the pancakes cooked, she told Jeff about the call from Karen. "She *wasn't* here, was she?" she asked, her eyes narrowing in sudden suspicion. Had Jeff smuggled the girl into his room last night?

Jeff groaned. "No, she wasn't here. Why would she be here this early?"

Marge didn't even bother to respond to the question, but glanced at the clock as she transferred the pancakes to a plate and set them down in front of Jeff. "I've gotta go," she announced. "And remember, if Julie shows up in the next hour or so, you two both go see Dr. Filmore. If she says you go to San Luis Obispo, you go. And you don't stir from here for any other reason. Understand?"

"Will you just leave me alone?" Jeff flared, jerking away from her touch. "What is the big deal? I'm eating breakfast, and I feel fine. Just go to work, okay?"

"Don't you speak to me that way, young man," Marge snapped.

"Well, don't act like I'm dying, then, okay?" Jeff shot back.

"I'm just worried about you—" Marge began, but Jeff didn't let her finish.

"Who *asked* you to worry about me?" he yelled. "Will you just get out of here and leave me alone?"

As Ben burst into tears and fled out the back door, Marge glared furiously at her older son. "Now look what you've done," she said. "What is it with you? Sometimes you act just like your father!"

"And maybe he was the smart one!" Jeff shouted. "Maybe he just got tired of you nagging at him all the time!"

His words stinging more than a slap would have, Marge felt her eyes fill with tears. Snatching her purse up from the counter, she hurried out the back door.

A moment later Jeff heard the engine of her car roar and the wheels spin as she jammed it into gear. Wishing he could take back the last words he'd uttered, he stood up from the table, knocking the chair over in his hurry, and went to the back door.

Too late.

His mother's car was already disappearing down the driveway, lost in a cloud of dust.

"Shit," Jeff said softly to himself. Going back to the table, he righted the chair, settled onto it once again, and began shoving the pancakes into his mouth. When the back door opened a moment or two later, he barely even heard it, but he did hear the words Vic Costas was speaking.

"I'll take the keys to the station wagon," the farmer said in a voice whose quietness bespoke his authority.

Jeff looked up at him in surprise.

"I heard you talking to your mother," Costas told him. "Your mother's a good woman, and she works hard to take care of you. That's the thanks you give her? Talking to her that way?" He shook his head. "Not on my farm. And boys like you don't use my car, either." He held his hand out.

Jeff hesitated, and for just a moment wondered what would happen if he refused. But as big as he was, Vic Costas was two inches taller, with wide shoulders and the muscles of a man who had been working the land all his life. As the farmer's eyes, so dark they looked black, fixed on him, Jeff reached into his pocket, pulled out the keys to the rusting Mercury, and handed them over.

"You apologize to your mother," Costas told him. "And

you think about how you treat her." Without another word, he turned and left the house.

Left alone again, Jeff finished the stack of pancakes, then made another. Drenching them with Karo syrup, he wolfed them down, then poured a bowl of cereal, and ate that, too.

Before he was finally finished, he'd scrambled half a dozen eggs and drunk half the can of pineapple juice his mother had opened for Ben that morning.

And now something else was happening to him.

He was starting to feel restless.

He began pacing through the house, then went out into the yard.

It seemed hot—way too hot even for the end of June.

He moved over into the shade of one of the olive trees Mr. Costas had planted years ago when he'd decided to experiment with producing domestic olive oil, and dropped down to the ground, leaning his back against the tree's trunk.

A hornet settled on his leg.

Jeff stared at it, instantly remembering the horse he'd watched die in the Owens' corral yesterday.

A cold shiver of fear made his spine tingle, and he moved his right hand slowly toward the hornet, preparing to brush it away in a motion so quick the insect would have no time to plunge its stinger through his skin.

His hand hovered in midair, but when he tried to flick the hornet away, his arm refused to respond to the order of his brain.

His hand remained where it was.

A second hornet settled on his leg, and then a third.

Jeff felt a lump of fear growing in his throat, and once more tried to flick the insects away, but once again found himself unable to make his hand obey.

The hornets began to move on his skin.

To move in a pattern that captured his attention.

The focus of his eyes began to narrow, until it felt as though he were looking through a long tube, and all he could see was the hornets.

They kept moving on his skin, repeating the same pattern over and over.

Then an image came into his mind.

Julie!

He saw a vision of Julie perfectly clearly.

Julie was smiling at him, and beckoning to him.

It was almost like a dream, except that Jeff knew he was wide-awake.

As the hornets rose from his leg and flew off, quickly disappearing into the distance, Jeff Larkin stood and began walking.

Moving quickly with long, steady strides, he set off across the field, heading northeast toward the Owen farm.

To the hills beyond the farm.

The hills, and Julie.

Kevin stepped out onto the porch, waving and yelling at Jeff Larkin, but the other boy didn't seem either to see or hear him. But that was nuts! Jeff wasn't more than fifty yards from the house, walking along the dirt road he and Julie had used when they'd come home the other night. "Jeff?" He yelled again. "Hey, Jeff!"

When Jeff still failed to respond, Kevin finally left the porch, jogging across the yard, yelling his name yet again. But only when Kevin was within a few feet of him did Jeff finally turn to face his friend.

Kevin stopped short.

Jeff's face had that same pallor that Julie's had the other day, and though he seemed to be looking right at Kevin, Kevin had the eerie feeling that Jeff didn't quite see him.

"What the hell's going on, man?" Kevin demanded. "I've been yelling at you for ages."

Jeff's brows came together in a puzzled frown and he

shook his head. "I guess I wasn't listening." Suddenly his eyes seemed to focus on Kevin, and he grinned. "Or maybe I'm getting deaf."

"Well, you want to tell me what's going on?" Kevin demanded. "Where are you going?"

"To Julie," Jeff replied.

Kevin blinked. To Julie? What the hell was he talking about? "You mean you know where she is?" he asked.

Jeff nodded.

Kevin glanced around, but no one else was anywhere to be seen. "Well, where is she?" he asked.

Jeff hesitated, then tipped his head toward the hills to the west. "Up there." He fell silent for a second, then: "Want to come with me?"

Kevin hesitated. His father had been clear that he should stay home, in case Julie came back. But if she wasn't coming back, if she was up in the hills . . .

But how could Jeff know where she was?

Unless they'd planned it. "Are you supposed to meet her up there?" he asked. "I mean, did she call you or something?"

Jeff shook his head. "I just know that's where she is, that's all. I'll show you."

Still Kevin hesitated. Jeff looked strange, but he looked more sick than spaced out.

"Why don't you come back to the house, and I'll find my dad," Kevin suggested, but even before he finished the sentence, Jeff shook his head.

"I can't. Julie wants me."

What was he talking about? Julie *wanted* him? He glanced around again, hoping he might catch a glimpse of his father, or maybe Karen.

But from what he could see, he and Jeff might as well have been alone on the farm, and now Jeff was walking away, starting up a trail toward the hills behind the farm.

Still, Kevin hesitated. But what if Jeff really did know

where Julie was? What if Julie was sick or something and needed help?

The way Jeff looked, Kevin wasn't sure he'd even be able to make it up into the hills, much less help Julie.

Making up his mind, Kevin cast one last look back at the farm, then followed Jeff, breaking into a trot to catch up with him.

The land rose steadily, and the trail kept branching, but at each fork Jeff seemed to know exactly which way to turn. Though the grade grew steeper, Jeff's stride never broke, and twice Kevin, who knew he was in better shape than Jeff, had to stop to catch his breath, then run to catch up with his friend.

Almost half an hour had passed when Jeff abruptly stopped.

Kevin nearly ran into him before he realized Jeff was no longer moving, and when he looked around, he saw no sign of Julie.

They were on the flank of a boulder-strewn hillside that looked no different from any of the other hills they'd hiked across. Below them was a small valley, covering no more than a few acres, which a stream ran through.

The same stream that came out at the farm? Kevin wasn't sure. Indeed, he'd been so intent on simply following Jeff that he really hadn't paid much attention to where they were going.

He scanned the valley but still saw no sign of his stepsister. "So where's Julie?" he asked.

Jeff pointed downward, across the valley. "Over there."

Kevin searched the hill opposite, then saw it.

Low down, just above the valley floor, there seemed to be a cave. "You mean she's in there?" he asked.

Jeff nodded and started down the hillside. Kevin went after him, skidding and sliding as he tried to hold his footing. Finally they came to the bottom of the valley and headed toward the cave, stepping easily across the narrow ribbon of water that was the creek. At the mouth of the cave, Kevin paused.

It didn't look too big—the entrance appeared to be no more than ten or fifteen feet high, and maybe twelve wide.

But how deep was it?

From here, with the sun shining in his eyes, all Kevin could see was a black hole.

"Julie's really in there?" he asked, his voice reflecting his doubt. How the hell would she even have found this place, especially in the middle of the night?

Jeff nodded.

"Prove it," Kevin challenged.

"She's there," Jeff insisted. "Come on."

Jeff started up the slope toward the cave, and Kevin went after him, but when Jeff walked straight into the blackness that was the entrance to the cave without even pausing, Kevin hesitated.

What the hell was going on? What were Jeff and Julie up to? Was this some kind of elaborate trick they were pulling on him?

He stood at the entrance, staring into the darkness inside.

Slowly, with the sun no longer shining in his eyes, he grew used to the gloom.

Then he saw Julie.

For a moment he froze, staring at his stepsister.

She was crouched down at the side of the cave, only a few feet from the entrance.

She was naked.

And she was staring at him.

But what made Kevin's groin tingle and his stomach contract in sudden terror was the sight of what surrounded Julie.

Insects.

Thousands of them.

Crawling on the walls.

Hovering in the air.

Not just bees.

Gnats, hornets, even wasps.

Creeping over Julie's naked skin.

He gazed at them, mesmerized, his heart pounding.

Then Julie raised her arm and beckoned to him.

"Come in," he heard her say. "Come inside."

A strangled whimper of pure fear rising in his throat, Kevin lurched backward, then turned to run away from the horrifying sight.

And found Jeff Larkin standing in front of him, his tall frame towering above him.

The two boys gazed at each other, and Kevin's barely controlled terror began to shatter into panic as he saw the look in his friend's eyes. His heart pounding, he tried to step around Jeff, but Jeff's arms snaked out and grasped his own in a far stronger grip than he'd ever remembered his friend possessing.

"H-Hey, man, what's going on?" Kevin managed to ask, his voice trembling.

But Jeff made no answer. Instead he bent forward and his lips curled into a twisted smile.

A smile that filled Kevin's soul with numbing terror.

As a scream rose in his throat and he opened his mouth to release it, Jeff's smile broadened and his twisted lips parted.

The scream died in Kevin's throat as the dark cloud that streamed forth from Jeff's mouth engulfed him.

His skin stung; his mouth felt as if it was on fire.

His throat and lungs burned.

And then the nausea struck.

Clutching his belly, Kevin sank to the floor of the cave.

CHAPTER 19

"Something really bad's happened to Julie, hasn't it, Mommy?"

Molly's voice quavered as she spoke, and Karen wished she knew how to answer the little girl.

How long had it been since she and Molly had set out from the house? Thirty minutes? An hour? She had no way of knowing, for in her anxiety to find Julie, she'd forgotten to put on her watch.

Over and over she'd told herself there was nothing to worry about, that Julie had simply gotten up early and taken off for a hike somewhere.

But even as she'd tried to cling to the thought, tried to tell herself that any second Julie would answer their calls or they'd catch sight of her—maybe just around the next bend in the winding stream—an image of her older daughter had risen in her mind.

An image that mocked her hopes.

Before her floated Julie's face as she'd seen it last night—the color washed from her skin, her eyes strangely flat and expressionless.

No matter what Julie—or Ellen Filmore—said, Karen had seen that something was clearly wrong with the girl.

Now, in the bright morning sunlight, she chastised herself for not keeping a more careful eye on Julie last night.

What if she'd awakened in the night, delirious?

262

She could have wandered away from the house, become lost in the darkness.

No! That was ridiculous—if she'd been that sick, she would have been too weak to go very far, and they'd have found her by now. Then where was she?

Runaway? The word echoed in her mind, and she thought of all the girls she'd seen on the streets of L.A., their faces haggard, their eyes older than their years, supporting themselves and their drug habits by selling their bodies.

No, not Julie! she told herself. She's out here somewhere, and we'll find her. But even as she repeated the words to herself one more time, a great wave of hopelessness washed over her and she sank down onto a large, flat rock that edged the pool into which a stream was tumbling from a narrow gorge above.

On any other morning Karen would have found the spot beautiful, but today she barely noticed it.

Now, though, Molly was gazing up at the cleft from which the stream emerged.

"What if she's up there?" the little girl asked.

"I don't see how she could be, sweetheart," Karen said. "It's so narrow, I don't think I could even get into it, and I'm not sure how she'd have climbed up, even if it was wide enough."

"Over there," Molly promptly replied, pointing to the other side of the pool. "See? It's almost like there's steps in the rocks." Kicking off her shoes, then dropping her socks on top of them, Molly waded into the water. "Look!" she cried. "It's not deep at all. I can wade right across!"

As the little girl waded farther into the pool, Karen scrambled back to her feet. "Honey, be careful," she fretted. Then she gasped as Molly slipped, lost her footing and flopped into the water.

"Molly!" Karen shrieked, instantly wading in after her daughter and plucking the little girl out of the chilly water.

"I just slipped," Molly complained, struggling to free herself from her mother's clutching hands. "The rocks are just real slickery!"

"Which means you're staying out of the water," Karen declared. "The last thing I need right now is for you to hurt yourself!"

"But Mom," Molly protested as Karen carried her back to the shore, "what if Julie's really up there?"

Karen looked once more at the cleft fifteen feet above the pool and shook her head. "She's not," she replied. "She couldn't possibly be." After pulling her soggy shoes off, Karen stripped her socks from her feet and wrung them out. "Let's just go back to the house, where at least we can put on dry clothes. And maybe Julie will be back. Okay?"

Five minutes later, abandoning the meandering streambed in favor of cutting through the trees, they emerged from the grove of oaks. Half a mile away they could see the house. They started across the field toward it, Molly dashing ahead of Karen, Julie forgotten for a moment as she chased a monarch butterfly as it flitted from blossom to blossom.

And for a moment, as Karen watched her younger daughter pursue the fluttering creature, her own worry about Julie eased. But as they drew closer to the house, she began to feel a new sense of trepidation.

She paused, gazing at the house, now only a hundred or so yards away.

Where was Kevin?

Surely he would have seen them coming across the field and come out to meet them?

Unless someone else had already come back to the house.

Hope surged in her heart. That must be it! Julie must have come home!

"Molly!" she called, breaking into a run. "Molly, come on!"

Molly streaked off toward the house, and Karen chased after her, her lungs quickly beginning to protest against the unusual strain. When she finally came to the front porch, Molly still ahead of her, she paused to catch her breath.

She pushed the front door open, about to call out to Julie. But her daughter's name died on her lips as soon as she stepped into the house and felt its emptiness.

Without even exploring it, Karen knew that not only had Julie not come home, but now Kevin was no longer there, either.

She moved inside, uncertain what to do. Finally, more for the sake of doing something—anything—she called out Kevin's name.

No reply.

"Mom?" Molly said. "Where's Kevin?"

"I-I'm not sure," Karen replied. "Maybe he went out looking for Julie."

Molly's brows knit into a deep frown. "But he was supposed to wait for her," Molly began. "He was supposed to—"

"I know what he was supposed to do!" Karen cut in, her mind spinning. Where would Kevin have gone? Surely he wouldn't have just taken off by himself?

A note!

If he'd gone somewhere, he would have left a note stuck to the metal door of the refrigerator with a magnet.

Relief flooding through her, Karen strode to the kitchen.

No note.

She went to the back door, her eyes darting around, searching for any sign of Kevin, but the yard was as empty on this side of the house as it had been in front. She was about to go back inside when her glance fell on the triangle. Seizing the rod that hung next to it, she banged on the metal as hard as she could, shattering the quiet of the morning with a dissonant clangor. She paused for a moment, then struck the bell again. Finally, in the far distance across the road, she saw a figure moving toward the house.

Five minutes later, panting from the run, Russell arrived on the back porch. "Where is she?" he gasped. "Is she all right?"

Karen gazed at him bleakly. "She's not back," she said.

"But the bell—" Russell began.

"It's Kevin," Karen interrupted. "Now he's gone, too."

"We have to call the police." Karen was sitting at the kitchen table, struggling not to lose her composure.

Russell, still trying to digest the news that Kevin was also missing, shook his head numbly.

"Why not?" Karen demanded. "They can put together a search party or—or something!" Didn't Russell care that both their children were missing? "We can't just—"

"They won't start a search party until the kids have been gone at least overnight," Russell interrupted, his voice bleak. He could imagine what Mark Shannon would say if he called the deputy so soon after the kids had left: " 'Kids take off all the time, Russell. Chances are they'll be back before the day is over, but even if they aren't, my hands are tied until tomorrow, at least. Department policy, no exceptions. Otherwise we'd all be out chasing kids twenty-four hours a day.' " But Karen was right—they had to do something, or they'd both go crazy. "Maybe I could take Bailey out—"

"Bailey!" Karen exclaimed, nervously getting up from the table to go stare out the window. "Bailey can barely find his own shadow!" Her words died away as she saw something moving in the distance, far up in the foothills.

"Karen?" Russell asked. "What is it?"

But Karen was already through the back door and moving out into the yard. Russell went after her, and in a moment saw the figure, too.

"Who is it?" he asked. "Can you see?"

Karen shook her head, then called out. "Julie? Kevin?"

Russell dashed into the house, reappearing a moment later with a battered pair of binoculars. He held them to his eyes, worked his thumb at the knob between the two lenses, then handed them to Karen. "I think it's Kevin," he said. "But I can't quite—"

Karen tried to quell the surge of disappointment that went through her. At least *one* of the kids was back, and maybe—just maybe—he'd found some trace of Julie. Maybe she was hurt and Kevin had come back to get help! Once again hope rose in her, and she ran forward, Molly chasing after her.

"Kevin?" she called again. "Kevin!"

She stopped abruptly.

Why didn't he answer her?

Surely Kevin could hear her—he wasn't more than a couple hundred yards away.

Then she knew! Julie!

Kevin had found Julie, but she was—

She banished the thought from her mind the instant it formed.

If Kevin had found Julie—even if she was only hurt—he wouldn't be walking along the trail as if he hadn't a care in the world.

He would be running, coming to get help.

She began running toward him, but long before she got to Kevin, Molly was already there, throwing her arms around her stepbrother, tugging at his arms.

Karen paused again, watching, barely conscious that Russell was now beside her, his arm around her, watching his son with the same strange misgivings that Karen was feeling.

Kevin knelt down, hugged Molly, and said something to her.

Then, holding Molly's hand in his own, he once more started toward the house.

Now Russell, his arm dropping away from Karen's waist, strode toward his son, the worry he'd felt only a minute ago giving way to anger that Kevin had taken off against his orders, and hadn't even left a note.

"All right, young man," he said as he approached Kevin and Molly. "I hope you have a good explanation for this one, because if you don't . . ." His furious words died away when Kevin finally looked up and Russell saw the look on his face.

His son's face was ashen, and his eyes had a strange look to them, almost as if he were in shock. Then, from beside him, Russell heard his wife's voice.

"Kevin?" Karen asked. "Kevin, what is it? Are you all right?"

Kevin hesitated, almost as if he hadn't heard the words, but then nodded. "I—"

But the words he'd intended to say refused to come out of his mouth.

What was happening to him?

He wasn't sure how long he'd been walking back down to the house, moving steadily along the trail, not really watching where he was going, but retracing the route he and Jeff had been using. All he knew was that at each branch in the trail, every fork, he'd known which way to go. In fact, as he thought about it now, Kevin realized he had no memory at all of any of those forks in the trail.

For as he'd walked, his whole mind had been consumed with trying to make sense of what he'd seen in the cave, trying to figure out how to tell his stepmother what he'd seen.

But now that he was home, and Karen was looking anxiously at him, waiting for him to say something about Julie, the words wouldn't come.

"I—I went looking for Julie," he said, thoughts and words suddenly coming unbidden into his mind. He gestured vaguely back the way he'd come. "J-Jeff came over, and we went up into the hills."

Karen's breath caught in her throat.

They'd found Julie.

They'd found her, and something terrible had happened to her.

She could tell by the tone of Kevin's voice.

Jeff was still up there, staying with Julie, and Kevin had come back to get help. "Where?" she finally managed to ask. "Where is she?"

Kevin only looked at her as he struggled against the irresistible urge to speak the lies that suddenly seemed to flow so easily out of his mind and off his tongue. What was happening to him? Was he going crazy? What had Jeff done to him up there?

"You found her, didn't you?" Karen pressed. Her voice rose, tinged with panic. "Didn't you find Julie?"

The image of his stepsister clear in his mind, Kevin opened his mouth to speak once again, determined that this time he would tell Karen the truth.

But again the power within him overcame his own will. "No," he heard himself say. "We looked, but we didn't find her."

Wanting to scream—not merely from frustration, but from the sheer terror of what had happened to him—Kevin struggled against the new will that had invaded his mind and body.

Struggled to scream, to speak—anything!

Struggled, and failed.

CHAPTER 20

"*I*'m telling you for the last time," Marian Bennett said, exasperation etched in her voice. "I'm already late for my hair appointment, and if Jolene gives my time to somebody else, you're going to be a very sorry young man!"

"So go get your hair done," Andy replied, barely even looking up from the copy of *Field & Stream* his father had left on the kitchen table that morning. "I already told you I don't need to go to the doctor."

Marian's level of exasperation escalated another notch, and she knew she was on the verge of getting really angry, which she hated to do. She had read an article in one of the tabloids last year—or maybe the year before—that said anger was very hard on the skin, and ever since then she'd been determined she would not let her temper age her prematurely. She simply wouldn't do it! But sometimes—and this was one of those times—Andy's attitude just annoyed her beyond human endurance! She could see that something was wrong with him—anybody could! But he just kept insisting that he was fine.

Just fine!

Well, she knew better, and whether he liked it or not, he was going to the doctor! Marian's lips pursed tightly for a moment before she remembered the tiny crease lines that were beginning to form around her mouth. "Do you want me to call your father? Is that what you want?"

His eyes still on the magazine, Andy tried to figure out

270

what to do. The truth was, he didn't feel well at all, despite what he kept telling his mother. And he didn't dislike Dr. Filmore—in fact, for someone who was always telling you about how bad for you all your favorite foods were, she was pretty nice. At least she didn't really expect you to quit eating hamburgers and french fries at the A&W every afternoon. So why was he refusing to go see her?

It had started yesterday, right after she'd given him that shot for the bee sting, and he felt like he was going to die for the first few minutes, even though he kept insisting he was fine. But then he started feeling better, and figured that by this morning he really *would* be fine.

But this morning he still felt itchy—like there were some kind of fleas or something that had actually gotten *under* his skin—and he was really hungry, too.

He'd already eaten three bowls of Fruit Loops, and a fourth one was sitting in front of him right now. Which was weird, because all he ever ate for breakfast was a piece of toast. In fact, he hated cereal.

Then why was he eating it?

And why had he kept telling his mother how great he felt, when it was a big lie? But every time he opened his mouth to tell her how he really felt, he just kept saying the same dumb words over and over again: "I'm fine! I'm fine!"

But he wasn't fine at all, and even though he wasn't about to tell his mom—or anyone else—he was starting to get scared. What if he really was sick? Even worse, what if he was cracking up?

Just the thought of that possibility sent a chill through his body, a chill, to his relief, that his mother didn't miss.

"That's it," Marian said, her eyes narrowing and her brows plunging into exactly the kind of deep frown she had carefully avoided since the morning last year when she'd discovered two vertical wrinkles starting to form just above her nose. Now, just to be on the safe side, she slept with heavy tape on her forehead, and a string running around the back of her head as a safety precaution against frowning in her sleep. Chuck might laugh at her—in fact he often did—but he'd appreciate it in a few more years when the other women in town started to show their years. Now, in the face of Andy's sudden shudder and the feverish look he'd had in his eyes all morning, the last of her beauty concerns was finally driven from her mind. Picking up her purse in one hand, she grabbed Andy's arm with the other and almost violently pulled him up to his feet. "Come on," she snapped. "No more arguing!" Her perfectly manicured nails digging into the flesh of Andy's arm like the talons of an eagle, she marched him out of the kitchen, through the service porch, and into the garage. As she pressed the button that would raise the garage door, she nudged her son—who was almost a foot taller and a hundred pounds heavier than she—toward the LeBaron convertible that Chuck had bought her for her fortieth birthday last year. "Get in."

"Let's put the top down," Andy suggested as she backed the car out into the brilliant morning sunshine.

Marian shot him an exasperated glance—aside from the fact that he was obviously sick, surely even *Andy* knew how bad the sun was for her skin!—and pulled the car into the street.

They drove in silence until Marian started out of town on Main Street and came to the foot of the park, where the enormous stanchions supporting the power lines marched down the hillside to run parallel to the road for the next ten miles. As always, Marian smiled at the sight of them. "I know everyone thinks they're a terrible eyesore," she said, parroting once more the identical words she spoke every time she drove this direction, "but I just love them. They remind me of . . ." She paused, waiting for Andy to finish the sentence she'd said so often it had become a family joke, but instead of groaning the words "marching giants," he said nothing at all. She glanced over at him, and seeing the strange expression on his face, her right foot left the accelerator and hovered over the brake. "Andy? Andy! What's wrong?"

Andy could barely hear his mother's voice, for as they'd come to the power lines, he'd begun hearing a strange humming noise.

A humming noise that affected him the same way as fingernails scratching across a blackboard, setting his teeth on edge and sending shivers down his spine. Except that this was even worse.

He hadn't any idea where the horrible noise was coming from, but it was almost like a dentist's drill screaming in his head. His hands went up to cover his ears and press against his temples, but it didn't seem to help at all.

Now he was starting to get sick to his stomach.

"Andy? Andy!"

He heard his mother's voice, coming as if from a great distance, and slowly Andy turned to look at her.

But the humming was getting even worse, making it feel like his whole body was buzzing with electricity, and he could hardly see his mother through a strange fog of black specks that clouded his vision.

Marian's eyes widened as she stared at her son.

His face had gone pasty white, and a sheen of sweat was standing out on his forehead.

His hands were clamped over his ears so tightly that his knuckles had gone white, and his whole body seemed to be trembling.

And though his eyes were fixed on her, she had the strangest feeling that he wasn't seeing her at all. She pressed hard on the brake, and the tires screeched as they lost traction on the pavement. The car fishtailed for a second, then came to a stop, its right-side tires kicking up a cloud of dust as they left the pavement. "Andy, what's wrong?" Marian demanded. "I swear to God, if you throw up in my car—"

But Andy had jerked the seat belt loose and was shoving the door open before the LeBaron even came to a complete stop. He scrambled out, then stood next to the car, his hands still clamped over his ears.

But the sound boring into his brain was even worse outside the car, building to a terrifying cacophony that made him feel as if his head might explode at any second.

"Andy?" Marian cried again as she jerked her own door open and got out. Leaving the door standing wide open, she rushed around the front of the car to her son. "Andy, what is it?" she pleaded, reaching out to him. "For God's sake, what's wrong with you?"

Andy twisted away from his mother, staggered a couple of steps, then turned and ran, dashing around the back of the car and across the road. Marian started to follow him, then stopped short as an air horn blasted a warning. Turning, she saw a semi rolling toward her and instinctively stepped back off the pavement. Then, as she looked to see where Andy was, the horn blared again, and this time she saw the driver frantically waving and pointing.

Too late, she saw both the oncoming car, and the open door of the LeBaron. Her hands flying up to cover her mouth as she realized what was about to happen, she took another step backward, then turned away, dropping into a protective crouch, her hands and arms covering her head.

Time seemed to stand still as she listened to the hiss of the truck's air brakes and waited for the impact when the semi struck her car.

When it finally came, the crash was much softer than she'd expected it to be.

Her heart pounding, Marian looked up, and for a moment thought nothing had happened at all. Then, as she rose to her feet and saw the truck slowing to a stop fifty yards farther down the road, she also saw what it had hit.

The driver's door to her beautiful convertible—her fortieth birthday present—was leaning against the fence across the road, so battered that she was only able to recognize it by its color.

And Andy, halfway across the field on the other side of the fence, was still running, oblivious to what had happened.

Karen paced restlessly from the kitchen into the living room then back again, her eyes automatically going to the clock, as they seemed to be doing at least every two or three minutes. Finally she went out the back door, circled the house as she had done half a dozen times in the last hour, then went back in.

As usual, all she'd seen were Russell and Kevin, working down by the barn as if nothing had happened.

How could they?

Didn't they care that Julie was missing?

An hour ago, when Russell told her he couldn't go on searching until he'd at least fed and watered the animals, she'd barely been able to believe what he was saying.

She'd had to struggle to keep from screaming at him in her fear and frustration, but in the end, when he explained that no matter what had happened, the animals still needed to be fed and watered, she reluctantly agreed.

Now, though, it was starting to look as if he had no intention of going on with the search.

The hell with him!

Maybe Julie was right after all! Maybe marrying him and moving back to Pleasant Valley *had* been the stupidest thing she'd ever done.

Well, when Julie came back, she knew exactly how to fix it. She would simply pack Julie and Molly up in her car, and the three of them would drive back to L.A. If she groveled enough, the law firm where she'd worked would take her back, and maybe they'd even handle her divorce at a rate she could afford!

But in the meantime, she had to do something— something constructive—or she'd go crazy.

The police!

Of course! Why hadn't she thought of it before? It was one thing for them to tell Russell on the telephone that they couldn't do anything until Julie had been gone for twenty-four hours, but if she was actually there, standing in front of them—

"Molly!" she called, galvanized by the thought that there was, after all, some positive action she could take. "Molly, come on!" She was already searching through her purse for her car keys when Molly came into the room, looking at her questioningly. "We're going into town, sweetheart," Karen told her. "We're going to make the police start looking for your sister."

"But Russell said—" Molly began.

"I don't care what Russell said," Karen snapped, instantly regretting both her tone and her words when she saw the devastated look on her younger daughter's face. Quickly, she knelt down and pulled the little girl close. "I'm sorry, darling," she whispered. "I guess I'm just upset, and I want to do something to find Julie. So you and I are going to go into town ourselves, and explain to the police that Julie isn't the kind of girl who would have run away. Okay?"

Molly, sniffling and wiping at her damp eyes with the sleeve of her shirt, nodded, and a moment later the two of them were in the front seat of the worn Chevy that had barely gotten them to Pleasant Valley in the first place.

"How come we're going in Kevin's car?" Molly asked.

For a moment Karen didn't have the slightest idea what Molly was talking about, and then it suddenly came back to her.

My God, she thought, I don't even have a car of my

own anymore. But even as the thought came into her mind, she decided she didn't care who the car technically belonged to. Julie was *her* daughter, and this had always been *her* car, and if she had to take care of herself and her daughters with no help from Russell, she would damned well use her car to do it!

Not bothering to answer her daughter's question, she started the car and headed down the driveway, ignoring Russell's shout as she passed the barn.

She also ignored the big semi parked on the edge of the road between the clinic and the village, along with the doorless convertible behind it, and the angry-looking woman who was standing by the damaged car, yelling at the truck driver.

Three minutes later she pulled up in front of the city hall across the street from the old Carnegie Library. Not bothering to lock the car, she took Molly by the hand and strode around the corner to the side entrance, where the tiny office that housed the local deputies was located.

Mark Shannon was sitting behind his desk, his feet up while he leafed through a catalog of various guns, holsters, belts, nightsticks, and other paraphernalia relating to his job. Looking up and seeing Karen, he guiltily dropped his feet to the floor and shoved the catalog into the bottom drawer of his desk. "Mrs. Owen," he began, automatically offering her a smile that faded as he saw the look on her face. Already certain he knew why she was there, he rummaged through the pads of forms on his desk, finally finding the one he was looking for. "I guess you want to fill one of these out," he said, offering her the missing person forms. "If you have any questions—"

Karen's jaw set. "I'm sure I don't have any questions that are on that form," she said. "You already know what Julie looks like—you met her when Otto died." She rummaged in her purse, found her wallet, and pulled out a picture of Julie that was less than a year old. She laid the picture in front of Shannon. "My daughter is not a runaway," she said. "Nor does she have a drug problem. If you don't believe me, you can call Ellen Filmore, who, as it happens, tested her for drugs just last night." As Shannon started to say something, Karen cut him off. "It wasn't just Julie she tested. It was Jeff Larkin, too. Both of them were looking ill, and Marge and I took both of them to the clinic." Briefly she told him what had happened and what Ellen Filmore had wanted the kids to do this morning. "But Julie was gone this morning," she finished.

She was about to tell him about Kevin going up into the hills with Jeff Larkin when the door opened and Marge Larkin walked in, her face pale. "Mark, something's happened. Jeff was supposed to go to the doctor in San Luis . . ." As Karen turned around and Marge recognized her, her words faded away. Then: "What is it? Have you found Julie? Is she—"

Karen shook her head. "It's like she's vanished off the face of the earth." Now she repeated to both Marge Larkin and Mark Shannon what had happened when Kevin walked out of the foothills. "I keep having this awful feeling that Jeff found Julie, but that something happened. Either to her, or to both of them, or—" The terrible strain of the morning closed in on her, and she burst into tears, dropping onto the chair in front of Mark Shannon's desk, burying her face in her hands. As Molly looked as if she, too, might begin sobbing, Marge Larkin went to Karen and put an arm protectively around her shoulders. But her eyes, still fixed on Shannon, turned hard as flint.

"Two children," she said. "We have two children missing now. And if you don't do something, you can bet there's going to be a very large story on the front page of the next issue of the *Chronicle*. Is that what you want, Mark?"

When the phone rang, Mark Shannon felt a wave of relief to have an interruption—any interruption—in which to figure out an answer for the two women.

"Mark?" It was Marian Bennett, sounding agitated. "Something terrible has happened. My car's wrecked and—"

"Is anyone hurt?" Mark cut in.

"No! At least—Mark, Andy's gone!"

Mark Shannon blinked as a cold knot of apprehension began to form in his stomach. "Andy's gone?" he repeated. "Marian, what are you talking about?"

Marian, despite her fury over what had happened to her convertible, carefully explained what had happened that morning.

How strange Andy had looked.

How she was on the way to the clinic with him when he suddenly started acting funny.

And how he had run across a field, finally disappearing into the hills.

Just like Jeff Larkin.

And possibly Julie Spellman, too.

Russell leaned on his pitchfork and stared down from the loft in the barn, watching Kevin pitching the dirty straw from the floor of the horse stalls into the wheelbarrow.

Something was definitely wrong.

Though Kevin was working steadily, removing the dirty straw with the easy rhythm that Russell himself had taught him, there was something about Kevin that just didn't look quite right.

Finally he plunged his own fork deep into one of the bales of hay that were stacked in the loft and climbed down the ladder, dropping to the floor directly from the fourth step up.

Kevin, despite the loud thump that Russell's feet made when they struck the barn's wooden floor, didn't even look up.

But he did pause in his work for a second—just as Russell had seen him do several times over the last hour—and peer out through the stall's open door, into the corral.

Peer out as if he were looking for something.

Russell followed his gaze, but the corral was empty. They'd turned the horses out into the field to graze.

As he was about to speak to Kevin, Bailey trotted into the barn, started toward Kevin, then paused, whimpering uncertainly.

"What is it, Bailey?" Russell asked, moving next to the dog and dropping one hand onto its head.

The dog whimpered again, took a tentative step toward Kevin, then seemed to change its mind. Suddenly it started barking, wheeled around and dashed out of the barn. For a moment Russell wasn't sure what had spooked Bailey, but then, at a pause in the dog's barking, he heard the sound of the old Chevy coming up the driveway.

So at least Karen was coming back. When she'd left, not even slowing down as he came out of the barn to find out where she was going, he'd had a terrible feeling that she might be taking Molly and leaving the farm.

Why else would she be taking the Chevy?

Then he'd decided that was crazy—she'd never leave until she'd found Julie.

Still, he'd almost decided to go after her, only changing his mind when he realized that if he did, there would be no one but Kevin at home should Julie return.

And Kevin, although he claimed nothing was wrong, now seemed to be coming down with something, too.

In the end, he'd stayed in the barn, and tried to concentrate on his work, but between his worry about Julie and the need to keep an eye on Kevin, not much was getting done, at least by him.

Now, following Bailey out of the barn, Russell planted himself firmly in the middle of the driveway. Karen would either have to stop or ruin the lawn by driving around him.

Or run right over him.

For a second, as the Chevy approached, he thought she might be intending to do exactly that. At the last minute, though, she stopped the car a few inches short of hitting him. She sat still for several seconds, as if trying to decide whether to get out or not, then finally opened the door. As she stepped out into the sunlight, Russell could see the redness of her eyes. He quickly moved to her side and put his arms around her.

She barely reacted to the gesture.

"There's another one missing," she said, her voice dull. "At least now I think maybe they'll do something."

Russell stared at her. "Another teenager?"

She nodded. "Andy Bennett. Another one of the kids Julie and Kevin went to the movies with."

"Oh, Jesus," Russell breathed. "Poor Marian. She must—"

Karen jerked away from him, her eyes blazing. "Poor *Marian?*" she echoed. "Why are you so worried about her? What about me? I have a child missing, too! Or have you forgotten?" Suddenly all the fear she'd been trying to control all morning, all the frustration and helplessness that had been welling up inside her, coalesced into rage. "I don't know why I ever came here," she yelled, jerking away from Russell and starting toward the house. "My mother was right! This is a terrible place! It's hot, and the people are horrible, and if the bees don't kill you, the scorpions do! God, why did I marry you? Why did I ever think any of this was a good idea?"

She broke into a run, her head down as she fled toward the house. Molly scrambled out of the car and chased after her, and a moment later so did Russell, catching up to his wife and stepdaughter just as they reached the front porch.

Kevin, coming out of the barn, watched for a moment as his father and stepmother stood on the porch of the house, arguing. From inside the barn he'd heard everything that Karen had said, and gotten more worried by the second.

More worried, and more frightened.

So now Andy Bennett was gone, too.

Had he gone up to the cave where Jeff and Julie were?

What about the rest of his friends?

Where were Sara McLaughlin and Shelley Munson?

Were they feeling the same way he was?

Were they getting sick, too?

Suddenly he had to know.

Abandoning the chores that still had to be done, Kevin got behind the wheel of the Chevy and was about to start its engine when he heard his father yelling at him. Twisting the key in the ignition switch, he pumped the accelerator a couple of times. The motor coughed, then started. Putting the car in gear, Kevin drove it on up to the house. From the porch his father and stepmother gazed at him.

"I'm going to go see if I can find Sara and Shelley," he said. "If Andy's gone, too, maybe they know where he went."

"You're not going anywhere—" Russell began, but Karen cut him off.

"Why not?" she demanded. "At least he cares that they're gone! Why shouldn't he go look for his friends?"

Russell hesitated, then gave in. "All right," he said. "But just be careful, Kevin, okay?"

Kevin smiled. "Don't worry," he said. "I'm fine."

Then he was gone.

Andy Bennett moved steadily into the hills.

The agonizing humming in his head was gone—had been gone almost from the second he'd jumped over the fence and fled from his mother and her car. He'd heard the crash when the truck hit the car door—even turned around to see what had happened. But seeing that his mother was okay—even though the door of her car was torn off—he hadn't gone back to find out what had happened.

In fact, he wasn't sure he'd have gone back even if someone had been hurt.

For now there was something new going on in his head.

A new sensation—not quite a sound, not quite an image.

Something else—something he'd never experienced before.

It was as if he was no longer in control of his own mind, or his own body, and as he walked up into the hills, he had no conscious idea where he was going.

But he knew he was going somewhere—somewhere he felt compelled to be—and as he moved along the paths, soon losing any real knowledge of where he was, that strange sensation of a presence in his mind seemed to guide him, seemed to know exactly where he should go.

Finally he came to the crest of a hill and found himself looking down into a valley. On the other side of the valley he could see a cave.

The cave, he suddenly knew, was where he needed to be.

His step quickening, Andy hurried down the hillside, crossed the stream that wound along the floor of the valley, and started up toward the cave.

He was still fifty feet away when he saw Jeff Larkin step out of the shadows that hid the interior of the cavern. Jeff neither waved nor spoke to him, but merely stepped back into the cave. When Andy finally was at the mouth of the cave, he wondered if Jeff had even seen him. But a moment later, as he stepped into the gloom within the cavern, Jeff fell in beside him.

Then he saw Julie.

She lay on the floor of the cave, near the back.

Her body was bloated, and every inch of her skin was covered with bees, whose wings vibrated steadily, filling the cave with the low hum of a hive.

Andy stopped, his stomach churning with nausea at the sight of her. He wanted to turn away, to run out of the cave, to flee back into the sunlight outside.

But he couldn't.

Something inside him—something he could neither understand nor resist—took control of him.

He started slowly toward Julie as her arms rose and reached out to him.

Reached out with fingernails that had grown long.

Long, and pointed.

Pointed ... like stingers.

CHAPTER 21

Carl Henderson pulled into the A&W stand, parking his car in the shade beneath the orange canopy over the drive-in service area. He'd been on the road most of the morning, dropping in on farmers as far north as Coalinga, and he was more than ready for lunch when Charlene Hopkins came over and rested her elbows on the window frame of the Cherokee. But before he could order, she sighed deeply, shook her head and clucked her tongue, which Carl knew was her habitual prelude to the announcement of bad news. Sure enough, a moment later, she brushed a stray wisp of platinum hair back from her forehead and said, "Isn't it strange about all them kids?"

Carl frowned and his heartbeat skipped. What was she talking about? What kids? Surely they hadn't found— But even before he could finish his thought, Charlene read the confusion on his face.

"You mean you haven't heard? Seems like kids are disappearing all over the place today. First that Julie Spellman—you know, Russell Owen's new stepdaughter? They say she was gone first thing this morning. And now Jeff Larkin and Andy Bennett are missing, too." Her voice dropping conspiratorially, Charlene passed on the various bits and pieces of gossip she'd picked up over the course of the morning, from the tale of Marian Bennett's convertible—which Charlene was pretty certain would result in Chuck's divorcing Marian—to the fact that both

Julie Spellman and Jeff Larkin had been taken to the clinic the night before. "And Dr. F. sent Roberto Muñoz over to someplace in San Luis Obispo with samples of their blood," she finished, flushed with excitement. "I guess something pretty awful must be wrong with them, huh?"

Carl Henderson, his pulse racing, struggled to reveal nothing of the fear surging through him. Instead he simply nodded in agreement and tried to show just exactly the right level of interest. "Roberto have any idea what they're looking for?"

"Search me," Charlene replied. "Maybe drugs, I guess. Or maybe some kind of new sickness. I mean, that girl Julie's been living in Los Angeles, and she could have brought all kinds of sickness up here, couldn't she?"

"I guess," Carl Henderson mused, his mind racing as he wondered if the lab in San Luis Obispo had already tested Julie's blood. If they had, and found traces of the stuff he'd given Ellen Filmore as a bee antivenin . . .

He felt an almost irresistible urge to drive over to the clinic right now—this instant—and do whatever was necessary to retrieve the vial.

But he couldn't give in to the urge, because he could imagine Charlene Hopkins telling her next customer: *And you know, that Carl Henderson, he got so upset when I told him they were checking Julie's blood! Why, he took off out of here like a bat out of hell!* Then she would give that annoying little chuckle of hers and shake her head. *I never did trust that man,* he heard her saying. *Always something strange about him.*

And that would do it. Mark Shannon would be at his house again, but this time he wouldn't just be asking questions.

Carl's jaw tightened as he had a sudden vision of Charlene Hopkins hanging from the wall of his darkroom, her gossiping voice silenced forever as millions of his tiny carnivores quickly devoured her, cleaning her bones as quickly as they had that of—

He put the thought quickly out of his mind.

Calm.

The main thing was to stay calm and behave logically.

Feigning boredom with Charlene's continuing recitation of the morning's gossip—which, he noticed, she was embellishing even as she repeated it for him—he broke into her stream of words to order a hamburger, fries, and a chocolate malt.

As Charlene went to put his order in, his mind continued racing, and by the time the food came, he knew what to do.

He ate slowly, forcing himself to show no signs of rushing, determined that when he left, neither Charlene nor her husband, who worked as a cook behind the counter, would have any reason to comment on him later on.

Except to say that he'd seemed perfectly normal.

As he was getting ready to pay Charlene, he winced, then uttered a gasp of surprise.

Charlene glanced up from her order book. "You say something, Carl?"

Carl shook his head and put on a weak smile. "Uh-uh. Just a little gas, I guess."

He winced again, and this time added a grunt, as if he were suppressing pain.

Charlene Hopkins's smile faded. Her penciled eyebrows came together in a worried frown. "You sure you're all right?" she asked. Then, with a guilty glance toward the interior of the drive-in, she leaned toward the window. "Maybe you better go over to the clinic and see Dr. F. yourself," she said quietly. "I keep tellin' George to make sure he cooks that meat real good, but I heard about another of those *E. coli* things just last week." She clucked her tongue in disapproval. "I swear, if you can't trust the meat anymore, I just don't know what to think!"

Nodding as if not trusting himself to speak, Carl Henderson gave Charlene a ten-dollar bill, waited for his change, then started the car.

Even better than he'd hoped—it had been Charlene herself who sent him to see Ellen Filmore!

As he pulled into the clinic parking lot five minutes later, the worst of his fears began to ease when he didn't see either of the town's two squad cars in the lot.

And when the anxious look on Ellen Filmore's face turned into a smile as she recognized him, Carl relaxed even more. No matter what she might have found out about Julie's blood, at least so far she hadn't put it together with the substance in the vial.

Even before he spoke, Ellen Filmore came out from behind Roberto's desk, where she'd been filling in for her nurse until he got back from San Luis Obispo. "I hear you might have gotten some bad meat," she said.

Carl feigned annoyance. "I don't believe it—Charlene already called here?"

"*E. coli* is nothing to make light of," Ellen told him, leading him into the same examining room where she'd treated Julie Spellman the day the bees had stung her. "And you can't blame Charlene for worrying—if they served you tainted meat, you could sue them."

"Right," Carl said, rolling his eyes. "And if I did, nobody in town would speak to me, and I sure wouldn't be able to eat anything anywhere. I think I'd rather take my chances."

"Well, I agree with Charlene," Ellen told him, handing him an examination smock. "Put this on, and call me when you're ready." She left the room, and Carl Henderson immediately checked the counter against the far wall, which was the last place he'd seen the brown vial he'd given Ellen Filmore less than a week ago.

It wasn't there.

Quickly taking off his pants and shirt and putting the

shapeless smock on over his underwear, Carl checked two of the drawers for the vial and was about to open a third when there was a sharp knock at the door.

"Are you all right?" he heard Ellen call.

"All set," Carl called back, moving hurriedly to the examining table. By the time the doctor stepped through a moment later, Carl was perched on its edge, his fingers pressed to his stomach. "Probably nothing but a little gas," he muttered as Ellen began going over him, checking his vital signs, then palpating his abdomen.

Ten minutes later she was done. "Okay," she said, picking up Carl's chart and jotting a few notes on it. "I think you can relax. If it's *E. coli*, it's the mildest case known to medical science." Opening one of the cabinets over the counter, she took out a bottle of antacid tablets, handed one of them to Carl, and winked. "This is what I always take after one of George Hopkins's burgers. If it doesn't work, call me. But I suspect you were a lot closer to a diagnosis than Charlene was. Come out to the waiting room when you're ready."

Ellen Filmore closed the door to the examining room as she left, leaving him alone again. Then Carl went to work again, searching through one drawer after another.

Was it possible she'd used the entire contents of the vial?

But if she had, why hadn't she called him, demanding more? After all, despite what he'd intended the contents of the vial to do, it had apparently proved as effective as the real antivenin. In fact, Carl still had no idea why the contents of the vial hadn't killed Julie, but he knew that it had done *something*. And if they found traces of it in her blood—

Quickly, Carl opened the last drawer, and was about to close it again when he spotted the tiny brown bottle.

Snatching it up, he replaced it with the vial of the real antivenin that he'd transferred from his briefcase to his pants pocket on his way to the clinic from the A&W drive-in.

Less than five minutes after Ellen Filmore had left him to put his clothes back on, Carl Henderson was back in the waiting room.

"Feeling any better?" the doctor asked, glancing up from the medical journal she was reading.

Carl smiled broadly. "I'm fine," he said, unknowingly repeating the same words Julie, Jeff, and Andy had all uttered over the last few days. "I'm just fine."

But unlike the other three, Carl Henderson meant what he said.

Kevin Owen slowed his car to a stop at the bottom of the road leading up into the park. His head was throbbing and the terrible itching sensation that had spread all through his body was getting worse by the moment.

He was almost sure he was going crazy, for the more he thought about it, the more certain he was that what he'd seen in the cave that morning couldn't possibly have been real.

But if it wasn't real, where had the image that was so vivid in his head come from?

Once again, as he'd been trying to do all day, he struggled to remember exactly what had happened up there.

Jeff had been acting strange—of that Kevin was absolutely certain.

That he'd barely spoken as they hiked up into the hills was weird enough, given how much Jeff usually had to say. But the way he'd just kept walking, like he'd known where he was going all the time, was almost eerie.

Was it possible that he'd been up there before? Could he have gone with Julie when she went, and then come back down?

How come, Kevin wondered, he hadn't been able to tell his father and Karen what had happened up there?

In fact, ever since that horrible thing had happened, when what had looked like a black cloud of gnats had swarmed up out of Jeff's throat—he'd felt like something foreign was inside him.

Sort of like those movies he'd seen where space aliens came down and got inside human bodies, taking them over so they could pass themselves off as human.

But it wasn't quite like that, either, because in those movies, the aliens always killed the real person and just used their bodies.

And he was still alive—he *knew* he was still alive!

Yet he still had that odd sense of something else being inside his body, and he knew that something had happened to him, because he couldn't say what he meant anymore.

In fact, he couldn't even *act* like he wanted to!

He'd worked in the barn with his father, even though he felt so bad he kept thinking he might collapse at any minute. And when his father had asked him how he was, he kept going on about feeling fine, even though he'd been ready to puke the whole time.

Once, he even tried to vomit, figuring that if he did, at least his father would figure out that something was wrong with him.

But he couldn't even throw up!

An hour ago he'd felt an urge to go back up into the hills. Twice, as he drove around town looking for Sara and Shelley, he found himself turning onto one of the streets that led toward the hills, but both times he'd managed to make himself turn back, determined that whatever happened, he wasn't going to go back up to that cave!

Then, suddenly, he'd gotten hungry.

It wasn't the kind of hunger he was used to, where he slowly began to feel like it would be nice to have something to eat.

No, this was something else—a ravening sense of starvation that made him feel that if he didn't eat right away, he'd die.

That was when he'd gone to the A&W, where he ordered twice as much food as he'd ever eaten before.

And while he'd eaten, he listened to Charlene go on and on about all the weird things that were happening that morning.

When she finally got around to telling him about Andy Bennett taking off up into the hills, Kevin knew right away where he'd gone—it had to be the cave!

He started to wonder, then, if maybe he was going crazy, or if maybe even a spaceship really had landed, and he and the rest of the kids were being taken over by aliens, like in those movies.

But that was stupid! There weren't any such things as spaceships or aliens!

Then what *was* happening to him?

After he finished the third hamburger at the A&W, he'd gone over to the grocery store where Sara's mother was a cashier. Mrs. McLaughlin had seen right away that something was wrong with him, but he insisted he was fine and just wanted to find Sara and Shelley.

"They're up in the park, I think," Mrs. McLaughlin told him. "Sara said something about them taking Shelley's sister and her friends for a picnic." Then, as she examined Kevin's sweating face, her tone had changed. "But I think you ought to go over and see Dr. Filmore," she said. "You look sick, and I don't want you going up to the park and spreading it all over the place. Okay?"

Kevin nodded, but when he got back to the car, he'd known he wasn't going to the clinic.

He headed straight for the park.

Now that he was here, he felt worse than ever.

A terrible humming was starting in his head, and he suddenly remembered the other night, when they'd all gone to the movies together and then come up to the park.

The night Julie had first started acting weird.

And she hadn't wanted to go anywhere near the power lines.

Now, as the throbbing in his head grew worse, he understood why.

He sat in his car for a few minutes, trying to clear his mind enough to figure out what to do.

The urge to turn away from the power lines was growing stronger, but he wouldn't give in to it.

Not until he'd talked to Sara and Shelley and found out if they were all right.

And warned them what was happening to everyone who had gone to the movies that night.

If he could.

Steeling himself against the terrible buzzing in his head, and battling the almost overpowering urge to turn the car around and drive away, he put the transmission in gear and started forward.

The power lines were almost directly over his head here—much closer than on the road that led out to the farm—and the buzzing in his head rose to the level of a power saw screaming its way through a piece of plywood.

Gritting his teeth, Kevin forced his right foot against the accelerator and the old Chevy surged ahead, gaining speed until he came to the crest of the hill and the parking lot. The instant he came into the lot, he swerved away from the high-voltage wires. As soon as he did, the howling screech inside his head began to ease. The lot was almost empty, and he drove all the way to the far end, finally turning into a spot near the swings.

Shelley Munson's sister was on one of the swings, and behind her was Sara McLaughlin, pushing the swing higher and higher as the little girl screamed happily. Kevin sat behind the wheel of the car, watching the little girl while he waited for the terrible throbbing in his head to ease.

A minute or two later Sara caught sight of him, waved, then came over to the car, her smile fading as she got a closer look at his face.

"Kevin? Are you okay?"

Kevin started to shake his head, but found himself nodding instead. "I'm fine," he heard himself say.

But it wasn't what he had intended to say at all! If he couldn't even tell her how he felt—

"I feel—" he began again, but the rest of the words—the ones about the fever, the itching, and the terrible nausea—died in his throat, choked off by the force that seemed to have invaded not only his body, but his mind as well. "Jeff's gone," he managed to say.

Sara frowned uncertainly. "Gone? What do you mean?"

Kevin formulated the words carefully in his mind. Maybe if he didn't try to tell her about himself, it would be all right. Maybe if all he tried to do was tell her that Jeff had gone up to a cave in the hills, where Julie was—

Maybe if he only told her that *Jeff* was sick, and so was Julie . . .

Maybe if he didn't try to talk about himself at all—

"You want to go somewhere?" he heard himself ask. "Somewhere we can be by ourselves?"

Sara's eyes widened. Was Kevin saying what she thought he was saying? He'd never been interested in her before! But the way he was looking at her now . . .

She glanced over her shoulder. Shelley's sister was off the swing now, playing on the rusting merry-go-round with her friends.

And Shelley was sitting at one of the picnic tables, keeping an eye on them. If she and Kevin just went off somewhere for a while . . .

"Sure," she said, pulling the car door open for Kevin. "Where?"

Don't get out! Kevin told himself. Just pull the door closed, start the car, and go away! But even as the thoughts formed in his mind, he found himself getting out of the car and taking Sara's hand. "How about over there?" he asked, nodding toward a thicket of shrubs in the center of which was a small clearing. "You got a blanket?"

Sara nodded, her heart beating. Was it really going to happen? Her and Kevin Owen? She could hardly believe it!

Hanging onto Kevin's hand as if her life depended on it, Sara led him over to where she and Shelley had spread their blankets two hours earlier. Picking one of them up, she folded it quickly, then fell in beside Kevin once more as he led her toward the dense thicket.

They picked their way through the foliage, emerging half a minute later into the clearing. Just large enough to spread out the blanket, the open area in the middle of the thicket was littered with empty beer cans and used condoms, all of which Sara tried to ignore as she spread the blanket out and sat down, pulling Kevin down next to her.

"I—I didn't even know you liked me," she stammered. "I thought—well, I guess I thought you liked Julie Spellman."

Get away, Kevin thought, screaming the words silently in his mind, struggling to give voice to them before it was too late. Get away before something awful happens!

Sara's hands were on him now, unbuttoning his shirt, her fingers gently stroking the skin of his chest.

"You're sweating," he heard her say. "Why don't you take off your shirt?"

His mind numb, his body refusing to obey the orders he tried to give it, Kevin stripped off his shirt, then lay down on his back, pulling Sara down with him.

It's going to happen! Sara thought. It's actually going to happen!

She leaned down, ready to kiss Kevin, then suddenly froze.

His eyes!

Something was wrong with his eyes!

All around the edges of them, creeping out from under his eyelids, were what looked like tiny gnats—hundreds of them!

Gasping, Sara tried to draw away from Kevin, but his fingers suddenly closed on her arms, his nails digging painfully into her flesh.

The black specks were flooding out of his nose now, and as a scream of terror rose in Sara's throat, Kevin's mouth opened.

Instantly, Sara's face was engulfed in a stinging, searing black cloud.

The scream that had been building in her throat died before the onslaught. And for Sara McLaughlin, as for Julie, Jeff, Andy, and Kevin, the nightmare began.

CHAPTER 22

*E*llen Filmore's patience was finally running out. She was about to cross what she called her "temper threshold"—the point when it became dangerous for anyone to cross her path. Normally in possession of what she liked to think was a fairly sunny disposition, Ellen could quickly turn into a holy terror once she was pushed across that threshold, and the lab in San Luis Obispo was just about to do it.

Six-thirty.

She knew there was no point in trying to call them—they'd stopped answering their switchboard at five-thirty, and the last time she'd talked to them their operator had assured her (in tones that Ellen had, frankly, found to be a bit less than polite) that the technician wouldn't leave until he had finished the job, and that—"for the tenth time, Dr. Filmore"—he would certainly call her with the results when he had them.

Well, what was he doing, counting every red and white cell in those samples one by one?

Ten minutes ago, when she'd begun to feel her temper starting to fray around the edges, she'd sent Roberto Muñoz home, seeing no reason to take out her hostility on him. After all, he had gotten the samples to the lab in record time—which was going to cost her whatever the price of his speeding ticket turned out to be—and had even volunteered to keep her company until the lab called. That, she'd decided, was truly beyond the call of duty, particularly since Roberto knew exactly what might happen to him if he stayed. "Thanks," she told him, managing a smile despite her already growing anger, "but you're too good a nurse for me to risk losing. Besides, you have a right to a decent night's rest, and if I blow up, you just might not get it."

Now, as her eyes remained fixed on the clock, and she felt her blood pressure rising a notch with each passing minute, the explosion was imminent.

At 6:58, with only two minutes remaining in her countdown to temper blast-off, the phone finally came to life and she snatched it off the hook.

"Dr. Filmore?"

"Yes."

"This is Barry Sadler. At the lab? I've been working up some samples for you?"

Oh, God, Ellen groaned silently. Not one of those people who makes everything into a question. "What do you have?" she asked. "Tell me about the blood."

"Well, that's the thing," Sadler said, hesitant. "I'm afraid—well, there seems to be something in it I can't identify. I mean, I know sort of what it is, I guess, but it's not like anything I've ever found in blood before. I think what I'd like to do is—"

"Stop!" Ellen Filmore commanded, the force of the single word cutting through the telephone wire like an ice pick sinking into balsa wood. "What do you mean, you sort of know what it is?"

"Well, it looks like some kind of organism. . . ." Sadler said in a strangely hesitant voice that sent a chill of fear down Ellen Filmore's spine.

"An organism?" she pressed. "What kind of organism?"

"Well, that's the thing," Sadler replied. "It's not like anything I've ever seen before."

The icy fingers of fear that had been playing along her

spine began to close around Ellen. What was he saying? "You mean it's not like anything you've ever seen in *human blood*," she corrected, her voice taking on a slightly professorial tone.

"It's not like anything I've ever seen at *all*," Sadler said, his voice trembling so badly that Ellen could picture the beads of nervous sweat that must be breaking out on his forehead.

"All right," Ellen said, struggling to keep from betraying her own rapidly rising fear. "Give me your best guess—what does this organism resemble most?"

For a long time Sadler said nothing, and when he did speak again, his voice was still shaking. "Larvae," he said.

"Larvae?" Ellen echoed. "I'm sorry, but—"

"Look," Sadler broke in, his voice gaining strength now that he'd spoken the words he knew were going to be hardest for the doctor to accept. "I'm a lab technician. I've seen a lot of things through a microscope, and I'm telling you that those samples you sent me are the weirdest things I've ever seen. They're pretty much normal when you test them for all the usual stuff. But when I looked at a slide under the mike, there were all these ... things! I mean, most of them—the big ones looked just like some kind of insect larvae. But there's other stuff, too. Much smaller. I'd have to have an electron microscope to be sure, but my best guess—and I'm a pretty damned good guesser—is that what I'm seeing are the remains of the eggs the larvae hatched out of."

Ellen Filmore's mind felt numb. For a long moment she said nothing at all, then: "Are you telling me that I have two patients who are infected with some kind of parasite that's living in their bloodstream?"

Now it was Barry Sadler who was silent for a moment. Finally he uttered a long sigh. "I guess so," he said. "If I were you, I think I'd get them into a hospital as soon as possible." He went on talking for a few more moments, explaining that tomorrow he would have some people from the biology department at the college look at the samples, but Ellen Filmore was no longer listening.

Not like anything I've ever seen before.

Larvae . . . eggs . . .

Her mind raced as she thought of the possible ramifications of a parasite living in the human bloodstream.

Living, and multiplying.

Feeding on . . . what?

And as they multiplied, what happened to them?

Larvae. If the technician was right, what did the larvae develop into? And where were the adults of whatever it was?

Her voice hollow, Ellen thanked the lab technician for his work and made him promise to call her the next day. "And I'll want to talk to your man at the college, too," she added.

"Don't worry," Sadler replied. "I have a feeling he's going to want to talk to you, too."

Hanging up the phone, Ellen sat at her desk for a moment, trying to sort it out in her mind.

The most important thing was to find the kids.

Flipping through her Rolodex, she picked up the phone and dialed the Bennetts' number.

Busy.

Stabbing one of the buttons for a new line, she flipped through the Rolodex again and dialed Russell Owen's.

Busy.

Her frustration growing, she tried Marge Larkin, wanting to scream with frustration when that line was busy as well.

The police.

Flipping through the Rolodex yet again, she found Mark Shannon's home number, dialed it, and drummed her fingers impatiently on the desk as she waited for him to answer. "What have you done about the missing kids?" she demanded without preamble when he finally answered on the seventh ring. "Julie Spellman, Jeff Larkin, and Andy Bennett?"

The deputy groaned. "Come on, Doc. You know the rules—we can't just go chasing after every kid who takes off for a few hours. Not unless—"

"Unless there are extenuating circumstances," Ellen finished for him. "How about if they're sick? Would that qualify?" Before he could respond to her questions, she added, "At least two of them have something more serious than flu. I already know that Julie and Jeff have something I've never seen before. Andy Bennett might have it, too, judging by what Marian told me this morning." As quickly as she could, Ellen explained to him what the lab had found in the blood samples she'd sent them.

Mark Shannon heard her out, then sighed his acceptance of her demands. Ellen Filmore wasn't merely an overwrought parent, and he knew her well enough to know that if he didn't give her at least some satisfaction, she might well badger him for the rest of the night. "Tell you what," he said. "I'll take a look around tonight, ask a few questions and see what I can find out. And if they still haven't turned up by tomorrow morning, I'll put together some people and take a look up in the hills. But you know as well as I do that kids who don't want to be found rarely are. All they have to do is get to the interstate and hitch a ride either way. They get to L.A. or San Francisco in a matter of a few hours, and that's that."

"But you'll see what you can do?" Ellen asked, intent on nailing him down. "You'll at least try to find them?"

Mark Shannon hesitated, then gave in. Better to spend a few hours cruising around in the car, checking the motels up and down the interstate and talking to the people at the cafés, than have Ellen on his case all night.

Not that it would do any good, he was sure, and he suspected that deep down inside Ellen knew it wouldn't accomplish much, either.

If the kids wanted to come home, they would.

If they didn't, the odds were that no one would hear from any of them until they did.

Unless, of course, the guy at the lab in San Luis Obispo was right and something truly weird was going on.

Mark Shannon didn't even want to think about that possibility.

Carl Henderson switched off the light in the kitchen, then moved quickly through the darkness to peer through the window into the night outside.

All evening, ever since the sun had set, he'd felt eyes watching him, but so far he hadn't been able to catch whoever was lurking in the darkness, spying on him.

Not that they would have been able to see anything, for he had been clever.

Very clever.

All evening he had resisted the urge to go down to the basement, where his laboratory was waiting for him.

Instead he had stayed upstairs, moving through the rooms of the main floor of the house, following what would appear as a perfectly normal routine to an observer.

As long as whoever was watching didn't suspect that he knew someone was out there, he would be safe. All he had to do, Carl thought, was be patient and make no mistakes, and after a while everything would be all right again.

Keeping that one imperative—that everything must look normal—firmly in his mind, he resisted the urge to come directly home after his visit to the clinic, refused to give in to the desire to begin working immediately with the contents of the little brown vial, to determine for himself how a compound that should only have affected the egg of a bee could also have had such a dramatic effect on a human being.

Had he created something even he didn't fully understand? And if he had, what were its full effects?

But he had controlled his scientific curiosity, and instead of going directly to the lab, had gone about his normal routine, stopping in at a couple of farms, even dropping by the Owen place for a few minutes to volunteer his help in locating Julie.

Julie, who, he suspected, might finally be dying out in the hills somewhere. Which was a shame, really, for if she was going to die anyway, it would have been nice to have put her in his darkroom for a while.

Nice to have listened to her screams as his colonies swarmed out of their nests to creep over her, exploring her body in the darkness.

Otto Owen's screams, which had only lasted a few short minutes, hadn't been nearly as satisfying as those of the girl. What had her name been? Dawn Something-or-other.

Julie's screams, though, would have been wonderful.

But it was probably too late, although he wouldn't truly give up hope for her until he'd determined exactly what the contents of the brown vial would do when injected into a warm-blooded creature rather than the incubation cell of a beehive.

Even when he finally allowed himself to come home, he'd sat at the kitchen table for a while, taking care of some paperwork, as if he didn't have a care in the world.

He hadn't betrayed his certainty that someone was watching him with even the briefest of glances out the window.

Now, he felt a chill of apprehension—had he been too careful?

Had he been acting abnormally normal?

No! Of course not! He rarely looked out the window at all.

Or did he?

Suddenly he had the horrible feeling that he usually unconsciously glanced out the window dozens of times in the course of a normal evening.

His body tensed as he wondered if he'd already given himself away to the unseen watcher.

Then another thought occurred to him:

Had he been in the darkened kitchen too long?

Of course! He should have gone through the house, turning out all the lights on the first floor, as if he were going to bed. Only then, when all the windows were dark, should he have made a second circuit, peering out to try to get a look at the hidden watcher.

But it wasn't too late. It couldn't be!

Carl moved quickly then, striding from room to room, turning out the lamps on the tables in the living room and parlor, and the chandelier in the dining room. Finally, when all the lights were off, he began his second patrol, peering out from the darkened rooms, gazing into the shadows of the yard.

And still he saw nothing.

But he could wait no longer, and finally he picked up his briefcase from the table in the entry and slipped through the door under the stairs. Pulling the door shut behind him, not daring even to turn on the light over the stairs, he felt his way down the steep flight through the suffocating blackness.

Even when he was safely in the cellar, he turned on only a single light over his worktable.

Taking the vial he had pilfered from Ellen Filmore's office out of his briefcase, he used a hypodermic needle to draw a few drops of its contents through the rubber seal he himself had applied to the vial only a few days ago.

He moved to the far end of the counter, where one of the rats he kept for experimentation—and to feed to the most carnivorous of his specimens—was eyeing him warily from the confines of its cage. Opening the cage, he carefully removed the rat, holding it gently as he slid the hypodermic needle into its skin. He pressed the plunger of the hypodermic needle, and instantly felt the rat begin to squirm in his hand. Dropping the rat back into the cage, he closed the lid, then stepped back to watch.

The rat backed into a corner of the cage, where it crouched, trembling, its nose twitching as it sniffed the air, its tiny eyes darting around as if seeking some unseen enemy.

Carl Henderson's eyes narrowed. Had he given it too much of the serum in the vial? Was it going to die?

Suddenly the rat began furiously scratching itself, and Carl's frown deepened.

An allergic reaction?

He tried to remember how Julie had looked and behaved after she'd been given her shot.

She had gone to the bathroom, he could remember that.

And when she came out to the waiting room, she'd looked strange.

Had she been itching? Or had the shot affected her differently from the way it seemed to be affecting the rat?

He didn't know.

As he watched, the rat seemed to calm down, and Carl Henderson's fear that it was going to die right then began to abate.

But what would happen to it in the morning?

He was tempted to stay up all night, to keep watch over the rat, so that he could take careful notes on everything that happened to it. But if he didn't sleep at all, the strain of staying up all night would show in his face.

No, better to go to bed, better to keep to his normal routine.

He turned away from the rat, then remembered something else he'd heard that day.

About Jeff Larkin.

Something Vic Costas had told him.

"He didn't look right this morning," the old Greek

farmer had said. "Like that girl, Julie. He looked this morning the way she looked yesterday. Just not quite right, you know? Just not right. I guess maybe he caught whatever she had." His brow had furrowed into a deep scowl. "Kids these days," Costas had added. "You just can't keep 'em away from each other."

Carl turned and gazed at the rat once more. If what he'd just injected it with was contagious . . .

He glanced around the room, then spotted exactly what he needed. On one of the shelves above the counter there was a Plexiglas box that he'd constructed himself when he'd experimented with breeding spiders a year ago. Sealed nearly perfectly, the only thing that could get in or out was air.

And even the air had to pass through a filter that was fine enough to meet hospital standards. Indeed, it was at a hospital supply house that he'd bought the air filtration system.

Carl Henderson picked up the rat—still in its cage—and placed it inside the Plexiglas box, sealed the box's top, then turned on the ventilation fan.

The hum of the fan's motor seemed to make the rat even more nervous than it had been before, and Carl watched it for a few more minutes. Then, deciding that the little creature would settle down as soon as it got used to the sound of the whirring fan, he turned off the light and went back upstairs.

Within the rat, responding to the vibrations emanating from the ventilating fan, the organism Carl had injected into its bloodstream began to reproduce. And the rat began going rapidly insane.

Long before morning, the rat would batter itself to death trying to escape from the colony growing within it.

Kevin bumped slowly along the rutted dirt road that skirted the western boundary of the farm, the headlights of the Chevy turned off, his speed never exceeding ten miles an hour. But no matter how slow he went, the car bottomed out every time he hit a chuckhole, its shock absorbers no longer able to take the jolts the road was giving it. Yet it was still better than the county road, where the humming from the power lines had become unbearable, finally forcing him to turn off even before he came to Vic Costas's farm.

At last, though, just after ten-thirty, he turned down the narrow track that would bring him almost to the back door of his house, and he finally shut the engine off, coasting the last few yards in the hope that perhaps no one would hear him coming in. Right now, the last thing he wanted to do was try to talk to anyone.

For a while, after he'd been with Sara in the park, Kevin had felt better. The chills that had gripped him all through the morning had finally eased, and when he drove back down from the park, even the terrible throbbing the power lines caused in his head had been almost bearable.

The thing was, he didn't really know exactly what had happened when he'd been with Sara. All he could remember was that he'd been feeling worse and worse, and that on the way up to the park he felt like he was going to die. But then he and Sara had gone into the clearing in the thicket where everyone went to neck, and she'd spread out a blanket.

He'd lain down, and she dropped down next to him.

Then she bent over, about to kiss him.

And something had happened to him. His lungs had suddenly felt as if they'd filled up with cotton. He hadn't been able to breathe, and a horrible wave of panic came over him. Suddenly he'd felt something almost like an explosion in his chest, and for a single terrible moment he thought maybe he was having a heart attack. But it hadn't been a heart attack at all, for a second later a great gasp burst from his throat—almost as if he'd been holding his breath beyond his own endurance, and then . . .

And then he felt a great sense of relief.

The sickness he'd been feeling all day suddenly left him, and for a while he simply lay on his back, staring up into the sky.

He had a vague memory of Sara leaving, but he'd fallen asleep, not waking up until the sun was already dropping in the western sky. And then, as the afternoon began to turn into evening, the sickness began to come back, and with it the terrible fear that he was losing his mind.

Now, getting out of the car, Kevin circled the house, his eyes scanning the dimly lit rooms for any sign that his family was waiting up for him. But the curtains were drawn, and only a few lights glowed softly in the downstairs rooms.

Kevin slipped into the house through the kitchen door. On the refrigerator was a note telling him to help himself to a piece of the apple pie left over from dinner, and Kevin wolfed it down, then took a second piece, and finally a third.

The terrible hunger that had left him for a few hours after he'd been with Sara was back again, and now it seemed to be growing worse by the minute. After he finished the pie, Kevin opened the refrigerator and began looking for something else to eat. It was while he was unwrapping the remains of a meat loaf that he felt someone watching him.

Turning, he saw Molly standing in the door to the dining room, the afghan from the living room sofa wrapped around her shoulders. Her eyes, large and serious, gazed worriedly at him.

"Did you find Julie?" she asked, her voice quavering.

Kevin hesitated, then shook his head. As yet a new urge began to rise within him, an urge that this time was somehow connected to Molly, he took a step backward.

Sensing nothing of what was happening to her stepbrother, Molly dropped the afghan and ran to him, throwing her arms around him as a great sob wracked her body.

Kevin stiffened. The urge within him grew stronger, and he wanted to pick Molly up—hold her—bring her face close to his own. . . .

"Hey," he said, his voice strangling in his throat as he struggled against the danger he felt growing inside him. "Just because I didn't find her today doesn't mean I won't."

"B-But what if something's happened to her?" Molly sobbed. "What if she's sick, or what if she got hurt or something!"

Kevin steeled himself, but the force within him strengthened. Picking Molly up, he carried her through the dining room. He was about to start up to the second floor when he saw his father asleep in the big brown leather chair in the living room.

There was no sign of his stepmother.

"Where's your mom?" he asked, his voice trembling as he struggled against the steadily growing urge to press his face close to Molly's and . . .

What?

Hurt her? Hurt Molly? But he loved Molly!

"I guess Mommy went to bed," Molly said, still not sensing the danger in Kevin. "When I woke up, she wasn't in the living room anymore."

Kevin said nothing, but moved silently up the stairs, carrying Molly into her room and laying her gently on the bed. He gazed down at her, the force inside him still growing. He wanted to bend down, to kiss her, as he had kissed Sara McLaughlin. . . .

Molly looked up at him, then reached out, stretching her arms toward him. "Hug," she said.

Kevin hesitated for a split second, the being within him nearly overwhelming him, then suddenly he jerked away, turning from Molly, certain that if he even looked at her again, he would lose the battle raging within him.

Molly, finally sensing something different about her stepbrother, shrank back. "I'm . . . scared," she whispered.

Kevin started toward the door. "Don't be," he breathed, his words rasping in his constricting throat. "You're going to be all right. I'm not going to let anything hurt you."

"Promise?" Molly asked, her voice quavering.

For a long moment Kevin said nothing at all, but then, as he hurried out of the room, he uttered one more word: "Promise." Then he was gone, but as he went into his own room, closing and locking the door, he knew he'd lied to Molly.

He wouldn't be able to keep the promise he'd just made.

CHAPTER 23

*K*evin Owen woke up as the sun was beginning to rise. Instantly, he knew he was sick—sicker than he'd ever felt in his life.

Sicker even than when he'd been up in the hills with Jeff yesterday morning, and suddenly . . .

What?

What was it that had spewed out of Jeff's mouth? All that remained in his mind was a vague image of a dark mist—like black smoke—that had boiled around his head for an instant.

For a fleeting second he had imagined his skin was actually on fire, and then—as now—he felt violently ill.

He lay in bed, held in the icy grip of a feverish chill, his skin covered with a cold sweat. Yet despite the terrible fever that raged in his body, he felt hungry.

Ravenously hungry.

But he was almost certain that if he ate anything—anything at all—he would simply vomit it up again, for suddenly his belly was churning with nausea.

He lay shuddering under the quilt, praying for the fever to ease, but as the seconds ticked slowly by, not only did the chill tighten its grip on him, but the hunger grew steadily worse, until even his teeth began to ache with it.

He had to eat—if he didn't eat, he would die!

Flinging the quilt back, he pulled on his clothes, then went down to the kitchen and began ravaging the contents of the refrigerator, devouring first the leftovers from the supper Karen had made last night, then whatever else came to hand.

Opening a package of thick bacon, he began cramming the raw strips of fat into his mouth, chewing them only briefly before forcing them down his throat.

His gorge rose in protest against the stringy, greasy mass, but in the end his stomach accepted it, and Kevin kept eating, devouring whatever he could find until at last the terrible hunger began to feel sated.

But as stabbing pangs of hunger eased, another urge began building within him.

The same urge he'd fought yesterday.

Now it was back, more powerful than ever, and this morning he knew he would be helpless to resist it.

It was the urge to return to the hills, to the cave he'd never seen before yesterday.

Return to Julie.

But why? What force was it that was drawing him to her?

Though he had no understanding of what the force was or how it might work, he knew there would be no way for him to fight it.

He started toward the back door, then hesitated.

When the rest of the family woke up, when Molly came down . . .

The promise he'd made to the little girl last night echoed in his head.

The urge to leave the house and go back up into the hills growing stronger by the second, he quickly went to the counter and scrawled a note on the pad that always sat by the telephone:

> Dad—
> Had an idea—went to look for Julie.
> Back by lunchtime.

He reread the note, then pinned it to the refrigerator with a magnet. He left the house, pausing when he was fifty yards away to look back.

Despite what he'd written in the note, he had a strong feeling that he wouldn't be back by lunchtime.

Indeed, he had a very strong feeling that he wouldn't be coming back, for as he'd started away and seen the golden brown hills ahead of him, a peculiar sensation had come over him.

A sensation that he was going home.

But why?

Where had the feeling come from?

Home wasn't up in the hills. And it had nothing to do with the cave he'd seen yesterday, where Julie, her body enormously swollen, stood with a cloud of insects swarming around her.

Yet even as that vision of Julie came into his mind—a vision whose reality had terrified him when he'd first seen it yesterday—he felt himself being drawn to her all the more strongly.

Something inside him wanted to be close to her, to bask in her presence.

As he moved up into the hills, his step quickened.

Mark Shannon rolled over, groped for the alarm clock next to his bed, and jabbed groggily at the button that would silence the alarm.

A second later the insistent ringing sounded again, and he finally opened his eyes to glare balefully at the telephone, his mind still fogged from the extra hours he'd put in last night, first cruising around the town, then going out to the motel to check out the register and the rooms, then finally settling in at the Silo, where he'd perched on a bar stool until closing time, lubricating the voices of every customer who came in with drinks he would charge to the county.

No one, of course, had known anything about the missing kids.

As the telephone jangled one more time, Shannon reached out and picked it up. "This better be important," he growled.

"I think you better get down here," Manny Gomez told him. "I got a whole office full of people, and they all want to know the same thing—how come we haven't found any of those kids yet."

Mark Shannon groaned. "What time is it?" he asked.

"Six-thirty," Manny replied, then began to list all the people who were crowded into their small office around the corner from the city hall.

The name that finally goaded Mark out of the comfort of his bed was that of Marge Larkin's boss, Jim Chapman. If the editor of the paper was there, then everyone else in town soon would be as well. "Okay," he sighed. "I'll be there in fifteen minutes." Hauling himself out of bed, he stumbled into the bathroom, turned the shower on cold, then stepped under the icy spray. Instantly, his head cleared and most of the hangover was driven out of his body.

Obviously, the department regulations were going out the window on this one, he thought as he shaved, and he was going to have to organize a search party. He'd been skeptical at first, but it was now clear that three kids were missing. There was something very strange about Andy Bennett having taken off the same morning that Julie Spellman and Jeff Larkin had disappeared. Two kids—one boy and one girl—was one thing. In fact, it was pretty obviously explainable to anyone except the parents involved, who never wanted to think their adolescent children might just want to take off and spend a night together.

Andy Bennett, though, added a twist that didn't make any sense. According to Marian and Chuck, he hadn't even talked to either Jeff or Julie since the night they'd all gone to the movies together.

Shannon put on the cleanest of his four uniform shirts, pulled on the same pants he'd worn yesterday, then added his belt, holster, gun, and badge. Ten minutes after the phone had jarred him out of sleep, he was in his squad car and on his way.

And half an hour after that, leading a caravan of fourteen cars filled with what seemed like every relative and friend the Bennetts and Marge Larkin had, he set out for Russell Owen's farm to begin the search.

When he got there, though, Karen Owen informed him that the search had already begun: both Russell and Kevin were already up in the hills. "Kevin left before breakfast," she told him, handing Shannon the note she'd found on the refrigerator door. "Russell went after him as soon as we found out he was gone."

Mark Shannon scowled deeply. "I wish you'd called us—" he began, but Karen cut him off.

"I called you yesterday," she reminded him, her voice quavering. "I even came to see you, for all the good it did me."

Abashed, Shannon turned away from Karen to study the hills behind the house. Covered with short grass that was already turning brown under the summer sun, they were crisscrossed everywhere with a tangled maze of tracks and paths. A few of them were man-made, but most of the trails had been worn into the earth by grazing cattle and foraging deer. To try to follow anyone up there would be nearly impossible. Still, a plan was already formulating in Mark Shannon's mind.

"Okay, here's what we're going to do," he told the crowd of men who had gathered around him. "I want you to spread out—you all know these hills even better than I do, so let's break up into groups of two. Then we'll stretch a line as far as we can without completely losing sight of each other, and we'll start up into the hills. Anybody sees anything—anything at all—start hollering. I'll be about a third of the way from the north end, and Manny Gomez'll be about a third of the way from the south end. Shouldn't take more'n a few minutes for one or the other of us to get the message." Then an idea struck him. "How many of you guys got cell phones you can take?"

Half a dozen hands went up, and Shannon began splitting the group into teams, spreading the men with cellular phones as evenly along the line as he could. "If anyone with a phone sees anything, call 911, and the dispatcher can patch me or Manny in on the radio. Okay?"

No more than fifteen minutes after the caravan of cars had driven up her driveway, Karen found herself standing behind the house, tightly clutching Molly's shoulders as she watched the cars leave again, this time moving slowly along the rough dirt track that edged the foothills, kicking a cloud of brown dust high into the air.

Russell paused on the crest of the hill to use the bandanna he habitually carried in his hip pocket to wipe the sweat from his forehead. The sun was high in the sky now, and the cool wind coming in from the sea only a little while ago had shifted, turning hot and dry and promising that by this afternoon the temperature might rise to over one hundred degrees.

And still no sign of either Julie or Kevin.

Why hadn't the boy given them some clue of what his idea had been? Couldn't he have at least provided a hint of where he might have gone? To attempt to "follow" Kevin into these hills, with their labyrinth of tracks, Russell realized, was futile. Yet he couldn't bear to give it up and head home.

If he kept at it—if he climbed to the top of just one more hill—he might find them.

Or, more likely, he would find himself gazing once

more, as he was now, over a series of grassy hills, an endless vista broken only by scattered stands of scrub oak and an occasional outcropping of rocks. Turning slowly, Russell scanned the full horizon once more, just as he had from the top of every hill he'd stood upon this morning.

Suddenly he froze as a figure appeared on a low ridge to the east where he himself had stood only twenty minutes ago. Though the figure was too far away for him to recognize, Russell was almost sure it was neither Kevin nor any of the three missing kids.

Cupping his hands around his mouth, Russell filled his lungs with air, then bellowed a single word: "Hello!"

The figure waved, and a moment later Russell heard faint words drifting back to him, almost lost in the building wind. "Find anything?"

Understanding that he was no longer the only person searching for the missing teenagers, Russell started back down the hill, almost breaking into a run in his eagerness to find out how many people had joined in the hunt.

He was nearing the bottom of the slope when he stopped short, his attention caught by something he'd barely glimpsed out of the corner of his eye.

For just a moment he stood frozen as the fragmentary image in his mind coalesced into a dark vision that made his skin crawl with dread.

Certain he must be wrong, praying that what he'd seen had been something else entirely—perhaps the bones of some kind of animal—he braced himself to gaze directly at the object that had set his skin crawling.

Even as he looked at it, part of his mind screamed out that he was mistaken, that what he was seeing wasn't what he believed it to be at all.

A human skeleton, only partially concealed by a clump of brush.

The bones were intact, except for the lower portion of the left leg, which wasn't there at all. Though the bones were picked clean of flesh, Russell could see they were fresh—not totally dried yet, they glistened in the morning sunlight. His gaze moved slowly, reluctantly, over the denuded frame, and finally, as he stared directly at the skull, he winced.

Ants were swarming over it, milling with seeming aimlessness, but as the focus of Russell's eyes sharpened, he saw the tiny fragments of matter gripped in their mandibles, infinitesimal scraps of brain tissue that they were taking back to their nest.

Maggots, their pale white bodies squirming grotesquely, writhed in the empty eye sockets.

But what gripped Russell's attention, what made him feel numb in his soul and nauseated in his belly, was the hair.

Still flowing from the scalp that was intact on the skull was a mass of dark, wavy hair.

Luxuriant hair, which, even though covered with dust, still bore traces of its original luster.

Julie's hair?

A sound boiled up from somewhere deep inside Russell Owen, partly a groan of terrible anguish, partly a pleading cry for help.

After a moment that seemed like an hour, Manny Gomez appeared next to Russell. Only the deputy's strong grip on his arm finally brought Russell out of the trance in which the grisly skeleton held him. At last, he tore his eyes away from it to turn and face the other man.

"How am I going to tell her?" he asked. "How am I going to tell Karen?"

Manny Gomez was silent for a few seconds, his dark eyes perfectly reflecting Russell Owen's anguish, but then his expression hardened as his features settled into the demeanor of a professional. "Let's not get ahead of ourselves, Russell," he said. "We don't know that this is Julie."

"Don't we?" Russell asked, his voice hollow.

As Manny spoke into his radio, quickly telling Mark Shannon what they'd found, Russell's gaze returned to the remains on the ground.

The leg.

What had happened to the missing leg?

A coyote, probably, roaming in the hills last night.

Maybe he'd heard it himself, howling over the meal it had discovered before gnawing the bones loose to drag them off to its hidden den.

He shuddered at the thought, then once more felt Manny Gomez's hand on his arm.

"Come on, Russell," the deputy said, the gruffness in his voice betraying his own emotions. "You don't know who this is. You don't know who it is at all." But even as he said it, Manny knew he believed, as Russell did, that these hideous remains had only two days ago been pretty, lively Julie Spellman.

CHAPTER 24

*E*llen Filmore had been fielding telephone calls all morning. It started the moment she walked into the clinic, arriving early just in case Barry Sadler or the professor at Cal Poly called. The phone had rung even before she put down her purse, and she snatched up the instrument on Roberto's desk, cradling the receiver against her shoulder while she hunted for something with which to take notes. It had not been the biologist from Cal Poly, but Lucy Meyers, wanting to know about rumors she'd heard of some kind of sickness being passed among the teenagers in Pleasant Valley. "I heard Karen Owen's daughter brought something up from Los Angeles, and now they're all getting it. Suzanne Munson says she's not letting Shelley go out at all." Lucy's voice dropped slightly. "Is it true that those three kids aren't missing at all, but that they're locked up in the hospital in San Luis Obispo?"

I only wish it were, Ellen Filmore thought silently. But when she spoke, she tried to reassure Lucy Meyers. "There seems to be something going around, but so far it doesn't look too serious. Even the kids who've caught it aren't really sick. They just get a little pale."

"That's not what *I've* heard," Lucy replied in a tone that let Ellen know that as far as Lucy was concerned, the information she'd gotten from her friends was a lot more reliable than anything a mere doctor might offer her. "I can

320

tell you, I'll be keeping my kids inside for the next few days."

"That's probably a good idea," Ellen said, realizing too late that within twenty minutes Lucy would have called at least ten other women to report that Ellen Filmore was now advocating a quarantine. "Not that I think there's really anything to be too concerned about," she hastily added, deliberately lying rather than risk adding fuel to Lucy Meyers's already panicky state.

No sooner had she finished talking to Lucy than someone else had called, and after that, someone else. By the time Roberto Muñoz had arrived, both lines were ringing steadily, and finally Ellen began to worry that the biologist from Cal Poly would not be able to get through to her at all. She cut each caller shorter than the one before, but by mid-morning rumor was running rampant through the town. Around ten, as she was trying to decide if Jan McLaughlin fretting about Sara should be taken seriously or not, Roberto motioned frantically to her through the glass panel that separated her office from the reception area and mouthed the words "Cal Poly." "Jan?" she broke in. "Look, a call just came in that I really have to take, so I'm going to give you to Roberto—believe me, he knows every bit as much about this as I do."

"But Sara's—" Jan McLaughlin began again, determined not to be put off.

"Tell Roberto," Ellen said, then punched the flashing button that would connect her to the caller from Cal Poly. "Hello? This is Ellen Filmore."

"Harry Matson here," a man with a deep, resonant voice replied. "I've been looking at some blood samples you sent to—"

"Thank God," Ellen interrupted. "You have no idea what's going on here. Both the kids those samples came from are missing." Realizing she was sounding very much like the panicking mothers she'd been trying to calm all morning, she cut herself short. "Do you have any idea what kind of bacteria we're dealing with here?" she asked, deliberately shifting into her most professional tone.

"From what I can see so far, we're not dealing with a bacterium at all," Harry Matson replied. "A bacterium generally reproduces by transverse fission, although in some varieties—"

"—some of them transfer nucleic acid between two cells," Ellen cut in, more impatiently than she'd intended. "I mean, I did go to medical school, Dr. Matson. But if it's not bacteria in those samples, what is it?"

Matson hesitated, and when he spoke again, his tone had lost some of its resonance and taken on a note of worried uncertainty. "I wish I could be sure," he said. "So far, my best guess is that it's a parasite."

"Best guess?" Ellen Filmore echoed. "For God's sake, Dr. Matson, I got a best guess from the lab last night. What I need now is an answer."

"And I'd like to give you one," Doctor Matson replied sharply. The hard edge softened somewhat as he went on, "But it's just not that easy, since what's in that blood is something I've never seen before. But I can tell you what it looks like. It looks exactly like some kind of insect larvae, but on a microscopic scale."

"Insect larvae," Ellen repeated. "That's what Barry Sadler said, too."

"The question is," Matson continued, as if she hadn't spoken, "what is it doing in blood? That's where the best guess that it's a parasite comes in. The whole thing is fascinating, from a scientific standpoint. The larvae are starting to die, but until I can actually look at one of your patients, I can't be certain why. What it looks like, though, is that the larvae feed on the blood, but need some other environment to metamorphose into adults. There don't seem to be any adults at all in the samples you sent to me.

If you can get some samples from some other parts of these patients' bodies—"

"I can't," Ellen broke in. She was just beginning to explain that both the patients had disappeared, when she saw Roberto frantically signaling her. "Look, I'm going to have to call you back." Quickly writing down Harry Matson's phone number, she jabbed at the second line just in time to hear Mark Shannon's voice.

". . . be there in five minutes or so. Just tell her we need her to look at them."

"Mark?" Ellen said. "Mark, it's Ellen. I'm here."

"It's okay," Shannon told her. "Roberto can explain. See you in a few minutes." He hung up, and as she was about to punch the first line, which was again flashing, Roberto called out, "I'm shutting them both off."

Putting both lines on hold, Roberto Muñoz got up from his desk, paused to pour her a cup of coffee from the pot on the table in the waiting room, then dropped into the chair next to her desk and scanned a pad full of notes. "Most of this is just bullshit," he told her. "You can look at it all later. Two things are important. I told Mrs. McL to bring Sara in. From what she says, it sounds like the same thing you had with the other three kids. I told her not to let Sara argue, not to let her out of her sight, and not to stop for anything. I did my best to scare the shit out of her. That okay?"

Ellen Filmore nodded. "Perfect." She ripped the top sheet off her own notepad and handed it to Roberto. "Call Matson back and tell him I may have some more samples for him, and ask him if there's anything specific he wants me to look for. And line up an ambulance, just in case we have to get Sara over to San Luis Obispo in a hurry."

"Got it." He paused only a split second, then went on. "The other thing is Shannon. He's on his way over here with something he wants you to take a look at."

"Something," Ellen repeated in a tone that let Roberto

know he'd better tell her exactly what it was that Shannon was bringing.

Roberto sighed. "It's a skeleton. It's human, and he's pretty sure it's fairly . . ." He hesitated, but saw no way to avoid the word. ". . . fresh," he finished. "He wants you to take a look at it." Dismissing the rest of his notes as being nothing that couldn't be put off until later, Roberto stood up again. "Great day so far, huh?" he said, then headed for his own desk to begin taking care of the details, leaving Ellen Filmore to sip her coffee and gather her thoughts for a moment or two before the next onslaught.

Her cup was still half full when she saw Mark Shannon's squad car pull into the parking lot, immediately followed by Russell Owen's pickup truck, and finally a small four-wheel-drive vehicle she didn't recognize. Car doors slammed, and a moment later Mark, Russell, and two other men stepped into her office.

Mark Shannon placed a large plastic bag on her desk. "Roberto tell you what we've got here?"

Ellen nodded and stood up, forcing a thin smile. "Let's take it into one of the examining rooms, all right? No sense putting it on display for anyone who might walk in here."

She led Shannon into one of the examining rooms behind her office, closing the door to shut the others out. Then she opened the bag and carefully removed the bones, laying them out on the counter that ran the length of one of the walls. Working silently, she listened as Shannon explained that the skeleton had been found intact except for the missing leg, and that the bones had still been lightly attached to each other by a few fragments of cartilage. "But they came apart as I was bagging them up," he finished.

Ellen nodded, first picking up the pelvis, then turning her attention to the skull. Her own mind was putting together an identification as rapidly as had Russell Owen's, but she struggled against the urge to jump to quick conclusions. "Well, there's no question it was a girl, and a fairly young one, too."

"How young?" Shannon asked, already certain he knew what was coming.

Ellen Filmore frowned. "Teenaged, I'd say. Anywhere from thirteen to fifteen." She pointed to the intact teeth in the skull and jaw. "It shouldn't be too hard to get a positive identification from those," she said quietly. Now there was no longer a way to postpone putting a name to the skeleton. "I think you might want to start tracking down Julie Spellman's dental records."

Flicking on his portable radio, Shannon spoke rapidly into the mouthpiece, then turned back to the doctor. "Am I right that they haven't been out there very long?"

"No more than a day or so, at most." Ellen sighed. "And possibly only a few hours."

"Any idea how they got so clean?" Mark asked. "It doesn't look like they've been gnawed on."

Ellen's jaw tightened. "Call me in an hour or so, all right? And you might want to check with Roberto about our other patients' dentists," she said. "I'm not about to positively identify this as Julie Spellman."

"Got it," Mark said. "I'll have a listing of every missing girl in the area by the time I get back to my office."

A few minutes later the examining room cleared out and Ellen set to work, measuring the bones, taking samples from them to send to the lab, and trying to discover how they might have been picked so clean while suffering no apparent damage.

A grisly thought came into her mind as she remembered what had been found a few years earlier in a Milwaukee apartment, yet as she examined the bones, they didn't appear to have been boiled.

Rather, the matter that would normally have been clinging to the bones appeared to have been carefully picked off, down to the last fragment.

Suddenly an image came into her mind.

One day a year ago she'd been out hiking and stumbled across the remains of a small animal. Most of the larger bones were already gone, and all that were left were a few vertebrae, picked fairly clean by the scavengers that fed on carrion. Yet even what was left was still serving as a feast, for the vertebrae had been covered with ants—thousands of them—reaping a final harvest of the last fragments of meat the larger scavengers had left. A few hours later, when she returned along the same route, she'd stopped to look at the bones again.

The ants were gone, the bones having been picked clean.

As clean as the bones on the counter in front of her.

She stared at the bones, and the words of Harry Matson came back to her.

. . . the larvae feed on the blood . . .

But what did the adults feed on?

A thought began to form in her mind—a hideous thought.

Was it possible that Julie Spellman had been totally consumed by something that had been living inside her own body?

Her thoughts were interrupted by the intercom, and Roberto Muñoz's voice. "Mrs. McL and Sara are here, Doc."

Grateful for the distraction from her ruminations, Ellen Filmore turned away from the bones on the countertop.

"It's not Julie!" Karen said, her voice louder than she'd intended it to be.

She sat at the kitchen table, flanked by Russell and Mark Shannon, who had just come back from town.

Karen had listened in silence, her jaw setting stubbornly, while a scream built in her brain. *No!* It was not Julie, could not be Julie.

"It simply can't be Julie," she said again, pushing away from the table and moving to stand, arms tightly crossed to stop herself from shaking, at the counter across the room. "If it was, I'd know. I'd—I'd feel it." She ignored the furtive glance Russell and Shannon exchanged. "You'll see," she went on, hearing the desperation in her own voice, which made her wonder if she truly believed what she was saying, or if she was only trying to convince herself. "As soon as Julie's dental records arrive, you'll both see." Russell stood up and came to put his arms around her. For a moment Karen leaned against his chest, but as her eyes began to moisten with tears, she knew that if she let herself give in to the impulse to collapse into his embrace, her emotional control, already stretched, would snap.

"You'll see," she said again, pulling away from Russell. Once again Russell and Shannon exchanged a glance, and this time Karen knew there was something they hadn't yet told her. "What is it?" she asked, her gaze holding on her husband for a moment, then shifting to the deputy.

Mark Shannon hesitated, then handed Karen a sheet of paper.

She found herself staring down into the face of a girl.

A girl who looked to be the same age as Julie.

A girl who had long dark hair.

Hair like Julie's.

"Wh-What is this?" she asked, though in her heart she already knew what Shannon was going to say.

"Her name is Dawn Sanderson," Mark said. "She disappeared from Los Banos a week ago. Last seen walking out of town, heading toward I-5. Presumably a runaway, and her friends seem to think she might have been heading to L.A. She wanted to be an actress."

"And you think this might be the girl whose skeleton . . ." She trailed off, unable to finish the sentence.

"We're checking her dental records, too," Shannon said. "We should have them by late this afternoon. But the thing is, even if the bones are Dawn Sanderson's, we might have a real bad problem. If it's a serial killer—"

"No!" Karen burst out, her voice rising. "That's not what's happening! It's not! I mean—what about Jeff and Andy? You thought they were all together, didn't you? And if they're all together—"

"We don't know what to think," Mark Shannon said. "All we're doing right now is exploring possibilities, and one of the possibilities we have to be prepared for is that—" He cut off his own words as Karen's face paled. "Well, we just have to be prepared for whatever we might find," he finished.

"I think they're together," Karen said. "I think that Jeff and Julie and Andy Bennett are all together, and that we're going to find them." She forced a smile. "For all we know, Kevin is finding them right now."

Karen and Russell both remembered the note on the refrigerator door, in which Kevin had assured them that he would be home by noon.

It was already nearly one. Nothing had been heard from Kevin; no one who had come down from the search in the hills reported seeing him.

Neither Karen nor Russell was willing to speak the thought they both shared, but each could read it in the other's eyes:

Another of their children was gone.

Vic Costas crested the rise and paused to catch his breath, gasping from the unaccustomed exertion. Pitching hay was one thing, but tramping through the hills was another. Still, he'd come to like Jeff Larkin in the months the boy had lived on his farm, and if he could help find him, he'd keep on hiking, out of breath or not. A minute or two to catch his breath and he'd set off again.

Swabbing the sweat from his forehead with an ancient red bandanna, the old Greek farmer surveyed the valley below him. He could not remember having been up here before, for surely he would remember the sight of a valley as pretty as this one, with a stream meandering across its floor, oak trees studding its hillside, and what looked like a cave on the opposite side.

A cave . . .

When he was a boy back in Greece, he and one of his friends had found a cave in the hills behind their village, and used it as a place of refuge, a place to hide from their parents.

Costas frowned, an idea forming in his mind.

Could it be?

Stuffing the bandanna back in his pocket, he started down the hillside, half running, half sliding as he struggled to prevent himself from losing his footing. Coming to the bottom of the steep slope, he paused to catch his breath once more, this time dropping to his knees to scoop water up from the stream and pour it over his sweat-soaked head. The dust cleaned from his face, he scooped up more of the clean, fresh water, sucking it thirstily from his cupped hands.

Then, his thirst almost quenched, he sensed something watching him. He glanced over his shoulder, half expecting to see a coyote poised on the hillside, one foot trembling in the air as it studied him.

There was nothing.

He bent to take a final drink from the stream when a movement in the shadows at the entrance to the cave caught his attention. Standing, he shaded his eyes, squinting against the glare of the sun. Nothing.

Then a figure stepped out of the shadows, and Vic Costas gasped.

Julie Spellman.

He was certain it was she, for her long dark hair was cascading over her shoulders just as he remembered from the other day when she'd come over to baby-sit Ben Larkin.

Yet except for her hair, she looked nothing like the image he now conjured from his memory.

Julie Spellman had been slim.

The girl he beheld now looked almost bloated, her body distended in an unnatural way that made Vic Costas's skin crawl and sent a strange anticipatory shiver down his spine.

The shiver coagulated into a stab of fear a moment later when her eyes fixed on him and she raised an arm to point a single finger directly at him, just as the ancient crone back home had when he was a boy.

The crone who cursed him when he and his friends called her a witch.

Suddenly the same irrational fear he'd felt when he was seven years old welled up in him, and he turned to flee from Julie Spellman's pointing finger just as he'd wheeled around and fled from the old Greek woman's gnarled hand more than half a century earlier.

He'd only taken a few steps when he stumbled, lurched on another two steps, then tripped once more, this time crumpling to the ground. He struggled to regain his feet and had started to push himself up with his hands when he felt a burning sensation on his right palm and yelped in pain. Dropping to a sitting position, he lifted his injured hand and stared at it.

His palm was covered with red ants. Even as he thrashed his arm, wildly trying to shake them off, he tried to imagine where they had come from so quickly: an army of them that continued to prick him, their tiny stingers bombarding his bloodstream with venom.

Now his ankles were beginning to burn, too. He looked down to see more ants—thousands of them—swarming over his shoes, disappearing up under his denim pants.

Gasping with shock and pain, Vic Costas began swatting at his pants, and tried once again to struggle to his feet.

Then he heard the hum.

Faint at first, it quickly grew into a loud droning. By the time Vic realized it was coming from the direction of the cave, the bees were on him, a dense cloud swirling around him, landing on his face, his hands, the back of his neck—attacking every inch of exposed skin.

As fast as one of them would pull away, leaving its stinger embedded in his skin, another replaced it.

Vic was screaming with pain now, his arms flailing as he tried to ward the bees off. Finally, he stumbled toward the stream, where the water, if it was deep enough, would protect him from the bees and soothe the burning agony that was quickly overwhelming him.

He was still a step or two short of the water when he collapsed. For a minute or two he lay in the dust, twitching like a snake whose back has been smashed with a rock, gurgling moans burbling up from his fast-constricting throat.

He clawed at his neck with his fingers as his windpipe closed and thrashed wildly, gasping for breath until, in mere seconds, his supply of oxygen completely cut off, he began to sink into a dark oblivion.

An oblivion where, mercifully, he could no longer feel the stings of the insects that were still attacking him.

The moment his heartbeat stopped and the last spasm of his diaphragm eased, the bees dispersed.

But now more ants came, welling up out of their subterranean nests, scurrying across the hard-packed ground to swarm over the corpse, already beginning their task of picking the meat from his bones.

Flies gathered, laying eggs which would soon hatch into maggots that would feed on Vic Costas's entrails and brain.

Within a few hours the corpse of Vic Costas, like that of Dawn Sanderson, would have all but disappeared, leaving only a few bones on the floor of the valley, from which the buzzards that were already wheeling overhead could pick a meager meal.

Then the coyotes would come, and soon the bones, too, would be scattered over the hills surrounding the valley.

From the entrance of the cave, Julie Spellman watched Vic Costas die, then turned and moved slowly back into the coolness of the cavern, following the orders of the force within her, just as the bees and ants had when they attacked the old Greek farmer and brought him to his sudden, pain-wracked end.

CHAPTER 25

*S*ara McLaughlin was terrified.

She was in a room in the hospital in San Luis Obispo. A private room, with a television set, which she could watch as much as she wanted.

Until this morning, that would have been Sara's idea of paradise.

But from the moment she woke up, she'd felt terrible—her whole body was itchy, and no amount of scratching relieved it. Nothing seemed to affect the burning, prickling sensation—not the calamine lotion she'd tried, or the sunburn spray, or anything else.

For most of the day she'd also been shivering with the same kind of chills she'd had ten years ago, when she almost died of scarlet fever.

A little while ago she'd felt so sick at her stomach she was sure she would throw up right there in bed, or maybe even pass out.

Yet no matter how hard she tried to tell the doctors and nurses how she felt, she couldn't.

She would rehearse the words in her mind, even repeat them silently to herself over and over before trying to speak them. Yet each time she opened her mouth, it was as if someone else was talking, as if someone she didn't even know had taken over her body and was speaking for her.

But at least no one believed what she was saying. At

least they could see that she was sick, even if she couldn't say the words.

But how could she feel so cold, so feverish, when her temperature kept registering normal?

She even *looked* sick. Every time she caught sight of herself in the mirror, her face seemed to have lost more color, and her hair was starting to look all damp and stringy, the way it did whenever she got the flu.

But that wasn't the worst part.

The worst part was the relentless restlessness that would not release her from its grip. A feeling that she must get out of this room, escape from the hospital, flee up into the hills that beckoned to her from beyond the window. From the moment she'd gotten up that morning, she felt an urge to go up into the hills. The urge had kept getting stronger and stronger. If her mother hadn't almost literally forced her into the car and taken her to the clinic, she was certain she would have given in to it.

But Sara hated the hills. She had always been afraid to venture away from town, afraid of becoming hopelessly lost, afraid of being bitten by a rattlesnake or attacked by a coyote.

Yet today the urge to climb up into the rolling brown wilderness was so strong she was losing the will to resist it.

Her stomach knotting with fear, Sara once more gazed up at her mother, and tried yet again to describe what was happening to her. But when she spoke, her voice once again betrayed her. "Why do I have to stay here?" she demanded, her voice taking on a petulant quality that made her want to scream with rage and frustration. Her fingers twisted and tugged at a lock of her hair. "There's nothing wrong with me! If my dad were here—"

God! Why had she said that? Her mother *hated* it when she started blaming everything bad that happened on the fact that her mother had thrown her father out of the house last year. And she'd stopped doing it three months ago! Why had it suddenly come out now? Sure enough, the sympathy she'd seen in her mother's eyes only a second ago now turned to annoyance.

"If your dad were here, nothing would be any different," Jan McLaughlin said. "Believe it or not, your father has nothing to do with illness. And you have to stay here because they don't know what's wrong with you."

Though Sara's lips twisted into an angry pout and she turned to stare out the window, inside she felt a wave of relief. Don't let them believe me, she prayed silently. No matter what I say, don't let them believe me! "But I keep telling you," she said out loud, helpless to keep from speaking the words that were tumbling unbidden from her lips, "there's nothing wrong with me! I'm fine!"

Jan McLaughlin's tortured eyes shifted from her daughter to Ellen Filmore, who had arrived from Pleasant Valley an hour ago to check on the condition of her patient. "Maybe I ought to take her home," she fretted. "If she's going to be this unhappy—"

No! Sara wanted to scream. Don't take me home! Don't take me anywhere! Lock me up in here! Please . . . please . . . help me.

Yet despite the anguished phrases she could cry only in the silence of her mind, she felt her mouth harden once more into an angry line. Don't give in, she silently begged once more, praying that somehow, by some miracle, Dr. Filmore would hear the message she was desperately trying to send.

To Sara's relief, Ellen Filmore held up a hand to cut the flow of Jan McLaughlin's words. "Until we know exactly what is happening to Sara, I can't approve her going anywhere. Not only do we not know what it is she's got, but we don't have any idea how she caught it, or how contagious it might be."

Kevin Owen! Sara wanted to scream. I got it from Kevin!

But as with everything else that Sara McLaughlin wanted to say, the words died silently long before she could force them from her throat.

It was late in the afternoon by the time Ellen Filmore got back to Pleasant Valley. The drive through the hills from San Luis Obispo had gone quickly, for Ellen had been busy trying to fit together the bits and pieces of the puzzle that confronted her.

While she was at the hospital that afternoon, three specialists had come in to examine Sara, but none of them were able to make any sense of her condition. Though they'd muttered a few comforting platitudes in the presence of Jan McLaughlin, their opinions had been much less hopeful when they finally met to confer with Ellen alone.

The gist of it was that while they had no idea what the source of Sara's disease was, they were very sure what it wasn't.

It wasn't a bacteria, but Ellen already knew that.

Nor was it a virus or a retrovirus.

They kept coming back to some sort of parasite, but even the specialist in tropical diseases—which were the most logical explanation of the presence of larvae in the bloodstream—hadn't been able to come up with anything to fit the facts.

Indeed, the only real facts they had were that the same larval forms that had been found in Julie Spellman's and Jeff Larkin's blood had also been found in Sara McLaughlin's.

Each of the specialists had ordered his own battery of tests, and samples had been taken from various areas of Sara's body.

Some of the tests had been merely uncomfortable.

Others had been downright painful.

And through it all, Sara had steadfastly insisted that there was nothing wrong with her, that she felt fine.

Ellen Filmore didn't believe a word of it, which was one of the things she was most worried about. What kind of disease would make a person who was obviously ill insist that he was not?

What kind of disease could mask itself so perfectly that its presence would not be betrayed by fever, or abnormal blood pressure, or a change in either respiration or heart rate?

Most frightening of all, what kind of disease could prevent its victim from even complaining of not feeling right?

The answer was that no disease fit the parameters of Ellen's questions. At least, no disease that Ellen Filmore or any of the specialists who had examined Sara that day had ever heard of, nor any disease that was contained in the data banks of the three medical libraries that Ellen had tapped into through the computer at the hospital in San Luis Obispo.

Ellen Filmore was beginning to understand exactly how the doctors who had encountered the first AIDS cases must have felt.

Puzzled, then baffled, then terrified.

As the car wound through the hills along Highway 41, Ellen reviewed over and over again what she knew.

And over and over again she kept coming back to Julie Spellman.

Somehow, it had all started with her. Was it something she had brought with her from Los Angeles?

But if that was true, then the organism she was carrying must have had a dormancy period, since Julie had been fine for the first week she'd been in Pleasant Valley.

Yet the other kids had begun showing symptoms almost immediately.

Could something have triggered the organism?

Ellen suddenly felt a chill, recalling the first time she'd seen Julie, after the girl had been attacked by the bees from the hives on her stepfather's farm.

She had treated those stings with the new antivenin that had saved Molly's life a few days earlier.

Could the antivenin have somehow triggered whatever organism was in Julie's blood, transmuting it from a benign presence into an active parasite, which she then passed on to Jeff Larkin, Andy Bennett, and Sara?

But if that were the case, why had they all begun to show symptoms at different times?

Neither Andy nor Sara had seen Julie since they'd all gone to the movies the day Julie had been stung. If she'd passed it on to them that night, why hadn't they all begun showing symptoms at the same time?

Varying incubation periods, possibly. But would parasitic life have a varying incubation period, particularly in environments so similar as various human bodies?

Instead of turning toward her house on Third Street when she came into Pleasant Valley, Ellen drove on through town, finally pulling into the parking lot at the clinic. Except for her own car, the lot was empty—even Roberto Muñoz had gone home for the day. She let herself in, going into her office and pulling the Rolodex to a position directly in front of her.

Then she began making telephone calls.

Shelley Munson, who had been at the movies with the rest of the kids the day Julie had been stung, was still feeling fine, and, more important, looked fine to both her parents.

Kevin Owen had begun looking a little strange after he'd gone up into the hills with Jeff Larkin yesterday morning, and was now missing.

And Shelley had seen Kevin with Sara yesterday afternoon.

Part of the sequence, then, was clear: Julie, to Jeff, to Kevin, to Sara.

But what about Andy Bennett?

If he'd gotten it from Julie the night they went to the movies, then why hadn't he been infected then, too?

Why Jeff, and not Andy, until later?

And then, from the depths of her mind, the truth suddenly came to her.

It had been there all along, of course. She had simply refused to let herself see it.

It wasn't that the antivenin had triggered anything.

The antivenin itself was the culprit.

She herself had injected it into Julie, and into Andy Bennett, and by the next day, each of them had fallen sick.

But what about Molly? Molly had been given the same antidote when she'd been stung, hadn't she?

Suddenly, scenes began flashing through her mind.

The vial in San Luis Obispo, labeled with a word so polysyllabic she hadn't even been able to pronounce it.

The vial Carl Henderson had handed her the morning he'd brought Julie into the clinic.

What if he'd handed her the wrong vial?

Alone in her office, Ellen Filmore groaned out loud.

How could she have given her patient a shot of something whose name she couldn't even pronounce? And not just one patient, but two?

Her heart pounding, she left her office and went into the examining room where she'd treated both Julie Spellman and Andy Bennett. Crossing to the counter, she pulled one of the drawers open, frantically searching for the tiny brown bottle.

There it was, exactly where she'd left it.

She snatched it up, her eyes fixing on the label, her memory scrambling to bring up an image of the label that had been on the vial in San Luis Obispo.

But even as she struggled to recognize the name of the chemical, she saw something else.

The level of fluid in the bottle.

After she'd given Andy Bennett his shot, the vial had been reduced to only half its capacity. She remembered it clearly, because she'd made a mental note to ask Carl Henderson for more.

The bottle in her hand was full.

But that was impossible!

Unless Roberto had called UniGrow and gotten more.

The small brown vial clutched tightly in her hand, she went back to her office, picked up the phone and rang Roberto's number. When the answering machine picked up on the sixth ring, she hung up, for now more memories were rising up from the depths of her mind.

The story Otto Owen had told, of finding Carl Henderson trying to rape Julie.

A story Otto had stuck to, even though Julie herself had denied it.

Denied it, but only after Ellen had given her a shot from a vial that Carl Henderson himself had given her.

Was it possible that Carl had deliberately given her the wrong bottle?

Her mind raced as she remembered Carl trying to take the vial back from her, and she refusing to give it to him.

And Carl had come in yesterday, complaining of a stomachache. She had examined him in the very same room from which she'd just taken the vial.

As the pieces all began to fall together, a terrible fury rose in Ellen Filmore.

If Otto had been right about what he claimed to have seen, then maybe Carl hadn't been trying to save Julie Spellman's life at all! Maybe he'd actually been hoping she'd die!

And when she didn't, he'd simply walked out, leaving

her to administer whatever had been in that vial to other
people!

Furious, she snatched up her purse, dropped the vial
into the jumble inside it, then left the clinic once more,
driving directly to the sheriff's office behind the city hall.

It was locked and deserted, and instantly Ellen knew
why.

The deputies were still up in the hills, searching for the
missing kids.

The kids Carl Henderson had poisoned.

Poisoned deliberately.

She sat in her car, seething with anger.

At last, gunning her car's engine, she pulled away from
the curb.

Part of her mind knew that what she was about to do
was a mistake. Instead of allowing her rage to dictate her
actions, she should simply go home, fix herself a drink,
get herself calmed down, and decide rationally on the best
course of action.

At least she should wait until she could talk to Roberto,
and make certain that he hadn't, after all, simply picked up
more of the antivenin when he'd driven over to San Luis
Obispo yesterday.

But even as the fleeting thoughts of rationality drifted
through her mind, her rage at Carl Henderson overpow-
ered all reason.

She had to confront him.

Now.

Carl Henderson was in his basement lab when the doorbell
rang. He was tempted to ignore it and let whoever was
there keep ringing until he finally gave up and went away.

But his car was parked in front of the house. So whoever was out there knew he was home, or at least close by,
and might not give up at all.

Yet what he was observing in his laboratory was so fas-

cinating that he hated to leave, even for the few minutes
it would take to get rid of whoever was at the door.

He was staring into the acrylic box that contained the
rat he'd injected the night before with the serum from the
vial he'd removed from Ellen Filmore's office.

The incriminating vial, which he couldn't allow to be
found there.

Now, staring through the transparent panels of the box,
he knew beyond a shadow of a doubt that he'd been right
to retrieve the tiny bottle.

Not that he understood yet exactly what had happened
inside the box. That would take hours, perhaps days,
studying the remains of the rat through his microscope.

The doorbell rang again, and Henderson finally turned
away from the acrylic box, shut off the bright lights above
the counter, and quickly mounted the steep stairs to the
first floor. Switching off the basement light before he
stepped through, he made sure the door under the stairwell
was closed securely before moving down the hall to the
foyer. There, he pushed aside the shirred linen that covered
the beveled glass panels of the front door.

Standing on the porch was Ellen Filmore—with a look
on her face that sent fear coursing through him.

Carefully masking his nervousness with his best smile,
Henderson opened the door. "Ellen," he greeted her.
"What a nice—"

"Don't," she cut in, her voice ice cold, her words sharp
as razor blades. "I know what you did, Carl. I know what
you gave me to inject into Julie Spellman wasn't the antivenin that saved Molly."

Henderson did his best to feign surprise. Pulling the
door wider, he drew her inside with a gesture. "The antivenin?" he asked. "What do you mean, it wasn't what
saved Molly? Of course it was. And it worked on Julie,
too."

"Did it?" Ellen asked, her voice turning bitter as her

rage swelled. "Is she dead now, Carl? *Were* those her bones they found up in the hills today?"

Carl felt another shiver of fear go through him. What bones was she talking about? Was it possible that—

He put the thought out of his mind. Even if they'd found a bone or two, what could it possibly prove? "Ellen, I'm afraid you've lost me," he said, his voice still betraying nothing of his roiling emotions. "Perhaps you'd better let me fix you a drink, and you can tell me exactly what's on your mind." He turned and started into the living room, switching on the chandelier as he passed through the door. The light, refracting through the crystal prisms of the fixture, made the iridescent shells of the hundreds of beetles glitter in the display cases that lined the walls. From every table arrays of butterflies seemed almost ready to rise through the glass panels and begin fluttering through the room.

Ellen Filmore, stepping through the doorway on the heels of Carl Henderson, stopped short, gasping at the display.

Henderson, already at the small butler's cart that served him as a bar, turned to smile at her. "You've never been here before, have you? Do insects interest you?"

"They didn't," Ellen Filmore replied coldly, "until today."

Even as she spoke the words, she realized her mistake, for something in Carl Henderson's demeanor suddenly changed.

Not much, really—just a faltering in his smile and a darkening in his eyes.

But it was enough to tell Ellen that he knew exactly what she was talking about, and that it had been a mistake to come here.

A mistake to give in to the fury that had possessed her when she pieced together what he'd done. Instinctively she took a step backward, then turned to start toward the front door.

Carl Henderson, though, was far faster than she expected him to be. She was barely reaching for the doorknob when his left arm snaked around her neck and his right hand grasped her wrist, easily pulling it away from the door and twisting it into a painful lock behind her back. "You can scream if you want," he said. "Believe me, no one will hear you."

"Let me go," Ellen demanded, but even she could hear that the anger that had strengthened her voice only a moment ago had now turned to fear.

"I don't think I can do that, Ellen," Henderson told her. He was propelling her down the hall now. For a moment she thought he was taking her into the kitchen. But he stopped abruptly, jerking painfully on her right arm, and opened a small door beneath the stairs.

Partly pushing her, partly restraining her, Henderson worked Ellen down the stairs into the basement. "If you really want to know about that shot," he said, his voice grating harshly in her ear, "I suppose there's no reason not to show you."

He propelled her across the floor. Then, still clasping her right arm in the agonizing hammerlock, he reached up and jerked the string that lit the fluorescent fixture above the counter.

Ellen blinked in the sudden glare of light, then her eyes focused on the acrylic box and the rat inside it.

The rat was dead.

Its skin was torn from the fury with which it had scratched the terrible itching that had afflicted it the night before, and its nose was bleeding from the battering it had taken as the swarm in its body had tried to escape the humming of the ventilation fan.

Now the remains of the rat lay on the floor of the cage, but it wasn't that bleeding pulp that drew Ellen's attention.

It was the black film on the side of the box farthest from the ventilating fan.

Though she couldn't distinguish one individual from another, she could see that the whole mass was moving, undulating, crawling across the acrylic panel to form an ever-changing mass.

"What is it?" she breathed, her eyes locking onto the dark mass.

"A swarm," Carl Henderson told her. "A swarm of something that seems to behave exactly like a hive of bees, or a colony of ants. They invade, they feed, they multiply, and then, when the swarm becomes too big, they divide. An invasion force sets out, conquers a new host, and colonizes." He smiled. "And I created it," he added. "A new form of life, which I created."

As the words sank into Ellen Filmore's consciousness, she stared numbly at the dead rat. "They killed it, didn't they?" she asked, her voice hollow as she realized what must be happening to the four missing adolescents.

"I'm not sure yet," Henderson replied, his voice reflecting no emotion at all. "They may have killed it, or they may have simply driven it insane, so that it killed itself trying to escape." He smiled again, but since he still stood behind her back, Ellen couldn't see the coldness in the expression. "I'll know more by morning," he said. "And perhaps I'll tell you what I find out."

He began moving her once more, propelling her toward a door at the far end of the basement. "You won't like it in here," he said as he opened the door. He shoved her inside, then pulled it quickly closed. "Neither did the girl I found on the freeway," he added more loudly, so she could clearly hear him. "And Otto Owen hated it, even though he wasn't really in it very long." He turned and started back toward the counter to begin his investigation of the organisms—*his* organisms—that were trapped inside the acrylic box.

A new strain of microscopic bee, if it truly was a bee at all, which Carl Henderson had developed in his basement lab. Even if it wasn't what he had intended to accomplish, it would still be the crowning achievement of his life.

A new form of life, never before seen on the planet.

His form.

Apis hendersoni.

He turned to speak to Ellen Filmore through the door once again.

"You'll learn to like my specimens," he said. "And they'll like you, too."

CHAPTER 26

"*I* don't think I can stand to go home," Marge Larkin said, gazing bleakly out into the gathering dusk. It was almost eight, and the search had been called off for the night, the last of the volunteers straggling down from the hills half an hour ago. Now Marge sat in the living room of Karen and Russell's house, her mind numb, her emotions exhausted. Even her body felt far more tired than it normally did at this hour. Though she wasn't really hungry—hadn't been all day—she reached out to the coffee table and picked at the platter of ham someone—she didn't even remember who—had brought over that afternoon.

"Don't go home," Karen told her, understanding how Marge would feel as the night wore on. Karen recalled the night after Richard had died, when she finally forced herself to go to bed, then lay awake all night, loneliness gathering over her like a physical force, a slowly growing weight that made her wonder if she would ever find the strength to get up again. Tonight it would be like that for Marge, she thought. Karen had Russell to cling to, while Marge had only Ben.

The little boy was now sprawled on the floor of the den with Molly, both of them staring at the television. As Karen glanced through the open doors into the other room, she almost envied the nine-year-olds their ability to lose themselves in the images on the television screen, to for-

347

get, even if for a few minutes, that something in their lives had gone terribly wrong. No, Ben simply wasn't old enough to help get his mother through the desperation that would come as the night wore on.

Turning back to face Marge again, Karen reached out and squeezed the other woman's hand. "We've got plenty of room, really." When Marge still looked hesitant, Karen said, "It's time for Molly to go to bed, so why don't we just have Russell tuck Ben in, too?"

"You're sure you don't mind?" Marge asked. "It would sure—well, it would sure just make things a little easier. The way I feel right now, I just don't know how I'd make it through the night."

"We'll make it," Karen told her, injecting a lot more confidence into her voice than she really felt. Even as she spoke the words, though, an anguished sob rose in her throat. She quickly got to her feet. "Molly? Time for bed."

"Not yet," Molly replied, automatically shifting into her bargaining mode, just as she did every night. "It's only—"

"Eight," Karen told her. As Molly started to argue again, Karen shook her head. "Not tonight Molly. Please don't argue, sweetheart." Moving into the den, she reached down, lifted Molly to her feet, then stood there for a moment, her fingers resting on the soft skin of Molly's cheek. Be all right, she prayed silently. If something happens to you, too, I won't be able to stand it. I really won't.

"But I'm worried about Julie and Kevin, too," Molly insisted, as if she'd unconsciously picked up on her mother's thoughts.

"I'm sure they're all right," Karen told her. "Maybe by morning they'll have come home. Wouldn't that be nice?"

Molly nodded, but Karen could tell by the look in her eyes that the little girl didn't believe the words any more than she herself did. "Ben's going to stay tonight," she said, grasping at anything to distract Molly's attention, certain that if they talked any more about Julie and Kevin, she would burst into tears. As she'd hoped, Molly's expression instantly brightened.

"Can he sleep in my room?"

Karen shook her head. "But he'll be in the room right next door, and tomorrow morning when you go out to take care of Flicka, he can help you. Won't that be fun?"

Just as Karen had hoped, the idea of having Ben stay the night distracted Molly enough so that she let Russell pick her up and carry her to the stairs with no further protest.

"You, too, Ben," Marge Larkin called from the living room. "Time for bed."

The little boy, detecting his mother's false cheer, got up from the floor and went to the living room, where he wrapped his arms around Marge's neck. "Don't worry," he whispered into her ear. "Jeff will come home. I know he will!"

Marge's arms closed around her younger son. "I know," she replied. "I know." But as Ben followed Russell up the stairs a moment later, Marge knew that she didn't believe the words she'd spoken to Ben any more than Karen had believed what she'd told Molly.

"Are Kevin and Julie and Jeff really going to come back?" Molly asked as Russell tucked her quilt snugly around her shoulders a few minutes later.

"I hope so," he told her, leaning down to kiss her cheek. Then he winked at her. "Who knows? Maybe your mother's right. Maybe by the time you wake up tomorrow, they'll be back. Wouldn't that be a nice surprise?"

Molly nodded, but she could tell that her stepfather didn't really believe they were coming back, either. Tears welled up in her eyes. "What if they don't come back?" she whispered, her voice trembling. "What if something bad happened to them?"

Russell felt helpless in the face of the little girl's misery.

"But they will," he said, barely able to mask his own desperation. "I'm *sure* they will." Hearing a soft whimpering at the door, Russell looked up to see Bailey standing there, one forepaw up, his tail wagging uncertainly. Russell frowned, then understood. "You want to sleep with Molly tonight, boy? Is that it?"

The big dog's tail began wagging furiously and he bounded into the room, leaping up onto Molly's bed, then flopping himself down next to the little girl. To Russell's relief, Molly's tears dried up. "Can he sleep with me?" she asked. "Can he really?"

Russell nodded. "I don't see why not." He leaned over and kissed Molly once more, then scratched Bailey's ears. "You two take good care of each other, all right?"

Molly nodded, slipping her arm around Bailey, and the big dog happily licked her cheek, his heavy tail thumping on the mattress.

Russell snapped off the light, closed the door, and went back downstairs.

Molly and Ben, at least, would sleep through the night.

The rest of them, he was certain, would not.

The moon hung low in the sky, casting a dim glow over the valley floor but leaving the interior of the cave swathed in a velvety blackness. Kevin Owen sat on the cavern's floor, his back resting against the cold rock wall that formed the inner limit of the chamber, his eyes staring vacantly toward the pale gray luminescence beyond the entrance, but his mind focusing only on stimuli he'd barely noticed until he'd come here today.

All around him, from every part of the cave, insects buzzed softly in the night. But tonight, instead of blending into a monotonous white noise that would drop quickly from the forefront of his consciousness, each sound remained clear and distinct.

Just beyond the entrance he could hear crickets chirruping, their musical note seemingly a beacon, not merely to members of their species, but to other creatures as well.

In sharp counterpoint to the crickets' gentle melody, elater beetles were clicking loudly, and each time Kevin heard one of the sharp snapping sounds, he could almost see the little creatures' bodies lifting off the floor, flipping in the air, then dropping back.

Though he couldn't see them at all, he could sense the presence of ants creeping over the packed earth of the cavern's floor. Indeed, he could even hear something he imagined might be their mandibles working as they discovered bits of detritus to break up and carry back with them to their nests, hidden below the ground.

The most distinct sound, though, was the sound of the bees.

From all around him the vibration came, a nearly subliminal tone to which something inside him seemed to be responding.

For the first time since the sickness had come upon him, the terrible sensations inside his body had eased.

The itching, the terrible itching that had permeated his entire body, had stopped, and the chills of fever that had held him firmly in their grip for almost two days had finally released him from their icy embrace.

A breeze, set up from the steady beating of millions of tiny wings, caressed his skin. And the fear that had been his constant companion since he'd first come up here with Jeff Larkin had finally faded away, and he knew that he had come to the place where he belonged.

He had come home.

He had no idea how long he'd sat with his back against the wall, how long he'd listened only to the narcotizing sounds of the insects that surrounded him, for his consciousness of himself as an individual had begun to fade.

No longer was he Kevin Owen, for the swarming organism that now inhabited his body had repressed all but a few scraps of Kevin's own personality, bending both his mind and his body to its own imperatives and those of the greater swarm of which it, in its turn, was only a minor part.

As he sat in the darkness, an urge began to form in Kevin, a primal instinct that he was helpless to disobey.

Following a set of instructions that seemed to have no distinct origin nor any true form that his mind could have recognized, even had he wanted it to, Kevin silently rose from his position and moved toward the entrance of the cavern. Emerging from the mouth of the cave, he paused, standing perfectly still, his eyes unfocused.

The night seemed to have come alive.

The air was thick with flying insects, and the floor of the valley seemed to have become a living entity, for in the dim moonlight a constantly shifting carpet of tiny creatures was barely visible, creeping and crawling in what the ordinary observer would have seen as no more than a random pattern. Something in the massive horde's movements penetrated the entity within Kevin, and he began to move once more, eastward across the valley toward the hill beyond.

Beneath his feet, crushed by the heavy soles of his shoes, thousands of insects died, but even as the life was pressed out of them, their bodies were instantly devoured by the other insects around them.

The carpet they formed remained untorn, the pattern in which they moved unbroken.

By the time he reached the base of the hill and began climbing, the pattern the insects danced on the valley floor had imprinted itself upon Kevin's mind.

And his body—no longer his own—had become a slave to it.

He walked through the darkness, oblivious to the lack of light, his own intelligence now totally suppressed by the alien consciousness of the hive that had invaded his body.

* * *

Molly woke up in the darkness of her room, certain that something was wrong. She was lying on her side, with her back to the window. Though she had not opened her eyes, had not heard anything, either, she still knew she was no longer alone.

Someone—or something—else was there.

Clamping her eyes more tightly closed, she tried not to move, certain that if she so much as wiggled a finger, whatever it was would leap at her, pouncing on her out of the darkness, tearing her apart like the ogres she'd read about in her fairy-tale books.

Time seemed to stand still, and finally Molly risked opening her eyes. Just a little—just barely enough to see the slight glow of the moonlight coming in through the window.

The moonlight, and a shadow!

Involuntarily she drew in her breath in a soft gasp, then held it, fearful that whatever was in the room must have heard her.

The shadow moved!

And now she heard it, too.

Something was moving toward her, coming from the direction of the window, moving around the foot of the bed—

A scream rose in her throat, but she refused to let it out, because if she did, whatever was coming for her would certainly leap onto her and—

And then Bailey, whimpering eagerly, licked at her face.

Her breath exploded as the paralyzing fear that had gripped her a second ago evaporated, and she threw her arms around the big dog, burying her face in the fur of his neck. "Don't *do* that," she whispered, as if the dog could understand every word she said. "You *scared* me!"

Bailey slurped at her face again, then pulled away from her clinging arms to trot back to the window. Putting his front paws on the sill, he whimpered softly, then turned and stared at Molly, who was now sitting up in her bed. "What is it, Bailey?" she asked, keeping her voice no louder than a whisper. When Bailey whimpered again, she slid out of bed and went to crouch by the dog, slipping one arm around him as she struggled to see into the darkness beyond the window.

Her forehead furrowing into a deep scowl, she tried to figure out what to do.

Ben Larkin was in the room next door to hers.

But where was everybody else?

Padding silently across the floor in her bare feet, she opened her door a crack and listened.

The house was silent.

Pulling the door open a little farther, Molly slipped out into the hall, then went to the room next door. Once again she stopped to listen, but still heard nothing. Finally she opened the door, crept inside, and shook Ben awake. "Ben," she whispered. "Ben, wake up!"

Ben rolled over, his eyes finally opening. "What?" he asked. "What's wrong?"

"It's Bailey," Molly said. "He's acting real funny. Come and look! Come *on*!"

Rubbing the sleep out of his eyes, Ben pulled on his pants and shirt, then followed Molly into her room, where Bailey was still at the window, whimpering eagerly. "Look at him," Molly said. "What's he doing?"

Ben, like Molly a few minutes ago, went to the window and peered out into the darkness, but saw nothing. "Maybe he has to go outside," Ben said. He turned and cocked his head at Bailey. "Outside?" he asked. "Want to go outside, boy?" Bailey wagged his tail furiously and dashed to Molly's closed bedroom door. "Get dressed," Ben told Molly. "We'll take him down and let him out. He has to go to the bathroom."

Molly scowled at Ben. "I'm not taking off my pajamas

with you in here," she announced. "Besides, if we're going outside, you have to put on your shoes."

Less than a minute later, with Molly clutching at Bailey's collar to keep him from bolting ahead of her, she and Ben stood at the top of the stairs, staring down into the glow of light spilling from the living room into the foyer. "What if our moms catch us?" Molly whispered. "They'll never let us go out this late."

Ben's lips pursed, then he motioned for Molly to follow him, and turned away from the stairs, tiptoeing rapidly back to the room. When both Molly and Bailey were inside too, he closed the door, then went to the window. "I bet we can jump off that," he said, pointing to the roof of the back porch, which slanted away from the wall only a couple of feet below the windowsill.

Molly gazed at the edge of the porch. It couldn't be any higher than the roof of the carport behind the building they'd lived in back in L.A., and she'd jumped off that lots of times.

Well, she'd jumped off it once, but she hadn't hurt herself.

"What about Bailey?" she asked Ben, who was already out on the porch roof, gingerly creeping down toward its lower edge. The boy glanced back and whistled softly, and the dog scrambled out the window onto the roof.

A moment later Molly followed, and a few seconds after that, the two children and the dog were all lined up on the edge of the porch, peering down at the ground eight feet below. "Can you do it?" Ben whispered, and Molly could tell by his voice that he didn't believe she would.

Instead of answering him, she rolled over on her stomach and slid down the roof until she was dangling from the rain gutter, only her fingers supporting her. She clung there for a second, then took a deep breath and let go. A split second later she was on the ground, grinning up at Ben.

"Come on," she hissed. "Hurry up, or they'll hear us!"

Suddenly Bailey, crouched next to Ben, stiffened, his ears pricking, his whole body quivering. An instant later he launched himself off the roof, hit the ground on all fours, and charged off toward the chicken coop.

"What is it?" Molly whispered to Ben as he dropped down beside her. "What's he doing?"

And suddenly the same idea occurred to both children, and Ben's eyes widened with excitement. "I bet he smells Kevin," he said. "Dogs can do that, you know. They can smell stuff from miles away!"

"But if he's around here, how come he doesn't come home?" Molly challenged.

Ben shrugged elaborately. "How should I know? Maybe he tripped and fell. Maybe he's lying out there with a broken leg or something!"

Following Bailey, the children were drawn down the slope toward the chicken coop. They were almost there when they saw a flash of movement, and a dark shape moved through the gate. Struck with fear, Molly froze in her tracks. But instead of dashing toward the figure, as she expected him to do, Bailey pressed against Molly's knees, a low growl forming in his throat. Terrified, Molly felt her knees begin to shake, but then the shadowed figure turned and moonlight fell full on its face.

"K-Kevin?" Molly gasped, her eyes widening as she recognized her stepbrother in the gloom of the night. And yet, even as she recognized him, she also knew Ben had been right.

Something had happened to Kevin.

For even in the moonlight, even though she could barely see him, Molly could see the smears of blood that covered his face and soaked his shirt.

* * *

Kevin stood perfectly still, the moon shining in his eyes. He had no real sense of time anymore, no true idea of how long it had been since he'd left the cave.

Nor was he consciously aware of where he'd been or what he'd been doing, for he was barely aware of anything at all, having almost ceased to function as a physical extension of his own mind, instead becoming merely a tool of the presence within his body.

He had hiked down out of the hills, his eyes barely focused on where he was going, his mind failing to register anything at all of his surroundings. He was following the imperative of the force within, carrying out the directions the patterns of the insect dance on the valley floor had imprinted on his mind.

Food.

He had to gather food, and bring it back to his hive.

He'd set about his task mindlessly, heading first toward the hives on the far side of the property. There, he'd opened the abandoned hives and broken as much of the honeycomb as he could carry out of the frames, stuffing it under his shirt until he could manage no more. Finally he'd turned away and moved on, foraging through the night until he came to the chicken coop, where he'd gone inside, pushed the hens from their roosts, and gone after their eggs, breaking some of them to suck the contents greedily into his mouth, putting others in his pockets to take back with him to the hive.

His pockets full, he'd turned to the chickens themselves, using his teeth to tear the heads off two of the hens.

He'd been reaching for another when he became aware of a presence behind him, though he'd neither seen nor heard anything at all. Moving instinctively toward the gate, he'd frozen as he suddenly came face-to-face with the danger.

And then, finally penetrating into the consciousness the

invader had almost totally repressed, Kevin heard a single word.

His name.

It registered slowly. For a moment he didn't quite realize what it meant. But then a little more of his own consciousness reasserted itself, and he saw Molly standing in the darkness, staring at him.

"K-Kevin?" she said again. "What's wrong?" She started to take a step toward him, then changed her mind, unconsciously dropping a hand down to rest on Bailey's head. "Y-You don't look right," she said.

Kevin's fingers flexed, and the corpses of the dead fowl fell into the dirt at his feet.

Within his body the teeming entity surged into frenzied activity, the intelligence of the hive sensing a new nesting place, a fresh site in which to colonize, and breed, and reproduce themselves.

Kevin began to move toward Molly, the black mist already gathering in his lungs, ready to spew forth on his exhaled breath as soon as he was close enough to the new host.

Molly, as if frozen where she was, gazed up at Kevin, transfixed by the strange expression on his face.

And then, just as he started to kneel down to put his face close to hers, to ready himself for the colony's transference, his own consciousness struggled to the surface and he realized what was about to happen to Molly.

"No!" he gasped, standing and backing away. "Go in the house. Just go back in the house and leave me alone!"

Gathering what few vestiges of his willpower he could still control, Kevin fought against the invader that all but ruled his mind and body. Turning, he staggered away toward the hills.

For a long moment Molly stood where she was, staring after Kevin, though he was already lost in the darkness. Then, from just behind her, she heard Ben's voice.

"We have to follow him," he whispered. Molly turned slowly around. Ben was gazing at her in the moonlight, his eyes glittering with excitement. "We can find them, Molly," he said. "I bet we can find all of them!"

Molly shook her head. "N-No," she stammered. "It's dark, and he's gone, and I'm scared. I want to go back in the house."

"But we can find them," Ben pleaded. "I know we can. We'll use Bailey. I bet he could follow Kevin anywhere!"

Molly's grip tightened on the big dog. "We should go back in the house," she said again.

Ben gazed steadily at her, then shrugged. "Then go. I don't care. I'll just take Bailey and find them myself." As if he'd understood what Ben had said, Bailey moved to the little boy's side, his whole body trembling as he sniffed at the spot where Kevin had stood a moment ago. "See?" Ben crowed. "He *wants* to go. So go back in the house if you want to, and me and Bailey will go find everyone."

Molly's eyes flicked toward the house, then up toward the hills. Kevin's figure emerged from the shadows for a moment, and in the glow of the moonlight she thought he beckoned to her.

But he'd told her to go back into the house, hadn't he?

But if he was sick, like Julie had been . . .

Molly struggled, trying to make up her mind what to do. If Ben was right, and Bailey could help them find Julie and Jeff, too—

Suddenly she pictured the look on her mother's face when they all came into the house together, and her last doubt evaporated. "Come on, Bailey," she said. "Let's find Kevin."

The big dog bounded toward the hills, Molly and Ben running to keep up with him.

Molly and Ben stood side by side on the top of the hill, looking down into the valley. Bailey crouched next to

Molly, trembling, a strange sound—part growl, part whimper—rattling in his throat. All around them the air was thick with insects, and their ears were filled with the chirps of crickets, the clicks of beetles, and the rasping sounds of the june bugs.

The moon was high in the sky now, and the night had brightened. Across the stream that cut through the little valley's floor, they could see the mouth of a cave, and standing just outside the cave was a dark figure.

As they watched, the figure started toward them, moving steadily across the valley, then starting up the hill.

"J-Jeff?" Ben called, not quite able to see who was coming.

After a moment of silence the figure spoke, and the little boy recognized his brother's voice. "It's okay, Ben," Jeff Larkin said. "It's me."

Ben ran down the hill, but as he got close enough to see his brother clearly, he stopped dead in his tracks.

Jeff's head was covered with a mask of bees, a squirming, humming mass whose constantly shifting form kept folding in upon itself as some of the bees burrowed deep into the swarm while others rose to the surface.

Ben stared at the terrifying visage, his heart pounding, his breath frozen in his lungs. His eyes widened with horror as Jeff came closer and closer, finally stopping only a few feet away.

As if on command, the bees rose away from his head, disappearing instantly into the night sky, leaving Jeff's features, pale and strained, illuminated in the moonlight.

"It's all right, Ben," Jeff said. "I'm fine. And you will be, too."

Ben stood as still as a fawn caught in the bright glare of headlights while his brother moved closer. Jeff knelt, and then, just as he was reaching toward Ben, a shout split the night.

"No!" Kevin bellowed. "Run, Ben! Run!"

Galvanized by the shout from the bottom of the hill, Ben turned and fled back the way he had come. Molly followed him, racing away as fast as her legs would carry her, her stepbrother's cry echoing in her ears, the image of Jeff's gray, drawn face imprinted on her memory.

Of her sister—of Julie—she had seen no sign at all.

CHAPTER 27

Sara McLaughlin moaned softly, rolled over in bed, then began thrashing out against the damp and tangled sheets that had become twisted around her body during the few minutes in which she had fallen into a restless sleep. One of her arms finally slipping free, she frantically ripped the rest of the sheet loose, then tore her nightgown from her body as well. Gasping for breath, her lungs feeling as though they had filled up with thick phlegm, she flopped, naked, onto her back, her body heaving as she struggled to draw air into her congested chest.

Freedom from the constrictions of the sheets and nightgown gave her only momentary relief from the chaos going on in her body, though, and a few seconds later she began frantically scratching at herself, desperately trying to stop the terrible itching that had grown steadily stronger as the night wore on. Finally she left the bed and went to the window, where she stared out into the moonlit night.

Once again the hills, now silhouetted against the night sky, beckoned to her, called out to her, something hidden deep within them summoning her with a force she could no longer resist. The urge to escape from the confines of the hospital room—to flee into the hills—bloomed into an obsession now.

Sara's fingers fumbled with the window latch until it came free. She pushed the window open and scrambled out onto the narrow strip of grass that separated the building from the parking lot. Though a cool breeze was blowing in from the ocean, it failed to ease the fever raging within her body or to soothe the chaos in her mind.

Whimpering to herself, oblivious to her nakedness, she dashed away from the building, instinctively dodging the bright pools of light cast by the lamps suspended over the parking lot. A moment later she disappeared into the shadows of a clump of scrub oaks. Threading her way through the trees, she ignored the sharp stabs of pain from the twigs and rocks upon which she trod. When her right foot began to bleed, she didn't notice it at all.

Passing through the stand of oaks, she came to a fence at the edge of the hospital property, all that separated her from the open rolling hills extending both north and east. The fence blocked her path. She ranged back and forth in front of it, moving first one way, then the other, like a tiger pacing insanely within the confines of a cage.

Within her body, the colony turned frantic as it continued to expand and began sending forth scouts in search of a new host.

Tiny flecks, invisibly black against the darkness of the night, emerged from Sara's mouth, nostrils, and eyes, hovered in the air for a few seconds, then quickly died when they found no new host within which to feed and breed.

And the colony infesting Sara's body, receiving no signals from its scouts, continued to expand within the confines of its host, reaching deeper and deeper into Sara's vital organs.

Then, from out of the night sky, a cloud of insects dropped down to surround Sara, and for a moment she felt calm once again.

Her eyes focused on the creatures as they buzzed around her head, and in her mind an image began to form; an image so abstract it could not have been replicated outside of her fevered mind.

Yet to Sara, and to the teeming being within her, it formed a map, a clear route to take her where she must go.

The skin of her hands ripping on the rough mesh of the fence, Sara scaled the single obstacle that kept her from the wilderness.

For Sara McLaughlin, the last fragments of her humanity were finally extinguished.

The homing became the single, unalterable obsession of her existence.

Alice Jenkins arrived at the First Floor West nurses' station at precisely ten minutes to midnight, ready to relieve JoAnna Morton, who was just finishing the final activity reports of her shift. "Anything going on?" Alice asked.

"All quiet," JoAnna replied with a smile. "Everyone's asleep." She gathered the various items that inevitably wound up on the desk—her keys, lipstick, a paperback book, two emery boards—into her purse while Alice made her habitual round of the ward, peering briefly into each room just to make sure that, as she always put it, "JoAnna hadn't misplaced anyone."

In Room 112, where a card on the door read MCLAUGH-LIN, S., the television was on, the bed seemed to be torn apart, and a nightgown was draped over the chair next to the bed. Of "McLaughlin, S." there was no sign at all.

Frowning, Alice pulled the door to 112 open and stepped inside. Shivering in the cool of the room, she went to the window, pulled it closed, then checked the tiny bathroom that connected 112 and 114. It was empty, and the patient in 114 was snoring peacefully.

Her frown deepening, Alice returned to the nurses' station, where JoAnna Morton was pulling on her sweater in preparation to leave for the night. "Didn't you say everyone was asleep?" she asked. JoAnna looked at her blankly, then nodded. "Well, would you mind telling me where you tucked McLaughlin, S. in? One-twelve is empty."

JoAnna Morton gazed at the other nurse for a moment, then turned and walked down the hall to 112. Just as Alice had said, there was no sign of Sara McLaughlin. "She was there half an hour ago," JoAnna insisted as she came back to the desk. "And I can't believe I wouldn't have either seen her or heard her if she'd gone anywhere."

Unless you were reading your romance, Alice thought, but was too tactful to say out loud. Instead she headed quickly toward the far end of the hall. "I'll check the lounge and rest rooms, you call the other floors."

Ten minutes later, when they had still found no sign of Sara in the hospital, they decided they knew what must have happened, even though it made no sense at all.

Leaving not only her nightgown behind, but every stitch of clothing as well, Sara had apparently gone out the window. Once outside, the teenaged girl—stark naked—seemed simply to have vanished into the night.

"All right," Alice sighed when she, JoAnna, the emergency room resident, and two orderlies had exhausted every other possibility, "let's start notifying people. Alice, you call the police, and I'll call her doctor." Her eyes shifted to the young resident from the emergency room. "And you can call her parents," she said. Before the resident had time to object, Alice picked up the phone and dialed Ellen Filmore's number in Pleasant Valley. On the fifth ring, an answering machine picked up the call.

"This is Ellen Filmore. I'm not at home right now, but please leave a message. If this is an emergency, please call 555-6472." When the electronic tone beeped, Alice left a brief message, then dialed the number she'd jotted down as Ellen Filmore's voice had spoken it. After four rings, a sleepy male voice came on the line.

"Hello?"

"I'm looking for Ellen Filmore."

Instantly, the sleepiness left the voice. "This is Roberto Muñoz. I'm her nurse."

Alice Jenkins quickly explained what had happened. "We're notifying the police, of course, and the girl's parents. If you can tell me where I might find Dr. Filmore, I'd be glad to—"

"It's all right," Roberto interrupted. "If she's not at home, I'm not sure where she might be, but I can find her a lot faster than you can. I'll take care of it."

Hanging up the phone, Roberto dialed the number of the clinic, starting to pull on his clothes even while the phone rang. When the answering machine there finally picked up, and Roberto heard his own voice beginning to deliver a variation of the same message that was on Ellen Filmore's phone, he hung up, thought a moment, then dialed the sheriff's dispatcher. "Carla? It's Roberto Muñoz, in Pleasant Valley. Any idea where I might be able to find Dr. Filmore? Has something happened with our missing kids?"

"We've got a couple of deputies out cruising around the area, but if something's happened, I haven't heard," the dispatcher replied. "And I haven't heard from Dr. Filmore in weeks. Is there a problem I can help you with?"

"I don't think so," Roberto sighed. "Another of our kids just turned up missing, this time from a hospital in San Luis Obispo."

"Oh, Lord," the dispatcher replied. "You're sure there's nothing we can do?"

"The cops over there are taking care of it," Roberto told her. "Talk to you later." Hanging up, he finished dressing while he tried to figure out what to do next.

The thing was, his boss never went anywhere without telling him where she could be reached, or leaving a message on her machine. In the three years he'd worked for her, this was the first time Roberto hadn't been able to tell a caller exactly how to get hold of her.

Picking up his wallet and the keys to his car, Roberto Muñoz set off in search of Ellen Filmore.

Something was wrong.

* * *

Karen Owen's eyes snapped open, and for a moment she wasn't quite certain where she was. Then she recognized the living room of the farmhouse, and as the fogginess of her restless sleep began to lift from her mind, she shifted stiffly on the sofa in an attempt to ease the dull ache that was throbbing in the small of her back.

In the big brown leather chair across from her, Russell was snoring rhythmically, his head lolling on his chest, his mouth partly open. Beside her on the couch, Marge Larkin had lain down, curled her legs up almost to her chest, and slept with her neck bent at an angle so severe it almost made Karen wince. Slowly, her muscles protesting every movement, Karen unfolded herself from the sofa and started toward the kitchen for a cup of the coffee it seemed she'd brewed a few minutes ago. As she passed the clock, it struck a single deep note, and she automatically glanced at it.

Twelve-thirty.

Which meant that she hadn't made the coffee a few minutes ago at all, and by now it would be stone cold.

How could she have slept for two hours?

The strain of keeping her emotions in check, when what she really wanted to do was burst into tears and collapse, had exhausted her.

She turned the heat on beneath the coffeepot, then reached for a mug on the counter. And stopped.

She looked around the kitchen, frowning as she tried to focus her mind. Something wasn't quite right. What was it? Was something out of place? Or something not there at all?

The silence of the sleeping household was unnerving her. That's all it is, she told herself. Still, something didn't feel right.

Her heart beating faster as a pang of fear twisted in her belly, Karen started up the stairs.

This is ridiculous, she scolded herself. There's nothing wrong. Why was she getting so upset?

But as she started down the hall toward Molly's room, she broke into a run, throwing open Molly's door and snapping on the light.

The room was empty.

"No," she whispered, already starting toward the room next door. "Not Molly, too." It was going to be all right. She would open the door and find Ben asleep, with Molly and Bailey curled up on the floor next to him, a blanket wrapped around them to keep them warm.

But even as she pushed the door open, she knew that Kevin's room would prove to be just as empty as Molly's had been.

Now a scream burst from her throat—a scream that was meant to be her husband's name, but erupted only as a formless howl of anguish. Frantically, she rushed from one room to another, calling out Molly's name, and by the time Russell arrived at the top of the stairs, followed a second later by Marge Larkin, she had checked them all. A sob of hopelessness racked her body, and she stared first at her husband, then at Marge Larkin. "They're gone," she breathed. "Oh, God, Marge, now our babies are gone, too."

Her frayed emotions finally snapping, she collapsed into Russell's arms. "They took Bailey," she sobbed. "Why would they do that? Oh, God, why would they do that?" But even as she asked the question, deep in her heart she already knew the answer.

Molly and Ben had gone out into the night to look for their sister and brother.

How long had they been gone?

Breaking away from Russell, Karen rushed down the stairs and out into the night.

"Molly! Ben! Come back! Oh, God, please come back. . . ."

As Russell dashed down the stairs to call Mark Shannon, and Marge Larkin burst out of the house to join Karen in the yard, Karen's screams slowly died away into the silence of the night.

Over the next half hour, as Mark Shannon began spreading the word that Molly and Ben were gone, lights came on in the homes of Pleasant Valley and men began to leave their houses, knowing they wouldn't sleep again until Molly and Ben had been found.

Or until they discovered exactly what was happening to the children of their town.

Roberto Muñoz pulled into the parking lot of the clinic, not because he expected to find Ellen Filmore there, but because he had no better ideas of where to look next. He'd already been to her home, checking her garage to make certain her car was gone. Next he'd driven slowly up and down every street in town searching, half expecting to see the doctor's car parked in the driveway of someone she knew.

Her car, though, seemed to have disappeared off the face of the earth.

Was it possible she hadn't come back from San Luis Obispo at all? No, she would have called him. Ellen took her responsibility as the town's sole doctor very seriously; if she were going to be out of town unexpectedly, he was always informed, no matter how late the hour.

Parking near the clinic's door, Roberto let himself inside, going first to Ellen's office, where he rifled through her calendar, searching for any clue as to plans she might have had.

Nothing.

He moved through the rest of the clinic, not certain what he was looking for, but knowing that if anything—anything at all—was out of place, his practiced eyes would spot it immediately.

The open drawer in one of the examining rooms drew his attention. The moment he looked inside it, he knew what was gone.

The antivenin that Carl Henderson had brought to the clinic the day Julie Spellman had been stung.

But why would the antivenin be gone? Why would anyone want to steal—

But it hadn't been stolen! He'd seen nothing to indicate that the clinic had been broken into, and no thief would have left a drawer standing open, where either he or Ellen would be sure to notice it first thing in the morning.

It had to have been Ellen who had taken it.

The connection clicked in Roberto Muñoz's mind just as it had occurred to Ellen Filmore a few hours earlier. He knew where she must have gone. Leaving the clinic, he drove out to Carl Henderson's house. There, parked in the driveway behind Henderson's gray Jeep, was Ellen Filmore's car.

He was about to get out of his car when he noticed that something was odd about the house.

Two cars in the driveway, but not a single light on in the house.

Roberto started once again to get out of his car, tempted to barge into the house, to break in if necessary, to find Ellen. But then he changed his mind. Henderson was six inches taller than he was, and outweighed him by at least fifty pounds. If Ellen were in danger, he alone could never rescue her. He had to get help—but he couldn't just leave.

Then Roberto remembered one of Ellen Filmore's habits, one that he had warned her, to no avail, that she should break. Leaving the engine of his own car running, he ran over to Ellen's car and opened the driver's door.

Just as he'd hoped, the keys were hanging in the ignition.

Switching on the ignition, he picked up her cellular phone and called Mark Shannon's number. The deputy answered on the first ring, and didn't sound as though he'd been sleeping at all, though only a few minutes ago, when Roberto had passed his house, Shannon's lights had been out, too. "It's Roberto, Mark," he said, keeping his voice down. Quickly, he told the deputy what had happened and what he now suspected.

"Okay," Shannon began, thinking quickly. Only minutes ago, he'd heard from Russell Owen that Molly and Ben had disappeared, and he'd been about to head to the Owen farm when Roberto's call caught him. Reaching a quick decision, the deputy said, "Stay there. I'll be out in a couple of minutes."

Shaking, Roberto put down the phone. And then, as if from a great distance, he heard it.

Though it was muffled to the point where it was barely audible, Roberto was sure it was the sound of a scream.

Ellen Filmore screamed once more, and scrabbled across the floor of the pitch-black chamber in which she was imprisoned.

She had no idea how long she'd been locked in the room, but as the minutes had turned into hours, and she'd heard Carl Henderson moving around beyond the locked door, she'd grown more and more terrified.

She'd tried to keep calm, refused to give in to the panic that threatened to overwhelm her when she'd first been plunged into the blackness of the chamber.

Instead she'd moved around it, carefully exploring, crawling across the floor on her hands and knees at first, then finally standing up to feel the walls, working her way slowly around the perimeter, taking the measure of the room with the span of her arm reach.

It seemed to be empty, save for some heavy spikes she'd discovered on the back wall, driven deep into the upright timbers that seemed to have supported the house before the concrete retaining walls had been added. One of the spikes had seemed slightly loose, and she'd spent a long time—she didn't know how long—working at it, trying to pull it free, until, sobbing with the exertion and frustration, she gave up.

There was a drain in the floor, too; and in the wall that separated her from the rest of the basement, there were some irregularities she hadn't yet been able to figure out.

Once she'd gone over the room with her hands and been able to discover nothing she might be able to use, she decided the best thing to do was simply to sit and wait.

And stay awake, and listen.

Sooner or later Carl Henderson would leave the basement. And when he did, she would go to work again, gouging at the door, prying at its hinges, until somehow she got it open.

Screaming, she knew, would do no good. No one was close enough to the house to hear her, and screams might very well induce Carl Henderson to kill her right now.

So, for what seemed like an endless eternity, she had sat on the floor, her back against the wall, forcing herself to stay awake and listen.

A few minutes ago Henderson had come close to the door and spoken to her.

"It occurred to me you might be getting lonely," he said. "So I thought I'd send in some company for you."

There had been a long silence, and Ellen had wondered if perhaps Henderson had gone away.

She was just about to get up and move closer to the door when she suddenly felt it.

Something crawling up her leg.

Instinctively she reached down to brush it away, but as her hand touched it, she felt a sharp stinging in her calf. She uttered a sharp cry of pain and surprise, and then Henderson had betrayed his presence.

He laughed.

Then he spoke.

"Do you like spiders?" he asked. "I hope you do, because there are several hundred of them in there with you now."

Though she could see nothing, she suddenly imagined the darkness to be alive with creatures creeping toward her from every direction.

Ellen shrank back against the wall.

A moment later she felt the first of the vile creatures crawling up her leg, and instantly a scream erupted from her throat.

Then she felt the spiders everywhere.

Dropping from the ceiling into her hair.

Creeping up both legs.

She could feel them on her hands and arms now, her face, her neck.

Another scream burst from her throat, building quickly into an agonized wail of pure terror.

CHAPTER 28

*J*ulie lay near the entrance to the cave.

She no longer had any sense of time, any memory of where she was or how she had gotten there. All she was now aware of, all she responded to, was a steady throbbing, a pulsating rhythm that came not only from deep within her grossly distended body, but from beyond it, as well.

Insects were everywhere now, bees lining the walls of the cave, clinging to the rock so closely together that they formed a solid curtain, their wings humming steadily as they worked in concert to keep the air within the cave fresh, its temperature constant.

Clouds of gnats and mosquitoes hovered in the air, something in them responding to the summons that was somehow issuing steadily forth from the entity that was steadily growing, steadily multiplying, within Julie's body.

Jeff Larkin and Andy Bennett knelt on either side of Julie, their minds now as numb as her own, their bodies slavishly following the orders of the masters that resided within them. They massaged Julie's body, their fingers gently, rhythmically working her flesh, moving slowly and steadily over her limbs and torso, tending to her as worker bees tend to their queen.

Kevin Owen crouched near Julie's head, methodically transferring food from his mouth to her own, relieving her of the necessity even to chew before she swallowed.

Though his own body was once again starving, craving nutrition, the needs of Julie came first, overriding even the most basic of his own. Not so much as a single morsel did he swallow.

The floor of the cave, too, was thick with yet more teeming masses of insect life. Ants were everywhere, crawling over Julie and the others, picking their bodies clean of any detritus they could find, scurrying away even with flecks of dead skin.

Outside the cave the hum in the valley grew steadily stronger as more and more insects responded to the pheromones that now exuded from every one of Julie's pores and emanated from her lungs on every breath she exhaled.

Then, as the moon neared its zenith and the wind began to shift to the east, a new force arrived in the cave, a force borne on the warm summer breeze that came up from the valley.

Julie stirred, then slowly got to her feet.

In unison, Jeff Larkin and Andy Bennett rose as well, each of them falling in on either side of their mistress.

As Julie moved out of the cave, Kevin followed behind her, obediently, mindlessly, playing his tiny role in the great mosaic of the being's existence.

Together the four adolescents emerged from the mouth of the cave and started across the floor of the valley, the carpet of insects parting as they approached, melding instantly back together to form an unbroken, seamless mass after they had passed.

The flying insects—the bees and gnats, the wasps and hornets, the clouds of mosquitoes—erupted from the cave as well, forming a hovering mass around Julie and her attendants as she crossed the stream and started up the hill on the other side—the hill where Bailey still waited, his hackles raised and a low growl building in his throat as the strange mass of teeming life, all of it now moving as a single force, came slowly toward him.

The dog, his muscles tensing, sniffed nervously at the breeze, and his growl dropped to a frightened whimper as he sensed the danger in the air. But at the same time, barely distinguishable in the miasma of strange aromas, Bailey detected the faint scent of his master, and it was this one familiar odor that kept him from turning and fleeing the oncoming tide of churning life.

Instead he waited, his body rigid, his eyes fixed on the shadowy mass that blotted out the stars above and dimmed the silver light of the moon. Finally even the faint whimper of fear died in his throat as the mass began to engulf him, and at last, as Julie—flanked by her attendants and followed by her feeder—drew closer to him, the big dog took a tentative step backward.

And Julie leaned forward, the long needles her fingernails had become piercing easily through the dog's skin and sinking deep into the muscles of his body.

As a great searing pain coursed through him, a single howl of fear and agony burst from his throat, only to be cut off a second later as the venom injected into him through Julie's fingertips reached his brain, instantly collapsing his nervous system.

The great dog fell in a heap to the ground, and as Julie passed, the creatures that dwelt beneath the surface of the earth surged over him, their mandibles working.

Within minutes the ants and roaches, all the scavengers the earth could spew forth, had done their job. Only Bailey's bones, picked clean of every scrap of muscle and ligament, every fragment of fat and skin, lay on the ground, still perfectly arranged, as they had been the instant he died.

Only much later, when the mass that had destroyed him had passed on, would a coyote finally arrive, sniff briefly at the skeleton, then pick up one of Bailey's hind legs, the trophy held high as it trotted back into the hills from which it had come.

For Bailey, the moment of fear had been short, the pain of death had lasted but an instant.

But Bailey's death was only the beginning.

Manny Gomez was dozing behind the wheel of his squad car. The sound that brought him instantly and fully awake was an unearthly howl of sheer terror that rose into a shriek of unspeakable pain, only to die away as quickly as it had come.

Manny jerked upright in the driver's seat. Getting out of the squad car, he stood in the pale silver light of the moon, listening.

The howl was not repeated.

Manny continued to listen, uneasy. Slowly, he began to understand what was wrong.

It was the quiet of the night.

The absolute quiet.

Tonight, the constant backdrop of sound the insects created during the summer was missing.

Manny frowned, and gazed around him. The moon was high enough and bright enough to have turned the landscape into a sharp chiaroscuro, with the stands of small oaks clearly etched against the star-filled sky, the hills delineated in dark relief.

Half a mile away the lights of the Owen house glowed brightly, and across the road, in the pasture, Manny could make out the shapes of a few cattle.

Every now and then he heard their soft lowing.

But the steady song of the insects had disappeared so completely that Manny Gomez almost wondered if perhaps his memory was playing tricks on him, and the insects had never created the constant hum of noise that he was now remembering. Then an idea came to him. He reached in through the open window of the car and switched on the headlights.

Normally, moths and june bugs would gather within seconds. The moths would flutter in the headlights' beams, spiraling steadily toward the lamps, finally battering themselves against the headlights' lenses as they tried to navigate off the false sun. And the june bugs would bumble through the light a couple of times, lose their bearings and tumble to the ground, their legs waving in the air, their wing covers buzzing their frustration as they tried to right themselves.

Tonight, though, there was nothing but total silence.

Suddenly the radio came alive, and Manny heard the department dispatcher paging him. Picking up the microphone, he responded with his unit number and position.

Somehow, even his own voice sounded odd against the unnatural quiet of the night. "Something weird's going on," he added. "It's real quiet out here."

"Well, it won't be quiet for long," the dispatcher told him. "You've got two more kids missing, this time little ones. A boy and a girl, both of them nine years old."

"Don't tell me," Manny broke in, now grasping the significance of the blaze of lights coming from the Owen farm. "It's Molly Spellman and Ben Larkin, isn't it? How long have they been gone?"

"We don't know," the dispatcher replied. "According to the little girl's father, they may have taken a dog and gone looking for the others."

Swinging into the car, Manny started the engine. "I'm on my way." If he cut across the Costas place, he would be able to cover the foothill road on his way over to Russell's. If they hadn't been gone long, he might actually run across the two children and their dog—

And then he remembered the agonized howl that had awakened him minutes ago.

The howl that could have come from the throat of a dog.

Turning up Vic Costas's dirt driveway, Manny Gomez pressed the accelerator to the floor, and the squad car shot forward.

Mark Shannon pulled into the driveway of Carl Henderson's house, killing the lights but leaving the engine running, as Roberto Muñoz, who had locked himself inside Ellen Filmore's car where at least he had the cellular telephone, finally ventured out, hurrying over to the squad car. "Have you seen anything?" Mark asked the nurse.

Roberto shook his head. "There was ... a scream. At least, I thought I heard a scream." Roberto hesitated, then added, "But I'm starting to wonder if I really heard anything at all. I mean, it *sounded* like I did—"

"I know," Shannon told him, eyeing the darkened house. If Ellen's car had not been parked in front of it, he'd have been tempted simply to send Roberto home and head on out to Russell Owen's place. "Things get weird at night. It could have been a cat, or a raccoon, or who knows what. Well, let's take a look around."

"Aren't you going in?" Roberto asked.

"Not until I check things out," Shannon replied. "It's not like TV, Roberto. I can't just go busting in. Carl Henderson could have my badge by tomorrow morning, and then sue the shit out of the county. Even if he has a dozen bodies in there, he's still got rights."

"But if—" Roberto began.

Shannon cut him off with a question that was almost a challenge. "You worried enough about Ellen to come with me?"

Given the choice of staying alone with the cars or going with the deputy, Roberto chose the latter, just as Mark Shannon had expected he would.

Taking a flashlight from the glove box of the squad car, but not turning it on, Shannon started working his way slowly around the house, checking each window as he came to it.

At the back door, the deputy tried the knob, found it locked as securely as the windows, then moved on, still checking each window as he came to it.

Everything was locked tight.

"Check around for a key," Shannon instructed Roberto as he reached for the doorbell at the front of the house. But before either of them could make another move, the same sound Roberto had heard earlier was suddenly repeated.

Muffled, indistinct, but definitely a scream.

A woman's scream.

The sound galvanized Shannon. He pulled his gun from its holster, while at the same time raising his right foot and smashing it below the doorknob. The frame of the door gave way, the old wood splitting cleanly as the striker plate tore loose from the jamb. The door itself slammed back against the wall, its crash immediately followed by the tinkling of glass as several of the beveled panes set into the old door shattered under the impact.

Groping for a light switch, Shannon pressed an old-fashioned button, and the chandelier in the foyer blazed on, flooding the room with brilliant light.

"Jesus," Roberto whispered as his eyes fell on the cases of mounted insects that lined the walls. "What's all this shit?"

"Bugs," Shannon grated. "He collects them." He pressed a finger against his lips as he listened for any sign that someone had heard them break into the house. For a moment there was nothing, but then they heard the sound of feet resounding on stairs. Instinctively, Shannon glanced up toward the darkened second-floor landing. He was just reaching for the light switch at the base of the stairs when Roberto jabbed him.

"Down there!" the nurse hissed, pointing down the hallway toward the kitchen.

A door beneath the stairs was just starting to open, but as Roberto spoke, it jerked closed again. Shoving his way past Roberto, Shannon dashed down the hall, yanking on the knob just as he heard the click of a lock.

"Police, Henderson!" the deputy shouted. "Open up!"

But instead of the lock clicking open, Shannon heard feet pounding back down the stairs on the other side of the closed door. Cocking his pistol, he stepped back and to the side, aimed carefully, then fired directly at the lock. The slug hit the brass plate then whined as it ricocheted back across the hall to lodge deep in the oak frame of the kitchen door. Prying the broken lock free with his fingers, Shannon twisted the knob and pulled the door open.

The sound of another scream—much louder now—rose from the depths of the basement. Shannon peered around the door frame and down into the darkness below.

Then, snapping on his flashlight, he started down.

Molly Spellman was running as fast as she could, but it seemed no matter how hard she tried to keep up, Ben Larkin got farther ahead of her. She didn't know how far they'd run, or even where they were. All she knew was that her heart felt like it was going to explode, and her legs hurt, and she could hardly breathe at all, but she had to keep running.

If she didn't, she might lose sight of him, and then she'd never find her way home.

The thought of being out in the hills all alone, lost in the middle of the night, spurred her on, and she managed to run a little faster. But still, with every step she took, Ben got farther away, and now he'd almost disappeared into the darkness.

Then she would be alone.

Just the thought of what might happen terrified her so much that she missed her footing, tripped, and sprawled headlong onto the path they were following. "Ben!" she screamed, his name bursting from her lips as a high-pitched wail. Lying on the ground, she sobbed from the pain of her skinned elbow, and with terror—not because Ben had left her by herself, but because his brother might find her here.

The image of Jeff, his face pale and scary in the moonlight, his fingers—with long, pointed nails—reaching for her, was still vivid in her memory.

"Ben, wait! Come back! Don't leave me here!"

Her whole body shaking, Molly curled up, tears streaming from her eyes, sobs choking her throat. She wrapped her arms around her legs, and for what seemed like forever, she simply lay there. Slowly, her sobs began to ease and her breathing evened out into its normal rhythm. But then the skin on the back of her neck began to tingle as she sensed that someone was behind her.

Some*one*, or some*thing*.

She froze, her heart pounding again, her breath caught in her throat. Then she heard a voice.

"Molly? Can't you get up?"

Ben!

It was Ben!

Sitting up, she rubbed her eyes with her fists, then peered up at him, his face clearly visible in the moonlight. His head was cocked and he looked almost as frightened as she felt.

"What's wrong?" he asked. "Did you hurt yourself?"

Now that she was no longer alone, Molly's fear began to ebb, and she rubbed at her skinned elbow. "I tripped," she said. Then her voice took on an accusing note. "How come you didn't stop when I called you?"

"I did," Ben told her. "Soon's I heard you, I came back.

And I've been right here all the time, too. You were just crying so hard you didn't see me."

Sniffling, Molly rolled up her pant leg, inspected her injured knee, then stood up. "Do you know how to get home?" she asked.

Ben hesitated, then slowly shook his head. But as Molly's eyes once more flooded with tears, he pointed off in the direction they'd been running. "I—I think we have to go that way," he stammered.

Molly looked around. In the darkness everything looked the same to her. "What if that's the wrong way?" she challenged.

Ben hesitated. Somewhere in the back of his mind a memory was stirring.

A memory of something Jeff had told him a long time ago, when they'd been outside one night, staring up into the sky.

"See that?" Jeff had asked, pointing up into the sky. "That's the Big Dipper." Carefully, Jeff had shown him how to recognize the seven stars of the constellation. "If you follow a line up the side of the Dipper away from the handle, the brightest star you see is Polaris. That's the North Star. And as long as you can see that, you know which way is north."

Now Ben peered up into the sky, and picked out the bright stars of the Dipper, then followed the line Jeff had told him about.

And there, shining brightly, was the star he was looking for. "There," he said, pointing to it. "That's the North Star, so that way's north, so we live that way!" His arm shifted around to the east.

Molly, her terror starting to abate in the face of Ben's certainty, slipped her hand into his. "But how far is it?" she asked.

This time Ben didn't hesitate at all. "Not very far," he declared, though the truth was, he didn't have any idea how far from home they might be. "It might even be right over the next hill. Come on."

Hand in hand, the two children started down the slope into the saddle between the hill they were on and the next one. Before they'd gone more than a dozen steps, the quiet of the night was shattered by a noise that froze them in their tracks.

The same howl of a dying animal that had awakened Manny Gomez at exactly that instant.

"Wh-What was that?" Molly asked in a quavering voice.

"I don't know," Ben replied, his hand tightening on hers. "But I think we better get out of here." Breaking into a run, he half led, half dragged Molly up the slope of the next hill, not pausing to catch his breath until they were both at the top.

And this time, as their panting slowly eased, they heard something else.

It was the same humming sound they'd heard in the valley in front of the cave.

Now, though, it was coming toward them, growing steadily louder every second.

CHAPTER 29

"*H*old it right there, Henderson," Mark Shannon said. He was standing at the foot of the steep flight of stairs that led from the foyer above, Roberto Muñoz right behind him.

Pinned like one of his own insects by the bright beam of the deputy's flashlight, Carl Henderson blinked, then started to raise one arm to shield his eyes from the glare.

"Don't move!" Shannon barked. "Tell me where the light switch is." When Henderson said nothing, Shannon spoke over his shoulder. "Find it, Roberto. It's probably on the wall right next to me." He heard Roberto moving behind him. A naked bulb came on, flooding the basement with harsh white light. Shannon's eyes darted around the basement, searching for Ellen Filmore, then bored in on Carl Henderson. "Where's Ellen?" he demanded.

Finally Henderson spoke, his voice trembling almost like that of a frightened little boy. "I didn't hurt her," he said. "I just locked her in the darkroom, that's all."

Almost before Henderson had finished speaking, Ellen's voice, muffled and distorted, came through the door that was all but lost in the shadows at the other end of the room. "Help! Oh, God, someone get me out of here! Please!"

While Shannon held his gun steadily on Carl Henderson, Roberto dashed to the far end of the basement, found another light switch, then fumbled for a moment with the dead bolt that was mounted on the outside of the door. A second later it turned in his fingers and he pulled the door open.

For a moment he thought he must be hallucinating.

Sitting huddled against the far wall, her face ashen, was Ellen Filmore.

Crawling on her skin, creeping over her clothes, caught in her hair, were spiders.

Dozens of them—scores of them.

Even as he watched, still more of them were dropping down from the rafters above her head, spinning out webs as they went.

Roberto gasped, his eyes darting around the room. The spiders were everywhere, spinning webs, creeping over the walls and the floor. A violent shudder seizing him, Roberto fought against a sudden urge to slam the door again, to rid himself of even the sight of the crawling predatory creatures. But instead he rushed in, brushing as many of the spiders off Ellen Filmore as he could, then lifting her to her feet and half carrying her through the door. Only when she was outside the room and Roberto had closed the door behind him did she suddenly come back to life, stripping off the long-sleeved blouse she was wearing and shaking it violently. Sobbing partly from the horror of what had happened to her in the locked and darkened room and partly out of relief at being released from her torture, she leaned over, shaking her head violently and running her fingers through her hair.

More spiders dropped to the floor and scurried toward the dark corners of the basement, away from the light that exposed them.

Finally free of her tormentors, Ellen at last gave in to the emotions she'd been struggling to hold in check through the hours of her imprisonment in the blacked-out chamber. Sobbing, she sank onto a worn and sagging chair. "I thought I was going to die," she breathed, her voice breaking. "Oh, God, I thought they were going to kill me!"

A few yards away, Carl Henderson laughed.

It was a dark, brittle laugh, the laugh of a man whose last few shreds of sanity were starting to unravel. "Kill you?" he echoed, spitting the words contemptuously from his lips. "I don't think so. If I'd wanted to kill you, I certainly would have. They were only spiders, Ellen! Just harmless spiders! Not even any of my lovely brown recluses."

Mark Shannon felt a shiver go down his spine, remembering what had happened to someone down south who had been bitten by one of the shy little spiders. Though the victim hadn't died, Shannon suspected she wished she had, since she'd been left armless and legless as one limb after another began to rot away under the poison. "Brown recluses?" he repeated. "You keep them here?"

Henderson turned to face the deputy. "Of course I do," he said, speaking as if to a particularly dense student. "Arachnids aren't my specialty, but that doesn't mean I'm not interested in them. I'm interested in anything that—" Henderson cut his own words off abruptly.

"Interested in anything that what, Henderson?" Mark Shannon asked.

When Henderson made no reply, Ellen Filmore spoke, her voice far more composed now, her sobs abating. "I think—" she began, then her voice faltered. Steeling herself as if she were about to tell a patient he was terminally ill, she went on: "I think he's been killing people down here, Mark. He said something about a girl from the freeway—"

Dawn Sanderson, Shannon thought. What in hell is he— But before he could even finish the thought, Ellen's next words hit him.

"—and Otto Owen."

"Otto?" Shannon echoed, suddenly puzzled. "He killed Otto?"

"Nobody will ever prove that," Henderson sneered.

As Ellen Filmore repeated what Henderson had told her of the life-form he'd created in his laboratory, Mark Shannon felt a dark rage take possession of him. For a moment he wondered what would happen if he simply executed Henderson on the spot.

Even as the fleeting thought went through his mind, he knew he wouldn't act on it. Yet with Molly Spellman and Ben Larkin now missing as well, he couldn't waste any time transporting Henderson to the nearest jail, either, not when it was forty miles away.

Then his eyes fell on the darkroom door, and he knew what he could do. There was an elegance to it, a certain justice to holding Henderson captive—even temporarily—in the same room in which he had imprisoned his own victims.

"In there," he said, opening the door to the darkroom and switching on the light so that the interior was dimly illuminated by the light of the bare bulb. "If Ellen couldn't get out, and Otto Owen couldn't get out, I don't think you'll be able to, either."

As Carl Henderson gasped, Mark Shannon gazed at him once more. All the confidence he'd shown a moment ago, all the superciliousness, was gone. In its place was a look of stark terror. "Move it," Shannon said, inclining his head toward the room at the far end of the basement. "And one word out of you, one complaint about your rights, and I won't just lock you in, Henderson. I'll turn the lights out, too. You'll be in the dark."

Though he uttered no complete words at all, Carl Henderson whimpered with terror as Mark Shannon propelled him toward the open door. As the deputy shoved him through, a dark wet stain spread across Henderson's pants.

Karen Owen had never felt more helpless in her life than she did at this very minute.

How could she have let it happen?

She had promised herself—sworn to herself—that she wouldn't fall asleep for even a minute, but now her baby, all she had left since Julie had disappeared, had gone, vanishing into the darkness so completely that she could still barely believe it had happened at all.

Why hadn't she heard them going? Surely they must have been talking to each other, whispering between themselves the way children Molly's and Ben's age did. And what had possessed them? What could possibly have lured them outside tonight?

Once again Karen found herself moving almost involuntarily to the door, going out onto the porch, staring into the darkness, searching.

She didn't know how many times she'd gone outside since Russell had called 911 to report that the two children had disappeared. She'd already been to the barn twice, searching every corner of it, just in case Molly and Ben had decided to play some game, never thinking how much it would terrify their mothers. But she had found no trace of them, not in the barn, or in any of the sheds, or even in the pigpen or the chicken coop, where she'd looked the last time she was out.

Then, perhaps ten minutes ago, she'd noticed that something about the night didn't feel right.

At first she tried to ignore the strange sense of something being different from usual, telling herself that of course things felt different—her baby was gone! But it was something else, something much subtler than that, and the more she tried to ignore it, the more it began to bother her.

It wasn't until Russell had come out that she suddenly realized what it was, and even when she did, she thought maybe she was mistaken.

The night was silent.

The soft cacophony of insect song she had grown so used to over the last two weeks was silent tonight.

She'd been just about to ask Russell about it when the

strange silence was broken by a sound that chilled her to the marrow.

An animal screamed.

It hadn't barked, nor howled, nor even bayed at the moon the way coyotes sometimes did in the hills above the San Fernando Valley.

This had been a short scream of terror and agony, cut off in an instant, gone so quickly she would have wondered if she had imagined it had Russell not tightened his grip on her shoulder, pulling her close.

"It's only some animal," he said. "It's not one of—"

He'd broken off before finishing the sentence, but Karen had had no trouble completing it in her own mind.

—*not one of the kids,* he'd been about to say.

She let him lead her into the house, but ever since then she'd been pacing back and forth from the living room to the kitchen, looking first out of one window, then another. From the kitchen window, which faced north and east, she could see nothing at all, and from the living room window, where the view was to the south and west, there had been only an unbroken curtain of darkness until a moment ago, when she spotted a pair of headlights moving slowly toward them.

So at last something was happening! "There's someone out there," she called. Russell and Marge Larkin joined her. Together they watched the car make its slow way along the dirt road that wound north from Vic Costas's farm and would eventually bring it to their own farm. "Who is it?" she breathed. "What are they doing up there?"

"Maybe it's Shannon, looking for the kids," Russell said. "I'll go see."

"We'll *all* go see," Karen told him.

Together the three of them went out the back door and got into the big pickup truck that, until a few days ago, had been Otto's. "There's a flashlight behind the seat," Russell said as he started the engine and put the truck in low gear. "See if you can get it out. It's a big halogen that plugs into the cigarette lighter."

As the truck bounced up the rutted driveway toward the foothills, Karen climbed up onto the seat and fished around among the jumper cables, flares, and other miscellany Otto had stashed in the space behind it. And suddenly, now that she was doing something, making some positive effort to find her missing children, some of the terror in her heart began to abate.

We'll find them, she told herself. We'll find Molly and Ben tonight, and tomorrow we'll find them all.

But even as she uttered the words, she wondered if perhaps they weren't more hope than reality.

Though Mark Shannon knew there was practically no chance of finding Molly Spellman and Ben Larkin until the sun came up, he also knew there was no way he could call the search off, either. By the time he'd joined up with Manny Gomez on the dirt road behind the Owen farm, Russell and Karen were already there, along with Marge Larkin, and for the next twenty minutes more cars and trucks had arrived, everyone determined to begin the search immediately. So, even while knowing that seeking lost children at night was only slightly less futile than the proverbial hunt for the needle in the haystack, he'd broken the searchers up into groups, giving them strict orders not to lose contact with each other. "I'm going to need all of you in the morning, and the last thing I'm gonna want is to have to send people out looking for my search party. Clear?"

For almost three hours the search had gone on, but so far, just as Mark Shannon had expected, there had been no results.

Now, from his command post midway between the Costas farm and the Owen spread, he was trying to stay in radio contact with everyone at once, producing an often unintelligible jabber of overlapping conversations.

Up in the hills, lights glimmered as the searchers made their way slowly along the paths, pausing every few minutes to sweep their flashlights in wide circles.

Clouds had begun drifting in, and the moon, so bright two hours ago, was now only intermittently visible. If it disappeared entirely, Shannon wasn't sure how the search could continue. Half an hour ago he'd started issuing warnings to the searchers to watch their batteries, to make sure they had enough light left to get themselves back down to the road in the event the moonlight failed.

Still, in a few more hours dawn would begin to break, and then at least they'd have a chance. Except that Shannon kept thinking about the sound he'd heard just before he and Roberto broke into Carl Henderson's house.

The sound that Manny Gomez had heard too, along with Karen and Russell Owen, and Marge Larkin.

"I don't know what it was for sure," Manny told him when he first arrived on the scene. "But I can tell you it sure sounded to me like something was dying out there. A coyote maybe." Then he'd glanced over to make sure Karen and Russell were out of earshot. "Or maybe that dog of theirs, Bailey."

"That's what I'm thinking, too," Shannon had admitted.

Now he glanced at his watch.

Quarter to three.

Three more hours, and it would start getting light.

A shout interrupted his thoughts, then another. When Shannon looked up into the hills, he saw the beams of several flashlights crisscrossing as they searched one of the slopes.

Flipping on the powerful searchlight mounted on the roof of his squad car, he began moving the beam slowly back and forth, working it up the hillside in a steady pattern. A moment later Karen Owen appeared next to him, clutching the halogen spotlight from the pickup truck.

"Did someone see something?" she asked. "What's going on?"

"Don't know," Shannon replied, not looking at her as he concentrated on keeping the pattern of his searchlight tight.

"Molly!" Karen called out. "Ben! Where are you?" Turning on the brilliant halogen light, she sent a bright beam all the way to the top of the hill, working it slowly along the crest.

Suddenly, at the very edge of the beam, she thought she saw a flicker of movement.

She held the light still for a moment, then slowly moved it back the other way. "Molly!" she called out again. "Molly, it's Mommy!"

And then—miraculously, it seemed to Karen—a tiny figure appeared in the center of the spotlight.

A tiny figure, wearing clothes that Karen recognized instantly.

A tiny figure that waved. And then she spotted another figure.

"It's them!" Karen shouted. "Oh, God! It's Molly! And Ben!"

Mark Shannon shifted his own light until its beam held steady on the two children. "Go," he said. "I won't let them out of the light for a second."

Karen, though, didn't even hear him, for she was already running, stumbling, up the hill, Marge Larkin scrambling after her.

Ten minutes later, their children in their arms, Karen and Marge were back.

Five minutes after that, in the safety of the Owens' brightly lit kitchen, Molly and Ben told the story of what they had seen that night.

And as they listened, Karen Owen and Marge Larkin began to cry.

CHAPTER 30

Sara McLaughlin stumbled along the track that was now only barely visible in the faltering moonlight. She no longer had any idea of how long it had been since she fled from the hospital, let alone where she was or where she was going.

There was only the imperative need emanating from somewhere deep within her, driving her on, compelling her to move toward an unknown goal she could not comprehend. In her haste, she tripped, her right foot—which had been bleeding steadily since she slashed her toe on a broken beer bottle an hour before—smashing into a rough fragment of granite. Sara grabbed reflexively at a large bush next to the trail, and the long thorns studding its twisting branches pierced her skin, sinking deep into the flesh of her palm.

Staggering, she lurched two more steps before losing her balance completely and dropping to the ground, scraping the skin from her left knee and twisting her right ankle as she fell. For a moment she lay where she was, her heart pounding, her lungs working feverishly to pump oxygen into her body.

Despite her bleeding foot, the stinging punctures in her left hand, and the throbbing pain in her ankle, Sara struggled to her feet and moved on, leaving the trail now to cut cross-country, her numbed mind oblivious to the jagged rocks and sharp twigs that tore at her feet, stripping the skin away until she was running on the raw tissue of her soles, every step so painful that another person—one whose mind still possessed some shred of sanity—wouldn't have been able to walk at all.

But Sara's mind had stopped functioning long ago, though her body kept moving, driven far beyond the bounds of endurance by the inhuman force dwelling within it, a force now grown so large that her slim body could barely sustain it; a force that now, responding to the directions of an intelligence far greater than the sum of its individual parts, was embarked on a last desperate attempt to rejoin the great mass of its being, and to search out a new host upon which to feed.

Sara McLaughlin, her mind and body totally subjugated to the demands from within, stumbled on through the night.

"Are you mad at me, Mommy?" Molly Owen asked, her voice quavering, her eyes moist.

They were upstairs, and though the sky was just turning gray with the first faint light of dawn, Karen was tucking her daughter into bed. As Molly's question echoed in her head, she laid her palm on the little girl's cheek and shook her head. "I guess not," she said. "But you have to promise me never to do anything like that again, darling. Don't you know how frightened I was when I woke up and found you gone?"

Molly's chin trembled. "I wanted to surprise you," she said. "We didn't know we were going to get lost! We were just trying to help!"

"I know." Karen sighed, remembering once more the strange story Molly and Ben had told of finding a valley far up in the hills, where their brother and sister had been in a cave, surrounded by insects.

Millions and millions of them, Molly had assured her.

The story couldn't possibly be true, of course, though surely they must have seen something up there. But what?

And what had happened to Bailey?

Karen still felt a chill as she recalled that terrible howl she'd heard a few hours ago.

A howl that had been cut short, as if whatever uttered it had suddenly fallen victim.

To what?

A swarm of bees attacking it as they had attacked the mare a few days ago?

A feeling deep in her gut told Karen that it had, indeed, been the big friendly mongrel with the constantly wagging tail whom she had heard screaming in terror and agony in the silence of the night. That same feeling in her gut whispered to her that whatever had attacked Bailey was nothing the dog had ever experienced before, something even more frightening than the scene Molly and Ben had described.

Part of Karen wanted to know what it had been, but a greater part of her hoped she would never find out. "I know you were just trying to help," she reassured Molly now, kissing her on the forehead and trying to keep her voice from betraying her fear. "But the way to help isn't to go up into the hills in the middle of the night by yourself, and I want you to promise me you'll never do it again."

Molly's big eyes fixed on her own. "I promise," she whispered. "Cross my heart, and hope to die."

No, Karen silently said to herself. Don't ever wish to die, darling. Not ever. But when she spoke, she managed to conceal from her little girl most of the pain and fear she was feeling. "Then everything's all right," she said. "Now I want you to go to sleep, and when you wake up, maybe—"

Maybe Julie will be here, was what she'd been about to say, but she could no longer bring herself even to suggest such a thing, for deep in her heart she no longer believed it.

"—maybe things will be all right again," she finished. But things wouldn't be all right, not if there were any truth at all to the children's bizarre tale, which sounded to Karen more like something they must have seen on television than anything they could possibly have actually witnessed up in the hills. Yet the children's voices had trembled with fright, even in the safety of the farmhouse, and their words had the ring of truth, rather than the hollow sound of a story they'd made up to extricate themselves from trouble. "Sleep, baby," Karen crooned. "Just go to sleep."

Staying with Molly until she finally drifted into an exhausted sleep, Karen at last turned off the light. She slipped out into the corridor just as Marge Larkin was coming out of the next room, where she'd been tucking Ben in. Neither woman spoke until they were both at the bottom of the stairs. Then Karen turned to face Jeff's mother.

"Do you think we're ever going to see Julie and Jeff and Kevin again?" she asked.

Marge hesitated, then shook her head grimly. "If we do," she said, her words barely audible, "I'm not sure we'll be able to recognize them." Her voice, then her whole body, began to tremble. "They're dead," she said. "Oh, Lord help me, Karen, I just know it. I can feel it!"

Karen put her arms around Marge Larkin. "I know," she whispered into Marge's ear. "I feel the same way."

For a long moment the two women stood silently together, supporting one another in their mutual grief.

In the basement of Carl Henderson's house, Ellen Filmore raised her head from the microscope, stretched her aching back, then rubbed her eyes with her fists. Refusing Shannon's attempts to send them away, she and Roberto Muñoz had worked together all night long on the chance that they could learn something—anything—about Henderson's creation that might help the infected children.

From Henderson himself they had heard little. So deep was their concentration that for minutes at a time they would forget about him completely, until the silence of the lab was suddenly interrupted by one of his sobbing pleas to be released from behind the locked door of the darkroom.

Pleas that neither of them had even been tempted to heed.

"Have you got that lung tissue ready?" Ellen asked Roberto, who was preparing slides for her as fast as he could.

"Almost," he replied. He carefully cut a tiny tissue sample from the rat's lung, transferred it to one of the thin glass slides they'd found on a shelf above the counter, then applied a drop of dye to it. Covering it with a second slide, he passed it over to Ellen. "Seems like this was a lot easier back in school," he said. The rat's internal organs had been so thoroughly destroyed that it was only barely possible to identify them.

Ellen Filmore pressed her eye to the microscope, adjusted the light and the focus, then found what she was looking for.

Under the magnification she could clearly see the alveoli. Though a few of them still looked perfectly normal, most of them did not. Rather than being the tiny empty sacs used by the rat's lungs to exchange carbon dioxide for oxygen, many of the alveoli she was now looking at were occupied by something else.

Something that, though invisible to the naked eye, was easily identifiable under the microscope.

Insects.

The final piece of the puzzle fell into place.

Throughout her long night's work, she'd begun to understand the life cycle of the parasitic colony that had infested the rat's body before it died.

In its blood she'd found something that looked to her very much like a larval insect form, which she had assumed was what Barry Sadler had found in the blood samples she'd taken from Julie Spellman and Jeff Larkin.

The larvae, though, seemed to have metamorphosed into various kinds of adults.

In the rat's intestines, she found what appeared to be some kind of workers, tending to eggs.

In its heart she'd found a queen, surrounded by attendants, which produced a constant stream of eggs, laying them directly into the bloodstream, which transported them to the nursery in the intestines. As the eggs hatched into larvae, they returned to the circulatory system, apparently taking their nourishment directly from the host's blood. Then, as they entered the pupal stage, they redistributed themselves once again, larval royal attendants returning to the heart, and nurses to the intestines.

But she'd found other kinds of adults as well.

The rat's brain had been filled with them, and though she had no idea what their purpose had been, the results were clear to Ellen under the microscope: they had been destroying the brain, burrowing through it, devouring it cell by cell. As she'd studied the damage the colony had done, Ellen felt a growing sense of horror, for the destruction of the brain had not been random. Rather, the organisms worked their way carefully through the tissue, riddling it with tiny passages so it almost resembled a microscopic anthill.

The rat might have felt nothing, for a while.

Then it would have begun experiencing phantom stimuli as the parasites devoured more and more nerve cells.

It could have felt pleasure, but more probably experienced excruciating pain.

Before it died, it would have gone both blind and deaf, for both the optic and aural nerve centers were gone.

Then, as the colony multiplied, expanded, and continued feeding, the creature's mental processes would inevitably have been affected. But the colony, behaving with the same peculiar intelligence as a hive of bees or a nest of ants, had begun their feeding with noncritical areas, leaving the most vital parts of the brain intact so their host would survive as long as possible. Indeed, the autonomic nervous system and the portions of the brain controlling it seemed still to be almost intact.

The question, though, was what would happen when the host inevitably died. It was when that question formulated in Ellen Filmore's mind that she finally turned to the lungs.

And found her answer.

The adult forms that were still present in the alveoli of the rat's lungs were different from any of the others.

For one thing, they had wings.

Wings, she assumed, that would fall off soon after the insects had taken their maiden flight, just as the wings of termites and ants are shed once the colony has split.

As she examined the alveoli more closely, she discovered that even among the adult forms in the rat's lungs, there were variations.

She discovered three pupae that were much larger than the others; these, she assumed, would be queens.

All of them were equipped with what appeared to be sharp proboscises.

Ellen Filmore shuddered, imagining what would happen if an uninfected animal came close enough to an infected one just as the swarm had prepared itself to split.

She could imagine a cloud of the microscopic insects erupting out the infected lungs, riding the air currents for no more than—what?

A foot?

Perhaps only an inch or two?

In an instant the attackers would bore through the skin and be safely into the bloodstream, ready to colonize a new host.

Colonize it, and kill it.

Still, as she examined the rat, Ellen Filmore found a few anomalies.

What, actually, had killed the rodent?

As she and Roberto dissected it, its brain didn't appear to be fatally damaged.

And why had the exhaust filter on the acrylic box in which the rat was held been covered with a film of the insects, all of whom were dead?

Obviously, the creatures couldn't survive outside a mammalian host for very long—from the observations she'd already made, they weren't adapted for anything else.

Then why had they deserted the host, only to die?

Because the rat was dying itself?

Exhausted in mind and body, she finally straightened up once more. "Come on," she told Roberto. "Let's go upstairs and see if Henderson has any coffee in his kitchen."

Roberto nodded toward the closed door at the far end of the basement, from which they had heard no sound at all for the last hour. "What about him?"

Ellen's eyes hardened as she remembered the hours she'd spent behind that door, locked in the darkness. Once again she felt the terror that had paralyzed her as the spiders crept up her leg. Now, as she thought about what this man had unleashed on the teenagers of Pleasant Valley, the terror she'd felt earlier dissolved once more into cold rage. She was tempted to cross the room herself, turn off the lights, and release some of Carl Henderson's specimens into the dark chamber to torture him as the spiders had tormented her. A moment later, though, she put the impulse down. "Leave him there," she told Roberto. "The way he's built that room, he won't get out until Shannon comes to take him to jail." She led the way up the steep flight of stairs, blinking in surprise as she stepped through the door into the entry hall and realized that dawn was starting to break.

In Carl Henderson's kitchen, she poked through the cupboards in search of a jar of instant coffee. Then she spotted a coffeemaker sitting on the kitchen sink. "Am I going to turn that on, or are you?" she asked Roberto.

Roberto grinned. "Sit, Doc. You look even more beat than I feel." But as he searched for a clean filter to put into the machine, he became aware of a noise.

A low humming, as if there were a swarm of bees somewhere nearby. When he looked out the window, he saw it.

"Holy shit, Doc," he breathed. "What the hell is that?"

Moving next to him, Ellen Filmore, too, gazed out the window. For a moment she wasn't certain what he was talking about. Then, in the steadily brightening light, she saw it.

Far off in the distance, hovering above the hills that lay beyond the field behind Carl Henderson's house, was what looked at first glance like a dark cloud. As she focused on it, her ears began to pick up the same sound Roberto had heard a moment earlier.

Insects.

Millions and millions of them, billowing out of the hills, rising into the sky, their sound droning louder by the moment.

Ellen Filmore's eyes widened as she realized what the steadily rising hum meant. "Come on," she told Roberto, grabbing his arm and starting toward the kitchen door. "Let's get out of here."

"Get out?" Roberto said. "But—"

"Can't you hear them?" Ellen asked. "Can't you see them? They're coming right toward us!"

Roberto tore his eyes away from the doctor to look out the window once more.

The cloud of insects appeared to be growing by the second, and now Roberto realized Ellen was right—already they were beginning to advance into the field. As he watched, the fence that marked its far boundary disappeared into the dark mass, exactly as if it had been swallowed up. He suddenly remembered his grandfather telling him about a plague of locusts that had swept through his village in Mexico when the old man had been a boy. *Like night, in the middle of the day, Roberto. You couldn't see, you couldn't hear, you could hardly breathe. We thought we were going to die. We all thought we were going to die.* Now the memory of his grandfather's words catapulted Roberto into action. The coffee forgotten, he followed Ellen Filmore through the foyer to the front door and outside.

"My car!" Ellen shouted, running to the driver's side of her Buick. "At least we can call someone!"

The first scouts arrived in advance of the body of the swarm, swirling around the car just as Ellen Filmore and Roberto Muñoz slammed the doors shut. The moment Ellen started the car, Robert picked up the cellular phone and stabbed 911 into the keypad, then hit the send button.

"Where's Shannon?" he demanded when the dispatcher came on the line. As the operator started to demand details of the problem, Roberto shoved the phone at Ellen, who was already speeding down Carl Henderson's driveway. "Pull rank," he told her.

"This is Dr. Filmore," Ellen shouted. "I need to know where Mark Shannon is, right now."

The dispatcher, recognizing Ellen's voice and the note of emergency in it, reacted instantly. "He's at the Owen farm," she said. "Do you know where it is?"

"I do," Ellen said. "About five miles from where I am. Can you patch me?"

"I already am," the dispatcher replied.

A second later Mark Shannon came on the line, only to listen numbly as Ellen Filmore tried to describe the cloud of insects still descending from the hill, making its inexorable way across the field toward Carl Henderson's house.

"I've never seen anything like it," she said. "There are all kinds of insects, Mark." She slowed the car as it entered the cloud, which was already engulfing the road. "I can see bees, and hornets and gnats, and there're grasshoppers and cicadas, too. Jesus! It looks like—I don't know—it looks like a plague." Suddenly the car emerged from the cloud, and once more she could see the road ahead, clear now. "We're out of it now, Mark. We'll be there in—"

"No!" Shannon interrupted. "If you're out of it, stay where you are. I'll be there in five minutes."

Stopping the car, Ellen left the motor idling in case the mass of flying insects changed direction and started toward her. But as she watched, she caught a glimpse of four figures walking slowly across the field, in the center of the living whirlwind.

Four figures—a girl and three boys—moving steadily toward Carl Henderson's house.

The place, Ellen suddenly realized, where the parasite within them had originally been spawned.

And now she realized exactly what the swarm was doing.

It's homing, she thought. It's homing, just like a flock of pigeons.

Except that this flock was deadly.

CHAPTER 31

"What is it?" Karen asked Mark Shannon as he hung up the phone, her heart pounding. Was it possible that someone had found the missing children? But when Mark turned to face the little group gathered in the Owen kitchen, his face was pale, his expression hard.

"Insects," he said. "All kinds of them—millions of them—just like the kids said."

"Where?" Karen breathed.

"What about our children?" Marge Larkin asked, her voice trembling. "Did they see them?"

Shannon was already starting toward the back door. "They're over near Carl Henderson's place," he said. "No one said anything about your kids, but that doesn't mean they're not there." He flicked his radio on, speaking rapidly into the microphone. "Manny? I've got a report of something going on over by Henderson's place. What's your position?"

The radio receiver crackled, then the second deputy's voice came through. "I'm about a mile from there. Me and Jim Chapman and some other guys. You wouldn't believe what's going on! Weirdest thing I ever saw! It's like those seventeen-year locusts! I think you better get over here!"

"I'm on my way, Manny," Shannon said. "Get everyone out there into cars. Those aren't just locusts, the way I hear it. There's enough bees, hornets, wasps, and other

405

stuff over there to kill the whole town. I don't want anyone doing anything till I've had a look."

"We're going, too," Karen said, in a tone that told Shannon she expected no argument.

Still, he was as determined to keep as many people away from Henderson's house as possible. "I'm not sure that's a good idea," he began, but now Russell spoke, his voice every bit as determined as his wife's.

"Our kids might very well be out there, Mark," he said. "You can argue until you're blue in the face, but there's no way you're keeping me, or Karen, or Marge away."

"And we won't leave Molly and Ben here alone, either," Karen interjected, her expression leaving no room for discussion.

"If you had kids of your own—" Russell began, but Mark Shannon, realizing there was no sense even trying to argue the point, held up his hands to stem the flow of words.

"All right, enough said. But just remember who's in charge, and stay in your car until I give the word. And make damn sure Molly and Ben don't even think about opening a door or window." He hesitated, then added, "There's something I haven't told you, but I guess you'd better know. I've got Carl Henderson locked up in the basement of his house."

Russell's mouth dropped open in shock, and Karen, who was already on her way out of the kitchen to go upstairs and awaken Molly once again, turned to stare at the deputy, her intuition telling her what was coming.

"Otto!" she breathed. "He was right, wasn't he? About Carl?"

Shannon nodded grimly. "Close enough so that Carl killed him, apparently. When I got there, he had Ellen Filmore locked up, and had turned a bunch of spiders loose on her. His 'pets' he calls them. He's got all kinds of insects down there—spiders and scorpions, too! God knows what. And it looks like he killed at least one girl, maybe more."

Karen, suddenly dizzy, reached out to steady herself against the door frame, her fingers clutching it so tightly her knuckles turned white. When Russell started toward her, though, she shook her head. "I'll be all right," she said. "Marge and I will get Molly and Ben, then we can go." Russell said nothing, but Karen could see a vein in his forehead throbbing with fury. Shooting her husband a warning look, she spoke once more, this time to Mark Shannon. "He'll stay in the car, Mark. We all will. No one will try to do anything, believe me."

Shannon hesitated, his eyes flicking toward Russell, but then he nodded and left the house through the back door, breaking into a trot as he headed toward his squad car.

Five minutes later, when Karen and Marge Larkin came down the stairs, carrying their sleepy children in their arms, Russell was still standing exactly as she'd left him, his expression a mask of cold fury.

"I'll kill that lying son of a bitch," he grated. "If I so much as see him, I swear I'll kill him."

Carl Henderson stirred, then slowly awoke from a restless sleep.

His body ached; every muscle felt stiff and sore, and when he moved his legs, pain shot through his hips.

Slowly he opened one eye, and for a moment felt totally disoriented.

At first he could see nothing, for all around him, despite the shadowless glare of a naked bulb screwed into a socket in the ceiling, there seemed to be nothing but blackness. It was as if he were lying on a cold stone slab in the midst of a massive cavern whose walls were too far away even to be faintly illuminated by the light from the glowing bulb above his head.

Then, as his mind began to clear, an ancient memory,

long forgotten, surfaced. And Carl Henderson remembered. . . .

He had been only four years old that day when he made his way through the gate in the back fence—a jar holding his very first swallowtail butterfly clutched in his hands—and went into the house through the back door, intent on showing his prize to his sister.

He could hear the television in the living room. He was sure that his sister must still be lying on the couch where she'd been when he'd gone outside an hour before.

Maybe, if he was really nice, she'd even help him put the pretty butterfly on the pin, so he wouldn't accidentally mess it up.

As he went into the living room, he heard another sound, a sound like a moan, which was louder than the sound from the television.

Still holding the mason jar, he went around the end of the couch.

And then he saw his sister.

She was still on the couch.

But she didn't have her clothes on, and the boy who lived down the street was there, too, lying on top of her.

For a second he just stood there, looking at her, staring at her thick black hair cascading over the arm of the couch, not certain what she and the boy were doing.

But then she caught sight of him, and he could tell right away that she was really mad at him.

Her face turned red and her eyes opened wide, and then she started yelling: "You little creep! What are you doing in here? Didn't I warn you to stay outside until I told you to come in?"

His eyes widened in sudden fear, and he took a step backward. "I caught a butterfly," he began. "I—"

"A bug?" his sister shouted. "You came back in just because you caught a stupid bug?" Suddenly she was off the

sofa, standing over him, glaring down at him. "I'll show you," she said. "Come on!" Knocking the jar out of his hands, she grabbed his arm and dragged him out of the living room. He struggled to pull away from her, but her fingers closed tighter on his arm, and instantly an image rose in his mind of the butterfly in the jar, which had been struggling in his own fingers only a few minutes ago.

"Let go," he pleaded. "I didn't do anything—"

But his sister didn't seem to hear him. Half dragging him, his feet stumbling beneath him, she pulled him out of the living room and into the hall, then through the door beneath the stairs, down into the basement. Propelling him across the concrete floor, she opened a door at the far side of the basement, behind which was a large, dark room where he knew someone used to make pictures. Its blackened interior had always terrified the little boy. From the first time he saw it, he'd been certain that goblins and witches and monsters occupied its shadowed corners, and that if he ever got locked inside, they would lurch out of the darkness and kill him.

"Stay in here if you like bugs so much," his sister said, shoving him through the door. "Stay in here with the cockroaches until you can learn to do what you're told!"

She slammed the door, and a second later the little boy heard the key turn in the lock. Before he could even cry out, he heard her footsteps as she walked away from the door, then climbed back up the stairs.

A scream rose in his throat, then died as the darkness closed around him.

All the demons that had ever existed in his nightmares lurked in the blackness around him, floating just beyond his reach. Though he could neither see them, feel them, nor hear them, he knew they were there.

He dropped to the floor and scuttled backward a few feet, until his back hit one of the walls. Then he inched sideways until he came to a corner and could move no far-

ther. His back pressed into the angle of the two cold concrete walls, the little boy drew his knees up to his chest and wrapped his arms around them.

He closed his eyes, doing his best to pretend that the darkness wasn't really there at all, that if he opened his eyes again, it would be light and he would be able to see.

But knowing the truth, he didn't open his eyes, certain that if he did, and saw the darkness everywhere, something would leap out at him, its claws sinking into his flesh, its teeth ripping him into shreds.

His body shook with a sob, and he buried his face in his arms as tears began oozing out of his tightly shut eyes.

Then he felt something.

A tickling, as if something were creeping up his leg.

He gasped, instinctively brushing at his leg with his right hand, and for a second the tickling stopped.

Then it started again, but this time it was on his other leg.

Now he began to hear something.

The sound was very faint at first, and for a minute he didn't know what it was.

But then, as he held his breath, it started to sound sort of like something he'd heard before.

Like a fly, buzzing at the window, trying to get out.

Now the sound was getting louder, and he could feel the tickling sensation again. On both legs now, and on his arms, too.

As if hundreds of insects were crawling all over him.

The humming sound got louder, and he could feel a faint breeze, as if they were flying all around him—more of them than he could even imagine—their wings moving the air enough so he could actually feel it on his face.

Then they began lighting on his face, and suddenly, as his panic built, the little boy had a vision in his mind.

A vision of the bugs in his cigar boxes.

The bugs he'd caught, and killed, and mounted on pins.

The hundreds more that he'd only killed, then thrown away when they fell apart as he tried to mount them.

Suddenly he knew what was happening.

It wasn't the monsters and demons from his nightmares that were in the darkness.

It was all the insects he'd killed.

All the tiny creatures he'd caught in his jar, and killed.

They were coming for him now, coming at him out of the darkness.

They were going to do to him what he had done to them.

He felt them crawling over his skin, heard their vibrating wings humming in his ears, felt them creeping into his ears and nose.

His howls of terror filled the darkened room, echoing off the walls to reverberate in his ears, but still the creatures crawled over him, swarming around him, the humming of their wings growing louder every second.

He began flailing his arms, thrashing out at his invisible tormentors, then rolling across the floor, frantically trying to escape the horde of creatures.

They were everywhere. He could feel them beneath him, almost hear their wings and shells crush as he rolled over them.

The floor was beginning to feel slick, but no matter what he did, where he tried to go to escape them, there were always more.

The air was thick with them now, and when he flailed his arms in the darkness, he could feel them, sense them preparing to bite and to sting.

His howls rose louder. He scrambled to his feet and stumbled around the blacked-out darkroom, his mind starting to shatter as he tried to escape his tormentors.

He lurched into a wall, his face striking the cold concrete, and he felt a warm gush of blood spurt from his nose.

Shrieking in pain, he dropped back to the floor.

Now the bugs were sticking to the blood covering his face, and he could even feel them in his mouth.

He screamed again, but his voice choked in his throat, and he sobbed helplessly as he scrabbled across the floor in a vain effort to escape the teeming, swirling mass.

They were going to kill him!

He was going to die, all by himself, and no one was going to come and save him.

"Mommy . . ." he sobbed. The word was barely audible. A horrible weakness coming over him, he crouched quivering on the floor, the terror within tearing at his mind.

"Mommy . . ."

Then, from somewhere far away, he thought he saw a ray of light.

He froze, certain for a split second that he must have died and the light must be God, come to take him to Heaven.

Then, as a brilliant glare burst over his head and the darkness surrounding him was washed away, he heard a sound.

His sister.

It was his sister, and she was laughing!

He sat up, blinking in the brightness.

Why would she be laughing?

Then he heard her voice again.

"What's wrong with you?" she was asking. "It's not even cockroaches, you little creep. It's only termites. Termites can't hurt you!"

His eyes slowly adjusted to the light and began to focus. Finally he saw them.

Thousands of them, swarming up from the cracks in the concrete floor, down from the timbers that supported the floor of the house.

They swirled around his head, and he tried to duck away from them, tried once more to brush them off his skin.

A shadow fell over the little boy, then he felt his sister's hand close on his arm.

He tried to pull away from her, sobbing loudly, the terror of the attack in the darkness still making his heart pound.

His sister dragged him to his feet, but he struggled against her.

"Will you stop wiggling?" he heard her say. "Just let me get us out of here!"

As he sobbed once more, his sister's hand lashed out, striking him across the cheek. He howled at the stinging on his flesh, but his howl only brought him another blow, and then another.

"Shut up!" she yelled at him. "What are you crying about? It's just a bunch of dumb termites!"

Again he felt her hand slash across his face, and he howled all the louder.

She kept hitting him, kept telling him to shut up, but he couldn't, for every time her hand struck his flesh, a new howl of pain erupted from his throat.

Then, when he was sure she was going to kill him, she released him instead, and he fell into a sobbing heap on the floor.

"Fine," he heard her say. "If you're going to act like a baby, you can just get treated like o . Stay here until you die, for all I care."

As he sobbed, the lights went out again, and once more the darkness—the horrible darkness that hummed with the terrifying buzz of thousands of beating wings—closed around him.

The bugs were crawling over his skin, creeping into his ears, worming up into his nose.

And as he lay in the darkness, the insects torturing his body and his mind, a hot spark of hatred began to smolder deep within his soul.

He concentrated on the glowing ember of hatred.

Concentrated on it, and nurtured it, and began to fan it into a raging flame.

And as he lay on the hard concrete, waiting for someone to come and rescue him from the darkness and the insects, the hate consumed him.

It was a hatred he would never let go of.

He would keep feeding it until it grew so large, so strong, that it would never go away, never be satisfied.

And always be triggered by the sight of a girl who looked like his sister.

A girl with a flowing mane of thick, dark hair. . . .

No!

It wasn't happening! It was only a memory, and he wasn't a little boy anymore, and the lights weren't even off.

Carl Henderson lay still for a moment, forcing himself to relax, closing his mind to the awful memory.

His heartbeat slowed and his breathing, which a moment ago had been rasping in panting gasps of terror, evened out.

He began to remember what had happened last night, and how he'd gotten here.

He listened, his ears searching for the sound of Ellen Filmore's murmuring voice.

Despite the insulation he'd installed in the room years ago, he knew the soundproofing wasn't perfect—he'd been able to hear the screams of the girl he'd killed, and Otto, and Ellen Filmore, and before exhaustion had finally overcome him, he'd heard her voice as she talked to Roberto Muñoz.

Now, though, there was nothing.

Nothing, except for a faint hum.

A hum, he realized a moment later, that sounded like the beating wings of millions of insects.

Carl Henderson sat up, the panic he'd fought off only a moment ago suddenly rising again.

Had they released his pets?

Were they working their way into the darkroom even now?

His eyes fixed on the little pass-through he himself had built. Was it about to open, triggered from the outside, and release some of the creatures he'd so lovingly nurtured into this room where he had no defenses at all?

Abruptly, all his senses came alive, all his nerves began tingling.

In his mind he saw once again the body of the girl he'd left hanging from the wall to be devoured by the ants.

And Otto Owen's body, covered with scorpions that had scurried off into the darkest crevices of the room when he'd switched on the light.

Were they still there?

What if the light went off now?

The spiders.

What about the spiders he'd released to torment Ellen Filmore? Where were they?

The hum of the beating wings grew louder, filling Carl Henderson's ears. Driven by panic, he struggled to his feet and lurched to the door, where his fists beat futilely against the panels he himself had reinforced.

"Let me out," he pleaded. "Oh, God, let me out. . . ."

But on the other side of the door there was nobody to hear him, and finally he sank once more to his knees, the hum of the gathering swarm growing ever louder in his ears.

The swarm that Carl Henderson did not yet understand was real . . .

Real, and coming home.

"My God," Karen said. "What's happening?"

Russell braked the car to a stop, as awed as his wife by what he was seeing beyond the windshield.

The air was thick with insects, swirling around the car, seeming to come from every direction. But ahead of them the churning, roiling cloud thickened and darkened, an impenetrable mass of teeming life advancing across the field from the hills, moving steadily closer to the old Victorian house in which Carl Henderson had spent his entire life.

"They're in there," Marge Larkin whispered from the backseat. She leaned forward, resting her hands on the back of the front seat, gazing between Karen and Russell. "I can feel it. The kids are in there."

"It's like what we saw, Mommy," Molly piped, standing up to get a better view. "Except there's even more of them now! Where are they coming from?"

None of the adults in the car answered her, for all of them were simply staring at the swirling mass, barely able to comprehend that it was there at all, let alone what force might be driving it.

For several long moments the five occupants of the car sat silently, the light of dawn slowly fading as the ever-building swarm moved eastward, blocking out the sun.

"I don't like it," Ben Larkin said, his voice quavering with the fear they were all feeling. "I want to go home!"

Marge Larkin slipped one arm around him and the other around Molly, drawing both children close. "It's all right," she soothed. "We're safe. They can't get into the car."

In the front seat Russell, hearing her words, reached out to the dashboard and began flipping the levers that would close all the car's vents.

Karen, catching the movement out of the corner of her eye, glanced over at him. "They can't, can they?" she asked. Now her own voice trembled as her eyes shifted away from Russell to fix on a mass of wasps that alighted on the windshield and moved across it, finally stopping at the edges where, to Karen's horror, their mandibles began gnawing the black rubber seal that held the window in place. Reaching out, she took Russell's hand, and he squeezed it.

"We're okay," he said. "Cars aren't like they used to be. They're sealed so tight they'll float these days." But even as he uttered the words, he wondered if he was speaking the truth.

Julie came to the picket fence separating the pasture from the yard behind Carl Henderson's house. Though her eyes gave no clue that she even saw the barrier, she stopped a foot in front of it and waited. With no break in their own pace, Kevin Owen, Jeff Larkin, and Andy Bennett moved past her and began tearing pickets from the two rails until enough of them were gone for Julie to pass through, moving inexorably on toward the house, oblivious to the dense mass of insects surrounding her, unaffected by the howl generated by the millions of wings vibrating within a few feet of her ears.

Yet inside her, the living mind of the colonizing swarm was steadily functioning, and from every pore of Julie's body pheromones were constantly emanating, directing the churning horde that surrounded her and her attendants.

As she moved up the steps onto the front porch of the house, yellow jackets and paper wasps responded to a nesting instruction and began gathering cellulose, stripping it away from the siding of Carl Henderson's house, each of them carrying off a tiny fragment, returning a moment later for another.

From the ground beneath the house, ants swarmed up, and in the timbers supporting the structure, the termites went mad, their mandibles working frantically.

As Julie opened the door of the house, the swarm funneled in as if drawn by a vacuum. Soon the whole house was vibrating with the pulse of their humming wings.

And in the basement, locked in his still-illuminated chamber, Carl Henderson began to sweat as the distant hum he'd first heard only moments ago rose to a pitch that seemed to drive into his brain like a hot spike.

As Julie moved toward the basement door—Jeff, Andy, and Kevin still following in her footsteps—the cockroaches hiding in the dark crevices of the kitchen scurried forth, disappearing into the electrical sockets, making their way into conduits, to chew on the already worn insulation of the old house's wiring.

Opening the door below the stairs, Julie and her attendants started down the flight into the basement.

Now the nests of insects that Carl Henderson had tended and nurtured for years also began to respond. The ant colonies teemed with activity, the workers who had for generations remained content within the artificial boundaries of their nests suddenly going mad, burrowing into the lead linings of their cases. As the workers dropped away from the task, their mandibles quickly worn down by the lead, their systems poisoned by it, others replaced them. Finally the barriers were breached and the creatures joined the hordes of other insects that were already welling out of the cracks in the ancient concrete floor and the riddled beams above.

Coming to the bottom of the stairs, Julie stopped. And then, eyes fixed in front of her, she began to move again.

Toward the closed door to Carl Henderson's secret chamber.

Carl Henderson stared in horror at the insects that seemed to be oozing out of the walls. From above him, termites were pouring out of the support beams of the house, while from the cracks in the floor, ants of every conceivable variety were emerging.

Cockroaches appeared out of nowhere, and as Henderson looked up in terror at the bare bulb above him, praying that its bright light might wash away the dark horror that was suddenly all around him, another roach crept out from beneath the socket itself and dropped onto his face.

As he screamed and brushed the scurrying creature away from his cheek, the light went out, plunging Henderson into a black hell.

The ants swarmed over him, their mandibles sinking into his skin, each of them injecting a tiny droplet of poison into him, until, within a few seconds, his skin felt as if it were on fire.

Screaming in fear and agony, he staggered toward the door, but the sound of his pounding fists was lost in the ever-rising howl of the insects that now filled the cellar beyond the door.

And then, miraculously, the lock was opened and Carl Henderson felt the door open in front of him.

For an instant—a moment so brief he barely had time to savor it—Carl Henderson felt the thrill of escape.

Then the swarm attacked, wasps and hornets sinking their stingers deep into his flesh as the mosquitoes settled on him to feast on his blood.

Drawing in his breath to scream, Henderson choked on a cloud of gnats, and, coughing, fell to the floor.

He scrabbled across it in a desperate attempt to escape his attackers, only to feel, a second later, a new presence.

Reaching out, his fingers closed on what he was certain was a human ankle.

But even before he had a chance to plead for mercy, Julie's swollen fingers reached down and her long, stinger-like nails sank into his flesh.

At that moment, the roach-stripped wiring short-circuited, igniting the tinder-dry wood with which the house was constructed. As he died, the last thing Carl Henderson saw, hellishly illuminated in the flames, was a face—bloated, pale, inhumanly distended but nevertheless recognizable as a young girl's face. A face framed by long dark hair.

Julie Spellman's face . . . his sister's face.

* * *

Carl Henderson's house, invisible in a dense cloud of insects only a moment earlier, burst into flames, the fire erupting as if from nowhere, the flames fanned by the millions of beating insect wings.

Within seconds the whole structure was a blazing inferno, the flames shooting a hundred feet into the air, even the insects around the house feeding the conflagration.

Less than five minutes after the fire burst forth, the entire structure collapsed, what was left of the already half-devoured siding and timbers dropping into the pit of the basement, sending a shower of sparks and embers in every direction.

Then, as the flames died away, leaving nothing where the house had stood but a mass of smoldering coals, the cloud of insects began to disperse.

Other cars had gathered, their occupants drawn to the site of the burning house by the black smoke rising into the sky. Now, the shaken residents of Pleasant Valley began to emerge from their cars, staring at each other, dazed, barely able to believe what they had just witnessed. Smoking rubble was all that remained of Carl Henderson's house.

As Karen and Russell, holding Molly, stood next to Marge Larkin, whose arms were wrapped protectively around Ben, Ellen Filmore emerged from the onlookers and came to stand beside them.

"It's over," Ellen said. "It was Carl who turned it loose on us, and in the end, it was Carl it came home to. But it's over now."

Karen Owen looked uncertainly at the doctor. "But our children," she whispered. "Julie and Kevin. And Jeff . . ."

Ellen shook her head, thinking of the rat she and Roberto had dissected only a little while earlier. There was no point, she decided, in telling these people what their children must have suffered. "They would have died quickly," she said. "They probably never even knew what happened."

For a long time Karen Owen stared at the rubble. Finally, the doctor's words echoing in her mind, she turned away.

Let it be true, she thought. Let it be over, and let them not have suffered any more than they could bear.

EPILOGUE

*T*he coyote stopped short, his hackles rising as the unfamiliar scent filled his nostrils. His body stiffening, one forepaw lifted off the ground, he sniffed at the breeze. Then, in the growing heat of the morning, he set off in search of the prey whose smell he had detected on the wind.

He stopped again, for now the scent was strong. His ears pricking, he listened for any sound, motionless so as not to alert the prey to his presence.

Then he heard it.

A barely audible sound, but familiar.

Something injured.

In pain.

Dying.

Nothing he would have to hunt, or even fear.

His tail rising above his hindquarters like a plume, he started forward, his body quivering with eagerness, his jowls already dripping with saliva in anticipation of his meal.

Now he saw it.

He recognized the form instantly, for he'd seen human beings often.

He hesitated again, for he'd also learned to be wary of them.

This one, though, smelled different from the others.

It looked different, too.

It lay on the ground, in a position of submission, its belly exposed.

Wary, the coyote moved closer.

The form on the ground moved slightly, its skin rippling as if something were beneath it.

Again the coyote heard the moan that told him the creature was dying. Emboldened by the sound and the weakness of the form's movements, the animal moved closer, sniffing once again at the scent emanating from the fallen human.

The smell of death was already starting to drift from its skin.

The coyote moved closer still, reaching out with one paw to prod at the creature.

Again it stirred, and again he heard it moan.

The coyote moved toward the head and the exposed throat, its instincts urging it to sink its teeth into the naked flesh, to rip the windpipe open, then stand back until the creature died and it would be safe to begin its feast.

Creeping closer, it paused one more time, hovering above the prey, its jaws agape.

And suddenly its victim's mouth opened and a black cloud erupted from its throat, engulfing the coyote's head in a stinging black mass, swarming into his open mouth, disappearing into his tongue and gums, burrowing into his skin and down his throat.

At that moment Sara McLaughlin, abandoned by the colony that had consumed her, finally died.

And the coyote, bearing its pain in unnatural silence, staggered as a wave of nausea swept over it. Then, regaining its footing, it turned and loped away.

Don't miss
John Saul's new novel
of psychological suspense—
in bookstores now!

BLACK LIGHTNING

He is the most notorious serial killer of our time. Now, Richard Kraven is about to be executed. The police and the public think the nightmare is over. So does Anne Jeffers, the fearless reporter whose work has helped bring him to justice. But the real terror is about to begin. . . .

**Read on
for a chilling sneak preview
of BLACK LIGHTNING. . . .**

Five Years Ago—
Experiment Number Forty-Seven

It was a ballet the man had danced so many times before that the first steps had become familiar enough to be performed automatically, with little if any thought at all. If he'd been asked, he couldn't have said exactly what it was about this particular subject that first caught his attention, what particularly had piqued his interest in including her in his study. Certainly not age—he'd never been interested in the relative youth of any of his subjects.

Nor did sex matter. There were nearly as many men as women among his subjects; whatever gender imbalances existed in his study group were purely a matter of chance, and, he was certain, statistically insignificant. Not that his critics would ignore whatever imbalances existed when they began analyzing his work—he was all too aware that every possible nuance of his study would be minutely examined, that every possible interpretation, no matter how outlandish, would be applied to his choice of subjects.

But the fact was that he really hadn't come up with any standard criteria for selecting participants in the experiments. Neither race nor gender, age nor sexual orientation, had counted.

Nor had he ever been particularly concerned about whether he invited the subject to join his study, or whether the subject was the one to make the first contact.

His current subject had made the first contact herself, as it happened, and he had almost rejected her on the basis that she seemed somehow familiar to him, that he knew her from somewhere. Familiarity was the single grounds for automatic ineligibility for the project, for he could never be certain of his own objectivity if he had previously existing feelings for the subject, whether positive or negative.

He'd first become aware of the woman a couple of weeks ago, when he'd happened into a shop near the university for a cup of coffee. He'd briefly noticed her when he'd come in, sitting near the door alone, a copy of the *Seattle Herald* spread out on the table before her. He'd paid little attention to her until he bought his own coffee and settled into a chair several tables away.

Had he subconsciously known even then that he would include her in the project? He would have to consider that.

It had been she who first smiled at him, then come over and asked if she could join him. As he recalled it now, she said something she seemed to consider witty, about them not taking up any more room on the planet than they absolutely had to, and he produced the expected smile for her. But instead of inviting her to sit down, he pleaded work, and she left.

For the next ten minutes he'd tried to figure out why she looked familiar, but it hadn't finally come to him until he opened his own paper to the editorial section and his eye had been caught by one of the columns:

It hadn't been the story that had caught the man's eye so much as the accompanying photograph of the column's author.

Anne Jeffers.

That was why the woman he'd spoken to a few minutes earlier had seemed familiar: she looked very much like the newswoman. He'd sat staring at the photograph for several seconds, considering.

The woman had been in her early forties, of medium height, with the same kind of even features reflected in the photograph. The woman's hair had appeared to be of a similar dark shade, too, though Anne Jeffers's was somewhat shorter.

Was it possible it had actually been Anne Jeffers he'd spoken to?

A patient man, he'd finished his coffee, refolded his paper, and gone on about his business. But he kept his eyes open, and a few days later, when he spotted the woman from the coffee shop, he realized that she was not Anne Jeffers, nor was she anyone else he knew.

Discreetly, he'd followed her.

She lived not far from the university, in an old Spanish-Moorish-style apartment building the man had always liked.

Afterward, he made a point of walking by the building every few days. He'd seen the woman several times, and nodded to her.

The dance had begun.

It had gone on for several weeks, the two of them circling around each other in a strange pavane that was almost like a courtship.

They began nodding to each other, then saying hello.

He had begun to absorb the routines of her life, and found her—as he found most people—to be pathetically predictable.

Today, for instance, being a bright and cheerful Sunday, he was almost certain the woman would take lunch in a bag and go to bask in the rare warmth on the lawn of the university, where she would pretend to be reading a book while actually watching for a man—nearly any man, he had discovered—to show interest in her.

Today he would be the man to show interest.

Today the dance would end.

He left his car at home that morning, taking the motor home he'd bought four years ago, when the study had commenced. Perfect for field trips, he often drove it into the mountains even on weekends when he wasn't working on his research, parking it near any one of hundreds of babbling streams while he indulged himself in his only passion outside of his project: fly fishing.

Today he drove the motor home up to the university, parked it in the nearly deserted depths of the cavernous garage, and locked it. Taking his own lunch and two bottles of lemon-flavored sparkling water with him, he climbed the stairs to the surface and started across the lawn toward the spot that was the woman's favorite.

Half an hour later, after she'd consumed half the contents of the bottle of sparkling water he offered her, she frowned, then shook her head.

"Something wrong?" the man asked, his gentle voice freighted with benevolent concern.

"I—I'm not sure," the woman replied. "Suddenly I feel—" She hesitated, then stood up. "I'd better get home!"

The man scrambled to his feet and began gathering both their things. "Maybe I should drive you," he suggested.

The woman started to decline his offer, but a second later changed her mind. He could see that the color had begun to fade from her lips.

"If you could . . ." she began, but then, feeling lightheaded and dizzy, her voice faded.

Gratefully, she accepted the man's proffered arm and let him lead her down into the garage, where his motor home waited.

Even before he drove it out into the bright daylight, the woman had drifted into unconsciousness, and was now spread out on the sheet of plastic he'd placed on the floor.

He pulled out of the garage, went west two blocks, turned right up to N.E. 45th Street, and headed west to Interstate 5. Taking the highway south, he exited at Route 520, heading east toward Redmond.

After a while he wound up into the foothills, looking for the right spot.

Somewhere off the road.

Somewhere secluded.

Somewhere near a stream, so he could do a little fishing after his work was done.

Finally he found the spot: a narrow road, one he'd used

431

before, but not for years. A half mile through the trees and he emerged into a clearing next to a fast-moving stream. He looked around.

He was alone.

Now he began his preparations.

First, he stripped naked, folding his clothes neatly and stowing them in the drawer beneath the queen-sized berth at the motor home's rear.

After pulling on a pair of rubber surgical gloves, he covered the bed with a sheet of plastic and moved the unconscious woman onto it.

He continued working with the sheets of plastic, methodically lining the entire interior of the motor home; one of his prime rules when carrying out an experiment was that nothing must be contaminated.

Finally he was ready.

Undressing the woman, he gazed at her naked body for a few moments, savoring the life that seemed to radiate from it even as she slept.

Her breasts moved rhythmically up and down as she breathed, and when he lay his fingers gently on her neck, he could feel the pounding of her pulse.

He laid out the tools he knew he would need, then picked up the instrument he'd purchased the day before for this specific experiment, and squeezed its trigger.

It squealed shrilly as its blade began to spin.

The man began his work.

The blade of the cordless saw sliced through skin and flesh, parting the woman's sternum in a single quick cut up the center of her chest.

Setting the saw aside, the man spread her ribs apart and closed off the largest of her severed blood vessels with some of the surgical clamps he'd bought years before, when the research was still in its planning stages.

The worst of her bleeding stanched, the man slipped his fingers into the cavity within. He felt the woman's lungs—

still working strongly—and nodded in satisfaction. Once more he'd succeeded in making the primary cut so perfectly that the subject's diaphragm remained undamaged.

He slid his fingers deeper, working them around the lungs until both hands rested against the gently moving tissue. He paused, thrilling to the sensation of life pressing against his palms.

But now the woman's breathing was beginning to falter. Time was running short.

The experiment must begin.

His fingers probed deeper, until at last he felt the familiar contours of a human heart.

Time seemed to stand still. . . .

When he emerged from the motor home an hour later, the man's hands were covered with blood. More of the glimmering red fluid oozed from the body he carried in his arms, drizzling slowly down his torso and legs, dripping onto the ground he trod. He carried the body into a thicket of woods, waiting only until he was fully screened from the clearing before dropping it unceremoniously to the ground. He gazed angrily at the woman's remains.

Her organs were all there, but no longer in their original positions, for when he'd realized that once again the experiment had failed, a dark rage of frustration had come over him, a rage he'd released by plunging his fingers furiously into the woman's lifeless body, tearing her heart loose from its veins and arteries, then pulling more of her organs through the incision in her chest as he searched for the reason for his failure.

Now he glared down once more at the lifeless body, its chest torn open to offer the world an obscene view of the carnage within.

He turned his back and walked away, finally abandoning the subject for whom, only an hour ago, he'd had such wonderful hopes.

Emerging from the trees back into the clearing, he went to the river and plunged in, letting the rushing water wash the blood from his skin and cool the burning rage that failure always caused in him. Only when he was certain no trace of the woman's blood remained did he emerge from the river and return to the motor home, where, still naked, he carefully began folding the sheets of plastic in upon themselves. Soon the vehicle's interior was again pristine, all evidence of his experiment wrapped in the sheets of plastic, which in turn he placed inside a large white plastic garbage bag.

The man went back to the river and washed once more, then dried himself, dressed, and drove the motor home out of the clearing. Leaving it on the edge of the pavement, he returned to the clearing, broke a branch from a tree and swept it methodically across the ground, obliterating every tire print the motor home had left.

The branch he'd used to whisk away his tracks joined the soiled plastic sheets in the large trash bag.

As he started back down the highway, the man glanced at his watch and was pleased: there was still plenty of time to stop for an hour or so of fishing before he went home.

And as he fished, he would begin thinking about the next experiment. . . .

In *Black Lightning*, John Saul strikes with a novel as electrifying as a jagged bolt from a pitch-dark sky, proving once again that he is a genius at both nail-biting suspense and the spine-tingling macabre.

Readers of John Saul now can join the John Saul Fan Club by writing to the address below. Members receive an autographed photo of John, newsletters, and advance information about forthcoming publications. Please send your name and address to:

The John Saul Fan Club
P.O. Box 17035
Seattle, Washington 98107